BLACKSHIRT DEATH ZONE

They came minutes later. Three trucks, escorted by armored personnel carriers. Ben let them come up closer, readied his Thompson, then gave the command to fire.

Streams of tracers slashed into the unprotected trucks. The APCs reacted instantly, disgorging a horde of blackshirts who spread out and returned fire as well as the darkness allowed.

"This is getting too personal," Jersey suggested from her position beside him. "Let's get back in the Hummer."

Ben saw movement to his left, and turned the Thompson that direction. Vertical tongues of flame spurted from the compensator on the muzzle of the tommy gun. The lethal hot lead chewed into the running men, who tumbled like rag dolls thrown by an angry child.

"It's just beginning to get exciting," Ben protested, a fierce grin spreading his lips.

FLAMES FROM THE ASHES

WILLIAM W. JOHNSTONE

Pinnacle Books
Kensington Publishing Corp.
http://www.pinnaclebooks.com

PINNACLE BOOKS are published by

Kensington Publishing Corp.
850 Third Avenue
New York, NY 10022

First Printing: August, 1993
10 9 8 7 6 5 4 3 2

Printed in the United States of America

Book One

There are some children who can say that they have been born and raised their entire lives under the protective umbrella of the Rebel way. Ben Raines, soldier, writer, intelligence officer, and sometimes political figure, hadn't started out to have it that way. What he wanted was peace and security for himself and his family. Like Topsey, that grew.

Ben knew that "things" were rotten long before the Great War. He saw corruption winked at for years, until it became the norm for politicians, judges, the prosecutors and police. Not that there weren't some damn fine policemen in the country. Even some laudable members of the FBI. Ben had tried, in his books and in his lectures, to call the alarm. He had been met at the best with indifference, at the worst with open hostility.

"Don't rock the boat" and "bend with the bamboo" had become the national philosophy. The Japanese were selling America televisions, VCRs, and what later proved to be cheaply made, and then buying up a whole lot of America with the proceeds. Every ayatollah and two-bit strongman in the Middle East thumbed his nose at America. The Chinese communists raped the minds of 600 million people and Uncle Sam paid the bill for it through "Most Favored Nation" trade status. Latin America made gringo bashing the national pastime. The European community looked down their haughty, pseudoaristocratic noses and quietly loathed everything American. Idiotic adventures in Africa had sent the deficit skyrocketing, while the recipients of American largess secretly hated their benefactors and plotted to destroy the nation.

Ben Raines saw all of this and recoiled in revulsion and disillusionment. There had to be a better way. Then came the Great War, and all that changed.

Ben Raines had been a soldier, as well as a teacher and author. Sometimes, he believed he would spend the rest of his life as a soldier. Particularly after the Great War. Out of the ashes of devastation and disorder, Ben soon formed a small gathering of likeminded people. They journeyed through the country, seeking others who shared their stern, but fair, beliefs and their dreams of rebuilding a shattered nation. While what was left of the central government (read: *politicians*) of the United States still staggered around and pointed fingers of blame at one another and appointed and staffed endless (and certainly useless) committees to study this problem and that, Ben Raines and his growing band of followers, who would soon be known as Rebels, were cleaning out and setting up their own brand of government in the northwest.

It was called Tri-States, and before the nitwit politicians who made up the new central government of the United States—its capital now in Richmond (Washington, D.C., had been destroyed, a condition that many Americans, whether a part of the Rebels or not, felt to be long overdue)—knew what was happening and stopped stomping on their hankies, they discovered that there was a country-within-a-country, and that everything was just fine in the Tri-States.

To their shock and horror, the Tri-States had a zero crime factor, zero unemployment, clean, pure running water, electricity, social services, schools that actually taught useful subjects to the young, medical

8

care for all, and all the other amenities that made life good for the law-abiding. Everything just hummed along peacefully in the Tri-States. And they did it all without help from the central government. They even had the audacity to tell the bureaucrats to keep their long, disruptive noses out of the business of Tri-States.

"Good heavens!" shrieked the politicians, shredding more hankies and stomping them furiously. "We can't allow this. Why, it's — it's subversive, positively . . . *unAmerican!*"

Then, horror of horrors, the politicians and their toady bureaucrats in Richmond learned that criminals were actually being *hanged* in Tri-States, for such innocent pursuits as murder and rape and armed robbery and other such minor offenses that every politically correct person knows are not the fault of the perpetrator, but rather the fault of everyone else.

After all, the bleeding hearts pointed out, if the homecoming queen won't date a person, why, rape the bitch, right? Or if somebody has a nicer car or newer tennis shoes or flashier jacket, if they have a larger TV set, or a CD player, or a better boom box or Walkman, why, it made perfect sense for that less-fortunate person to go out and steal a gun to blow somebody away. For they all knew that the mental scars left by these horribly traumatic inequalities would certainly mark for life the afflicted individuals, and positively justified violent acts against such an uncaring society.

So after the liberals in Congress ended months of hand-wringing, snorting, and weeping, and trod to shreds a ton of hankies, and after forty-seven committees had concluded five thousand five hundred and ninety-three meetings and fact-finding junkets (all at taxpayer expense), the central government reached its decision: the Tri-States must be compelled to cease and desist and disband and stop all this unpatriotic foolishness.

9

Derisive laughter came from the citizens of Tri-States, who, through their elected leader, Ben Raines, told the President of the United States and the members of both houses of Congress to go fuck themselves.

Well! those august beings snitted with a limp flip of their wrists. Nobody tells Congress to do *that!*

Immediately the government of the United States declared war on the Tri-States. After extensive and expensive effort, they thought they had wiped out all those malcontents who had the nerve to think they knew more about running a government than the professional politicians.

Wrong!

Ben Raines gathered a handful of survivors around him and proceeded to rebuild his army. Once he had accomplished this, the Rebels set out to kick the crap out of the thugs and bullyboys the central government sent after them. With victory came fame.

The Rebel philosophy spread and the Rebel army grew rapidly. Right when Ben Raines and the Rebels had seized control of the central government, tragedy of another sort struck the world. Like the horror of the Middle Ages, a rat-borne plague spread through the world. When it was over, there remained not a single stable government anywhere in the world.

For a few years, anarchy reigned. Gangs of hoodlums and warlords ruled the cities and countryside, wreaking havoc and misery on the battle-worn and weary population. Everywhere except inside the borders of the new Tri-States, that is.

Ben Raines took his Rebels to the Deep South. There the rednecks and the black racist juju artists came on every bit as ferociously as the depraved warlords of the north and west. When the Rebels had their sector cleaned out and running smoothly, they began the job of sweeping out the dregs of the nation, coast to coast and border to border. It would take them years.

Meanwhile, down in isolated areas of South America, an even more deadly and virulent cancer had metastasized. Field Marshal Jesus Dieguez Mendoza Hoffman had built and trained an army of black- and brown-shirted Nazis. Like himself, many of Hoffman's officer corps came from the result of fraternization between the local ladies and the "pure" Aryan survivors of the collapse of the Third Reich who had fled to Argentina, Bolivia, Brazil, and Paraguay.

Now the New Army of Liberation, as Hoffman styled his *Wehrmacht*, controlled most of the continent, Central America and had inroads in Mexico. Their *Führer* had given them a new mission: to conquer what was left of North America and reeducate its citizens . . . those that would be left after a bloody purge of men, women, and children they considered to be *untermenschlich*, subhuman.

How, one could ask, could Nazism once more rear up its ugly face and be on the march, its ranks tightly closed, goose-stepping its way north? It all had to do with the infusion of Latin American genes into the Aryan supremacy madness.

The new leader of Hitler's rantings and ravings was much more subtle in his methods of indoctrination. Within the ranks of the New Army of Liberation could be found men and women of all races, all nationalities, all colors. Hoffman's mad psyche told him he must use people of all colors in order to win. After the battle was won, he shrewdly advised his backers and civilian bureaucrats, then he would start his new putsch, which, as the Night of the Long Knives had once purified the ranks of the SA, would rid his own *Sturmabteilungen* of racial and mental inferiors. Yet, in order to do that, once the battle was won, he would need the help of a certain type of North American . . . a rather ignorant and bigoted type of person.

Unfortunately that type still existed in large numbers in North America. People who hated "spicks" and "jigs" and "kikes" and "slopes." Men, women, and

11

even children, who lusted after their mythical Aryan ideal. Hoffman felt confident they would rally to his cause.

So the modern-day Hitler invaded Mexico and the United States. His superior numbers and blitzkrieg tactics overwhelmed General Payon and his Army of Mexico. General Payon never really had a chance, because those who remained of the aristocratic upper class of Mexico, who were also the government and thus controlled the army, fawned on the Nazis and treated them as liberators. The Rebels had hardly begun their task of restoring order and steady commerce to the United States, after their prolonged odyssey over the oceans and continents of the world, but they had soon found themselves facing the Nazi menace on the Rio Grande.

The massive size of the invasion force caused Ben Raines to break his light divisions into smaller units and fight a delaying, guerrilla battle against Hoffman. His watchword: "Make them pay for every inch they take."

From the outset, the storm troopers of Hoffman's Army of Liberation paid dearly. Even with the support of American Nazis, rednecks, and juju leaders, Hoffman soon found himself starring in the punchline role of that old British Army joke, with his thumb up a tiger's arse.

In short, Ben Raines and his Rebels, with a little help from unexpected allies, kicked the living shit out of Superman Hoffman and his Nazis. In the initial engagements not a Rebel life was lost, and only a handful wounded. Later, as Hoffman expanded his foothold into the breadbasket of America, it got grimmer. Even so, Hoffman's Nazi army lost ten to fifteen men for each Rebel wounded, a hundred or more for each one killed. At last Ben concluded that they simply could not fight worth a damn and had an idiot for a commander.

He turned up the heat and soon had a total rout on

his hands. Nazis fled singly, in pairs, in platoon-sized units, and finally entire divisions surrendered. Those that remained fled in terror to the Pacific Northwest, or split for South America with the only seasoned military mind, General Frederich Rasbach. A few remained in Mexico.

Ben and his Rebels soon encountered and wiped out pockets of stubborn resistance. As the number reported fleeing the "free" part of the United States to join Hoffman grew, they knew full well that the Rebel army would have to contend with the Nazi monster again.

So they rolled up their sleeves and made ready.

What they didn't know was how soon they would once again be thrown into the crucible of war.

One

"The tree of Liberty must oft-times be watered with the blood of patriots."

Benjamin Franklin

Ben Raines stood outside his Hummer. A lot more gray showed at the temples of his black hair; more than a decade of combat accounted for that. His jaw had lost none of its firmness, nor had the square cut of his chin diminished. His eyes squinted as he looked over a wide expanse of rolling landscape that had once more filled with undulating fields of amber waves of grain. This wheat had been planted by farmers living peacefully under Rebel protection. Big fists on hips, Ben turned to study the land. He and his headquarters team, Ben knew, were situated not far from what used to be Concordia, Kansas.

Their Humvee was parked along the cracked two-lane U.S. Highway 81. They had just come off old I-135. Ben stood alone, except for Jersey, on a knoll overlooking the rippling prairie. Somehow it . . . calmed him.

He needed the calming, considering what Intelligence had compiled in their latest summary. It consisted of three items, none of which pleased him. Carefully, he combed through them again.

First, Field Marshal Jesus Dieguez Mendoza Hoffman had rallied his demoralized troops in eastern

15

Oregon and northern Idaho. The mountain valleys and passes to the east were held by the fanatic survivors of SS *Brigadeführer* Hans Brodermann. Something new had been added: reinforcing Brodermann were the American SS counterparts under SS *Hauptsturmbannführer* Peter Volmer, who led the ambitiously named *Leibstandarte Hoffman*. Volmer had been a neo-Nazi skinhead before the Great War, raised by Nazi-loving parents to hate since infancy. Peter had sworn a sacred oath on his SS dagger to bring to his commander the head of Ben Raines.

Second, General Frederich Rasbach was reported as having taken ship from South American seaports, destination unknown. It had taken him only six weeks to reorganize an army.

And third, what scattered meteorological data were available indicated that unseasonably early storms were building in Canada and the Pacific Northwest. They could threaten to close the passes in the Rockies and Big Horn Mountains.

"We can't afford that," Ben said aloud at this last reflection.

"Sir?" Jersey prompted, no longer surprised at Ben starting a conversation in the apparent middle.

"If we're compelled to wait until spring to dig out Hoffman and his Nazis, we'll have lost the campaign. I have an uncomfortable feeling that Jesus Hoffman is not going to wait for warmer weather."

"Yeah," Jersey agreed. "Like now he has all these homegrown scumbags to help him. We've been in the Pacific Northwest before, General. For my part, he's welcome to winter in Oregon." Jersey shifted the M-16 in her hands to give an impression of severe shivers.

Ben's thoughts returned to how things had once been around here and how they had become that way again under Rebel rule. No, not *rule*, exactly, more like guidance. Only now the Rebel troops had left, called up to fight Hoffman and his New Army of

16

Liberation. Ominously, the fields were abandoned, void of people. A faint brush of cold crossed Ben's heart. Chaos could return again.

Too bad Hoffman had chosen to pass this way. Too bad there had been so many Americans willing to follow him. He wondered which ones were responsible for the missing farmers, their wives and families. Static crackled from the backpack radio Corrie had sitting on the seat of the Hummer, its antenna stuck out a window.

"Roger that, Far Eyes." She shot a hard expression toward Ben. "Scouts on the horn, sir."

Ben sighed. He never had time anymore to look at the beautiful and peaceful. With measured, catlike strides, Ben returned to the Humvee. He filled his hand with the mike. "This is Eagle, go," he announced, using his longtime call sign.

"Eagle, this is Far Eyes. We have contact with the local citizens from around this area. At least those who didn't join the Nazis. Over."

"I copy that, Far Eyes. What is their Twenty? Over."

"It's bad, Eagle. A mass, open grave, just outside Bellville, over."

Ben's brows knitted. He had dreaded something like this since first becoming aware of the emptiness and quiet of this farming region. "We'll join you ASAP, Far Eyes. Oh, any fix on those homegrown Nazis?"

"Ah, yes, sir. Right across the line in Nebraska. They seem to be holding some sort of rally. Over."

"We'll tend to them soon enough. Eagle out." To Cooper, his faithful driver of so long a time, "Fire it up, Coop. You have maps that show Bellville?"

"Yes, General." Coop delved into a map case, not unlike those once carried by airline captains. "Here it is. Thirty miles north of where Concordia used to be."

"Good. Take us there, and don't waste time on the

17

scenic route."

"You got it, General," Cooper sang out.

Jersey was last to enter the Hummer, her dark hair abristle, eyes cutting from point to point. Her small stature made her a hard target for anyone over three hundred meters off, but her superb marksmanship could easily outdistance the 350-meter maximum effective range of the M-16. And do it by a good 175 meters. Her round, firm bottom had barely touched the seat when Cooper made the Humvee roar to life and spirited motion.

"Maniac!" Jersey shouted at him as she tumbled against the backrest.

Field Marshal Jesus Dieguez Mendoza Hoffman sat behind the wide ironwood expanse of his conscripted desk, his feet up on an open drawer and his tunic unbuttoned. A fire crackled cheerily in the large, fieldstone fireplace of a large, rambling, ranch-style house that had miraculously escaped the ravages of time and turmoil. It had the good fortune of being located on the shore of Wallowa Lake outside Enterprise, Oregon. Isolated in the Wallowa Mountain Basin, the small horse ranch had been by-passed by the plunderers, creepies, and even Ben Raines's Rebels. Field Marshal Hoffman listened with intense interest to the reports of his staff. Personnel came first. Col. Rupert Hertl, the G-1, stood in place at his chair and consulted a sheaf of papers in his hand.

"SS *Brigadeführer* Brodermann has been reinforced with three thousand American Party members, they call themselves the SS *Leibstandarte Hoffman* regiment." Everyone effected not to hear the snicker from Maj. Karl Richter, Hoffman's senior aide. "They are commanded by *Hauptstandartenführer* Peter Volmer."

"Ah, yes, the ambitious and idealistic American who has kept the flame of our *Führer's* dream alive in this country. I must say that I am impressed by him,"

Hoffman added the praise generously.

"There are reports that some four to five thousand more American Nazis or sympathizers are en route here as we speak. Not counting them, we have an effective force of somewhat over ten thousand fighting men. Ten thousand three hundred ninety-seven, to be exact. There are, of course, the usual support elements and air."

Hoffman gestured to his most junior aide to refill his teacup. "Thank you, Hertl. You have greatly restored my vigor for the continuation of this contest with that barbarian, Ben Raines. Now, what can you tell me, my old friend, Joaquin, to make my day even better?"

Col. Joaquin Webber rose and dusted his palms together. He spoke from memory. "Indications are that morale has disintegrated in Mexico. The scorched-earth policy of both sides has left the peons starving. They are ripe to join whoever it is that first offers to fill their bellies." He paused, eyed the delicate bone china teacup, and wished it was filled with schnapps. "The Rebels, under Ben Raines, have completed the eradication of those pockets of resistance south and east of Kansas."

"Where is Ben Raines?" Hoffman coldly asked his G-2. His short stature, puffed-out chest, Hitlerian mustache, and lock of black hair over his left eye made Hoffman a ludicrous caricature of the former master of the Third Reich. Although no one would dare to tell Hoffman that.

"In company with a reinforced battalion, screened by scouts, Raines has outstripped the main Rebel advance, General. He has raced a third of the way across Kansas and then turned north. It is believed that concentrations of our American allies can be found in what was Nebraska and South Dakota, headed our way. Reins must be after them."

"Well, he can't have them," Hoffman snapped petulantly.

"He won't, sir," the G-2 assured him. "Peter Volmer

19

has departed your headquarters to make personal visits to these American units. He will contact you by secure radio net following this staff meeting."

"Go on."

"By our best estimates, the Rebels have broken off contact with General Payon to the south, and are spread on an entirely too thin line across the Midwest and Plains states. It is our estimate that they now constitute no immediate threat to us, nor in the near future."

Hoffman cut him a gimlet eye. "You're sure of this? Your predecessor made the mistake of underestimating Ben Raines too often. You know the near disaster that caused."

Webber bristled. "I made a careful study of Ben Raines, *Herr Feldmarschall.* I am certain I know his quirks far better than the officer who held my post previously."

"Then pray continue," Hoffman said coolly.

"There is little more," Webber advised, and launched into the minutiae of the intelligence analysis.

The G-3 came next. He gave information on the status of training and condition of equipment. He also suggested tactfully that Hoffman announce his strategic and tactical requirements soon so that plans could be drawn and orders cut. Hoffman said he would, after he talked with Brodermann and Volmer.

Food supplies and fresh water were the subject of the G-4. He noted that the stripping of farms had provided ample fresh meat for all troops, as well as eggs, butter, and milk for the staff. In all, Hoffman felt quite pleased with their accomplishments. Smiling, he passed around the plate of fancy tea cakes.

A strident *beep-beep!* on the command net advised Corrie that she had an incoming message. The Hummer whizzed along the cracked, uneven surface of

U.S. 81 at an acceptable speed of 45 mph. Corrie keyed the mike and spoke quietly.

"This is the Eagle's Nest, go."

A built-in scrambler unit converted the twitters and chirps into understandable language to which Corrie listened for five seconds before switching on the speaker unit. "It's Overseer," Corrie identified the Headquarters Company Intelligence radio-intercept van. "They're picking up a lot of traffic on Nazi freqs, General," she explained before the voice of the distant radio operator cut into the rumble of the Humvee.

". . . seem to be gathering in large numbers along a line from Geneva to Silver Creek. Best estimate, if they ever got together, some five thousand. There's more to the north, in old South Dakota. Over."

"What's the nature of the traffic? Over," Ben queried.

"Mostly pep talks. There's something about some big wheel coming to give them the word from on high. We haven't been able to figure that one out as yet, Eagle. D'you want a verbatim?"

"Not at this time, Overseer. I'll get a briefing from the Two Shed later," Ben dismissed. "Anything hot comes along, bump me like yesterday."

"Roger that, Eagle. Oh-oh, have something priority one coming in now. There's a fix on it, seems to be coming from somewhere around close to you."

FMJ rounds rattled off the armored sides of the Hummer to emphasize the words of the radioman from G-2. "There seems to be some hostile intent—"

"That's a rog-O, Overseer," Ben said dryly over the trashcan-lid clangor of the light auto fire.

Yellowish flickers spurted from the weapons in the hands of camo-clad figures on the ATVs that raced across a pasture toward the highway and the Hummer that made so tempting a target. Already Jersey had her M-16 pointed out the window and cut off crisp, three-round bursts. More of the snarling, balloon-tired little vehicles appeared on the opposite side of U.S. 81. Ben unlimbered his old faithful .45 Thompson and let go on full rock-and-roll from the fat drum magazine.

Flame rippled from the slots of the compensator as the subgun spit fat .45 slugs at a line of five advancing ATVs. Ben watched one Nazi get flung away from the back of the three-wheeler as he and the driver took rounds that ripped and tore. Undirected, the racing all-terrain vehicle crashed into the one on its left.

It upset, the gas tank ruptured, and the hot engine did the rest. A huge balloon of red-orange flame engulfed both rigs. A screaming human form, wrapped in a blanket of fire, ran from the conflagration. Ben ended his agony with a quick three-shot burst.

"Awh, shit, there's more of 'em, General," Cooper advised as he crested a low swale and saw a roadblock of old, rusted cars ahead.

Ben checked it out, gritted his teeth. "Crash through it, Coop."

"Yes, sir." Cooper didn't question the ability of the beefed-up Humvee to do as General Ben Raines wanted. He'd done it all too often before.

Bullets splattered against the thick windshield and Cooper gave brief thanks for the R&D staff at Base Camp One who had come up with a passable substitute for Lexan. Only trouble was that after a month or so in the field, it tended to pit and spiderweb when hit by fast-moving slugs. Now he would have to look around the edges and guide the hurtling Hummer in the bargain.

Some bargain, Coop thought as another slash of incoming opaqued the whole right side of the windshield. "Everybody brace; we're gonna hit hard," he sang out a moment before the welded I-beam that had replaced the usual bumper slammed into corroded metal. It yielded like a willing woman to her lover. Back when they were producing these things, Cooper thought frivolously, the Japs must have made the body panels out of old beer cans.

Then the obstruction that flung jagged bits into the air gave a lurch and screeched past. Beside him, Beth had her window down and cut off precise bursts with her H&K 7.62x42 assault rifle. Behind her, Jersey's .223 M-16 chattered steadily. Already corpses, the results of their efforts, did grisly dances of death.

Ben let the thunder roll from his Thompson, the muzzle oscillating in an upward-right oval. Impacted by two, sometimes three 230-grain .45 slugs, bodies flew to left and right. A tiny corner of Ben's mind kept note of the uniforms this unexpected enemy wore. So very like the camo gear of his Rebels. A short distance further to the west of the highway, Ben watched a man rise to a kneeling position, a long, flat green tube over one shoulder. RPG!

Before the Nazi could trigger the rocket-propelled grenade, Ben swung his Thompson to blitz the blitzkrieger into eternity. The Chicago piano chopped out five rounds and the bolt racked back in the open position. Empty. Ben Raines fought against time, a battle he was certain he would lose, to slide the drum from its keepers and insert a fresh one. He had wound up two before departing from the reinforced battalion that traveled with his headquarters. That might prove the deciding factor.

Sharp barks from the front seat halted Ben's hand. Cooper, his window down, fired an H&K P7M10. Chambered for the S&W .40 Magnum round, it spat a nasty slug. "Jeez, it's bad enough I got to drive through this mess, I've gotta do the shooting, too," Cooper complained with a quick wink over his shoulder to Ben.

"Thanks, Coop," Ben said tightly. "I owe you one."

"All in a day's work, General," Cooper said brightly, steering blind down the highway while he checked his handiwork with the rocket gunner.

The cammo-clad Nazi lay sprawled in the weeds and sunflowers. His unfired weapon rested across his chest. Ben inserted the magazine and rested the muzzle on the window frame in the sudden silence that washed over the Hummer. He noticed Jersey staring at him, openmouthed.

"What are you gawking at?" Ben asked in mock irritation. "Can't a man load his weapon in peace, without the distaff element of this team commenting?"

"Ben—General, that Nazi creep almost blew us away," Jersey squeaked.

"Close only counts in horseshoes and hand grenades, Jersey," Ben admonished jokingly.

A radio voice squawked in Corrie's ear. "Overseer wants to know if we made contact, General."

Ben chuckled softly. "Tell that mother hen that his warning wasn't quite timely enough. Those jokers made a mess out of my Hummer."

Two

A terrible stench rose from the pit — an odor so foul that it gagged Ben Raines, who had hunted down the creepies, up close and ugly. An awful sorrow and rage welled up in Ben's chest. These had been good people, peaceful farmers, their wives and children. Slaughtered for no more reason than someone figured them to be "racially inferior" to the Nazi monsters who put them here.

"The rest of R Batt will be along in a couple of hours. Close this . . . grave, and have the padre say some words. Small comfort for these folks . . ." Ben concluded with an absent stare. Then he slammed a fist that would have served as a fielder's mitt into the side of the Humvee. A wild light glowed in his eyes. "I want to find those Nazis that Far Eyes told us about. We're heading north."

"With this windshield, I'll be lucky to make ten miles an hour," Cooper protested.

"Then transfer us to another," Ben growled.

"It won't be armored. The spare's with R Batt," Cooper reminded, referring to the reinforced battalion that accompanied the Rebel headquarters.

It had begun life as Ben's One Battalion and consisted of the usual three infantry companies, one heavy-weapons, augmented by a company of M-1 Abrams tanks on lowboys, and a pair of Hughes AH-64 Apache gunships. Their main rotor blades could be extended and locked in place, the helicopters ready for takeoff from their transport trucks, in fifteen minutes. Then, alone or together, they could rain terror from the sky on anyone below. That is, anyone without IR heat-seeker SAMs.

"No time," Ben snapped, conscious of the stress put on him by the ambush and the carnage of the martyred farm families. "Get to humping, Coop."

Ten minutes later, Ben's mobile headquarters had been transferred to an available Hummer. The motor warmed and ready, Cooper took the squat, ugly, wide-wheelbased vehicle out of there, headed, he well knew, into a bloody confrontation with the Nazi butchers.

"This is Alien Secretions," a husky voice crackled through on what Field Marshal Hoffman's intelligence thought to be a secure channel.

Fifty miles away, the young Rebel on enemy traffic watch in Overseer glanced over at his friend on the duty desk. "What the hell have we got here?"

"Sounds like the name of a studded-metal band," the buddy suggested.

"Go ahead—ah—Alien Secretions," a Teutonic accent, faded by distance, responded.

"We had—ah—a hostile contact with one of the target's vehicles. No idea who was in it, but they fought like fiends. Broke through the roadblock and killed a bunch of my people."

A feathery whisper of chuckle came back. "You can't make an omelet, as they say. Have you made a positive identification on the main target? Over."

"Negative, it's not just that they're usin' code names, the Rebels have every transmission scrambled."

"Then get out there and use your eyes, you stupid American *schwein!*"

Gabriel Trasher slammed the microphone stand

hard on the Formica tabletop. "Gawdamned South American kraut," he snarled.

"You're the one wanted to throw in with these Nazis," Numb Nuts Nicholson, Trasher's second-in-command, reminded.

Trasher's close-set, beady eyes flared with anger. He had so far held his band of outlaw bikers together by sheer force of personality. Hugely gross, his belly slopped over the thick black belt that held up grubby jeans so grease-impregnated they could not rot away.

"I don't need you to tell me that." Trasher worked thick, wet lips, exposing crooked, yellowed teeth that sported a green fringe. "What choice did we have? It was that or face Ben Raines and the Rebels on our own. Goddammit, I hate Ben Raines." It would have done no good to tell Gabe Trasher that those who had spoken that phrase numbered in the thousands. He moved his lard butt with two grunts and a sharp gasp. The tumbledown farmhouse his Alien Secretions used as a flop and shelter for their Harleys had been furnished with items scavenged elsewhere. It stank of mildew, and the ceiling leaked in half a dozen places. Yet most of the city-bred members of the gang preferred it to sleeping out on the ground. There were snakes and other crawly things outside. Not to mention mosquitoes big enough to carry off a fair-sized man.

From another room came pitiful cries of anguish and horror. Some of the boys were punking out that peach-fuzz-faced farm kid they had snatched along the way. Give him a week, Trasher thought, and he'd be beggin' for it.

Gabe Trasher spoke from experience. He had been introduced to the far-from-subtle aspects of the drop-the-soap game long ago. It had been in juvenile hall at the tender age of twelve. He had punched out a teacher and stolen a car for a joyride to make himself feel better. The pigs had caught him and hauled him in to juvie.

27

He had never known fear until he ran into the older studs in that place. They'd had their way with him; and Gabe, over the years he'd spent behind bars, had taken his own share. Let the guys have their fun, he thought with a shrug. They had something important to do.

"Look, we've been given the assignment to track Ben Raines by the big honcho himself, Field-fucking-Marshal Hoffman. "We'd best perform. I hate to give that prissy kraut dork credit, but he's right. We gotta get out of here, whiz around the countryside, and make an ID on one General Ben Raines. Then we report it and wait for orders."

Short and stocky, with black hair and bluish-green eyes, Numb Nuts Nicholson showed the world a blank bulldog face that clearly revealed that his ship had sailed without him. "Whaddaya suppose they'll have us do next?" he asked in a vacant voice.

"Probably go terrorize some sissy-pants farmers, burn their crops so the Rebels won't have 'em," Trasher theorized.

A grotesque, choking whinny came from Numb Nuts, what passed for him as a laugh. "Oh, I like that. Maybe they'll have some cute little daughters," Nicholson slobbered.

Trasher winced. He knew what Numb Nuts meant by "cute" and "little": girls of eleven or younger. Not to say that when he'd been a long time without, ol' Gabe didn't enjoy a little lusty buggering, but when it came to women, he wanted them full-blown, busty, and with the legs of an acrobat. The obvious need to regain the upper hand goaded Gabe Trasher to action.

"Tell those horny fucks in there to leave the kid alone for a while. Have them get out and about and find me Ben Raines."

At least satisfied with the performance, Cooper

tooled the Hummer north along the dilapidated U.S. 81, now crossed over into Nebraska. With the big run-flat tires giving off pops and snaps, they entered the rubble that had once been Chester, Nebraska. Although they had seen it a thousand times, the occupants of the Humvee rubbernecked over the ruins.

More than curiosity motivated them. In their haste to contain and crush the loathsome creepies, the Rebels had flattened a lot of towns. Some of the noxious, cannibal monstrosities may have escaped in cellars, linked by networks of tunnels. If they or any other undesirables—by Rebel standards—existed in the piles of plaster and masonry, Jersey and Beth wanted to be aware of it long before it became a problem.

"Looks clean, so far, boss-man," Jersey sang out with obvious relief.

Cooper kept his eyes fixed on the narrow lane through the jumble of crumbled houses and downed power poles. To his right, Beth kept watch and spoke from the side of her mouth.

"There's a time to count chickens, and a time not—" Her barbed quip ended in a loud *wham,* that came from under the front right wheel.

Blast shock slammed Beth's head into the roof of the GP vehicle despite her seat belt and shoulder harness. Cooper white-knuckled the steering wheel and cursed hotly when his nose made violent acquaintance of the hub.

"Gawdamned mine," he shouted, mush-mouthed over the ringing explosion.

Ben found himself in a heap on the floor of the Hummer, with Jersey astraddle him and Corrie folded in half beside her, bootheels on the backrest. Fortunately good luck held. The Hummer came with a scatter shield as well as run-flat tires, Ben sorted out of his racing thoughts.

"Get us the hell out of here," he barked to the back of Cooper's neck.

"Can't, General. That sucker blew the wheel clean off."

"Corrie, get yourself upright and radio our situation to R Batt."

"Yes, General," her voice came tiny and distant.

A lot of wriggling produced the desired effect. Jersey made a production out of apologizing to Ben. He tut-tutted and endured it as he helped her to the seat cushion. Then he unraveled himself. Corrie had the window down by then and bumped the RT operator at R Batt.

"Yeah, Falcon, we hit a flogging mine. Disabled the Hummer," Corrie said in a decidedly stronger tone. "We're in Chester, just across the line. What's your ETA?" Her earphone squawked and she cut her eyes to Ben. "Falcon says two hours, General."

Disgruntled by the sequence of events so far that day, Ben grumbled and reached for the mike, then thought better of it. "Tell them goose it and make it in half that time. I want to catch up to those goddamned Nazis."

Corrie relayed the message and added, "Bring up the reserve Humvee for Eagle. Roger. Eagle out."

"Now we wait," Ben said in a sour mood.

"We can always have lunch," Cooper suggested, his mind always on his belly.

"*Whaat!*" Ben sounded outraged. "You mean some of that green-eggs slop Lamar Chase laughingly calls field rations?"

Ben meant the laboratory-concocted recipe of Dr. Lamar Chase, senior medical officer of the Rebel army. It was filling and nutritious, the good doctor never failed to point out. Jam-packed with vitamins, minerals, basic carbohydrates, and protein. But in the eyes of the Rebel soldiers, the miracle meals had a number of prominent drawbacks: No matter what label the manufacturer back at Base Camp One slapped on it, one meal looked and tasted exactly like any other. And they had a tendency to turn a sickly

30

green when heated.

"Not this time, General," Cooper eagerly informed him. "Right after that land mine went off, I spotted some big brown birds trying to fly out of the rubble over there. Looked like chickens."

"Probably diseased," Ben complained, still fixated on the ugly green goop his friend had invented.

"I don't think so," Cooper persisted. "They had all their feathers and beat their stubby wings like crazy hedgehopping blocks of concrete."

Ben thought that over a moment and brightened. "Prairie chickens — grouse." They had returned. Now was no time to quibble over his reverence for wildlife. "Go for it, Coop."

Ben Raines badly needed to lighten up, Beth thought as she brushed at a stray strand of dark hair and promoted a smile. "I can have coffee ready in five minutes, General."

"Do that. And I'll see what else is growing around here. We can dine on grouse and wild vegetables."

Jersey cocked a dubious brow. "Such as what, General?"

"Wild turnips, onions, maybe that creek over there has watercress growing. Without people to screw it up, it should have," Ben waxed enthusiastic.

"Uh — General, I hate to bring this up," Jersey began tentatively. "But someone had to put that land mine there in the road. What if they pay us an unfriendly call while we're slurpin' up that prairie chicken and nature-boy veggies you're talking about?"

Ben gave her a face of innocence. "Why, we follow Ben Raines's Golden Rule: we do unto them exactly as they are trying to do unto us."

By long-ingrained habit, and plain common sense, everyone took his or her primary weapon along when they departed the wounded Humvee to search for luncheon goodies. Ben located what had once been a tidy garden plot in the backyard of a lot that formerly contained a comfortable single-family dwelling of

31

sturdy brick.

Long ago reduced to piles of decayed mortar and broken bricks, the house held no interest for Ben. The cluster of dark green tops in one corner of the garden did. Tough, prolific volunteers, what his mother had used to call "winter onions," had escaped even the gleanings of starving human dregs. Ben laid his Thompson aside in order to pluck a suitable number without disturbing the rest.

In the same instant he bent forward, Ben heard the clatter of a falling brick. Hardly unusual, considering the recent shock-wave effect of the exploding mine. Yet, while his left hand continued downward, covering the action of the right, he eased back to the holster at his side. Another brick rattled down a low pile. Ben tensed.

Hissing frightfully, a filth-encrusted creature in a long, tattered black robe flung itself at Ben Raines. In a blur, the IMI .50 Desert Eagle auto Mag came out of its sheath. Ben rolled onto his right shoulder and whipped the powerful handgun across his body. His thick index finger flexed on the trigger and the world became a roar.

Screeching in fear and pain, the apparition landed hard on its butt. Long, blackened nails, chipped and broken, waved clawlike in the air. Instant imprint of memory identified the hideous being as a creepie. Yet, Ben's nostrils did not report the accustomed carrion stench of the repulsive flesh-eaters.

Ben had to shove analysis aside as the loathsome thing came to its boots and hurtled itself at him again. The second .50 round popped a neat hole between the eyes of the offensive attacker and blew away the larger portion of the back of his head. So much for body armor, Ben thought. How had the monstrosity survived?

From a short ways off, Ben heard the chatter of Jersey's M-16. Ever faithful to her charge, she had drifted along with Ben and now engaged a trio of gaunt spectral beings who appeared to wear trailing fragments of lace curtains and nothing else. This was turning into a drama of the weird, Ben acknowledged to himself. He gave Jersey a wave and called out.

"I'll watch your back."

"If I wasn't watching yours, General, these curtain-queens would have had you."

"So noted."

Ben's attention immediately focused on half a dozen skinny, completely naked men, their upper torsos painted blue, the lower part bright red, who lumbered over the irregular rubble toward Jersey. Had they stepped into the Twilight Zone? Ben wondered, recalling a favorite old television show from his youth. Chinese red, Ben decided as he turned the belly button of one armed specter into a half-inch-diameter figure eight.

Howling, the painted man dropped the Kalashnikov he had been clutching and turned partway to the right. He tottered a few steps, eyes fixed on Jersey, then fell facefirst into a pile of dirt. Ben quickly dropped three more of the weird sextet, while Jersey chopped down the other two.

In the silence that followed, Ben heard a piercing scream from back by the Hummer. It had to be Corrie, Ben realized, but he'd be willing to bet she would never encounter anything to make her do something so pointedly feminine. He scooped up the Thompson and reholstered his Desert Eagle.

"Let's go," he curtly told Jersey.

"What in god's name are these things?" she panted as they trotted toward the Humvee.

"I was asking myself the same," Ben admitted. "We've stumbled onto some sort of freak show," he suggested.

Ben began to believe his jest when they reached the roadway. Corrie stood in a ring of three men who were naked except for loincloths and moccasins, their long blond hair done in braids, feathers sticking up from the back of their heads. They danced around her, each with one hand slapping his mouth, making a woo-woo sound, the other hand holding a gaudily painted, rubber-headed tomahawk, which they all moved in jerky up-down gestures.

"Jeez," Jersey said, impressed by the mad gyrations. "The loonies are running the asylum."

"We can't shoot, Jersey. We might hit Corrie."

"Yeah, down and dirty, huh, General?"

Twenty pounds of Thompson, wielded by Ben Raines, butt-stroked one man in the back of the head. It split his skull and he dropped like a stone. Jersey slid an M-5 bayonet into the kidney of another. The third continued his manic dance, careful to step over the bodies of his fallen comrades. Corrie broke her entranced state to reach into the Hummer and retrieve the baseball bat Ben kept there. She hit the last white Indian square in the mouth with it. He went down twitching and gagging. Ben looked to his left from where an eerie screech came.

Dressed all in black, an old, wrinkled crone sat hunched over a cast-iron kettle. Long, dirt-laden fingernails wove strange figures over the empty container. "Bubble, bubble, toil and trouble," she cawed.

Suddenly she jumped up and leveled an AK-47 at them. Ben's Thompson roared to life a fraction of a second too late. Jersey beat him to it and cut the crazed woman in half with a long burst from her M-16. Slowly the sounds of battle echoed away in the ruins.

"Can you explain this to me?" Jersey groused. "Can you just freakin' explain any part of this?"

Cooper approached from the direction of the creek. He looked about absently and giggled. His eyes were glassy. An open canteen dangled lazily from one hand.

"It's something in their diet," Ben said tightly. "Has to be." He eyed Cooper. "Or the water. There's something in it, a hallucinogen maybe. These people must

34

be a pocket of survivors. Part of the time they are straight. They plant land mines, dig hidey-holes, their weapons are obviously well-cared-for. The rest of the time they're blown away on . . . something."

Jersey eyed Cooper suspiciously. "You must be right, General. What'll we do about this one, General?"

"Sober him up. We can't stay here." Then Ben added, "Who knows how long that will take."

"I'll drive," Beth offered.

Ben and Jersey exchanged glances. "Never mind. I will," Ben offered. Jersey groaned. "First we have to get the other Hummer from R Batt. By then, maybe Cooper will be all right."

"We can always hope so," Jersey offered sincerely. Ben's driving threatened to give her ulcers every time he got behind the wheel.

"Meanwhile, we had better keep a sharp eye. There may be more of this merry band. And—ah—ladies, don't drink the water."

Three

Gabe Trasher keyed the mike and spoke directly to the head-honcho Nazi himself. "We found him, ah, Field Marshal. We sure as fuck found Ben Raines. Over."

A long hiss of static did well to convey the mood of Jesus Hoffman. "Positive identification? Why wasn't he eliminated?" the CO of the NAL asked icily.

"Well, shit, we wasn't tol' to—ah . . . er—that is, our orders were to locate and identify, report in, and wait for instructions, Field Marshal Hoffman."

Gabe could almost see the icy smile of that smug bastard. "Excellent. You are learning to be a soldier, Mr. Trasher. Discipline, order, unity. They are what we, as you Americans so crudely put it, are about. Very well. You will stand by for orders. My adjutant will give them to you."

"Oh, one other thing, Field Marshal. This Ben Raines ain't such hot crap nohow."

Recalling his recent and almost endless string of disasters, Jesus Hoffman framed his question in a dangerous purr. "Oh? How is that?"

"When they hit that land mine, Raines and his personal team got jumped by a bunch of loonie-tunes."

"What do you mean, ah, *loonie-tunes?*"

"Some kind of druggies. Smashed on something, all of them doin' their own weird thing. Three of them was done up like Injuns, only they were blond and as pink as you or me. Real stoner assholes, 'cause they were carryin' rubber tomahawks."

"What has this to do with the military capability of Ben Raines?" Hoffman bit off. Talking with this *untermensch* was like rolling in slime.

"M'boys who was watchin' said they got out of their vehicle—not an armored job, at that—and went sightseeing. Then the freakos showed up and nearly creamed their asses."

"But Raines came out of it unscathed?"

"Un-*what?* Oh, if you mean he didn't wind up with his nuts in a sack, yeah. Him an' those chicks with him blew away all the stoners. His driver . . ." Gabe paused to chuckle, kept the mike open. "His driver got wasted on the same shit those freaks were takin'. Came back to the Hummer glassy-eyed and giggling. Raines about had a cow."

Field Marshal Jesus Dieguez Mendoza Hoffman tried to envision Ben Raines giving birth to a bovine. Disgusting animal, this Trasher. But these motorcyclists were highly mobile, and they did manage to obtain detail in their observations. He cleared his throat.

"My adjutant has specifics on your area of operation, but I can tell you to hold back on Ben Raines for the time being. Maintain visual contact, but do not, I repeat, *do not* engage. Do you understand, Mr. Trasher?"

"Uh—yeah, yeah I do. Thank you, Field Marshal."

After receiving map coordinates of their AO, resupply points, and medical facilities friendly to the Nazis, Gabe Trasher had his fill of the sneering superior attitude of his South American allies. He signed off and set the mike aside. He turned a seething snarl on Numb Nuts Nicholson.

"You watch and see. One day I'm gonna fix the clock for that simpering Nazi cunt."

"But first we gotta take care of Ben Raines, huh,

Gabe?" Numb Nuts gobbled.

A faraway look came to Gabe Trasher's eyes. "Yeah. First we finish off Ben Raines."

Corrie passed the handset to Ben. "Got an update from Far Eyes, General."

Ben had been patting the head of Smoot, his full-grown Siberian husky who had been brought up with the reserve Hummer. The armored vehicle purred along the pothole-studded U.S. 81 at a steady 40 mph. "Thanks, Corrie." Ben keyed the mike switch. "Eagle here."

"The black-shirts have moved out, Eagle. They're makin' good time north on 81 toward York. That's seventy-three miles north of Bellville, Kansas. Over."

Ben frowned. He still outranged the R Batt by a good five miles, but he had plans for these particular Nazi scum. "Eagle copies that, Far Eyes. Keep visual contact and report every hour on the half-hour. How's the road up your way? Over."

A soft chuckle answered him. "Better than where you are. The Nazis are makin' fifty miles per. They must have scrounged up every rust-bucket and junker in five states. We can follow them from ten miles off by the blue smoke."

"Hang in there, Far Eyes. If they go to ground, mark the place and fall back. Our ETA for York is an hour-forty. Eagle out."

Ben returned the handset to his lovely RT operator and resumed petting Smoot. "I'm glad you're here, girl." Then he added for Jersey what she already knew: "She can smell dope at a hundred yards since that dog handler worked with her while I was away. There may be more of those unfortunates around. Stirred up by Hoffman's Nazis, no doubt. Or their American counterparts moving northwest."

During the long run north, Ben Raines spent the silence in a review of what he knew of Field Marshal

Jesus Dieguez Mendoza Hoffman. Hoffman had a sound background in military customs and tradition, that much was obvious. He also had a solid knowledge of tactics—on a battalion commander's level at least. The man had a hard time thinking strategically. Too often he let his arrogance get in the way of the facts.

Hoffman had committed a light brigade to the initial invasion of the U.S. and had lost them nearly to a man. From there on, he had reacted rather than initiating positive action to negate the hit-and-run tactics Ben had relied upon. In so doing, he suffered losses in divisional size. Hoffman was subject to rages, Ben noted. Question: Were they real or self-induced in emulation of his hero and god, Adolf Hitler?

Ben's days with the CIA and before had made him wise enough to recognize that Hitler's rug-chewing episodes were figments of American and British propaganda. The opinion makers had taken a German idiomatic expression for being furious and translated it literally. Thus, Hitler "chewed the rug" when he got bad news. Ben accepted as fact that the *Führer* did not drop on the floor and gnash his teeth in the carpet. But did Hoffman?

Interrogations of prisoners indicated that Hoffman frequently threw objects against the walls of his mobile headquarters, dashed fine china to the floor in a rage. One defecting general had even recounted how a direct, insulting exchange with Ben himself had sent Hoffman to the floor to kick his feet and pound his fists on the carpet like a three-year-old with a temper tantrum. No doubt Hoffman played the game with a few cards missing from the deck. But that didn't make him any less dangerous. Ben sighed and looked out the armor-glass window of the Hummer.

Desolation greeted him. The American Nazis were burning fields as they advanced northward. Other signs of their contemptible behavior began to appear. Grease-stained food wrappings littered the verge of the highway, lifted into the air by the passage of the Humvee. Boxes and scraps of cardboard lay where they had been dropped. Here and there he saw cast-off items of clothing and some toys. Obviously the loot from the unfortunate people of the Concordia and Bellville area.

When things came too easily, Ben knew, people quickly got bored. Back before the Great War, far too many of his fellow Americans had fought to get a free ride. Welfare fraud and fraud against Social Security Disability were rampant. Ben recalled with grim humor a report on a commentator's noontime radio program one day.

It seems this fellow reported to the police that his Cadillac had been broken into and vandalized. When the officers arrived, the man gave a list of missing items. Included were an expensive CD player/stereo system and the contents of his glove compartment: $600 in food stamps. Then there was the example of the bears in Yellowstone.

They had been raiding garbage cans and getting handouts from the visitors for several years. A new park administrator decided to put an end to this. He had the bears humanely trapped and transported far away from the public areas of the park. Those who did not find their way back to their soft-hearted benefactors simply sat down and died. They had been on the dole too long to be able to return to a normal way of life.

The "Gimme!" creed and "Me first" mindset, coupled with a wimpy, bleeding-heart toleration of outrageous criminal activity, had created a deficit for the nation that tolled its death knell long before the lunatic politicians in America and abroad became tempted beyond restraint to put their fingers on the buttons . . . and push. For all its horrors, the Great War had been a cleansing for a sick society. By god, you're becoming a cynic, Ben chided himself.

Beyond the window, the countryside rolled past.

* * *

Twilight lingered a scant hour away when Ben's spearhead rendezvoused with his headquarters scouts. They met in a copse of cottonwood trees to the east of U.S. 81. Lt. Bob Fuller, the section leader, made a crisp report.

"Colonel Gray is holding his Three Batt short at the intersection of Nebraska 15 and I-80. Now, the enemy, sir. They're on the outskirts of what used to be York, Nebraska, General. About six hundred of them. There are more coming in all the time. Men, women, and kids. Some sort of meeting, like down south. They've occupied an old tumbledown drive-in theater. We can lead the battalion there within twenty minutes of their getting here."

"Thank you, Lieutenant," Ben responded. He was enjoying stretching his legs outside the Hummer after a long ride. "You can lead me there right now. I want to recee the place while the R Batt gets in position. Have your men do that, if you will."

"Yes, sir. It's only three miles. Uh—you plan on bringing that dog with you?"

"Smoot? Of course," Ben said blandly.

"The Nazis have some pooches with them. If they get a whiff of your, ah, Smoot, they'll set off a racket."

"Take us in from downwind. I only want to be close enough to check out the place through binoculars."

"Very good, sir. If you'll come with me, sir?"

Ben and team followed in the Hummer. Lieutenant Fuller's silenced moped made not a sound as he took rutted dirt roads that led Ben's party first away from York, then back on what Ben assumed to be the downwind side. Near the crest of a ridge that put them back close to U.S. 81, the brake light flared briefly and Cooper, now recovered from his brief experience with the hallucinogen, stopped the Hummer. Ben eased from the back of the vehicle and followed Fuller to the crest of the ridge.

41

There he eased down on his chest and belly and produced a pair of light-gathering night glasses. Ben fitted the lenses to his eyes and scanned the terrain between them and the sagging corrugated metal fence around the drive-in. Amateurs, Ben thought contemptuously a few minutes later. They had failed to put out any security. Next he examined the tall structure that housed the screen.

A few boards were missing, and others had warped enough to wrench free of their nails. The paint had faded and chipped; large, scabrous splotches had flaked off entirely. He could still make out the sign that identified it as: 81 DRIVE-IN THEATRE.

"Looks like the Nazis have taken their families out to a movie," Ben whispered to Fuller. "I'd like to slip along this ridge a ways and take a better look at the people inside."

"Nothing to it, sir," Fuller assured him.

Ten minutes of slow, cautious movement put them in total darkness and at an angle that exposed the occupants of the drive-in and the screen. Ben scanned the people first. They had come in all sort of vehicles. Far Eyes — Fuller — had been accurate, as well as picturesque, in his description. Rusting pickups lined up on the ridges of the drive-in beside old, spring-sagging sedans and two-ton stake trucks. Here and there a battered van stood out in blocky silhouette. The people were a shock.

Crew-cut kids, clean and neatly dressed, sat beside equally respectable looking adults. Most of the males had crew-cuts, or shaved heads. The women wore their hair close-cropped, but in feminine styles. Most of the men wore short-sleeved black shirts and trousers. The boys wore brown shirts and black shorts. All, men and women alike, wore the red-white-black armbands so chillingly familiar to the whole world for more than a half-century. In the center of the white circles sprawled the *Hakenkreuz* — literally, the bent cross, Ben reflected. Twisted was more like it. Portable generators coughed to life, and a powerful beam of light speared from a large step-van.

Images flickered to life on the damaged screen. Against a cautionary tug from Lieutenant Fuller, Ben edged closer to get a better fix on detail. As he watched, a sea of puffy, roiling clouds filled the frame. The angle changed and the shadow of an old Fokker Tri-Motor airplane was cast on the clouds. Slowly the scene dissolved to a very-medieval-looking town.

Tall stone buildings, gray and mossy with age, came into focus. A cathedral with Gothic arches and flying buttress supports filled the screen, sped on past below the point of view of the camera. Ben could almost hear the Wagnerian music swell and segue into the strident notes of the "Horst Wessel Song."

He knew this movie well. He had seen it a couple of times before the Great War. One of those had been at a film festival, could you imagine. Touted as the cinematic genius of director Leni Riefenstahl, *Triumph of the Will* was the title. Commissioned personally by Adolf Hitler, she had used her directorial skill to elevate to an almost-religious rite the proceedings of the 1934 Nazi Party Congress at Nuremberg.

When Adolf Hitler deplaned on the screen and was met by an obsequious covey of sycophants, Ben pulled back. "Let's get to my mobile CP, it should be up here by now," he urged Lieutenant Fuller. Ben could clearly hear Fuller's sigh of relief.

Back with his team, he found Jersey fidgety. No doubt she was miffed at being left behind. He'd rarely gotten away with that since the Battle for New York. As he had anticipated, the big eighteen-wheeler that served as his mobile command post rolled in and hissed air brakes to stop short of a ridge that concealed it from the Nazi mob in the drive-in. Quickly he outlined what he had observed.

"Our black-shirt friends are having a night at the movies. There's about seven hundred of them in there

43

now. I suggest we wait and see what comes next." He consulted the aviator's chronometer on his wrist. "We have a while until Stan McDade gets R Batt in position. Corrie, get on the horn and tell Dan to hold Three Battalion where it is. Then bump Buddy and tell him I want him here with me."

"Right away, General." She began muttering softly into the mike.

What happened next was that six more generators wound up and the area in front of the screen, in the old days a playground for the kiddies to while away the time until darkness and the movie, lit up in bright lights. An old World War II carbon-arc searchlight illuminated the large stage constructed there.

A military band of boys eight to fourteen lined the back of the stage. Their drum major, who was a good three years shy of having to shave, raised his long baton with its ball and tip of gold, and chrome shaft. He brought it down sharply and the musicians struck up. The boys, all towheaded and crew-cut, with clear eyes, from cobalt to cerulean, their thin lips set in lines of concentration, each in the brown shirt and black shorts of the youth uniform, slammed sticks to drumheads and tootled trumpets and fifes. A glockenspiel tinkled merrily. Ben scratched his memory and identified the music as "Die Jugend Marchiert," anthem of the Hitler Youth, Adolf's junior hate league.

"Damn them," Ben swore vehemently. "Damn them all for what they are doing to those children."

When the music ended, a tall, lean, deathly pale man crossed the stage in the cone of actinic light from the carbon-arc and stopped at the podium behind a bank of microphones. Cheers and shouts of *"Sieg Heil!"* came from the darkened recesses of the drive-in. The man, in the ebony uniform of the SS, raised his hands to silence the crowd.

"Many of you know me. For those who do not, I

44

am SS *Hauptsturmbannführer* Peter Volmer." He pronounced his first name *Pet-ter*. "I command our glorious American SS *Leibstandarte Hoffman*. I come to you in the name of racial purity. I come to you in the name of a nigger- and Jew-free America. I come to you in the name of *Feldmarschall* Hoffman of the New Army of Liberation. To bring you good news!"

At a near-hysterical pitch, the chanting of *"Sieg Heil!"* rose in monstrous waves into the Nebraska night. When the mob, which is what they had become, quieted, Volmer went on with his message of hate and Aryan supremacy. By that time, Buddy had arrived and the R Batt was deployed.

"What do you have laid on, Pop?" Buddy asked irreverently. He had come to take a liking to British idiom while they had fought in England.

"We have a nest of some seven to eight hundred American Nazis in that theater. Less than three days ago, it is believed they slaughtered several hundred of their neighbors who didn't buy the super-race crap."

"I know. We saw some of Bull's scouts covering the grave," said a subdued Buddy.

"I think they need a lesson in friendly neighborhood relations," Ben went on glibly, in an effort to contain his outrage.

"In other words, kick-ass time," Jersey translated.

Four

Buddy studied the interior of the drive-in with his own long night glasses. He turned back to Ben with a drawn expression. "What about the kids?"

"Yeah, General," Beth said softly in that particular way of hers. "What about those kids?"

The ball had settled solidly in Ben's court. It was his call. He knew it and didn't like it. Then the images of those small, twisted bodies in that charnel pit outside Bellville rose behind his eyes. Hadn't enough kids died? Then, as though she had divined his thoughts, Jersey spoke up.

"What about all those kids around Concordia and Bellville?" she asked. "Good Rebel kids."

Renewed outrage choked up in Ben Raines. "I owe them," he declared before he could stop himself. A shrug and he went on. "I—we—the Rebels promised them a safe place to live and grow up."

He raised his field glasses again and studied the set faces of the juvenile Nazis in their band formation. They are all so squeaky-clean, Ben thought. And so proud of their uniforms. Are they as proud of their cause? he wondered. He lowered the binoculars thoughtfully.

"Kids can run fast. And they have good reactions," he allowed. He turned his back, shut off the sight of those files of cherubic faces in back of the podium. He signaled for Lt. Col. Bull McDade and Lt. Fuller

46

to join himself and Buddy. "Stan, set up the mortars and instruct the gunners to walk the rounds in from the back. Frag rounds and willie peter."

"Yes, sir," Bull McDade delivered in an easy drawl.

"One Apache up to dust off that place." McDade nodded. "Fuller, I want scouts in the lead at each exit to that place. Full assault gear for everyone. I want to wipe out this Nazi scum here and now."

"I already have them in place, General," Fuller informed Ben.

"Buddy, I want you and your light company to come with me."

"Not still mother-henning me, are you, Pop?"

Tension and stress narrowed Ben's eyes. "You know better than that, son. I've saved the hardest job for you. I need you to make for the stage and terminate this Peter Volmer. Intel says he ranks second only to General Brodermann now. Make that *Brigadeführer;* Volmer's even got Hoffman using the old SS titles."

"How can a sickness like this take such deep root?" Buddy asked.

"Ours not to reason why, son," Ben quipped, pulled out of his earlier doldrums by the prospect of action. "Ours but to kick ass."

"One people! One State! One world!" Peter Volmer roared in conclusion.

"Sieg Heil! Sieg Heil! Sieg Heil!" screamed the assembled Nazis.

"Open the dance if you please, Bull," Ben Raines spoke into the mouthpiece of Corrie's handset.

Twin turbines spooled up in the squat AH-64 Apache and the main rotor began to turn. It rapidly became a blur. Then the heavily armed craft lifted off, tail-high, its nose appearing to sniff the ground like a bloodhound. The pilot in his right-hand seat leveled the bird and it *whop-whopped* away toward the theater.

Rebel mortar rounds *thunked* and their fins shivered spines with their ringing sound as they exited the tubes. With feathery whispers they arched high in the night sky and turned end over, to plummet into the 81 DRIVE-IN THEATER. Deadly blossoms opened over the heads of the occupants, white at the center, then pale yellow and duller orange on the edges.

The Cobra peeked over the top of the screen housing and opened up with two 40mm rocket pods and a pair of 20mm chainguns. The red lines of tracers terminated in exploding projectiles that set off new horror among the Nazis. The chorus of "Sieg Heils" cut off in midfrenzy.

Screams of terror replaced it. Passenger cars, pickups, and stake trucks made fiery ascent as gas tanks ruptured and exploded in a scalding rain of white phosphorus. Body parts went skyward with them. Ben Raines gave the go-ahead and the Hummer raced toward the nearest exit. Buddy's multiwheeled light scout vehicle bounded along beside. Rebel scouts appeared out of the dark brush near the unlighted gate and rushed to block passage. Ben and team, with Buddy, charged inside. The flash from the last mortar rounds had barely faded when they reached the scene of bloodshed and devastation within.

"Out," Ben clipped his command.

"Everyone unass this thing," Cooper elaborated.

Ben's team exploded into pandemonium. Wounded people screamed and writhed on the ground. Others, blood streaming from shrapnel wounds, ran by with blank faces and glassy eyes. Ben learned that the Nazis had not come unarmed when a bullet cracked by his head. He swung up the Thompson one-handed and bucked out a five-round burst.

Fat .45 slugs slammed into flesh and sent the offending Nazi into a giddy dance of death. He had not been alone, Ben noted, as the "Supermen" began to fight back. Individual shots came to Ben as little more than pops and crackles. His mind concentrated on the overall rhythm of battle.

Somehow this one played like an orchestra without a conductor. One hoarse-voiced man shouted down the mindless shrieking of a dozen Nazis and began to organize the resistance. Ben pointed and Jersey knew what he wanted.

Together they cut three-round bursts into the gathered enemy. American crapheads fell to left and right. Satisfied at the level of confusion that had been restored, Ben chanced a glance toward the stage and podium.

Peter Volmer was no longer there. A Walther P-38 in his left hand, he stood at the edge of the stage, firing into the air and bellowing for his Nazi horde to rally around him.

"For the Reich! For the Reich!" he screamed. "Stand by me."

Armed American hatemongers began to gather at the foot of the stage. So far, Ben saw nothing of Buddy. Worry lines creased his forehead. The battalion could take care of itself, he reasoned. Already they would be jumping off to mop up this vast collection of slime. Buddy was another story. He had spread out his company to sweep from front to rear of the parking area. Only three of his scouts accompanied him on his mission to scoop up Volmer.

He would have to fend for himself. Ben let go as more Rebels began to pour through the points of egress. The sweet-faced boys in the band produced shiny-bladed daggers, complete with spread-winged eagles and swastikas on the pommels, and made ready to die for *Führer* and fatherland. They formed a skirmish line between Buddy and Volmer. Ben bit his lip and shot the oldest of them, who had an SKS assault rifle in his hands.

On full auto, it ripped holes in the sky as the junior Hitler died from three .45 slugs in the chest. Suddenly four men appeared amid the smoking wreckage of mangled cars. Snarling their hate, they leapt into an attack on Ben Raines.

"Would you shoot our kids, now, you yellow bastard," one of them accused in a County Armagh accent.

Funny, he sounded more like IRA material than a Nazi. Maybe he was both, Ben considered in the flash of time it took him to swing the long barrel of his Thompson 1927 A-1 subgun and smack the nearest of the quartet in the side of his head.

The man rubber-legged his way into the side of an overturned Mustang and pitched headfirst through the window into the space behind the front seat. A bullet, from close range, jerked the beret off Ben Raines's head, and he shot the assailant with a tight trio of .45 justice.

To his right, Ben heard the chatter of Jersey's M-16 and a shriek of pain from her target. Beth held her own on Ben's left. She had two men down on their knees, hands laced behind their heads. With a neat wing shot, she cleared a charging Nazi off the hood of a car. Another gas tank exploded and the searchlight went out with a blue-white flash and plume of smoke.

"Hold fast," Volmer exhorted his followers. "Hold them here."

"Where's Buddy?" Ben took time to ask, worried that Volmer remained operational.

"I have him on the honk," Corrie said from behind Ben. "He says that with all of the lights out, he can't find Volmer."

"Tell him to keep trying." Then with a father's concern, "And to keep his head down."

Corrie spoke and laughed. "He says he can't do both."

"Smart-mouthed whippersnapper!" Ben said in an old-codger voice.

Peter Volmer had never before heard the sound of incoming mortar rounds. Their fluttery passage through the air could not be distinguished at first, over the chanting of the crowd. When he became conscious of the first few, they produced a brief *whuffle-BAM!* The effect was enough to make an impression he would keep the rest of his life.

Terror grew within Peter Volmer as rapidly as the white-hot flashes of exploding rounds. They began in the back and the screams of his people marched forward with them. A warm wetness spread at Volmer's crotch and he felt the trickle of liquid down his leg.

"Incoming!" shouted someone in the audience with more experience than himself.

Incoming what? Volmer wondered. Then one of his SS officers grabbed his arm and yanked him toward the far side of the stage. "Someone—the Rebels are mortaring us. We gotta get out of here."

Peter Volmer stared at a shower of smoking white globs that splattered across the roofs and hoods of cars, where they ignited instant flames. Fountains of blazing orange geysered from split gas tanks. Behind him the young musicians added shrill pandemonium. Concussion shattered the incandescent bulbs of floodlights. From above and behind him, Volmer heard the *whopping* sound of rotor blades, and a stream of tracers streaked past and sought out targets among the crazed mass of people. Then armed men in ballistic helmets appeared in the exits. Seemingly without provocation, they opened fire on the terrorized Party members. A detached arm flew into the air less than halfway to the stage.

"No—nooooo," Volmer moaned.

Another insistent tug set him in motion. He reached the center of the stage when an exploding gas tank took out the searchlight and plunged the theater into darkness. He had a fleeting impression of more men pouring into the drive-in. Suddenly the mortar shelling ceased. The crackle of small-arms fire punctuated the eerie scene that remained imprinted on the retinas of Peter Volmer's eyes.

51

"What do we do? What do we do?" he asked, totally disoriented.

"We get out of here," the hard voice of his adjutant rasped in his ear.

Right then, that sounded like the best suggestion Peter Volmer had ever heard.

Lt. Col. Stanley Bull McDade watched the progress of his R Batt troops through a tripod-mounted IR scope. A rueful grin spread the full lips under a neatly tended white brush of mustache. How he envied Ben Raines for being right down there in the thick. Hell, Ben should be in the rear, running this show, not out cowboying it with those kids.

"What am I saying?" he blurted aloud, waggling the thatch of his Vandyke. Ben Raines could never resist mixing it up with the bad guys. And these Nazis, *American* Nazis, were nearly as odious a lot of baddies as the creepies.

The wiggly green glow of the IR scope revealed scouts and some of his troopers in position at the exits and rear entrance. He keyed the microphone clipped to his battle harness. "Cease firing," he commanded the mortar crews. "Now the fun begins," he grunted to the young RT operator standing next to him.

"How's that, sir?" the youth asked. A replacement after the devastating battles with Hoffman's blackshirts, he had been a recent graduate of the basic training program at Base Camp One.

"That's right, you've never been in on one of General Raines's big operations. There aren't a lot of combat soldiers among Hitler's little helpers down there," McDade launched into an explanation. "When we get enough people in there, those that are left will start to surrender." At the RT man's quizzical expression, Bull chuckled. "Contrary to popular belief, the Rebels do take prisoners. It's how they are sometimes

52

disposed of that gives us our bad reputation among what bleeding-hearts are left. All of the leaders of any captured group are questioned personally by Ben Raines. It can be quite an education," he added dryly, "to those who live through it. Now, get the companies on the move. We have to contain that lowlife scum down there."

Ben Raines found he had a lot to handle, and all at once. A huge follower of the deranged Volmer came at him from between two overturned cars. The man had upper arms like most men's thighs. His legs churned on the uneven gravel of the theater, flexing muscles many people don't even know they have. Thick, stubby fingers groped for Ben's neck, and the Rebel commander smelled the fetid stench of rotting teeth in a widely stretched mouth.

Ben butt-stroked a mountain of belly with his tommy-chopper and found it contained mostly muscle. The giant grunted and grinned at Ben, who knew he was in trouble. Let go of the Thompson and make a try for his sidearm? Foolish. Ben shifted his balance and planted a boot toe in his attacker's crotch.

A piglike squeal came from a crimson face. Found a weak spot, Ben exulted. He stepped back and snapped the steel buttplate of his subgun into the man's lips. Small, reddened eyes rolled up and squeezed shut. Slowly the gargantuan leaned forward and fell at Ben's feet, his brush of crew-cut on the tips of Ben's boots.

"Sorry, General," Jersey offered from his side. "I missed that one."

McDade's R Batt troops arrived at that moment. They swarmed inside the drive-in with a raw roar that cast many a spine in ice. Charged-up Rebels, eager to settle scores, fell on the American Nazis. A series of flashes lit the darkness close-by, and Ben heard the crack of bullets punching through metal only inches from his head.

He squatted at once. The big Thompson snarled in crisp bursts. A scream rewarded Ben's marksmanship. Two more Nazi slime rushed at him out of the darkness. One held a hastily improvised Molotov cocktail. Jersey ran a .223 zipper up his torso. The last slug shattered glass and drenched the dying man and his companion with flaming gasoline.

"You'd think they would be giving up by now," Ben commented.

"They outnumber us, remember, General?" Jersey jibed.

"I've got Buddy again on the RT, sir," Corrie informed Ben. She crouched nearby.

"What have you got, Rat?" Ben asked.

"Nothin', Eagle. That head Nazi and the kids in the band skinnied out through a hidden entrance at the base of the screen."

"Send someone after them?"

"Already done, Eagle. Don't know if it'll do any good. In all this confusion and the dark, it took us a while to realize they were gone." Buddy hated to admit defeat.

"Keep working on it," Ben advised. "From here it looks like we've cut down the resistance."

"Roger that, Eagle. Only a couple of pockets down here by the stage."

"Do what you have to, Rat. Eagle out."

Lights began to come on randomly around the drive-in. With growing frequency, camo-clad troopers passed Ben's position prodding defeated "supermen" ahead of them. A final fusillade came from the direction of the stage, and then general silence. Only the crisp orders of the Rebels, the cry of the wounded, and the wail of the vanquished could be heard.

Gabe Trasher slammed a big fist on the cracked

Formica table. "I don't give a shit about your fucking orders, Adlerhoff. I wanna talk to the field marshal at once. Or at least Colonel Webber. Fuckin' Ben Raines is goin' ape."

With a muttered curse, the NAL radio duty man said he would contact one of the staff aides. Gabe sat back and rolled a joint. He liked this part of the country. Wacky tobaccy grew wild along the roads and in pastures. He cut his eyes to Numb Nuts Nicholson.

"Hey, Nuts, it's a good thing we didn't decide to take on Raines and his Rebels." It was as close to admitting that what they had seen at the drive-in had scared the living hell out of him that Gabe Trasher would get.

"Yeah. Them Nazis got blowed up real good. Boom! Oh, shit, *boom!*" His gobbling pig-squeal of laughter filled the room.

Gabe winced, then turned his attention back to the radio as General Webber's voice sputtered over the speaker. "This is the G-Two."

"Trasher here, Webber—er—Adlerhoff Two. Ben Raines and his Rebels just hit some of your American friends at a drive-in outside York, Nebraska. That's on U.S. Highway 81."

"I know where it is," Webber responded in a tired tone. "Do you have an assessment of the damage?"

"Total fucking loss, Webber buddy. I mean, like those Rebels creamed them."

After a long pause, Webber spoke in a subdued tone. "I was more concerned with Rebel losses."

"Maybe a dozen wounded. Two of them blown away trying to stop your boy Volmer."

"Did—did the *Hauptsturmbannführer* get away?" Webber asked, and Trasher could almost believe he hoped the news would be bad.

"Yeah. Him an' a bunch of little boys in short pants hauled ass in a Mercedes and a transcon bus."

"A bit of misfortune for the *Herr Hautman,*" Webber

said idly. "Why did you not engage to relieve them?"

"I got my orders, Webber. I'm to stand by until told otherwise by your field marshal."

"Yes, I see. I shall convey this information to the field marshal first thing in the morning."

"I'd think he would want to know right away."

Webber sighed disdainfully into the mike. "If the Americans are lost, they're lost. No need to disturb *Feldmarschall* Hoffman's sleep for that." He must have handed the microphone back to the RT operator, for it was his voice that came next. "Adlerhoff out."

Gabe Trasher turned to Numb Nuts Nicholson. "That's one cold fucking fish, my man. But, not as cold, I'm thinking, as Ben Raines."

Five

Ben Raines had no desire to lose a night's sleep. He knew the troops could use a good rest, also. They'd been on the hump for three days. He also knew that in the first hours after an engagement and subsequent capture, prisoners in an expectably shocked and demoralized condition talked more readily and freely.

Might as well get it going and over with, Ben decided, rousing himself. He walked to the chair set for him on the stage. Rebel generators provided the juice now to light the area at the center. Below him, in an area cleared of wrecked cars and trucks, the prisoners sat in glum defeat. They had been segregated by sex, and children from adults. The leaders among them who had identified themselves or were suspected by the Rebels had been lined up on the stage. They stood with hands behind their heads, glaring defiance.

Another everyday interrogation scene, Ben thought. Yet, this time Ben experienced an aspect of unreality about it. His unyielding eyes swept over the men, and a few women, culled out as leaders. He didn't see the rabid dogs of creepies, or scruffy bikers, full of bluff and bluster. Not even dim-witted, slovenly rednecks, their kids' bellies swollen from malnutrition and bones bowed by rickets. These are normal-looking, clean-cut folks, Ben told himself for the fifth time.

57

They would be right at home at any Rebel outpost. In fact, Intelligence had informed him, some of them had been. That's what galled the most. Many of these leaders, and the ones who followed them, had lived undetected right among them. What separated these "average Joes" from his Rebels and the good people they protected was the deadly poison of Nazism. Abandoning that line of thought, Ben took his seat at the small table.

He cut his eyes to Jersey, who stood upstage, at the ready with her M-16. Corrie hovered close behind him, with the radio. Ben carefully laid his recent find, a mint-condition IMI Desert Eagle .50 caliber Action Express autoloader, on the table. Cocked and locked, the smooth parkerized finish and half-inch bore gave it a very no-nonsense appearance. It took a big hand to control that much pistol, and Ben Raines had all he needed. He nodded to Buddy, who shoved one of the captives forward.

"What is your name?" Ben demanded.

"I don't have to say anything to you, whoever you are."

"I'm Ben Raines." It came soft and quiet, cloaked in menace.

The Nazi paled slightly but retained his defiance. "I am a prisoner of war. All I have to give is my name, rank, and serial number."

"That so? Seems I asked for your name, didn't I?"

"Dalton, Gerald R."

"Don't try to tire me out by being tedious, asshole. Give me the rest of it. And I want the name of your unit."

"Dalton, Gerald R., *Standar*—ah—Captain." He rattled off a meaningless string of numbers.

Ben's eyes narrowed. *"Standartenführer.* So you're SS, eh? Your bunch that stage-managed that massacre back down the road?"

"I don't know . . . I have nothing more to say," Dalton blurted.

58

"Oh, but I think you do, *Standartenführer* Dalton. I think my Intelligence people will get a great deal out of you."

Dalton paled even more. "Torture is against the Geneva Convention."

Ben Raines laughed softly. "Neither the Convention nor Geneva exists anymore, you hopeless bastard. Lucky for you, the Rebels don't use torture anyway. My G-2 people have nice, thin needles and vials of chemicals that do far better."

"You can't use chemical interrogation," Dalton stated with heated conviction. "It's—"

"Against the Convention? Can and will. You're trying my patience, *Standartenführer*." Ben made the SS rank sound like something that floated on the top of a septic tank. "Sergeant Bourchart, take him away."

A burly noncom in the rank to Ben's right stepped forward, grinning. "My pleasure, General."

Panic seized Dalton. "What are you going to do to me?"

Ben gave him a cold smile. "We're going to use those chemicals on you and find out if you had anything to do with the butchery of those innocent people. If you did, a squad of my Rebels will hang you."

"You caaaaan't dooooo thaaaaat!" Dalton wailed until silenced by the extended, stiffened fingers of Sergeant Bourchart striking him in the solar plexus.

"Next."

Scarlet hatred blazed from this Nazi's eyes. "You are a mongrelizing bastard, Ben Raines. You lie down in the stink of nigger sweat. You allow pure Aryan children to rub their bodies against the disgusting flesh of the yellow, brown, black inferior races. You promote degeneracy and glorify perversion."

Ben Raines laughed in his face. When he recovered his composure, he pointed a long, thick finger at the Nazi, who quivered with indignation. "Wanda would

59

love that. She would just fall down and roll around in hilarity."

"Who—who is Wanda?" the fanatic demanded.

"It's—just Wanda. She commands a company of Rebels known as the Sisters of Lesbos."

The Nazi actually gagged. His face wore a mask of horror and revulsion. "You're the scourge of America, Ben Raines!" he howled. A sudden transition occurred in his expression and a light that said he knew it all now glowed in his eyes. "Ben? *Benjamin?* You're a filthy, Jew-boy prick, Raines."

"No. Some people may see me as a *schmuck,* but I am not Jewish. Corporal Schultz, pick three men and take this . . . thing over against that wall and shoot him." To the others he said, "Listen up, people. We don't have time to finesse this moral-outrage crap with all of you. You are going to answer questions quickly and concisely or you are going to die. Is that *fucking* clear to all of you?"

As though on cue, three rifles cracked on the far side of the stage. The indignant Nazi fell in a heap, twitched, and went still. Ben signaled for another to be brought forward.

The American Nazi had a bloody shirtfront and started talking even before being placed squarely in front of the table where Ben sat. "I am Walter Utting. I am an SS *Standartegruppenführer* in the *Leibstandarte Hoffman.* My serial number is 559-34-6877. You are going to be sorry you did this, Ben Raines. *Hauptstandartenführer* Peter Volmer will see to that."

"Where has Volmer gone?" Ben asked conversationally.

"I don't know. But, when he comes after you, his vengeance will be terrible to behold. I understand you have two children, General? A boy and a girl. Volmer will save them for his *Sturmabteilungen,* his storm troopers. The troops will use them in every orifice of their bodies, and when they tire of the game, Volmer will personally cut out the hearts of

60

your diseased offspring."

"*Not!*" There were many things Ben could have, or perhaps should have, said to this arrogant asshole. But that made his point quite well, backed up by his swift uplifting of the big .50 Desert Eagle handgun. His thumb snapped off the safety and a fat, half-inch, 305-grain, jacketed hollowpoint bullet blew away the back of Utting's head from behind the ears. Utting's blood, brains, and bone splattered his fellow Nazis.

"Excuse me," Ben said to the gagging prisoners. "I tend to get overprotective of my children. Now, who has something worthwhile to tell me?"

That loosened the tongues of several smaller fry. They literally babbled their names and unit identities. Three of them positively identified the dead Utting as commander of the SS battalion that had engineered the bloodbath outside Bellville. He had brought a company of them with him to the theater, they told Ben. Ben immediately sent Buddy's company among the other captives to root out Utting's troopers. They went about their task with his laconic comment ringing in their ears.

"I don't know where you'll find enough rope, but I'm sure you'll manage."

Shortly, storm troopers began to dangle from the support posts of the twelve-foot-high fence around the drive-in, to kick and choke out their lives. In the middle of the grisly round of executions, a portly man came forward to talk with Ben. He might have been a banker in any normal sort of world, Ben considered.

"I am Major Richard Wagner—ah—no known relation to the composer, of *Hauptsturmbannführer* Volmer's staff. Perhaps I can provide you with the information you seek."

"I'm willing to wager one of Lamar's field rations that you can," Ben responded dryly.

"The *Hauptsturmbannführer* is making a tour of all of the gathering Party members. It is considered a momentous occasion by we American Nazis that the heir to Adolf Hitler has at last come to North America. Even the smallest tactical unit is eager to join in the great work. Our families, naturally, wish to reach Field Marshal Hoffman's interior zone in the northwest for reasons of safety. The *Hauptsturmbannführer* is selecting a few key people and taking them with him. The rest he is ordering to proceed due west."

"Why is that?" Wagner had Ben's interest.

"They are to establish a line of resistance points from the ruins of Miles City, Montana; south through Cheyenne, Wyoming; Colorado Springs; Santa Rosa, New Mexico; then Alamogordo; and on to El Paso, Texas."

"There are how many of these American Nazis?" Ben probed.

"Somewhere between ten and twelve thousand of combat age."

Intelligence had told him that, but the blunt answer stunned Ben. Yet, they had ambitions to cover a distance of a thousand miles. That made ten men to a mile.

"Hoffman's spreading them a little thin, isn't he?"

Wagner looked Ben straight in the eye. "That is my belief, also, General Raines. However, they are to be reinforced by a *Standartegruppe* of *Brigadeführer* Brodermann's SS."

"A battalion." That amused Ben Raines. "Thinks rather highly of them, doesn't he? Especially considering what we did to them two months ago."

A terrified scream interrupted Wagner's reply. "Noooooooo! I don' wanna die like that!" One of Dalton's SS troopers broke away from Buddy's executioners and raced for the wall. Ben and the cooperative Nazi watched with mild interest as another of the rank-and-file Nazis stuck out a foot and tripped the frightened wretch.

"Gawdamned coward," the prisoner snarled.

Three of Buddy's company picked the fallen SS man and carried him to the wall. In a trice they had the rope around his neck and hauled on the bite end.

"*Gaawk!* Hail Mary . . . *aawk* . . . full of . . . *gaaaak!*" the doomed man choked out.

"And a closet Christian at that," the Nazi who had tripped him said scornfully.

Ben turned from the scene. "You have been very helpful, Major Wagner. Is there anything else you have to tell me?"

He did. He spoke earnestly for ten minutes. Ben listened, his frown deepening. At the conclusion, Ben motioned a guard to his table. "Keep this officer segregated from the others. He is to be treated as a bona fide prisoner of war." He came to his boots and gestured toward the remaining Nazi leaders. "Find out what you can and then deal with them accordingly. I have some serious thinking to do."

In accordance with a lifelong habit, Field Marshal Jesus Dieguez Mendoza Hoffman awakened half an hour before sunrise. By the time the east blazed with white light and pale pink blushed the western slopes of the Cascades, he had showered and shaved and taken care of bodily eliminations. Dressed in knee-length, shiny black boots, with Junker spurs, gray-green trousers with a field marshal's black and silver stripes, picked out by a center line of red, matching tunic, and tall peaked hat with its spread eagle and swastika, he strolled from his sleeping quarters to the officer's mess. A riding crop grasped in his right hand slapped idly at the leather-gloved left.

He had just settled in at a comfortable table with his first coffee of the day and a delightfully plump *Sachertorte,* when G-2 Colonel Webber brought him the news of the disaster at York. He listened with a growing frown, and brushed irritatedly at the hanging lock of hair over his left eye. After Webber had stammered his report, Hoffman raised an eye and its brow at the chubby colonel.

"What a pity. We could have used another seven hundred men. You believe Utting was captured? At least most of his men got away?"

"Yes, Field Marshal."

"Ah! Ah, yes," Hoffman said brightly. "I have this very morning come to a decision about that. I have promoted myself. Henceforth I will be referred to as *Generalfeldmarschall*. Do you understand, Webber?"

"*Zu Befehl, Herr Generalfeldmarschall.*"

"Excellent, Webber. Now, our estimable *Hauptsturmbannführer* Volmer also managed to escape?"

"It was so reported, *Generalfeldmarschall.*"

"Wonderful. And I do hope those dear boys in that band he takes around with him managed to avoid capture and indoctrination by the Rebels."

"Absolutely, *Generalfeldmarschall.*"

Generalfeldmarschall Hoffman's benign mood evaporated in a cloud of rage. "Then can you tell me by all that's holy, how in the hell did this outrage happen?" Webber gaped. He had no answer. "With an SS regiment, albeit an American one, in the vicinity, along with Volmer's usual security, and you say at least three hundred effective soldiers in that theater, I should be viewing the corpse of General Ben Raines right now, not listening to another in a long litany of defeats." He spotted Karl Richter entering the mess, waved him over.

"*Jahwohl, Herr Feldmarschall. Was wollen Sie?*" Senior aide or not, Richter learned about the promotion in acid terms. "*Generalfeldmarschall,*" he corrected.

Then Hoffman told him what he wanted. "Staff meeting in half an hour. I want all troops put on alert. I want immediate contact with this Gabe Trasher person and his Alien Secretions—*Liebe Gott*, what an outlandish name—never mind. I want him now, now."

"Zu Befehl, Herr Generalfeldmarschall," Richter managed to choke out. He of all the staff at least spoke German without an outrageous Latino accent.

"It's the head kraut, or kraut-head, whichever," Numb Nuts told Gabe, and gobbled his obnoxious giggle.

Trasher took the microphone. "You've got the head Alien Secretion, come back," he brayed into the mike in a style reminiscent of some eighteen-wheelers on the superslab.

"This is General Field Marshal Hoffman. You are to go to full alert. Put your unit in the field and stand by to initiate a diversionary action on orders of this headquarters. Over."

"Well, well, the old fart's promoted himself," Trasher said to the four persons in the room with him and Numb Nuts. Into the mike, he replied, "Yeah. I copy that. But we don't have any long-range radio rig that's mobile. How will we hear when and what we're supposed to do?"

"You will be informed by other NAL units nearer your location. Tune your mobile radios to 137.45 MHz and monitor at all times. As to what your mission will be, set your recording equipment to receive a burst transmission at once."

"At once," Trasher mimicked, with limp wrist bent on one hip and mouthing the words in a grotesque manner. At a nod from Little Dick Bentley, he told Hoffman, "Send away, we're ready."

Little Dick Bentley, named for an unfortunate characteristic of his anatomy, watched the needle on the recorder's VU meter climb into the red and winced. He understood the practical application of burst or "squawk" transmissions, but the physics behind them eluded him entirely. He had always been taught to keep his modulation out of the red. How could these split-second transmissions peg the old needle every time and not come out distorted? Never mind, he dismissed, it worked and that's what counted.

So they were gonna see some action at last. That's what Little Dick hungered after. He also hungered after some of the fine mommas who hung out with the gang, but they knew of his legendary under-endowment, and viewed him with contempt.

It wasn't fair, he thought resentfully. It wasn't his fault he was hung like a stud mouse. But that left him only the preteenies they sometimes scooped up to lust after, and of course the small boys. Which wasn't such a bad selection, Little Dick allowed, when he looked at it in the proper light. Yeah, real action, man. How he longed to spill some Rebel blood.

"Everybody out," Gabe Trasher bellowed when he finished with the radio. "I gotta listen to this and decide how we go about it."

They shuffled out into the sunlight and Gabe played the tape twice. He listened carefully both times. A wild light filled his beady green eyes when he stepped out onto the crumbling porch of the old house.

"Listen up, everybody. Ol' Hoffman baby says that Ben Raines has a habit of striking out ahead of his main column. Well, he's given us the job of tweaking the nose of that bastard Raines. We're gonna fan out and find him, then we sting him good and run away. And sting him and run again and again, until we sting him to death."

A chorus of drunken and narco-crazed voices raised in a ragged cheer.

Six

Ben Raines sat scratching Smoot's big, triangular ears. The woolly Siberian husky had flopped her seventy pounds down on the toes of Ben's boots. The intelligence Ben had developed from interrogation of the more cooperative American Nazis troubled him greatly. He had summoned this council of war, and now, Ben had to admit, he didn't know exactly what he wanted to propose.

They had only just completed a protracted guerrilla-type war against Hoffman and his black-shirts. In the culmination of that, the units had been drawn back together. It was obvious what Hoffman, and his new military genius, Peter Volmer, wanted the Rebels to do. The logistics alone made it nearly impossible to grant Hoffman his expectation.

Take gasoline, Ben ruminated while he waited for the nearby commanders to arrive. Tanker trucks not only delivered fuel, they consumed it while they rolled. Already the line had been stretched mighty thin between the refinery and the troops in the field. In his campaign against the loathsome creepies, nearly all of the underground storage tanks scattered around the nation had been sucked dry, or blown up along with the creepie centers in the towns where they were located.

It would be sheer happenstance to locate sufficient quantities on a thousand-mile front. Ammunition resupply presented another problem. Groceries for over seven thousand combat troops and their support elements staggered the imagination when contemplating locating and distributing them. For all of the Rebels' stabilizing and civilizing efforts, the United States sadly lacked adequate supplies and the means to transport them. The nation had been laid to waste, mostly at the hands of the Rebels themselves.

That had been necessary to exterminate the cannibal cult of the Night People. Ben didn't harbor regrets for what he had ordered. To the contrary, it had been necessary and he had stood up to the challenge. Some men would have been content to rest on their laurels. Not Ben Raines.

He had quixotically gone off to clean up the rest of the world. Or at least as much of it as his Rebels could touch. In the unsteady peace that descended on the United States, agriculture enjoyed a revival, as did commerce and trade. Left alone, people exerted their efforts positively. At least some.

Because during that hiatus, there had been a secret resurgence of the old, much-discredited American Nazi movement. What in God's name attracted people to that shopworn socialist claptrap? *Nazi,* Ben reminded himself, was an acronym for *Nationalsozialist,* a member or supporter of the *Nationalsozialistische Deutsche Arbeiter-Partei* — National Socialist German Workers' Party. Over the years, since that cancer erupted in Germany in 1933, the "Socialist" had been cunningly dropped from any references in Great Britain and the United States to fit the politically correct espousal of socialism and Marxism by those nations' left-leaning liberals.

Truth was, Ben mused, Hitler's brand of socialism was anything but "right-wing" and as morally and economically bankrupt as all the others. Time proved that; the Soviet Union went broke and collapsed, and Marxism died in its client states. Germany was reunited, he reminded himself, and what the hell happened? The neo-Nazi movement flared up in astonishing numbers. But not here, never in America. And Ben had deluded himself with that smug assurance also. Now he and his Rebels were paying the price.

"Coffee on?" Dan Gray, the former SAS man, asked as he ducked his head to enter the small side door of the semi trailer Ben had been using as a mobile CP.

"Help yourself, Dan," Ben broke off his troubled reflections.

"I saw Buddy outside," the tall, lean, always dapper Rebel colonel added as he poured a earthenware mug of steaming real coffee. Dan nodded at the cup. "One good thing about fighting an enemy from South America. We must have captured twenty-five tons of coffee beans. Oh, Georgi sends his regrets, he and the battalion commanders in his sector will be joining us by radio net." He referred to General Georgi Alexandrovich Striganov, formerly of the Soviet Army, now a citizen of what was left of Canada.

A longtime ally of the Rebels, General Striganov had a sardonic wit and droll sense of humor. He was also a damn fine soldier, Ben Raines acknowledged. Striganov had been engaged in covert operations in the Hudson Bay region for the International Peace Force before the Soviet Union collapsed and the Great War came crashing down on the world. A Party member out of necessity, he didn't experience any great moral struggle to cast off Communism and the Soviet high command and embrace a new way of life. Once an implacable enemy of Ben Raines and his Tri-States country, he had become a fast friend.

"Ike McGowan is right behind me," Dan went on, one finger brushing at the pencil line of mustache below his patrician nose. "So's Captain Thermopolis." Dan winced. "He has Emil with him."

"Good. I have plans for both of them," Ben said levelly.

Not everyone in the Rebel command had bought Emil Hite. Emil did little to modify such opinions. He still saw himself as guru of his brand of mumbojumbo quasireligion. It was all a scam, and Emil Hite the prince of con artists, and Ben Raines had seen through it the first time he met the five foot one inch "Prophet." Dizzy and ditzy as he might be, Emil had shed his gaudy robes and any pretense of worshiping the Great God Blomm and proven one hell of a good soldier. Competent troop leader, too, Ben admitted silently.

"Word is, our chief medical officer is gracing us with his presence, too," Dan dropped his final dollop of news.

"So I've been told," Ben responded. He immediately extinguished the cigarette he had been smoking and waved the air in front of his face to dispel the cloud of smoke. "He'll no doubt tell me I've been eating too much, exercising too little, and smoking again. Not to mention that I've been exposing myself recklessly to danger. All of which is true."

"What's true?" Ike McGowan and Dr. Lamar Chase asked together as they entered the trailer.

McGowan, the ex-SEAL, slouched into a chair and snagged a mug of coffee from Beth. Pear-shaped Dr. Lamar Chase remained in the doorway, immaculate hands on hips. The retired Navy captain, although well into his seventies, refused to retire again from service in the field with the Rebel command. He cut his gaze from the top of Ben Raines's head to his heels. Then he spoke tartly.

"You've been eating too much. Not enough exercise. You've been smoking again, I can tell it. And you've been out racing around like a teenager, risking your life and the future of the Rebel cause."

Ben cut his eyes to Dan in a "Didn't I tell you?" glance. Then he laughed, a sort of snort. "Guilty as charged. If you want the truth, I drink whiskey and smoke to kill the gawd-awful taste of those 'nutritionally superior' field rations with which you insist on burdening us."

"I said nothing about your consumption of alcohol." Chase sounded wounded.

"Get your coffee and sit down, Doctor," Ben invited.

Thermopolis and Emil entered next. Ben Raines had once described Thermopolis as "Nature's prototype hippie." Thermopolis had shed his headband featuring the yin-yang symbol for a ballistic helmet, but he remained lean, long, and tanned. A stout set of Rebel hobnailed combat boots had replaced his sandals while on duty.

Since being made CO of Headquarters Company, he had shortened the length of his hair and trimmed beard and mustache. A camo outfit covered his psychedelic shirt and purple trousers. His droopy eyelids and laid-back attitude still marked him as the quintessential hippie.

Ben and the others greeted Thermopolis and Emil, who beelined for the coffee. Emil added a large spoon of honey to his. Then he turned his eyes and mouth on Ben Raines.

"Greetings, O sublime and magnificent Commander General of all the Americas. Emil Hite, guru extraordinaire, is at your disposal. Of course, I don't mean actual disposal, as in a large green garbage bag, but in your great wisdom you understand all that, Mighty Slayer of the Unfit."

Ben developed a pained expression. "Can the shit, Emil. This is a staff conference. Which reminds me. Corrie, will you open the command net and we'll begin this conflab."

"Yes, sir. General Jefferys is standing by, as are General Striganov and Colonel West."

"Thank you, Beth."

And no doubt Cecil Jefferys would be wanting to get back in harness, Ben reasoned. The huge black man, ex-Special Forces, had only recently undergone radical heart surgery, a triple-bypass—once a relatively simple procedure, but under the conditions of "modern" medicine, still somewhat of a risk. He had been assigned to Base Camp One, in command of the gigantic installation, while he recuperated.

When Hoffman and his black-shirted horde invaded, Cecil strained at the bit to be included in the operation against the Nazi vermin. Cecil Jefferys, like Ike McGowan, and Lamar Chase, had sided with Ben Raines from the first. In his more candid moments, Ben allowed as how he could never have done it, any of it, without them.

Colonel West was somewhat of an anachronism, Ben

considered. There had not been nations or multinational corporations rich enough to hire a battalion of mercenaries in a long time. West had been intelligent enough to see that and had gladly thrown in his lot with the Rebels. His men, all professionals, fought well and gained a lot of glory for the Rebel cause. That is, after he and Ben had had a knock-down, drag-out, head-butting row over the few, but stringent, rules that passed for law and morality in Rebel-held territory.

"Gentlemen," Ben began once the RT operators at the various far-flung locations had completed their ritual. "For want of any better term, you constitute my staff. I've called this little gathering to discuss what we have learned. It's alarming, to say the least. Oh, Jersey, would you ask Buddy to join us now, please?"

"Sure, General."

Buddy entered, poured coffee, and took his seat. He sipped, and breathed a sigh of contentment. He had yet to grow jaded by this treat of only four months' duration. Idly he ran big fingers across the brush-cut top of his head and then fixed his attention on his father.

Quickly Ben outlined the result of the interrogation of the American Nazis captured at the drive-in. Ike McGowan, Dan Gray, and General Striganov, in particular, asked pointed questions during the presentation. Ben concluded by listing their options.

"I'm open to suggestions," he stated at last. "Anyone have a favorite strategic plan, or know of something I haven't mentioned?"

"Not so you'd notice," Colonel West said through the static of distance. "You covered it rather well, as usual, General."

"I agree," Dan Gray chimed in. "And I get the feeling you are not in favor of splitting the command into small tactical units and engaging Hoffman's Nazis piecemeal?"

Ben smiled as though at an apt pupil. "You've seen through me, Dan. You're right."

"So then I would think an attack in depth is called for," General Striganov supported from his position in North

Dakota.

"Hoffman has too many men, and more coming, according to the Nazis we captured, for that to work," Ben contradicted. "What I propose is establishing two theaters of operation and rolling over them with what we've got." He went on to elaborate. When he finished, Dr. Chase raised a finger to be recognized.

"The medical difficulties are going to be astronomical. It will require at least four MASH units, and I mean complete."

"We have six," Ben reminded him.

"And I need three of them to maintain what we hold at this point," Lamar Chase snapped testily. "We simply don't have the personnel for this kind of scheme."

Cecil Jefferys boomed from the speaker. "We have those Nazi POWs who surrendered located here at Base. They've been through two months of intensive de-Nazification. Most, remember, were Latinos, who didn't buy into Hoffman's Aryan-supremacy crap at all. Among them are a lot of medical personnel. We can use them in the rear echelon and free up bona fide Rebels for field service."

"Good idea, Cece," Ben injected cheerily. "I was hoping you'd have a little something to add."

"Like my taking command of one of those theaters," came the Rebel general's growl.

"I'm afraid that's a forlorn hope," Lamar Chase snapped sharply. "You should still be in bed, if you want my opinion."

The sound of a big black hand slapping a hard, flat cammo-covered belly came through the airwaves. "I am as fit as the proverbial fiddle."

"Even a Stradivarius can have a crack in it," Chase complained.

"But it would still sound as sweet," Cecil Jefferys countered. "I'm tired of being babied. Your people down here are—"

"My people down there, as you put it, are doing exactly what I told them to do. Two more months. At least.

73

And then only if I find not a trace of myocarditis. Just because we've rerouted the freeway doesn't mean you're safe from any other infarction."

"Spare me the fancy medical words, Dr. Chase. My ticker is doing a Big Ben act all the time now. Your chief pill roller down here says so."

"I'm going to side with Lamar on this, Cecil," Ben Raines said, putting an end to the pointless banter. He needed Cecil Jefferys badly.

Always determined to have the last word, Cecil Jeffery pushed that aside. "Well, *shoot,* Ben. What chance does a guy have when you gang up on him like that? I've got cabin fever bad, son. You hear that? I've worn out two decks of cards playin' solitaire. All I have to do is boogie over to the office each morning, sign a few papers, then go waste my afternoon on that treadmill and the Nautilus equipment at the hospital."

Dr. Chase gave an impatient snort. "You'd better be reporting for your therapy sessions, General Jefferys. It's that or I have you checked back into the hospital."

"You and what ten military police types, Doctor? I'm *all right* now, I tell you. I've even rediscovered my lovely lady and we're working real hard on making a baby."

"Conjugal activities can put a strain on your heart," Chase snapped.

"That's enough. Both of you," Ben spoke sharply. "You sound like a pair of five-year-olds in the sandpile. Let's get back to the matter at hand."

"So, okay, I can use ex-Nazis to replace Rebel medical personnel," Cecil said at once. "You'll have your four MASH units, Doctor. The people will be on their way to you tomorrow morning. Now, what about supplies?"

Ben outlined what he had in mind. "Everything that we have that can roll will be moved up to near the front. The two theaters, code-named Asgard for the north, which will consist of Four, Five, Six, Seven, and Fourteen Batts. Sultan for the south, will have Two, Three, Eight, Nine and Thirteen Batts. They will be established starting at once. The R Batt will remain with me, of course, and be on the float. Each theater commander will take advantage of the latest intelligence summaries, the terrain, personnel, and supplies at hand, and give me a workable estimate of the situation and operations order within forty-eight hours.

"You will include in those a two-pronged mass assault on the enemy," Ben continued. "Time is of the essence; we don't want them to get too well dug in." He paused, drew a breath. "I would suggest that Asgard's main task will be to smash through at what used to be Cheyenne, Wyoming, advance westward, seize, and hold the passes. Sultan will determine the greatest concentration of enemy in the Southwest and attack accordingly. Georgi, you will command Asgard; vice, Colonel West. Ike, you will command Sultan, with Dan as deputy commander. Therm, coordinate logistics, intel, supply, and troop movements with the appropriate members of each TC's staff. That's it, gentlemen, short and sweet. You know your jobs, done them a thousand times. Meanwhile, I will be formulating my own strategic overview and tactical operations. We'll compare notes exactly forty-eight hours from now. That's all. Oh, no. One more thing. Buddy?"

The younger Ben Raines rose to his feet, puzzled. "I'd been wondering why you had me in on this, Pop."

Ben smiled warmly. "Promotion time, son. Effective now, you are promoted to lieutenant colonel and assigned as XO for Dan Gray during this operation. Your battalion will go to your exec."

Buddy actually blanched. "My—good—God, I don't . . ."

"Yes, you do deserve it and you can do the job," Ben said firmly as he ushered his commanders to the door.

From the air, the Rebel outpost three miles outside the ruins of Billings, Montana, looked a little like an old collective farm in Russia, or maybe an Israeli *kibbutz*. The high walls that connected the buildings into a stockade were not of frozen manure; rather, like those built by the

75

Israelis, they were of stone and mortar, with razor-wire concertinas on the top. Also, the roofs bristled with antennas and the comm shack was always manned.

"Something's up," the corporal on watch announced to the duty officer. "Or this set is on the fritz."

"How's that, Higgins?" the young lieutenant asked.

"Well, sir, the black-shirts were running a whole lot of traffic. All of a sudden it dried up. There's nothin' on the air."

"I suppose even they have to eat," the officer observed. "Which reminds me, it is that time. I'll spell you while you go get a tray."

"Thanks, sir. My belly thinks my mouth went on strike." Corporal Higgins left the radio console and walked to the door.

He swung it open as the first incoming rounds detonated. A hailstorm of shrapnel shredded Higgins's chest and abdomen. He fell where he stood. Ears ringing from the explosions, the lieutenant recovered from his abrupt trip to the floor and scrambled to the radio table. He hit the transmit pad and shouted into the microphone as the second salvo thundered into the compound.

"Eagle, Eagle, this is Billings. We're taking incoming. I say again, incoming. Heavy mortars and one-five-twos from the effect. Eagle—"

Eagle was the last thing the twenty-year-old officer said as a direct hit turned the comm shack into a cloud of flying masonry. Heavy tanks rolled out of a coulee to the west and fired point-blank into the main gate to the Billings outpost. Troops in *feldgrau* uniforms advanced behind the behemoths. Behind the walls, the Rebels recovered quickly and fought with a special ferocity.

They knew they had nothing that would stand up to such a determined onslaught. Their small supply of TOW, wire-guided AT missiles soon ran out. They left a dozen burning tanks behind on the field, huge columns of black smoke pouring from ruptured hatches. Still, the Nazis came on.

Shoulder-fired, laser-guided ERIX missiles, obtained in France, did more damage, as did the big .50 machine guns, M-60s, and small-arms fire. A hundred black-shirt corpses littered the ground between the coulee and the compound within the first two minutes of the unequal battle. Yet the enemy didn't hesitate.

A roaring surf of shouts rose from the throats of an entire company of Hoffman's Nazis as they charged the wall and began hurling grenades over the wire fringe. The small hand bombs chipped paint and scoured holes in the stone buildings, breaking what windows the artillery had left whole. Rebels in flak jackets and body armor poured from the barracks to bring deadly fire down on the attackers.

Counterbattery fire began. The sole remaining radar dish had tracked the big 152mm shells from the foreign guns and a reliable computer in an underground bunker had computed the trajectory, projected the location of the weapons. Barely within range of the 4-inch mortars of the outpost, these redoubtable arms opened fire to a ragged cheer from the doomed garrison. Voices in Spanish and German reached the Rebels from the main gate.

It had been blown off its hinges and sagged forlornly into the compound. The huge glacis of a MBT pushed through and troops poured after. They shouted as they came.

"Tod mit aller Rebellen!"

"Matalos!"

"Shit," a seasoned Rebel sergeant spat. "They say they want to kill us."

"Damned unfriendly, Serge," the nervous private beside him declared. He squeezed the trigger of his H&K assault rifle and killed two black-shirts.

"D'you ever hear of a place called Querétaro?" the sergeant asked.

Blank-faced, the private shook his head. "No. Where's that?"

"Down in Mexico. A long time ago, the Mexicans, led by Benito Juárez swarmed over the Foreign Legion, the

French Foreign Legion, and kicked a lot of ass. Ended up with a phony emperor named Maximilian being captured and executed. I got a feeling this is gonna be another Querétaro."

Corrie turned away from the radio in the mobile CP, her face drawn. "Billings, Montana, has just fallen, General. Other reports coming in indicate that Field Marshal Hoffman has attacked along a broad front from Billings south to Grand Junction, Colorado. His SS brigade is pushing eastward along nearly every usable artery."

Ben Raines sensed a sickness welling inside him. They had come so close to gaining the initiative. "So now it begins," he said softly, his words weighted with sorrow for the lost Rebel lives.

Seven

Ben Raines turned from the situations map. "We can always send in air," he stated flatly to his subordinate commanders. "Hoffman has pushed us into making do with what we have. I don't like it, but we are going to have to divide the theater commands into company-sized units to deal with this threat. It's that or concede the western third of the U.S. to that Nazi bastard."

"I agree in principle, Ben," Dr. Lamar Chase offered. "My only concern is how we handle the casualties."

"As it ought to be, Lamar," Ben assured him. "We're taking unusually high casualties right now due to the surprise nature of these attacks." He paused when Corrie pushed back earphones and raised a finger. "What is it, Corrie?"

"Our people outside Cheyenne weren't caught by so much surprise. They are offering stiff resistance. Hoffman has committed more troops. A lot more. A third of Brodermann's SS, two companies from Volmer's American SS, and two companies of tanks."

Ben smiled for the first time in thirty-eight hours. He rubbed his hands together in anticipation. "That makes a tempting target. One rich enough for us to act on it. Georgi," he said to the speaker microphone on the command net, "I want Colonel West to take this one. His three battalions will move out at once

79

for Cheyenne. You continue to push northward toward Billings. Now . . ." He turned to Dan Gray without waiting for Striganov's reply.

"Dan, I want your people mobilized at once. Ike, get your heavy stuff on the road immediately. Your light infantry and assault guns can pass though them en route. You will push the Nazis south of Cheyenne, at Denver, Colorado Springs, Pueblo. Let's gear up, folks. Cecil? You copied this, right?"

"Every word, Ben. I assume you want me to put the air on alert status?"

"Correct. Do it yesterday. If we get the right conditions we can give Hoffman a major headache." He turned to his G-3. "Colonel Shields, I want operations orders drafted ASAP. I'll review and sign them during lunch, for immediate transmission." Again he rubbed palms together. "Hoffman may have just overextended himself. Now, get out of here and get cracking people."

At one-thirty, on the road to Cheyenne, Wyoming, in the Humvee, Ben isolated a stray thought that had been nagging him: Perhaps Hoffman had not overextended. It might be he had learned from past mistakes. The field marshal could be sucking him in.

Oh, wow! Oh, glorious, Gabe Trasher thought fuzzily. They had received their alert plan and taken the indicated positions a day ago. With time on their hands, the Alien Secretions gravitated to what they did best. They got high on marijuana and homemade wine. Incredibly, Gabe had maintained presence of mind enough to monitor the radio.

A sudden burst of increased, scrambled Rebel traffic tipped him off that something was happening. He had no idea of what, until he tuned to NAL frequencies. The kraut was on the move. No doubt of that. Nazi troops attacked all along a front from up in Montana down to the southwestern corner of Colorado. Kickin' tail and bringin' scalding pee down on the Rebels. That called for a celebration, so Gabe broke out some of their last remaining good wine: Midnight Special, Ripple, and some MD 20.

Some of the Secretions cut it fifty-fifty with that rotten homemade stuff and smoked hash with it that they had processed themselves. Their hangovers would be totally monumental, Gabe thought. And, yeah, he joined in their fun. So what if his head would feel like a mud-filled lead ball when he came down? It would be worth it.

Because Gabe had a strong impression he and his bikers were about to become the fair-haired boys of Nazi Hoffman's army. Puffed with confidence, Gabe just knew that the Secretions would be the ones to collect the head of Ben Raines. Any time now.

For once, Ben Raines remained with the main Rebel force. He had listened to the implorings of his staff and subordinate commanders and kept the Hummer within three miles of the mobile CP and the troops of Ike's rump-regiment.

Severely restricted to 40 mph, compared to earlier standards, they rolled along I-80 toward Cheyenne. Dan would cut south on U.S. 183, a straight shot through Kansas to U.S. 54. Ike would peel off onto I-79 at Julesburg and head for the Denver area. Ben, with his Headquarters Company and R Batt, would continue on to rendezvous with Colonel West and his three battalions. Ben looked to his left where a soft *whoof* drew his attention.

Smoot occupied the window seat in the rear, fascinated by the hilly scenery that past by the vehicle. Ben scratched a tall, pyramidal ear absently. Smoot shot his head to the right and licked the back of Ben's hand. A methodical person, Ben Raines did not like being rushed into anything. Hoffman must be a lot stronger than suspected, he reasoned as he examined

81

the intelligence summary for the tenth time. Or he simply wanted to get the jump on the Rebels.

Either way, he had precipitated action on Ben's part that was decidedly unwelcome. Smoot caught sight of a bounding rabbit and woofed interrogatively. Ben took time to pet him again.

"No, boy, we don't have time for you to chase after any rabbits. Corrie, what's coming out of Cheyenne?"

Corrie removed the earplug from one pink ear and wet her full lips. "Not much. Comm-center is keeping on the air while rolling, and they relay to me. Our people are holding, only barely. Heavy casualties."

"Hoffman's learned how to fight," Ben speculated aloud. Then he considered the situation faced by the Rebels on the small preserve outside Cheyenne. No one had ever said Ben Raines had any backdown in him. Tactically, he grudgingly admitted, there was a time for hit and a time for run.

"Have them pull back." Ben reached for his map case.

They could use Kimball, right inside the Nebraska panhandle from Cheyenne, as a staging area. If the Cheyenne outpost fell back far enough, fast enough, it would leave Brodermann's SS holding a bag of air. Would he pursue?

Ben thought not. Whatever the case, he would have to gamble that they would not. "Tell the outpost CO to put everyone in everything that moves and haul out of there on I-80 to Kimball, just over the line in Nebraska. First pour on everything they have to force the storm troopers to break off their attack—we'll re-supply them when we reach Kimball—then use the time the Nazis are reorganizing to skinny out of there."

"Done, General," Corrie told him a minute later.

"Then bump Colonel West and tell him to turn his men to take U.S. 385 south to 80, then on to the rendezvous at Kimball."

"Getting on it, sir," Corrie sang out cheerily. For all

her protestations against violence, she loved combat every bit as much as Ben Raines did.

Ben leaned back in his seat. Damn, he hated fighting an engagement like this. He wanted to be there, out front, with a finger on every aspect of the battle. The line officer, in the field, always saw everything clearer than some REMF. Ben laughed inwardly. Time was he would have had the guts for garters of any man who thought of him as a rear-echelon MF. Now he was fast becoming that, thanks to a kindly conspiracy by Ike McGowan, Lamar Chase, and, before he'd gotten sandbagged with that heart attack, Cecil Jefferys.

Now Cecil wanted to get out, and about every bit as much as Ben. A low growl came from Smoot, who raised his muzzle and sniffed curiously at the air.

"What is it, boy?" Ben bent to ask.

Right then, three Harley-Davidsons came howling up the sloping concrete walls of an old flood-control channel. The one in the lead had a sidecar attached and an M-60 machine gun spitting angry slugs at the Hummer.

Kevlar lining between the panels and the light armor of the Humvee's skin absorbed the punishment. This time Cooper had time to react. He touched a button on the instrument panel and one 40mm-grenade-launcher cluster on the roof blooped out a spread of three projectiles.

They went off directly behind the scruffy bikers and lifted them from their saddles. His back shredded by piano-wire-like shrapnel, one did a full flip over his handlebars, his own machine running over the corpse. Another did a header onto the road that ground down his chin by a quarter-inch. He never felt it; a large piece of grenade casing had penetrated the base of his skull and obliterated what little consciousness he had possessed.

83

Smoot had hit the floor, and Ben lowered his armor-glass window enough to get his Thompson in service. He didn't need it; the grenades had washed the sidecar with blood and cleaned the driver off the hog. It careened forward to crash into a bridge abutment. A loud metal-meets-concrete grinding reached into the Hummer a moment before a soft *whumpf* accompanied an orange ball of exploding gasoline.

"There's more of them," Jersey said from Ben's right. "A whole damn swarm."

"Well, screw this," Ben said hotly. "Coop, wait until they get at optimum range and empty those bloopers into them. We've got a schedule to keep."

"Who are they, General? They aren't wearing any Nazi regalia," Corrie asked, anxious to relay the information to the main column.

"I would gather they are the Alien Secretions intel has listed in enemy radio traffic," Ben advised her.

"I'll let Falcon know," Corrie threw over her shoulder.

More rounds of small arms slammed into the beefed-up Hummer. A hillside on their right seemed to swarm with dark figures on frenetic motorcycles. Like a pissed-on anthill, Ben thought. Their antics made it impossible to make an accurate count. Around seventy-five, Ben estimated. Too many for them to handle alone. Reluctantly he leaned forward, sighed heavily.

"Better bump Falcon back and tell them exactly where we are and that we want them up here ASAP."

"Already done, General," Corrie said, grinning. "You know how I hate senseless violence. And our getting killed by these scumbags would certainly be senseless."

Ben framed a hot retort, thought better of it, and asked instead, "Where'd you pick up on that pre-Great War slang, Corrie?"

"Back then my dad was a cop, before he took up playing survivalist. I was a late-life surprise."

"Some of the best always are," Ben said, thinking fondly of Buddy.

Buddy Raines had been an unexpected, and for a while unknown, result of a one-night stand in Nashville some ten years after Tina had been born. Ben and his first wife, Salina, had thought themselves doomed to childlessness and had adopted twins, a boy and girl, Tina and Jack. Jack and Salina had been killed in the early fighting for the Tri-States. Tina had been battling at his side ever since. But Buddy came as a total surprise.

He had the height and spread of his father. Also his dark hair and intense eyes, the square chin a mark of the Raines influence. After an initial mutual uneasiness, father and son got on famously. Buddy's mother turned out to be a complete wacko, who called herself Sister Voleta, leader of the Ninth Order. She blamed everything and anything bad for her on Ben Raines and fought him implacably. Now she was dead and the Ninth Order was no more. All that Buddy had apparently inherited from her was a natural curliness to his thick black hair. Ben turned loose of it; time to concentrate on the immediate threat.

"Pull onto that bridge and broadside us, Coop. We're going to make it damn hard for them to come at us."

"We gonna kick a little ass, General?" Jersey asked through her grin.

"Damn right, Jersey."

Gabe Trasher cursed the throbbing in his head and tried to concentrate on what the hell that crazy bastard Ben Raines was up to. The bulky vehicle had pulled out onto the bridge over the Platte River and broadsided. Goddamn that Raines, he was up to something, but the little men with their tackhammers in his head wouldn't let Gabe figure out what. The receiver button in his ear crackled.

"You sure that's Ben Raines?" Numb Nuts Nicholson asked.

"Fuckin'-A I am. That thing's armored, right? An' Raines runs around in an armored set of wheels, right? An' it's way an' hell out in front of the main column, right? So it has to be Raines."

Numb Nuts gobbled his peculiar laughter. "Only, what's he up to?"

"I don't know," Gabe answered back. "I'm tryin' to figger it out."

"Best do it fast. We gotta shit or get off the pot," Numb Nuts put the situation elegantly.

"I know, I know," Gabe rapid-fired. "He has to have sent for help. Okay," Gabe hurried on, desperate for a solution. "We're gonna hit him from both sides. Ever'body with ears, hear this. Close in on the ends of the bridge. When ever'body gets in place, we hit this fucker hard."

"We'll be shootin' at each other," one Alien Secretion protested.

"Huh? Oh, yeah, I guess you would." Gabe thought fast, for Gabe. "So, here's what we do. We leave enough people here to keep Raines on that bridge, and we go back an' hit whoever is coming up to help him." A rattle of acknowledgments came to Gabe. "You'll be in charge, Fart Bucket. Let's do it now."

Ben turned from the window. "They aren't falling for it. Somehow I had the feeling we could sucker them into shooting at each other."

"One of them must still have a functional brain," Jersey agreed. "What now?"

Frowning, Ben mulled over that. "First we break out of here. Then we run west and keep them after us, concentrating on this juicy plum, until Falcon hits them in the rear. Corrie, bump Thermopolis and tell him I want Wanda and Leadfoot up here right after we break out. Have them wear their old colors."

86

"Huh?" Jersey asked from his right. "Seems like only yesterday we got them to looking civilized."

That brought a smile to Ben's lips. Big, thick fingers massaged his square chin. "Now, Jersey, you wouldn't want the Alien Secretions' new recruits to look out of place, would you?"

Jersey nodded. "Gotcha, boss. Just how do you figure to keep them focused on us?"

"Easy. Corrie, can you break in on the frequency that bunch of assholes are using?"

"Sure. Simple."

"Then do it. And hand me the mike."

When she had accomplished this, she handed the microphone to Ben Raines with a wink. "This is General Ben Raines. I want you to listen closely to me, you stupid, unwashed sons of bitches."

Gabe Thrasher sat gape-mouthed. He didn't believe what he was hearing. "I say again, this is General Ben Raines. I want you to break up and get the hell out of our way. We're coming through, and when we do, if you are still in the way, we'll tear you new assholes."

"Not fucking likely, Raines," Trasher snarled into the handset of his radio. "We got you cold. My guess is you're outta them nasty grenades. You ain't got shit and you ain't worth shit. We're gonna dust you right off this mudball. I'm gonna eat you for breakfast."

"Effing wrong, whoever you are. The Night People tried that and they're extinct."

"I'm Gabe Trasher, president of the Alien Secretions," Gabe growled.

Ben's soft laughter came back to him. "Biker shit, huh? Well, Gabe Trasher, you wouldn't make a pimple on a creepie's ass."

"That does it, gawdammit! That does it," Trasher blared with a rage. "You boys on the west side, take that son of a bitch. Later, Raines. I'll swing by and

87

take a look at your ball-less corpse."

Immediately a dozen Harleys snorted to life and began a slow advance on the Hummer that straddled the wide bridge across the Platte River. They rumbled at a stately pace, weapons at the ready. Leading them was a greasy slob named Fart Bucket. The stubble to both sides of his cleft chin, as well as his thick pursed lips, bore the yellow-brown stain of his smokeless tobacco habit. When his hyena pack of bikers had reached a distance of a hundred feet from the Hummer, he spat a long puce stream of home-cured leaf juice that splattered against a crackled and worn support column of the bridge. Another twenty-five feet and he uttered a guttural grunt of speech.

His biker brigands spread out and halted. Their hogs and choppers braced on one booted leg, they leveled their weapons at the Humvee. At Fart Bucket's command they loosed an explosive volley.

Hot lead slammed into the side of the armored Hummer. Thin armor plate made noisy protest. A couple of 12-gauge rifled slugs flatted enough to howl mournfully through the air when they richocheted off the curved front fender. Then the windows on the near side came down.

Three weapons, Jersey's M-16, Beth's H&K, and Ben's faithful old tommy-chopper, opened up on them in full rock-'n'-roll. Bits of filth-stained, rotting denim cloth flew in a cloud, along with chunks of flesh and gallons of blood. A pink haze hung in the air while Harleys went out from under dying Alien Secretions.

After the initial fusillade, Ben and team settled down to neat, accurate three-round bursts. Cooper risked exposing his back to step out of the driver's side and take aim with an M-209—a CAR-15 with a 40mm grenade launcher under the forestock. The blooper made its characteristic hollow sound and launched from a high-impact plastic casing a small green spheroid with a pale blue nosecone and a white band around its widest circumference.

White phosphorus from the exploding round ignited spilled gasoline. Fart Bucket, who had so far avoided contact with any ordnance, turned into a sprinting torch. Howling in agony and terror, he ran crazed in circles for a moment before lining out for the bridge railing. With a throat-burning sob of desperation, he flung himself over the side. Contact with the bed of the Platte River broke Fart Bucket's neck. At least it put out the fire. All except those pesky flecks of WP.

"Oh, Jesus, no. Oh, shit! Oh, fucking shit!" Gabe Trasher screamed from the hillside where he observed. Then he yelled into the mike. "Go, east side. Go-go-go! Get that motherfucker."

They did no better than their comrades. Worse, in fact. Cooper scooted around to the opposite side of the Hummer and began to lob 40mm blooper shots into them even before the first Harley rolled onto the bridge. Ben, Beth, Corrie, and Jersey climbed from the Humvee and took positions that offered good fields of fire.

Little Dick Bentley, who was going to get himself a little piece of Ben Raines got three little pieces of .45 JHP from Ben's Thompson. Arms flung wide, he reared backward and the Harley hog rolled out from under him. Several bikers had presence of mind enough to halt and dismount so they could return aimed fire.

A slug from what had once been an expensive, well-cared-for deer rifle cracked through the air an inch from the head of Ben Raines. Ben settled accounts for the former owner of the Weatherby with a Thompson tornado that would leave the biker singing soprano the rest of his life, if he didn't die of shock and blood loss.

Two-twenty-three hornets from Jersey's M-16 buzzed angrily off the receiver of an AK-47, which sent up a spray of 5.56x28 lead to puncture the sky. Before its owner could override the sudden numbness in his hands, Jersey finished him with a single shot between the eyes.

Bodies sprawled grotesquely on the floor of the bridge. Once again, Jersey wondered at the quantity of blood in a human being. Awash in it, the bridge gave up the crimson tide to the drain holes along its verge. It poured into the Platte, to be lost in its murky brown current. Two bikers came straight on, kamikaze style.

Beth straightened out one of them with a short burst from her H&K. He left his bike sideways, with an unrepentant curse on his lips for Ben Raines. "Goddamn you, Raines. This is all your fault," he yelled before his head made contact with concrete and scrambled what was left of his brain.

"Mount up," Ben snapped. "Coop, ram this thing over the top of those burning bikes and let's head for Kearney." He put a comradely hand on Cooper's shoulder. "Only slowly. We want to keep this chicken-shit trash on our tail."

Eight

Ben Raines directed Cooper to pull off I-80 at a rest stop. It had been badly vandalized long enough ago that the broken edges of concrete table supports had been rounded by weather and erosion. Ben stepped from the Hummer and stretched. Then he walked around behind what had been neat brick restrooms to relieve himself.

When he returned, he shared his suspicions with his team. "I think we did too good of a job. No sign of Trasher and his Secretions. No loss. The less of that filth we have to deal with, the better. Corrie, bump Falcon and find out what's going on."

"Something coming in now, sir. It's Falcon." She gave the handset to Ben.

"Eagle here, over."

"We've got some of what looks like bikers taking potshots at us," Stan McDade's voice rumbled over the connection.

"Anything you can't handle?"

"An annoyance," Bull McDade dismissed. "Your people pulled out from Headquarters Company ten minutes ago."

"They should be in position any time. After I brief them, I want you to open up with everything you have. Run those dirtbags out of there. Meanwhile, keep your heads down."

"That's a big roger, Eagle. Falcon, out."

Ben spoke as much to himself as to the team, all of whom knew the routine only too well. "With Leadfoot and Wanda under radio silence, I'll be pitching in the dark. I hope the reception is good around here. Well, here goes," he ended as he keyed the talk switch. "Outlaw, this is Eagle. Do you copy?"

A faint click interrupted the carrier wave on that frequency. It signified that Leadfoot heard the transmission. Ben nodded and launched into his specific instructions. "In a short while, some biker trash—ah, present company excepted—will be heading your way, thoroughly shocked by our big guns with Falcon. I want you in position near where we had our firefight within ten minutes to give them a little surprise. Do you roger that?" Again the click came. "Stand by for a change in orders, depending on what this Alien Secretions outfit decides to do." Another momentary silencing of the carrier static. "Eagle out. Falcon, this is Eagle. In exactly ten minutes . . . do it."

Leadfoot looked over the streamlined receiver of the M-60 light machine gun. He had the weapon pintle-mounted between the handlebars of his motorcycle. A pair of closed boxes, welded to the steering shaft above the fork, fed it. He had seen the carnage at the bridge and commented laughingly to his second-in-command, Beerbelly.

"Ben Raines having fun again."

Leadfoot, Beerbelly, and their collection of misfits had been implacable enemies of Ben Raines and the Rebels. Their enmity had caused them to swear allegiance to the Night People and their daytime stooges. It didn't take a lot of the awesome firepower of the Rebel army to convince them that following the rules of Ben Raines wasn't so bad a thing after all. It *did* leave you alive. Wanda, who sat across the highway in a screen of trees, had been the same, Leadfoot recalled.

They had formed a sort of unholy alliance, vowing to fight "that damned Ben Raines" to the death. Leadfoot, his unwashed bikers, and the Sisters had set up defenses outside the ruins of some of California's most beautiful cities. At least they had been until Ben Raines brought his Rebels howling down on them to exterminate the creepies. The Rebels kept dislodging the outlaw bikers, boys and girls alike. Wanda and her Sisters of Lesbos had resisted taking orders from Leadfoot—from any man, for that matter—until Ben Raines got them on the run.

Rapid attrition is an excellent mentor. Leadfoot and Wanda soon realized that the battle was lost for their disgusting masters. Raines had offered a generous chance to any who would throw in with his Rebels. Leadfoot and Wanda had talked it over and agreed to check out what the Rebel general had to offer.

They liked it and stayed. Now, the veteran of hundreds of hours of combat, Leadfoot could but vaguely recall what it had been like not being a Rebel. But what about these bikers? They were brothers, right? They should be given a chance to join, sure. But Ben had said there was no time for that.

So Leadfoot would do what he had to do. He stiffened suddenly and listened keenly to a distant rumble. The guns of the R Batt had opened up. Leadfoot could imagine the fat shells lobbing through the sky. He checked again to make certain the ammo belt ran right to feed properly. Any time now the Alien Secretions would come runnin' down the road.

Leadfoot tensed again a pair of minutes later. Leaning forward, he peered harder at the road. What was that? Gradually a figure solidified out of the heat waves rising from the concrete slab of I-80.

Long, grimy hair streaming out behind him, he rode laid back on a three-prong sissy-bar that featured a big swastika at the top, feet on high-rise pegs up on the frame near the belly tank. Leadfoot put binoculars to his eyes and saw the look of utter terror on his target's face. Half a dozen more crested the rise, their faces ghastly white. Another eyeblink, then they filled the road from side to side.

A quick adjustment of the sights and Leadfoot keyed his microphone. "They're here," he said crisply. "A whole shitpot of them."

"I see," Wanda responded.

Two seconds later, Leadfoot opened up with the M-60. He sprayed the shell-shocked bikers most thoroughly. Men and machines went tumbling along the superslab. Showers of sparks rose, and a tracer set off a gas tank. In a fatally long minute, the fear of what lay behind them became conquered by the terror of what they had run into.

Without regard for the rules of the road, the Alien Secretions reversed course and fled. The dying and wounded littered the highway, writhing in misery. At the first off-ramp, Gabe Trasher directed his thoroughly demoralized gang away from the sure knowledge of eternity. Their hogs sprinted out between open fields, on a secondary road, in an attempt to escape ruin.

Howling gleefully, Wanda's Sisters and Leadfoot's Sons of Satan streamed after them. Leadfoot had been cautioned not to get close enough to be recognized, but he didn't as yet know why. He merely followed the orders of Ben Raines. In a minute, Leadfoot had his answer.

"Leadfoot, this is Eagle. Any time now, those scum are going to run into Tina, who's been flanking them. That should shatter any organizational control remaining. When they break, I want your people to ease up among them and join in. You know the drill. All these fucking Rebels around, you've been getting run off every road for days. I think they'll take you in like long-lost brothers."

"Then what happens, O Great Eagle?" Leadfoot asked.

Ben grimaced, he got enough of that from Emil. "That's when we give them another surprise." Leadfoot could almost hear the smile in Ben Raines's voice.

"How the hell did they get ahead of us?" Gabe Trasher asked the wind.

Gabe led his demoralized outlaws south on a dirt road, away from the horror on the interstate. His stomach churned and his mind retreated in terror from the image of Rubber Duck, his chest bristling with those little, gray, ugly dart things. What the fuck did the Rebels have? That kind of shit wasn't fair. Jee-sus, he'd lost twenty people in less than thirty seconds. Then, somehow, some way, the fuckin' Rebels had gotten ahead of them and blown shit out of eleven more good men. But he had outsmarted them now.

They wouldn't come after him on these shitty roads. Not with all that heavy equipment. And there was a little town not far from where they left the slab. Name of Clay Center. He and his boys used to go there and terrorize the locals in the town's only beer bar. He wondered if it was still there.

Gabe and his outlaw bikers didn't get the chance to find out. They topped a long swell in the prairie and came head-on into more Rebels. Goddamn, they seemed to be everywhere! Big .50 caliber machine guns chuffed and snorted and their fat slugs tore up the sod all around the bikers.

Already shaken by their encounter with beehive rounds from R Batt, the dope-fogged brains registered this new chapter in devastation and wanted nothing to do with it. Gabe Trasher and Numb Nuts led the way. Gabe raised one hairy arm, a wide, spike-studded wristband sparkled in the sunlight, and he signaled for the Alien Secretions to take to the fields.

Roostertails of dirt spurting behind them, they ran for their lives. A cascade of copper-jacketed death followed them from the guns of Tina's Nine Batt. Gabriel Trasher so feared meeting his name-saint that he slobbered and whimpered. Fortunately for his reputation with the outlaws, the roar of his tonepipe-outfitted Harley drowned out the unmanly sounds. Gradually the hell-roar of automatic fire diminished.

When it cut off with the same suddenness with which it had begun, Gabe Trasher discovered he could think clearly again. They'd head on west, get past that goddamned bridge on I-80 outside Grand Island, then take to the superslab again. Yeah, that sounded good. They could outrun the Rebels easy then. Soothed by the brilliance of this idea, Gabe eased back and propped his boots on the high-rise pegs.

They'd have to take State 44 north, Gabe continued to plan. The only way to get across the Platte. That would put them in what was left of Kearney. A rotting shithole of a place. Even if Ben Raines was ahead of him, he wouldn't stop there, Gabe reasoned. Best wait until Raines was for sure and gone from the area, and his goddamned Rebels, too.

Inspiration came to Gabe. There was an old park sort of place not far from the junction with 44. A tourist joint back before the bombs fell. Pioneer Village, that was the name of it. They could hole up there, take care of the wounded. And fuck Ben Raines! Let him go as far west as he wanted to. Fuck that superkraut, too.

Gabe Trasher couldn't put an exact time to when the strange bikers started straggling in. He had a vague impression two or three joined them on the run over country roads toward U.S. 6/34, which led them to the rundown Pioneer Village.

A couple of the tall outer walls remained standing,

the parking lot long ago grown over, only a few shards of blacktop thrusting up through the weeds and dandelions. Gabe and Numb Nuts led the outlaws in among the buildings of what some promoter had imagined a pioneer town to look like. Most structures were burned-out hulks. A stone fireplace and chimney stood starkly against the light blue of the afternoon sky. A prairie breeze whispered through the tall grass covering mounds that looked like graves for elephants.

They found a picnic area in a grove of mixed maple and oak, grown large now and venerable with age. It had survived most of the ravages of the lawless, the uncaring, and the ignorant. Several tables remained intact, their tops weathered and splintered from lack of maintenance, but usable. Two of the ubiquitous sheet-metal barbecues still rested on their pipe pedestals, and a fire ring of native stone fronted a shelter house.

The roof had several holes, Gabe soon discovered, but the shelter had sidewalls that would break the wind. It would make do for his band of outlaws. More of the strangers rumbled in while the Alien Secretions unloaded and set up. Gabe started taking note of them, and decided they would do. Especially that great big dude with the machine gun between his handlebars.

"Don't think I know you," Gabe offered by way of introduction to the huge, burly man with the M-60.

"Handle's Leadfoot. These are the Sons of Satan. Who might you be?" he said, dropping easily into the outlaw role.

"Gabe Trasher. These are my folks, the Alien Secretions."

Leadfoot studied them for a long minute, then nodded and put on a droll face. "They'll do."

"What brings you this way, Leadfoot?" Gabe probed, conscious that it wasn't the politest or safest thing to pry into another outlaw's business.

"What do you think? Those fuckin' Rebels!" he punched out hotly. "They're every-fuckin'-where. They've run us off every road we tried to travel. Same's with you, I reckon, from the sounds of that firefight a while back."

"You got that right. What got the Rebels pissed at you people?"

Leadfoot hoisted both eyebrows and made a slow turn in front of Trasher. "Look at us, man. D'you think those squeaky-clean Rebel bastards would welcome us with open arms and want to play kissy-face?"

For the first time that day, Gabe Trasher laughed. A long, loud belly laugh that shook his girth. "Brother, you got me there. They sure as shit got no love for our kind. Hang in here a spell. Might be I have an idea that could appeal."

"Thank'e kindly," Leadfoot replied with a straight face. "Oh, there's some more people comin', a gang of mommas. Only they ain't exactly mommas. They've got a girl-girl thing goin'."

Gabe easily took it in stride. "Can they fight?"

"Like the fuckin' Harpies," Leadfoot replied earnestly. Thermopolis had him reading the classics.

Trasher paled. "Say what? They got the herpies?"

Leadfoot wanted to laugh, but stifled it for the sake of the mission. "Naw. Harpies, man, real bitch-kitty fighting ladies from a long time ago. Like in Homer, y'know?"

"Homer? What comic book was he in?" Trasher betrayed his ignorance.

"Weren't no comic book. Homer was a blind poet. He wrote about Ulysses, an' Helen of Troy, all that ancient shit. The Harpies fucked up Ulysses and his crew."

"Well," Gabe dismissed, totally lost now, "if they can fight, they're more than welcome. We took some heavy losses with them goddamned Rebels."

Leadfoot gave him a shrewd glance. "You aren't tryin' to say that you'd consider our throwin' in with you, are you?"

Gabe drew a deep breath. He'd already committed himself further than he had planned at this point. "Just what I'm sayin'. We got a shitpot full of vacancies. Whadda you say?"

"Who gives the orders?"

"I do, Leadfoot. The Secretions have this contract with that big Nazi dude, th' one runs the New Army of Liberation. He gives me my orders, I pass them along."

"Not to the Sons, you don't," Leadfoot stated belligerently. Inwardly he hoped the years with the Rebels hadn't taken the edge off his ability to gauge biker leaders. "*I* give them their orders." He narrowed his eyes, formed an expression of shrewdness. "We talkin' a partnership, you got a deal. Otherwise, we'll rest up a bit and ride on."

So desperate had Gabe become to fill his devastated ranks that he did not even withhold an answer for the time required by outlaw protocol. "Done."

He put an arm, the one with the spiked wristband, around Leadfoot's shoulder, reaching up from necessity to do so. "Now, come on, we've got some prime weed. We'll have us a little toke and wait for your lezzie friends to show up. I suppose the Bull Dagger who runs the outfit will want the same terms I gave you?"

"No doubt," Leadfoot answered dryly.

"She'll get it, too." Gabe gave Leadfoot a conspiratorial wink. "Hey, people, listen up. We got reinforcements," he called to the Secretions. "This calls for a party. Break out the wine and the grass and let's get crazy."

"How about food?" Martian Mucus complained. "Smokin' dope gives me the munchies."

"It gives *everyone* the munchies," Gabe shot back. "Okay, so whatever we brung along is what we've got. We can't go back to our old place."

"I've got sunflower seeds," a willowy momma who

99

looked to be about fourteen announced.

"I have a bag of dried sandhill plums I've been savin' back," another Secretion volunteered.

"Scrounge, you dumb fuckers," Gabe growled at them. "Set up a hunting party. See if you can shoot a couple of rabbits or something."

"It'll take more'n a couple of rabbits to feed all of us," Martian Mucus objected.

"I've got some jerked beef, a whole two pounds of it," a Secretion who called himself Venusian Snot offered.

"The only jerked meat you've got is between your legs," his momma quipped.

That brought laughter from all around. "I'm serious," Gabe pressed when it died down. "We gotta lay in supplies. Hunt around. Find wild stuff we can eat. Nuts, maybe."

"Acorns is bitter," the pouting teeny momma objected.

"Not if you fix them right," Leadfoot contributed.

"Okay—okay, we get what we can. An' clean out that fire pit," Gabe commanded. "We gotta get a fire goin'."

Within an hour, the party was in full swing. Wanda and her Sisters of Lesbos had arrived and been "convinced" to join with the Alien Secretions. The wine flowed freely, that homemade beverage giving off a sour, yeasty smell. Leadfoot and Wanda compared notes. They fondly hoped they would not have to stay here long.

It took less time than Leadfoot had expected. The wine and weed and the robust outdoor cooking took a heavy toll of the combat-wearied Alien Secretions. By ten-thirty, only half a dozen remained upright, arms linked around necks, by the fire. They swilled the edgy-tasting wine and talked of earlier conquests. Fired by the bold tales, they began an unsteady, shuffling dance around the rock pit. Leadfoot cut his eyes to Wanda.

"Time for some of our people to start pulling out. Your girls know where to go. I'll get on the radio to the general and to R Batt. We wait until they are in position and all our people get clear of the field of fire. Then we stomp this stupid shit into the ground."

"I like that," Wanda responded. "They remind me of someone I once knew. Someone I don't like much anymore."

"I hear you, gal. Me, too, I guess. Well, so much for that. Let's spread the word."

Half an hour later, the last Son of Satan and Sister of Lesbos wheeled bikes away from the old tourist attraction. Walking did not agree with their booted feet, but they endured a mile of it before kicking to life the big choppers and rumbling off into the night. They found the bulk of the company at the rendezvous.

"Any time now," Leadfoot was saying to Wanda.

Then the horizon behind them lighted up. A carpet-thick salvo of 155s, 105s and 4-inch mortars did a Long Island Express over their heads a moment later, followed by the sullen mutter of the guns. Leadfoot whistled softly.

"That's a lot of heavy traffic," he opined. "Gonna make jam outta those Alien Secretions creeps."

"You can say that again," Wanda agreed. "How long's that going on?"

"Five minutes. Then we hit them from this flank, R Batt covers the other three sides, and General Raines mops up any who survive to run away."

Hell came to visit at midnight. For five minutes it rained down on the coordinates provided by Leadfoot in the form of artillery shells that burst and showered everything living in the old Pioneer Village with shards of metal, screeching flechettes, and searing

101

white phosphorus. Not a man or woman of the Alien Secretion escaped without at least one minor wound.

Ears ringing and deadened by the tumult of exploding rounds, dizzied and disoriented, they were unable to fully appreciate the utter silence that followed. Few even had sense enough to reach for weapons when grim-faced young men and women in the camo uniforms of the Rebels swarmed out of the smoke and dust, weapons at the ready.

"Oh, shit, oh, Jesus, they're comin' after us again," Numb Nuts Nicholson wailed when he saw their approach. Blood streamed down his face from a cut above one eye. A flechette had fully penetrated his left forearm just below the elbow. The pain somewhat dulled his pig-squeal whinny giggle.

Nine

Tina's battalion had been assigned to establish a cordon completely around the area occupied by the Alien Secretions. To her disappointment they took no part in the brief fighting. Troopers of R Batt walked through the old tourist spot, eyes alert. Only a few brain-jumbled outlaw bikers offered resistance. Those they gunned down mercilessly. While the Rebel presence increased, Gabe and Numb Nuts set the example.

Whining, on his knees, bloody face upraised, Numb Nuts cried for mercy. "Don' shoot me, soldier-boy. I ain't done nothin' to you. I give up," he wailed.

"Don't shoot! Don't shoot. I surrender," Gabe Trasher appealed as he sank to his knees, arms raised above his head.

He knew that even while the frightening shells slammed into their campsite, some of the Secretions had kicked life into their Harleys and sped away to the west. Gabe fondly hoped that when things sorted themselves out, they would come back in a rush and pull him and Numb Nuts out of the hands of the Rebels.

While the Rebels rounded up the rest of the survivors, Gabe heard the distant sound of a firefight over the ringing in his ears. It smashed his hopes into ruins.

From the darkness to the side of the road, Cooper whispered into the handset of the AN/PRC-6 field radio. "About eight of them, General. Comin' on slow."

"Let them get good and close," Ben Raines responded. "There may be more got out of that barrage."

Beside him, Jersey nodded with an enthusiasm Ben could not see. "Don't want to tip our hand too soon."

Ben patted her on the shoulder. How, she wondered, could he see so well in the dark? "Always one up on me, aren't you, Jersey?"

"Huh? I was only thinkin' out loud about why you want them close."

"Good enough. I'd gleefully kill for a cup of coffee right now," Ben added wistfully.

"When this is over, General."

Two bikes showed darker silhouettes against the lighter curtain of night. They rolled along barely above idle. The riders hunched low. Ben eased the buttstock of his Thompson into the pocket of his shoulder. A couple of hours shy of moonrise, he would have to use the old point-and-shoot technique. Steadily, he squeezed on the trigger.

Muzzle blast brightly flamed the darkness. One biker, his bullet-scrambled brain giving confused signals, torqued the grip throttle of his Harley and it leapt forward. A thin, high scream came from his lips as the cycle scooted out from under him and he rebounded off a tree trunk. Blackout covers whisked off headlights illuminated the gory scene, and yellow-orange blooms winked from outlaw weapons.

"Damn, that's close!" Ben advised as a trio of rounds impacted the embankment much too near his body.

Outlaw bike lights revealed the Hummer blocking both lanes of Highway 6/34 on a narrow bridge. One Alien Secretion gunned his Harley in an effort to escape the ambush, certain he could outwit his attackers. He whipped to one side of the road and leapt the ditch. He hurtled the rising bank on that side, and a moment later a loud splash announced that he had lost his bet that the creek would be dry.

His scoot settled to a depth of twelve feet at midchannel and carried the unconscious Secretion to a watery grave. Rebel rounds sprayed the remaining six outlaw bikers. Only one avoided wounds. Instead of wisely surrendering, like his companions, he charged toward Ben Raines.

An ancient AK-47 spitting hollow-base steel-core slugs, he bore down on the dark figure on the verge of the road. The bullets popped noisily into Ben's body armor. He'd count the bruises in the morning, Ben thought with disgust as he brought up the muzzle of the Thompson.

Three rounds chopped the front wheel of the bike. Spokes bent and the fork set itself in the macadam surface of the highway. Venusian Snot got a lesson in applied physics as he catapulted over the handlebars and skidded along the roadway.

"Everyone belly down on the road, arms above your heads," Ben commanded.

Quickly his personal team secured the five bandit bikers. Jersey kept an eye on the surroundings as she gained the road and walked backward to Venusian Snot.

"This one is still alive, General," she informed Ben with a chuckle. "He's picked up one hell of a case of road rash."

"Scrape him up and bring him along. Time we joined the party with R Batt," Ben told her.

Gabe Trasher had recovered part of his shattered ego by the time the Hummer arrived with Ben Raines and the prisoners they had obtained. He had already figured out that he and the other identified leaders were not to be killed outright. That encouraged him.

Before everyone had gotten stoned out the past evening, he had radioed to Adlerhoff to report that they had been in a sustained firefight with an advance column of Rebels. Also that Ben Raines was along. Field Marshal Hoffman had not been overflowing with praise. Ben Raines still lived, seemed to be his main bone to worry.

Trasher had dismissed it. Now the full realization of just how much of a tricky bastard Rains could be dawned on him. He felt the fool. And nobody made a fool of Gabe Trasher. No one had since the fifth grade, when he'd cut that sissy preacher's kid, Bobby Smythe, who spelled his name with a "y" *and* an "e" yet.

"Why you grinnin', Gabe?" Numb Nuts Nicholson asked glumly. "We're fuckin' prisoners of the Man."

"Yeah. But maybe not for long," Gabe informed him. "I still have a trick in my boot that'll get us out of here, eliminate Ben Raines, and spell the end for this whole damned Rebel slime."

Nicholson blinked stupidly. "You're playin' head games, Gabe. Raines is one tough bastard. How you gonna work it?"

"Just watch and see. I'm gonna fix his ass yet."

General Field Marshal Jesus Dieguez Mendoza Hoffman danced around his desk in glee. "It's working, it's working!" he crowed in delight to his assembled staff officers.

Orderlies had rousted them out of sound sleep with a summons to the august presence in the middle of the night. None had the least idea why. This manic performance had so far failed to further enlighten them. Hoffman waved to three silver buckets of iced-down champagne on their glittering stands.

"It's only from the uplands of Argentina, gentle-

106

men, hardly the fabled Dom Pérignon. But it will have do for our celebration."

"If I may be so bold as to inquire, *Herr Generalfeldmarschall*," Colonel Webber boldly asked. "What is this occasion we celebrate?"

Hoffman stopped his giddy dance. "Why, the fall of Cheyenne, gentlemen. The Rebels have abandoned their farms and village and the compound, and the survivors are in full flight to the east."

"Are our troops pursuing them?" Webber asked, afraid of the answer.

"No. Why should they?" Hoffman responded, surprising and relieving his G-2. "It appears to me that General Ben Raines has conceded to us the entire western third of the nation."

"What, with one minor retreat?" Col. Rupert Hertl demanded.

General Field Marshal Hoffman produced an "I'm so clever" expression and snapped fingers for an orderly to open the sparkling wine. "Hardly. Billings is ours, Greeley is crumbling, Denver will be ours by noon tomorrow. Ben Raines has been outsmarted. He had no expectation of an attack this late in fall."

"Perhaps with good reason, *Herr Generalfeldmarschall*," the G-4, Gomez, prompted. "The weather is decidedly deteriorating."

"To our advantage. We hold the high passes, where I am told some snow is falling; we will now hold the lower ones as well. Raines can't get at us and we have no reason to overextend our lines. General Rasbach is racing our way with reinforcements. Come spring, we will overwhelm all of the old United States. We will smash Ben Raines, and with him his Rebels. You can take my word on that."

Flutes of champaign came into hands that raised in salute not altogether sincere. Col. Joaquin Webber had serious doubts.

* * *

They loaded the survivors of Trasher's outlaw gang into trucks and started back to where the mobile command post had been left off. Ben led the way in the armored Humvee. Along the way, as the rising sun banished darkness, Trasher saw medics tending to the wounded. Always Rebel wounded. None of his own men had received the least consideration.

Gabe Trasher chewed through the bitter ashes of defeat and found hot anger on the other side. He'd see about that. He would force the issue of humane treatment as soon as they got to wherever it was they were going. Morning was an hour old when the trucks pulled into a cleared field on the opposite bank of the North Platte River. When everyone had been unloaded, Gabe Trasher asked permission, although it galled him to do so, to speak with Ben Raines.

Two armed Rebels escorted him to where Ben sat munching on a savory-smelling breakfast. The aroma made Trasher's stomach knot. There was the matter of food, too, he thought uneasily.

"General Raines, I demand . . ."

Ben held up a hand filled with fresh, hot biscuit and honey, to halt the flow. Brow furrowed, he asked, "You do . . . what?"

"I—I demand to know why my people are not receiving proper medical care."

"Oh, it's 'demand,' eh? You are in no position to demand anything."

"But my people are wounded, some seriously. I'm wounded, too, can't you fuckin' see that?"

Ben finished the biscuit, wiped his lips on a napkin. "Oh, yes, I can see quite clearly. I gather that you are Gabe Trasher, leader of this scrofulous collection of dirt bags?"

"Ye—yes, I am." Driven by his own pain and his clever plan to get rid of Ben Raines, Gabe fought to keep his words and tone reasonable. "Surely you can't refuse to treat them for their injuries."

Ben bounced off his folding canvas stool, energized

by this exchange. "Oh, I can and will. You've not encountered any Rebel forces, so I'll explain it to you. We have a simple and reasonable policy governing the expenditure of our limited medical supplies. Any Rebel wounded in action has received injury defending the whole. He is entitled to immediate and complete care. Next are any children who happen to be in the area of conflict. Following that, adult civilians. After that comes enemy wounded who have been cooperative. There simply aren't supplies available for anyone beyond that."

For a moment a post-Great War sense of indignation awakened in Trasher as he stared up at Ben Raines, who towered over him. "Everyone is entitled to medical treatment," he grated.

"No. Certainly not your kind. Only those who out of loyalty, innocence, or cooperation received their wounds are entitled. You and this biker trash wallow in filth, decadence, and perversion. You glory in how much cruelty you can devise to visit on your fellow man. You live to see others hurt. Your kind aren't worth the powder to blow you away. You're less than the scum that floats on a septic tank. And you are definitely not deserving of medical treatment."

Panic started to touch Trasher. He pointed to Venusian Snot, writhing on the ground, most of the skin on his front ground away. "But my men are going to die."

"Some of them. The women, too. And good riddance to them."

Gabriel Trasher's hand began to shake as he sank to one knee. "Look, it's not like that at all. We're not the sort you say. I know these people, like them, love some of them. Sure, we're a little wild, but we don't go in for any of what you accused us of. Please, you've got to give us a chance."

While he spoke, Gabe surreptitiously moved his hand to one boottop. From it, he cautiously and skillfully drew a small, flat, .25 autopistol. Eyes fixed on

109

Ben Raines and the short dangerous-looking young woman near him, Trasher flexed the muscles of his legs and made a sudden, desperate leap toward Ben's nearer side.

He grabbed the point of Ben's shoulder and used it as a pivot point to swing himself around behind the Rebel general. All in the same motion, he jammed the blunt muzzle of the little .25 Browning in Ben's right ear.

Ben Raines heard a soft groan from the direction of Jersey. Her anguish and shame registered plainly on her face. "Sorry, Chief. I screwed this one up real good," she spoke calmly, eyes fixed on Trasher. "He moved so fast, I woulda hit you if I shot him."

"You'll get your chance," Ben assured her.

Everyone nearby froze and stared unbelievingly. The only sound came from Venusian Snot, who screamed away what life he had left. A Rebel medic raised his eyes to search Ben's face.

"No, she won't," Gabe hissed. "She shoots me, I turn your brain to fuckin' pudding."

"Think it through, asshole," Ben snapped gruffly. "You shoot me and she chops you into fine pieces."

"No, goddammit, no. It don't work that way," Trasher shouted in a babble, unnerved by the image that generated. "I got the gun on your boss, you bitch, an' he's gonna do what I say. You're gonna order my wounded taken care of, Raines, you hear me?"

"I hear you, but I'm not going to do it."

"You will or I'll blow you away. I'll splatter your brains all over the ground!" Trasher added as his voice rose to a shrill shriek.

Ben remained silent for a while, then sighed and sagged in resignation. "All right," he said softly. He caught the eye of the immobile medic. "Medic, take care of that vermin over there."

110

"Sure, no problem, General."

Walking cat-footed, the medic approached Venusian Snot. With slow deliberation he took an H&K P-9 double-action 9mm pistol from its holster and shot the wounded Secretion between the eyes.

In the stunned moment following, Ben employed his rusty command of *aikido* against the gaping leader of the Alien Secretions. With a rising butterfly he swept the .25 auto away from his ear. Ben sank on flexed knees and closed his hand over the weapon after its first discharge. Pivoting, he used Trasher's reactive force against him, bending the gun back and removing it from Gabe's hand, after breaking his index finger with the trigger guard.

Gabe Trasher howled in pain as Ben continued his pivot, which brought him face-to-face with his enemy. In a blur, Ben drove stiffened fingertips into Trasher's solar plexus. Foul wind gushed out of Trasher's mouth and his eyes bugged. He went deathly white and gagged in desperation against a paralyzed diaphragm. For good measure, Ben did a cross-over sidestep and chopped Trasher at the base of his neck. In a flare of red and black, the lights went out for Gabe Trasher.

"You should have let me pop him, General," Jersey gasped out as she stared in awe at the recumbent Trasher.

"No. It became suddenly personal. I'm getting out of practice. That round he got off cut hair from the top of my head. That made me take more of an interest in him."

Jersey wanted to laugh. She also wanted to cry. This made a second time she was just a hair slow in judging a situation and taking the proper action. Was she losing *her* edge? Corrie approached with a portable radio.

"I've got General Striganov on, sir."

Ben took the handset and settled at the table again. "This is Eagle, Bear, go."

111

"We are moving along briskly, old friend." Georgi Striganov came across jovial even through the mechanical rendering of the scrambler. "So far we have met little resistance. I'm wondering if they aren't making an elaborate mousetrap for you?"

Ben ran that over in his head, in light of what had just happened. "You may be right, Georgi Alexandrovich. So far Hoffman has thrown a large gang of biker garbage at me. I mean me, personally," Ben related the attacks by Trasher's Alien Secretions.

A blurt of static answered Ben. A scrambler doesn't know how to translate a whistle. "You are still short of your objective, I gather," Striganov inquired.

"That's a roger. Too damn short, I think," Ben responded.

"Our mercenary friend is well on his way."

"Good. We'll be through here in a short and back on the road," Ben advised his northern-theater commander. Because transmit and receive were on separate frequencies, the two men could converse rather like on a telephone. "We took a few casualties. Too many, to my way of seeing it," Ben added curtly.

"Omelets and eggs, my friend. But I know what you mean. Hoffman seems to grow troops out of the ground, while every loss we take spreads us thinner. There's a reported concentration of black-shirts in the area of Glendive, Montana. I'll contact you when we clear them out. This is Bear, out."

"Roger, Bear." Ben sighed, and handed Corrie the handset.

At Ben's feet, Gabe Trasher began to twitch and show other signs of life. He groaned after a couple of seconds, then doubled into a fetal position and vomited. Gagging, he cried out in misery and clutched his head with both hands. Slowly, consciousness swam back into focus.

"Goddamn, what did you do?" he croaked up at Ben.

Ben's response went not to Trasher but to Sergeant

112

Bourchart. "Sergeant, get a couple of men and take this filth over there and hang him."

Gabriel Trasher started to scream in abject terror. He kept on screaming until the rope cut off his wind.

Ten

General Field Marshal Jesus Dieguez Mendoza Hoffman looked up at his G-2 and G-3, standing at rigid attention in front of his desk.

"*Herr Generalfeldmarschall,* we wish to report that everything is in readiness. Operation *Adlermeister* can commence at your word."

Hoffman clapped his hands in enthusiasm. "Excellent! This spells the end of Ben Raines. Let *Adlermeister* begin at once. You have your duties to attend to, I'll not keep you."

"*Zu Befehl, Herr Generalfeldmarschall! Heil Hitler!*" they cho_rused.

"*Heil Hitler!*" Hoffman responded, wondering when the world would start hailing him like they still did the master of the Third Reich.

Bemused, he turned away to a large sand table on which the symbols of his various units had been laid out. Ben Raines was in for a major surprise. Volmer had done well in leaving behind convincing evidence that the NAL forces would be thinly spread along a thousand-mile front. From all reports, Raines was reacting as anticipated.

He had already split his forces. The only item that bothered him, Hoffman reflected, was that rather-large concentration of troops under the Russian bastard, Striganov. They were at that moment reported to be overwhelming the NAL garrison at Glendive.

Had the old communist son of a bitch had a falling out with Raines? Could it be that Raines had already been weakened by this loss?

No matter. His brilliantly conceived, two-pronged blitzkrieg would put the finish to General Ben Raines. A worthy opponent, though, Hoffman thought in his conceit. One befitting a contest with the most capable, powerful general in all the world. When he was master of the entire Western Hemisphere, he might, in his magnanimity, graciously pardon Ben Raines and let him live out his life in genteel exile.

Outside his office, Col. Joaquin Webber confided to Col. Manfred Spitz, "I think he's taken on more than he can handle."

"You mean our brilliant leader?" Spitz asked with a sneer. "I think he does that every morning when he undertakes to pull on his boots."

Webber looked around suspiciously. "Be careful. There are some of those SS big-ears everywhere."

"Not out here in the open, Joaquin. At least not unless they are close enough you can see them. It remains that I have a bad feeling about this Eagle Master operation."

"Time will tell, Manfred," Webber said gravely, his own doubts resurfacing.

During the first campaign against Field Marshal Hoffman, Ben Raines had left strong Rebel outposts at secure compounds outside of what had been Colorado Springs and Pueblo. Over the ensuing months, the Rebels who occupied them had enlarged on their defenses. Dragon's teeth had been set up in depth, randomly armed with contact-detonating explosive charges powerful enough to disassemble the best tanks Hoffman had. Lateral trenches, deep, steep, and wide enough to trap any armor that got past the concrete pylons. The ground all around had been sown with antitank mines and nasty little daisy-cutter AP mines.

Each outpost possessed a stockpile of beehive rounds for their 105mm howitzers. They also had the standard issue of CNDM—nausea and tear gas—canisters for the 81mm mortars and in hand-grenade form. Colorado Springs enjoyed a special advantage.

It sat atop the huge underground complex that comprised the central supply depot for the Continental Defense Command. For a long while, its copious inventory provided for all the munitions, supplies, vehicles, and spare parts the Rebels needed. A respectable amount remained on the shelves and forklift pads.

Entrusted with the security of this cornucopia, the Rebels at Colorado Springs remained doubly alert. Their sensors picked up the rumble of heavy armor at 0830 hours the next morning. Passive IR and other stealthy surveillance equipment soon verified that a major troop movement was under way and they were the target. Instantly the compound went to full alert. Condition Red warnings were radioed to Eagle's mobile CP.

"We have a Level One alert from Colorado Springs," Ben Raines was told a minute later.

"Dammit," Ben snorted. "I have a feeling the fecal matter is going to hit the rotor blades. Tell them to hold with what they've got, but not at the cost of all their lives. No, let me tell them."

"Understood, Eagle. That's a big roger. We've got this place nicely covered. It would take a major offensive to penetrate to our main bunker," Capt. Victor Sanchez of the Rebel command at the Springs responded to Ben's call. When Ben signed off, he turned to his four platoon leaders.

"I know we're what could be considered Reservists. But now we've got the shit in our left hands and it's headed for our faces. Start in with the LTDs and 'smart' AT mortar rounds at maximum range. I want the fifties set up with the Norwegian ammo General Raines brought back. That shit will penetrate up to seven inches of armor and do a real number on the inside of a tank *pronto*."

"We have everyone in body armor, Vic. What about you?" Lieutenant Price nodded to the sweat-stained OD tank top the captain wore.

Sanchez shrugged. "Yeah, I guess I'd better dress for the dance. Before I do, though, I want all of you to see that your men have a double issue of ammunition. We want to keep those fuckers as far away as we can. Have the gun crews gotten in from their R & R at the farm?"

"Last one is due in five minutes," Price informed him.

"Good. Then, quick like bunnies, get this show on the road. The general's counting on us."

Sgt. Emilio Sandoval didn't know what the hell to make of that little green spot of light on the rear deck of his MBT. Maybe he should button up just to be sure, he considered. He never heard the incoming mortar round. The hardened, armor-piercing nose of the projectile landed within an inch of where the laser target designator beam had "painted" the main battle tank.

It slammed loudly into the motor compartment and detonated in less than an eyeblink. The resultant massive explosion blew the top half of Sandoval out the commander's hatch. Like a huge Frisbee, the turret set sail through the smoke and exhaust-fumed air when the magazine let go.

Instantly deprived of their arrogance, the Nazi tankers began a wild, erratic series of evasive tactics. It did little good. Every time an LTD painted a tank, the high-angle projectile that locked onto it killed the MBT.

117

Such sophisticated equipment was a mystery to the South American black-shirts. It resulted in terrible confusion. "Fire! Fire on them. Open fire!" the company commander screamed over his radio. He said to the gape-mouthed infantry officer beside him, "Nobody can adjust his guns that fast. How are they hitting my tanks?"

"I don't know," the black-shirt captain responded. "Magic, maybe?"

A third of the initial armor reached the dragon's teeth. The first tank to nudge into a pyramid of concrete went up in a flash-bang of intense white light. The plastic explosive blew the main gun off the turret and stripped the treads with rippling blast effect. Inside, concussion did for those in the turret.

Eyes blinded and streaming from dust and paint chips, the driver threw the monster in reverse and rolled out of his treads. His head throbbed and blood ran from his ears. He could hear nothing and didn't know the tank commander lay dead in his harness above. All he knew was he wanted the hell out of there. When the bogies ground to a stop in the soft earth, he threw open the hatch over his head and squeezed out.

A short burst from an M-60 stitched across his chest and ended his anxiety. The infantry fared better. A daisy-cutter took off a leg here, disemboweled a man there, machine-gun fire raked the open spaces and sent deadly ricochets off tank obstacles. Slowly, sheer mass began to tell.

"We've stopped their armor cold," Price informed Sanchez.

"Now what's the good news?" Captain Sanchez asked facetiously.

"There's a hell of a lot of them out there. More than a company, for sure. I think we've got our nuts in a crack."

"You're saying we should pull out?" Sanchez probed.

"No. Not yet, Vic. We can hold, like the general said. For a while."

A similar drama unfolded outside what was left of Pueblo, Colorado. Two full battalions of infantry flung themselves at the Rebel defenses. Backed by tanks and light armored vehicles equipped with twin 40mm autoloaders, they slashed through the lesser defenses to a depth where individual riflemen engaged each other at eyeball-to-eyeball range. These massive attacks had not been in the planning done by Ben Raines.

It went against everything his efficient intelligence personnel had developed. Peter Volmer was spreading men thin through a wide corridor, intended, Ben believed, to suck him in and then slam shut on his main Rebel command. That, or force him to weaken his own position to counter them. Then Hoffman hit two vulnerable Rebel outposts early and with massive strength.

He had set Ben up all right. Gotten his attention and hooked him and now played with him like a big bass on a limber rod and nine-pound line. Ben fumed in impotent anger while he listened on the radio as the attacks unfolded. It was all his fault, he chastised himself. Hoffman and this Volmer had played him for a sucker, sure enough. And he'd gone for it. He should have anticipated this, Ben cursed silently as he listened to the last broadcast out of Pueblo.

"They're in the compound now, Eagle. We—we didn't have time to pull out, over."

"You mean you didn't want to, you gutsy bastard," Ben said thickly, his throat working hard.

"What's that, sir?" Corrie asked. "Do you want me to transmit that?"

"What? Uh—no, Corrie. No."

A loud blast came over the speaker. Coughing followed, and a weak voice. "Th—they've blown the manhole cover, General. I'm going to wait until this place fills up and . . . send them . . . all to hell."

"No!" Ben shouted. "Don't waste your life like that." His eyes felt hot and dry. Funny that his vision was distorted by a liquid film.

"Jesus, I've got an SS major down here," came the voice of the last living Rebel at Pueblo. "Here comes more of the bastards. I think now is a good —" The sharp edge of an explosion and sudden burst of static filled Ben's mobile CP.

Torn by powerful emotion, Ben stared at the speaker box. All of a sudden he wanted to put his head down on the table and bawl his heart out, something he hadn't done since he was eight years old. Instead, he turned hot, haunted eyes on Corrie.

"I want General Jefferys ASAP. Bump him now."

Corrie switched to the big, long-range radio set and spoke quietly into it. After a second she nodded.

"Have you been following this thing, Cec?" Ben rasped.

"As closely as possible, given the distance. What's up?"

"Hoffman's screwed the pooch. He's made an idiot out of me and I damn well intend to fuck over him for that. How fast can you get six Puffs in the air?"

"Half an hour, Eagle."

"Do it. I want them up, carrying a full load of every nasty thing they have. Two of them to Colorado Springs and Pueblo. I want them to clean the goddamn black-shirts out of there. Kill anything that walks, crawls, or wiggles. They can refuel at the old McConnell Air Force Base in Wichita on the way back. The other four to the north, to cream Cheyenne. We'll establish a refueling spot for them while they are en route. I want every one of these Nazi bastards dead. That goes too for their wives, kids, cats, dogs, and canaries."

Concerned for his old friend, Cecil Jefferys tut-tutted a bit. "You're taking this personally, Ben."

"Damned right I am," Ben snapped. "Just do it, Cec. I'm counting big on you."

A long moment of carrier wave answered. Then Jefferys spoke softly, a hurt tone in his voice. "I think you can, Ben. Without question."

Misery painted Ben's face. "Oh, shit, yes, Cec. I'm sorry I gnawed your headbone. I'm so—damned mad. At me, at Hoffman, at everything that delays cleaning the clock of this Nazi dung pile. FACs and FAGs will be sent forward with the refueling team. The pilots will be briefed in flight. Eagle, out."

Ben reached Tina next. "Take one company, stripped down for speed. I want you to draw two fuel tankers from Thermopolis and set out at once. Make an end run around Cheyenne and locate a functional airfield capable of handling C-47s. Heavily loaded C-47s."

Tina's eyes sparkled and Ben could see it in the tone of her voice. "You're going to bring in the Puffs," Tina said excitedly. She *loved* the big flying gun platforms. "They . . . smash things up so . . . efficiently," she had commented once.

"I'm tired of wasting lives," Ben answered curtly. "Hoffman seems to have an inexhaustible supply of ground pounders. What he doesn't have is effective SAMs. Without a surface-to-air capability, we have him by the short and curlies. I want to kick his ass all the way back to the mouth of the Columbia River."

"I—heard about Pueblo," Tina said cautiously.

"That's part of the reason," Ben admitted. "The rest is plain common sense. We're stretched so tight now that the balloon is about to pop. If we chase around to every little spot Hoffman's troops choose to hit, we'll run ourselves into the ground. I know it worked before. But Hoffman's staff and field commanders have learned, even if he hasn't. We aren't going to pick up the marbles without losing a few along the

121

way. I want to make it as few as possible."

"And I love you for it, Daddy. Every — well — I mean, that's what makes you so special to every Rebel. I remember reading in one of your books that there was a time when it seemed British officers calculated how great their victories were by the casualty lists. The more casualties, the bigger their success. Sort of winnow out the lower classes, don't chew know."

"Dan would be deeply incensed by that," Ben chided with a chuckle. "Okay, sweetheart, lighten that company and haul out with those tankers soon as you can. And, Tina, duck your head and keep your pretty little tail down."

Scandalized, Tina all but shrieked. "Daddy! You haven't seen my tail since Jack and I outgrew those evening bath sessions. You have no idea whether or not it's pretty."

"If it's attached to you, it is," Ben kept up the repartee, his mood lightened by doing something. "Need I mention, we are going to make all possible speed for Cheyenne. Hoffman's stuck his foot in our door, I'm gonna hand it back to him, chewed off at the knee."

Eleven

Rolling south on Nebraska 71, Tina and her small convoy blew into Colorado an hour out of Kimball. It would be another hour and a half to Colorado 14, where they would turn west to what used to be Fort Collins. Hell of a way to bypass Cheyenne, Tina considered.

Necessary, though. County roads closer to Cheyenne would be patrolled by the black-shirt army of SS General Brodermann. The whole trick was to avoid detection. Her tentative goal was the airport at Laramie. That or the small military airbase outside the metropolitan ruins of the city. They would be spotted at either, she had no doubt. And there would be fighting. Like before, her musings reminded.

That had been back before the crusade to liberate Europe. Back when the Rebel army fought the Night People. Tina recalled the desperate situation that had developed at the airbase. Memory of the fetid odor of the creepies could still wrinkle her nose. They had swarmed like a black human tide from the large hangars, to be chopped down with automatic-weapons fire. For once, Tina remembered, there had been more meat than air to shoot at. She had commanded a company then. Damn fine troops.

It still hurt to think of those who hadn't survived. A sudden chill rippled over Tina's skin as she saw images of the loathsome creatures grabbing and pulling at her in the security building. A young Rebel had given his life to save her from becoming creepie breakfast. But they had whipped the Night People, kicked the snot out of them, and exterminated their odious confraternity. Not only in Laramie, but everywhere in the United States.

"We'll have to make a refueling stop at Ault," the driver beside Tina informed her.

"Better make it along the roadside before there. Might find some Nazis in the ruins of Fort Collins."

"Right, Colonel, I never thought of that," the blushing driver responded. Although she had only a company along, Tina still commanded a battalion and retained her rank. The young Rebel wasn't used to having lieutenant colonels riding in the lead truck of a convoy. Especially one who carried a wicked-looking little gun like that.

Tina had noted his frequent darted glances at the compact automatic weapon she carried and softened her face into a smile as she decided to enlighten him. "It's something Ike McGowan picked up down in the Southwest. Albuquerque, as a matter of fact. It's called a Sidewinder. Nice thing is, it's a convertible."

"Huh—um—sir?"

"Using the tools built into the sling fasteners, you can change it from .45 ACP to nine-mil in a little over thirty seconds. I'll spare you all the details, but you can see the advantage of being able to use more than one caliber ammunition. The cyclic rate is twelve hundred rounds per minute in both configurations and it has a progressive trigger. Fires single shot, three-round burst, or full auto."

"M'god, that's a whole lot in a little package," the driver observed.

"You're O'Brien, right? Well, O'Brien, the Sidewinder gives a whole new meaning to *nasty*. The front barrel retainer plug is threaded on the outside to fit a suppressor. They found twenty Sidewinders, and the suppressors for them, in an old root cellar that had been converted into a vault. Whoever built those silencers sure knew what he was doing. All you hear is the cycling of the bolt and the brass hitting the ground. When Da—the general said to strip down a company to travel fast and light, I thought it might be useful to have along."

"I'll say," O'Brien answered enthusiastically. "What's it take to get ahold of one of them?"

Tina's smile was gentle and not at all patronizing. "They're special issue out of Headquarters Company, R Batt. I had to promise Captain Thermopolis my right arm to draw this one. They are rare birds and very much special operations equipment."

"I, ah, I'm kinda glad you've got it with you, Colonel."

"So am I, O'Brien. I've got a feeling we might need it sooner than you'd think."

Tina had sent two scouts ahead of the column, on silenced motorcycles. Painted flat black, they purred along with no more sound than an electric lawn-mower. Nightfall had come by the time they ghosted into the rubble that had been Fort Collins, Colorado. Dressed in dark clothing, their faces coated with ebony camo stick, hands gloved, the scouts could not be seen except for their movement.

Their precautions proved wise shortly after drifting through the center of the old town. The Nazis had come to Fort Collins. They traveled in style, the scouts made note. A large gooseneck trailer served as a barrack. It had an oddly foreign essence to its design; it had come up from South America, no doubt. With his companion covering him, one scout stealthfully opened the door and slid inside.

He came back three minutes later. In a soft whisper, up next to his partner's ear, he revealed what he had found. "There's a dozen of them sacked out in there. Must be the American brand of shitheads.

125

They have cammies exactly like ours."

"Why no sentries?" the other asked.

"Count your blessings. There isn't anything in there to cook with, so there must be more of these around."

They found them within a hundred yards of the bunk trailer. Two had been pulled into the hollow shells of old buildings — a decidedly unsafe undertaking, in the scouts' experience. Another, parked behind the solitary rear wall of an old muffler shop, showed a dim light and emitted a variety of tweedles and squeaks that they interpreted as radio communications. Nodding thoughtfully, they returned to their bikes and tooled out of Fort Collins before contacting the column.

Tina's RT operator sat tailor-fashion in the sleeper bunk behind the contour seats of the military-style tractor. She tapped Tina lightly on one shoulder and passed over the handset. Tina got the skinny on Fort Collins in short, terse sentences.

"Hold where you are," she told the scouts. "I'll be up shortly." To O'Brien, "Signal for a pull-over. I'm taking one of the BFVs."

Small and speedy the Bradley Fighting Vehicles had been hailed as the battlefield answer to moving infantry quickly and in at least minimal protection. Once in general issue, back in the 80s, from top brass to rear-rank grunt, the Army didn't quite see it that way.

They only held six troops, aside from the crew, which required committing two of the rather-expensive wheeled vehicles to each squad, with a vacant spot in one. Most considered the BFV a prime example of military-industrial complex boondoggles. Then some ordnance johnnies got to playing around with them, retrofitted the light armored vehicles with 4-inch mortar tubes and 30mm gatling guns. The mortars could fire on a flat trajectory, which effectively made them a 75mm tank gun. With "smart" ammo, and LTDs, they became awesome. The gatlings could traverse better than 200 degrees from the right-side hatch, providing adequate covering fire. When resurrected by the Rebels, with their more liberal rules of engagement, the BFVs survived contact with the enemy and generally spread terror on the battlefield. Tina had chosen wisely for what she had in mind.

"Corporal," she told the driver. "I want to be in Fort Collins yesterday afternoon."

"Can do, Colonel," he responded cheerily.

She gave further instructions about watching for the scouts while she took the suppressor from her alice pack and screwed it on the muzzle of her Sidewinder. One of the crewmen gawked at the potent weapon and blinked.

"Am I imagining things, or does that magazine rotate?" he asked.

"Sure does, trooper. There's several positions, controlled by ball detents around the receiver housing. To make it short, that allows the shooter to fire right- or left-handed around the corner of a building without exposing himself."

"Wouldn't want to be on the receiving end of that," he blurted.

"Haven't yet met anyone who would," Tina replied dryly.

In fact, the weapons being so scarce, she had only qualified with it. This was the first time she would use it in the field. If it proved out, production would gear up at Base Camp One. Tina had brought along the other three scouts with the company and turned now to the sergeant in charge.

"We'll leave the Bradley where we contact your scouts. Unlimber that bike stowed on the outside and we'll go in piggyback. I'll ride with you."

They completed the handoff without incident and arrived in Fort Collins twenty minutes later. Tina used a small hand-held radio to direct their operation.

"We'll take the comm van first. I'll do the shooting, the rest of you use knives. That way we can leave sleeping dogs lie," she added with a dry chuckle.

Tina eased open the door to the trailer five minutes later. A chill night draft of air drew the attention of one Nazi radioman. He looked up into the end-wipe of the suppressor. A silent .45 slug took him in the forehead. Immediately, Tina leapt into the communications van, followed by two of the scouts.

She shot another man at the counter along one wall, where he frantically tried to get off an alert transmission. Knives flashed to either side of her and the remaining two Nazis died with only soft, pained sighs. A burst from the Sidewinder trashed the radios.

"The way I like it. Not a sound." The scout sergeant noted a strange light in Tina's eyes. "Now we move fast. Neutralize that machine-gun position first. One of Carson's thermite tabs in the receiver should do the job. Then we hit that sleeping trailer and call in the Bradley."

Hans Brauer had been with the American Nazi movement since his teenage years. Growing up in the general anarchy that followed the Great War, he had developed into a selfish, bigoted, ignorant lout. Membership in the movement did little to change that, except for the worse. He hated the regimentation that had suddenly been thrust upon him by this call to arms. Although he felt great serving the new *Führer*. Jesus Diguez Mendoza Hoffman was like unto a god to Hans. Except, the dull-witted Hans wondered, why did he have to have all those spic names?

That question came to Hans after he had awakened in the middle of the night with a full bladder. Grumbling at the anticipated cold outside in the Fort Collins area, Hans pulled on trousers and boots—he had never toughened his feet by going barefoot; only sub-human children went barefoot, his parents had admonished. Doing a little dance of urgency, he headed for the door to the trailer in which he slept.

Only half-awake, Hans stepped out and instantly froze in shock. Three dark figures came purposefully toward him. About all Hans could determine was that their faces, as well as their clothing, were black. A low snarl formed in his throat and he sucked air to call the alarm.

He wasted the effort. A silenced three-round burst from Tina Raines's Sidewinder popped into his chest so fast blood had not flown from the first before the third struck his heart. In his death throes, Hans voided his uncomfortably full bladder before he went off to Hitlerland.

"No sense in being quiet now," Tina told the two scouts who accompanied her. "You, Evans, stay out here and pop any of them who try to jump out a window. We'll go in blasting," she told the other scout.

The remarkable combination of unique SMG and superior suppressor of Sid Garris spat silent death into the recumbent forms in the trailer. One man, alerted by the slightly noisier blast of the scout's silenced Uzi, got to his sidearm. The 9mm pistol cracked in loud inaccuracy. One slug did pass by Tina's head with a sharp crack. It only served to draw her attention. She cut a three-round burst that quieted the opposition.

One American Nazi, stark naked, made a leap for the nearest window. He crashed through to the waist before his head was sieved by Evans. His legs thrashed and pounded loudly against the thin wall of the trailer. Vaguely, Tina could hear firing from the other barrack trailer. Subjectively it seemed to take forever to quell the eleven men in the trailer. Actually the firefight lasted only eleven seconds. Tina stepped outside and breathed deeply to banish the coppery smell of blood.

"We'll mop this place up and move on when the column arrives. Trade off scouts and set them on the road now," she said calmly.

"Jesus, she didn't even turn a hair," one of those selected to take the point said to his companion when they rode away from Fort Collins.

"That's the boss's daughter," his companion responded with a grin of pride.

That night seemed the longest in the memory of Ben Raines. His daughter had her neck stuck way out. Colorado Springs still held out, barely. Reports of attacks on three more outposts gnawed at his patience and conscience. When he climbed from the contour chair in the mobile CP for his tenth cup of coffee, he expressed his doubts to Lt. Col. Stan McDade.

"Bull, should I have split the command into company-sized units and sent them to every outpost even remotely likely to be attacked?"

Colonel McDade was his usual miser with words. "It was your decision, Ben. For what it's worth, I think you did the right thing."

"Enlighten me," Ben said with a slight edge.

"I have a gut feeling that Hoffman wants you to divide your forces. He has numbers on his side. I've said it before, but maybe not clearly enough. When he loses a man, he loses a man; when we lose someone, we lose combat effectiveness."

Ben bit off a curse, swallowed coffee instead. The RT operator who had relieved Corrie after a long, hectic ten hours turned from the console.

"General, the Puffs have reached Pueblo. I have the command pilot on the line. He wants to know about forward air controllers."

"Tell him he doesn't need any. Anything that moves down there is the enemy." Ben looked relieved. Now things would start happening.

* * *

Major Alvaro Barron awakened to the drone of old piston engines. He blinked and tried to put meaning to the sound. Barron had occupied the small wooden building that had been the Pueblo, Colorado, outpost commander's quarters. He turned on a bedside lamp to check the time.

"Odd," he said to himself. "We don't have any cargo aircraft operating around here."

In the sky a quarter-mile from the compound, the big twin radials throttled back and the pilot touched a switch on the instrument panel. A green light flicked on and a grinning gunner swung the barrel of his electric gatling down and acquired a target.

Major Barron did not hear the metallic ring of the barrels as they began to turn, loading up with 20mm rounds. He also didn't hear the deafening roar when the gatling opened fire at over 2,000 rounds a minute. The table lamp beside his bed had provided a perfect beacon. All Major Alvaro Barron knew about the arrival of the Rebel Puffs could be measured in the enormous shock he felt when the building around him began to disintegrate.

Twenty-millimeter rounds turned the walls into showers of splinters and plaster dust. The one-in-three explosive rounds blew out windows and sliced the flesh from the major's orderly, sleeping on a cot in the hall. First one, then a dozen more three-quarter-inch slugs slammed into the Nazi major and pulped his corpulent body into a red smear.

Troops bivouacked in the open met a similar, if more grisly, fate when the 30mm chainguns belly-mounted on the second Puff raked their tents and shelter-halves with exploding rounds. Shrieks and howls of agony sounded thin and tinny in the presence of that awesome destruction.

To Rudolfo Quintaro, a carpenter until called up by the NAL for this campaign, it sounded like a huge table router working on a piece of Brazilian iron-wood. Bemused by the comparison, he walked into a hail of steel shards from an exploding round from the swivel-mounted 75mm autocannon belly-slung on the first Puff.

After four devastating passes, the winged death duo lined up in formation and made a run directly over the compound. Oblong gray objects dropped from their open doors. Battered and benumbed, the survivors of the initial onslaught stared upward in fascination while the containers descended upon them. When the first one hit in a long skid, spewing a trail of flaming napalm, their bewildered state ended in pandemonium and the screams of the dying.

Now the Puffs targeted vehicles. Trucks, utilities, APCs, and tanks erupted in fountains of blast and flame. They maintained a steady carpet of slugs of several calibers. At one point not a single inch of the ground did not have a bullet strike. After their final pass, huge halogen floodlights sprang to life and bathed the scene of slaughter in unearthly white.

"Tango Alpha Six, do you seen anything moving down there? Over." the command pilot asked his wingman.

"Negative, Tango Alpha Three. We really creamed them. Over."

"Roger that, Six. Lights out and turn to course two-niner-five. We'll go pay the Springs a visit. Over."

"Tango Alpha Six, roger. These birds are gonna need a drink soon. Over."

"It's all downhill from the Springs. Tango Alpha Three, out."

They came in at treetop level and demolished the tanks first. Turrets leapt into the air under the reign of terror from the 75mm autocannon. Ammo magazines added to the overall effect. At a distance of twenty miles from Colorado Springs, the radio crackled to life with a stranger's voice.

"Tango Alpha Three, this is Lone Wolf."

"Go ahead, Lone Wolf," the command pilot spoke.

"We're in the bunker at the Springs. We're still alive and well down here. We can mark targets for you with willie-peter mortar rounds. Over."

"Good show, Lone Wolf. Hang in there; company's coming fast. Tango Alpha Three out."

Grinning at the tenacity Rebels always showed, the pilot contacted his wingman and they began a rapid descent. "We'll make one flyby, Six, let 'em know we're there, then look for the white spots."

Reacting to the pyrotechnic showers of smoking white dots of phosphorus, the Puffs unloaded everything they had left. It gave new meaning to the old Vietnam-era slogan "Death from the Skies." Somewhere in the middle of the hell-on-earth, panic developed among the black-shirt troops. While men ran shrieking with blobs of WP burning through their flesh, others began to just run.

Walleyed with terror, they rammed vehicles into one another and scrambled in manic haste to be anywhere else than Colorado Springs. The surviving Rebels in the compound added their carefully horded supply of ordnance to the inferno of flying steel spit out by the Puffs. Incredibly, Capt. Victor Sanchez realized, a counterattack would carry the field. Laughing wildly, he ordered it.

Ben Raines heard the first good news from the three new hot spots. "They're pulling back, General. It looks from here as though it was only a probing action."

"You've made my day," Ben responded dryly. "Keep a close watch on the enemy. This might be a ruse."

A soft, relaxed chuckle answered him. "They're five miles down the road, sir, and not slowing down. There's not a black-shirt within sight of the compound."

Similar reports came from the other two. Then the stunning news came that Captain Sanchez had led a counterattack that had driven the surviving Nazis out of the Colorado Springs area. Ben reached into his desk and retrieved a disreputable bottle that contained Base One brandy. He poured a dollop into his coffee and sat grinning, an unlighted cigarette in one corner of his mouth.

Ben went to bed when the RT operator announced, "The Puffs are turning final to land at Wichita and refuel."

Twelve

Bone china flew in tiny fragments from the wet spot on the wall of the Oregon ranch house. The saucer followed the cup and General Field Marshal Jesus Dieguez Mendoza Hoffman shrieked in outrage.

"I can't believe he did this!"

"In all due respect, General Field Marshal, it seems that the Rebels have done exactly that," Colonel Webber stated dryly.

"He won't get away with this! I want Ben Raines dead—dead—dead!" Hoffman ranted.

"Ben Raines was nowhere near our, ah, ignominious defeats, General Field Marshal," Webber reminded him.

"His was the mind behind them. His is the evil genius that is disrupting my plan. His will be the life that pays for it." Hoffman stalked around the room in long, slouched strides, hands behind his back. "I want to go to the front. I want to see with my own eyes how he accomplished the impossible."

"It's hardly advisable for you to do so, General Field Marshal. The situation at the front is, ah, fluid, sir."

" 'Fluid'? It's a goddamned flood tide! Then send Volmer. Where is he, by the way?"

"Outside where Denver used to be, General Field Marshal," Gen. Kurt Kreuger answered.

"Have him go, make a full report to me by this afternoon."

"At once, Herr General Field Marshal," Kreuger assured him with clicking heels.

"Then I want him to come up with plans for capturing Ben Raines," Hoffman added, eyes glowing with madness.

At 0320, the convoy led by Tina Raines reached the airport on the edge of Laramie. Scouts had located only six storm troopers in the administration building. They appeared to be regulars, not some of the American traitors. That gave Tina an idea.

"We'll use a bit of a ruse," she explained to Lieutenant Novak. "What we need are some of those Nazi flags to put on our radio antennas. Hoffman's regulars can't possibly know all of the American traitors who have joined their ranks. And, if you've noticed, the American Nazis wear the same pattern cammies that we have. We'll just drive up as a reinforcement column, then jump them when they're off guard."

Lt. Kelly Novak nodded his understanding. The longer they avoided a firefight, the better their chances of remaining undetected. At least until the Puffs arrived to refuel.

So it was that the Rebel vehicles rolled into the airport twenty minutes later and dispersed to their required locations. Tina, Lieutenant Novak, and three scouts went to report to the ranking Nazi. He turned out to be a swarthy senior sergeant, with a moon face and pronounced Indian features.

He greeted them somewhat condescendingly and with a puzzled attitude. "I do not understand," he complained in Spanish. "Nothing came on the radio about reinforcements."

Tina almost blew their cover then, answering in the banter of veteran soldiers. "You know these rear-echelon types. Probably out slopping down beer when he

136

should have been transmitting orders to you."

For a brief moment, suspicion flared in the sergeant's eyes. "Yes, I know them only too well," he replied agreeably at last, then added in his native Paraguyan idiom, *"Te confieso que no puedo verlos ni en caja de fósforos."*

What the man had said was that he confessed he could not stand the sight of them. Translating it literally, Tina couldn't understand why the man would not have them in a box of matches. She did understand that the time had come to end this farce. By now the key players would be in position. Swiftly she raised the suppressed Sidewinder and plopped a three-round burst in the chubby sergeant's chest.

His eyes went round and filled with wonder. Full lips formed an "Oh" that never got said. The other two in the room with him reacted in confusion to the unfamiliar sound of the cycling action and the clack of empty casings hitting the tiled floor. Their hesitation cost them their lives.

Lieutenant Novak cut down one with a suppressed Uzi. The second caught another three-rounder from Tina. Reflex continued his draw and his sidearm—an Argentine copy of the old Walther P-38—clattered to the floor. From outside came the sound of a scuffle and a scream chopped off short.

"We now have us an airport," Tina said lightly. She went out of the administration building and located her RT operator. "Bump Eagle and tell him we are in control of the Laramie municipal airport."

General Field Marshal Hoffman received better news when he entertained his minister of information (propaganda) at breakfast the next morning. Over sweet rolls, juice, and coffee, the minister acquainted Hoffman with a new project his office had been working on during the conquest of Rebel outposts.

"We have obtained some video cameras, General

Field Marshal. Also the equipment necessary to use the products of their employment. I have had specialists recording what your troops and interrogators have done with the Rebels who fell alive into our hands." He produced a brief, neat, vulpine smile. "Copies are being made to be sent to every place your intelligence man — ah — Webber thinks Ben Raines might happen to go."

General Field Marshal Hoffman considered a moment the torture and degradation to which captive Rebels had been subjected. "I should think that would make General Raines absolutely furious, Keller. Raving mad, in fact."

"Precisely what we had in mind, General Field Marshal," Minister Keller responded with another flick of V-shaped smile.

"He has already killed to the last man the troops sent to Pueblo, Colorado. Driven the others from Colorado Springs. And my experts tell me that he is only mildly annoyed. To what good purpose do we drive him into a rage?"

Keller shot the wolfish grin again. "Our psychologists suggest that were he to become unmanageable in his outrage, actually lose touch with his reason, he might be likely to do something rash and unplanned, and thus expose himself."

Beaming in anticipation of such an event, Hoffman patted Keller affably on one shoulder. "My dear Minister Keller, you are balm for frayed nerves. I think that a simply marvelous idea. I will see to it that your technicians have anything they need to further this brilliant scheme of yours. My day is brighter for hearing this. Come, let me get the brandy and we'll take our coffee *royal*."

Static came from the speaker set up in the old control tower at Laramie Municipal Airport. Tina Raines stood behind the only intact piece of tinted glass in the tower's full run of windows. Binoculars to her eyes, she searched the sky to the southwest. A particularly loud hiss of background noise came to her ears, then words, broken up by the steady bellow of two radial engines.

"Laramie Approach, this is Tango Alpha One. Do you copy? Over."

"Roger, Tango Alpha One. How do you read us?"

"Five-by, Laramie. Do you have us on radar?"

"Negative, Tango Alpha. Funny man. Nothing works here except our tactical radios. We don't have you in sight, either. What's your ETA? Over."

"About five minutes, give or take five. It's a bitch-kitty navigating by railroad tracks and highways. I'd sell my soul for a VORTAC that worked. I've got a panel full of instruments that aren't worth a pinch of coon puckey, except on approach for Base Camp One."

Tina turned from the window a moment and shook her head. She knew the pilot, a chatty sort who took almost as much pleasure from his long-winded stints as he did from flying. He was also one of the best dead-reckoning navigators in the small fleet of Rebel aircraft. She indicated to the radio operator that she wanted to take over. When a break came, she spoke crisply.

"Chuck, can it for now. We're in the middle of outlaw country down here. I suspect we'll be under attack the minute you land. So make it a straight-in and hold the landing gear until you cross the threshold. We don't want landing lights advertising your presence from five miles out."

"Tina? That you?"

"You got it, Chuck. See you on the ground. Approach out."

Tina's estimate of the situation proved to be almost exact. Both C-47s had landed and rolled out to turn onto the taxi lane before activity began in the Nazi encampment two miles from the airport. There the commanding officer's curiosity got trucks loaded with a platoon of storm troopers.

They rolled past Tina's outer screen of security because of her admonition that the longer it took for anyone to find out something was up, the better. The lead truck turned through the gateway to the airport terminal before a well-placed projectile from a rocket launcher put a finish to the vehicle and its occupants.

A huge ball of flame marked the spot. The second driver slammed on brakes and got rear-ended by the third. Alarmed, the troops started jumping over the tailgates. That brought them into lines of crisp, measured fire from light machine guns. A couple of grenade launchers made hollow blooping sounds and whizzing shards of piano wire soon filled the air. The initial encounter ended after 93 seconds, with 43 men lying dead on the ground or converted to crispy critters in the burning truck. Not a Rebel received a scratch.

"We won that round," Tina said to the worried-looking pilots. "But they'll be back. After that, I'm sure of it."

"We can't have three-inch hoses running av gas into our wingtanks in a firefight," Chuck protested to Tina.

Tina's stubborn streak surfaced. "That's exactly what you'll have to do if you want to complete this mission today. Because, Chuckie baby, we're going to get hit by those Nazi bastards any second now."

"One hot round and it'll blow those fuckin' aircraft into confetti."

"There's one hangar that's in good condition," Tina offered. "Can you refuel in there?"

"If it's very well vented," Chuck persisted, understandably overprotective of his precious birds.

"Then, that's what you had better—"

"Tiin-coooming!" shouted a Rebel nearby, cutting off Tina's sentence.

140

Fluttering wings of the Angel of Death brushed over the airport, in the form of mortar rounds dropping on the field in random pattern. With a 4,800-foot runway, there was a lot more space than inbound bombs. The mortar shells exploded harmlessly enough. That would change, Tina knew.

"Get those planes under cover," she commanded. "Those Nazis may be assholes, but they're smart enough to get an FO up where he can walk those mortars in on something that counts."

Two drivers fitted jerry-rigged towbars to their Hummers, and the aircrews attached those to the nose-wheel struts of the C-47s. Slowly the tall-tailed craft disappeared inside the hangar. All the while the mortar rounds kept falling, although with little more precision than the first salvo.

Deployed to protect the critical-services area of the airport, the company had made sandbag bunkers and set up in an overlapping pattern that provided interlocking, enfiladed fire. The company's SAWs opened up while Tina and the pilots still anxiously watched the huge doors of the hangar slide shut on the Puffs.

Three M-60 LMGs per platoon, augmented by two more in the weapons squad, and .50 calibers on the pintle mounts of Hummers, brought a great volume of scalding pee on the heads of the charging Nazi troops. The router roar of the 30mm chainguns in the BFVs sang a death song that could be heard on the far side of the ruin of Laramie. Grenade launchers made their hollow barks and added to the carnage.

Storm troopers of Volmer's Bodyguard division made it halfway along the main runway before the steam went out of their assault. In withering fire they began to falter. The regulars of Brodermann's division yelled and tried to rally their American counterparts. Deadly Rebel accuracy gradually changed their minds.

"They're breaking!" a Rebel sergeant shouted.

"Pulling back all along the runway."

Tina had set up her CP in the control tower. From there, she had an excellent overview of the disintegrating assault. Part of her mind remained alert to the flow of radio traffic. When the last of the blackshirts streamed through the gaps in the sagging cyclone fence at the perimeter of the airfield, the call she had anticipated came through.

"We got it," came the calm voice of a scout. "Those assault troops led us right to their CP." He read off coordinates.

"Good work. Pull back far enough to direct fire," Tina ordered. Then she got on one of the cigarette-pack-sized radio to the four-inch-mortar crews. "I have a fire mission." Quickly she conveyed the elevation and declination. "Fire one for effect."

Two seconds later the big mortar round left the tube. It arched through the sky and descended on a block of rubble-strewn, but-still-standing buildings on the west side of Laramie. Its explosion sent a shower of brick chips whizzing along the deserted boulevard.

"Right two, up one," crackled from the scout. Tina relayed it.

The second and third rounds slammed into the gutted second floor of what had been a brick bank building. They blew out two of the remaining three walls and brought cries of alarm from those below, in the underground vault.

"Right on," the scout reported cheerily. "Right on the button."

"Fire ten rounds, alternate HE and willie peter," Tina commanded.

In pairs, the 4-inch rounds descended on the building that sheltered and concealed the Nazi CP. It and the ones to either side came down in a crashing roar. The dust cloud they raised could be seen from the airport. Nodding in satisfaction, Tina spoke again. "Now drop in four AP rounds."

Three men in the command post, out of fifteen,

survived, severely wounded and deafened. For the time being, the threat from Hoffman's black-shirts had ended. Tina Raines had time to think of other matters.

"I wonder how Dad's doing?" she asked herself aloud.

Ben Raines stood beside the Humvee on a slight knoll along I-80 and watched the long column of troops and heavy weapons stream past. They were only some twenty miles east of Cheyenne. By late afternoon the artillery would be in position to pound Hoffman's occupying force. The radio report from Tina had been promising.

She and her company had been able to fight off the Nazi attack, and the Puffs were being refueled. A little behind schedule, but still in time to paste the large concentration of enemy around the ruins of Cheyenne. Elsewhere, things moved well also.

Buddy, as the new XO of the rump-regiment formed for Dan Gray's command, would be well into Kansas and on the way to forestall any attempt by the black-shirts to retake Pueblo or Colorado Springs. Ike McGowan reported good progress in that direction also.

He would take Denver and then sweep southward to link up with Dan for the big push to the Mexican border. By splitting the Nazi line and hitting on the flanks, Ben expected to roll them up easily. He intended to keep his headquarters and R Batt with the northern theater under Georgi Striganov. Ben breathed deeply of diesel and gas fumes in satisfaction and clapped his hands together to summon Smoot, who had been off watering trees.

"Time to go tear off Hoffman's ass and hand it to him," he announced.

"All the way, General," Jersey urged through a grin.

* * *

By three that afternoon, Colonel West reported that his troops held the ground to the west of Cheyenne. General Striganov had his people in position to the north and east, supplemented by the R Batt. There had been a few minor skirmishes, though the two competent commanders had handled it easily. The big guns had been laid and waited only for the command to open fire.

General Striganov generously gave that honor to Ben Raines. "This is Eagle, you may commence firing," Ben spoke into the mike.

One hundred three 155s opened up on the doomed enemy deployment around Cheyenne from three sides. The fat shells whistled over the heads of the outer perimeter, whitening faces as they sailed by. Five rounds from each gun had taken to air before an answering rumble came from the Nazis.

"They've got counterbattery fire going," Ben snapped. "Tell the SPs to haul ass. Fire hit-and-run from now until I say stop. That should give the rest of the guns time to limber up and get the hell out of there."

Georgi Striganov shared a comfortable chair with Ben Raines in the mobile CP. He raised a stubby finger and bristly eyebrow to emphasize his soft reminder. "Ben, their 130s and 126s don't have the range of our 155s."

"That's right, though the 126s do if they add an extra powder bag and stress out the breech locks." Ben grinned. "It's good drill for our people, and they damned well need it. Some of those artillery boys are getting fat and lazy."

A few 126mm shells fell among the artillery batteries. They caused few casualties, mostly a lot of ringing ears. Within half an hour, Ben took the handset from Corrie, along with her summary of the incoming call.

"It's Colonel West. He wants to know when you're

gonna stop jacking his gunners around and get serious."

"Are you serious?" Ben asked.

"No. Just wanted to see if I could rile you, General."

"Eagle here, Merc, go."

West's voice came tinnily over the scrambler. "We've got a lot of black-shirt shit doing a bug-out our direction, Eagle. What do you advise?"

"Stomp butt on them, of course. But keep those shells dropping in. We want those Hitler-loving assholes to think they have the whole Rebel army on their nines."

"From their uniforms they appear to be the American variety."

Ben's eyes glittered. "Take no prisoners, Merc. No time, no facilities."

"I hear ya, Eagle. What was it your friend Peyon called it? *El Desgüello,* the Cutthroat Song? No quarter."

Ben thought of the tough, competent soldier from Mexico, every inch a man, without the swaggering pretense of *machismo,* yet strangely gentle, scholarly, a reflective man. "Yeah. That's exactly what I want," he told West.

Thirteen

For three hours the artillery duel raged on. The slightly more mobile self-propelled 155mm guns whipped around the city to give fits to the counterbattery radar operators of Hoffman's command. Sometimes they fired singly, others in groups of up to five, like a static battery.

By the time the return salvo had been plotted and loaded, they had dashed away to other locations. Repeatedly the Nazi commanders heard the jubilant news that another battery of Rebel guns had been silenced. After the count exceeded twenty batteries, they began to have serious doubts about the accuracy of their information.

A mounting tide of desertions had been halted when a number of sergeants shot down men fleeing the utter terror of an artillery bombardment. Gradually, the high-velocity 126mm guns of the NAL began to actually score on Rebel positions. A stream of wounded and dead began to pour into Rebel field hospitals. Ben Raines had awareness of this turn of events brought forcefully to him by Dr. Lamar Chase.

"Goddammit, Ben, you are spending men's lives like lead slugs in a penny arcade. I have two field hospitals and they are both full to overflowing."

Ben's eyes burned like shovelfuls of sand had been dumped into them. He stared blankly at his old friend for a moment without registering the doctor's complaint.

"Yes, I know," Ben said regretfully.

"Then what are you going to do about it? You haven't even launched an assault as yet. The troops are spread too thin. We're going to have increased casualties. There's a shortage of whole blood, bed space, and medical personnel."

Smarting from what self-criticism told him—that he was fighting a losing campaign—Ben failed to guard his tongue when he responded to Lamar Chase's criticisms.

"I haven't any choice. We have to break through Hoffman's line and go at them from the flanks or it's all in the toilet. Now, I strongly suggest, Doctor, that you confine yourself to the healing arts and let the strategy and tactical decisions be made by those qualified to make them."

Chase went white. Ben's harsh words deeply hurt him to his crusty soul. He turned on one heel and stalked to the door. There he paused to throw words back over one shoulder.

"I—well, I—at least you know how I feel."

Ben cursed himself silently, eyes squeezed shut. He had not intended to be so preemptive with his old friend. He was, Ben admitted, mad at himself, not at Lamar Chase. He had a way of fixing that. He always felt better when out mixing it up with the troops.

"Corrie, bump West and tell him I'll be over his way in a short. The first assault wave is to jump off in twenty minutes."

Major Dieter Furst, known before his conversion to Nazism as Wally Whipple, stared at the panting young American Nazi standing at his desk. "Their artillery has stopped firing, Major. What do we do now?"

147

Every bit as much a neophyte as the youthful storm trooper, Major Furst didn't know how to answer that. "They may have run out of ammunition. God knows they dumped enough on us." He gestured beyond the command trailer.

Dust, flame, and smoke still hazed the air so thickly that visibility had been reduced to thirty feet. Dazed men, not yet recovered from the ferocity of the Rebel shelling, wandered aimlessly around the small cut between low hills that bordered U.S. 85 at its junction with I-25. Elated that the terrible explosions had stopped punishing his ears, Dieter Furst hoped sincerely that the silence would go on forever. Then a horrible new thought burst in his head.

"They—they wouldn't fire on their own men, would they?" he asked uncertainly of the shocked, silent men in the command center. Suddenly, fearfully, he knew the answer. "They're coming! They are going to attack us. You, Trooper, get out there and tell the sergeants to roust their men out of their shelters."

"I c-can't tell sergeants anything, sir," the nonplussed storm trooper pleaded.

"That's right," Furst's rattled brain made him say. He rounded on two lieutenants, barely out of their teens. "You two, get out there and get those sergeants' whistles blowing. Turn out all the men to repel an attack."

Whistles began to blow along the Nazi positions. Men came reluctantly from their hastily dug shelters. Many had been all but buried by the ground heaves of the exploding Rebel shells. They stood alone or in clusters, dumbstruck and fearful of a resumption of the bombardment. What came instead were the feathery whispers of mortar rounds.

They fell as a sprinkle, then a shower, then a deluge. Whizzing fragments of shrapnel sliced through vulnerable flesh and men screamed their last amid the sharp crack of exploding rounds. Right behind the thunderous hail of death came a low roar, filled

148

with menace, that grew louder. The brutalized soldiers of the American Nazi movement turned stark faces to the direction of this clamor and, in utter dread, witnessed the swift, ground-covering approach of the Rebel infantry.

Some of the quicker-minded among them leapt to man machine guns and make an effort to save themselves. Belatedly the sergeants kicked and bullied the storm troopers into some sort of order and directed defensive fire.

Ben Raines's Hummer careened around a shell hole with one rear wheel hanging over the rupture in the ground. Corrie looked back at Ben and offered the handset. She made a chastened little girl big-eyed expression.

"It's Dr. Chase for you, General. *And boy is he mad.*"

"This is Eag—" Ben began, but Lamar Chase already had his sails filled and ran before the wind.

"Listen to me, goddammit, Ben Raines. You can't go out hot-rodding around in the middle of an assault. I won't let you."

Hot-rodding? Ben asked himself. At least the testy old fart had gotten over his hurt feelings, Ben mused. He wouldn't be on that tired old high horse if he hadn't. He spoke with a prim, schoolteacherish voice that he knew aggravated Chase.

"It seems that I am already out here, Doctor. I don't propose to run back through what we've already encountered just to return to the CP."

"It's crazy, Ben. It's damnfoolishness," Dr. Chase hurled at his commanding officer. "You're going to get yourself killed. We can't afford that. The Rebels need you, Ben. I—need you."

Enough of this, Ben thought. Next thing he'll be admitting he actually likes me. "Get a grip, Lamar," Ben said gruffly, moved by his old friend's show of emotion. "Before I know it, you'll be crying crocodile tears and stomping on a hankie."

"You're a prick, Ben Raines," Lamar Chase responded, the tension draining from his voice.

"Is that anything like a *schmuck,* Doctor?" Ben asked lightly, recalling the outburst of the captured American Nazi in the drive-in.

"Damn you, you always could push the right buttons. Have it your way, Ben, as I'm sure you will. But, damn it, man, be careful."

"We link up with West in about five minutes and I'll have three battalions around me."

"I still won't rest until you're back here," the doctor groused. "You tell that little lady that watches over you to make you keep your butt down. Chase out."

Ben spoke to his team. "That, boys and girls, was lecture number one thousand five hundred seventy-nine on covering the commander's ass. I want to gauge the caliber of men Hoffman has on this thousand-mile front of his. And that means going in and mixing it up close and personal."

"You mean get in their face, General?" Beth asked sweetly.

"You got it, Beth. When we reach West, we go into Cheyenne to kick ass and take names."

Word of the Rebel attack on Cheyenne reached General Field Marshal Hoffman within minutes of the opening of the artillery duel. Immediately he summoned his staff. Striding about the room in a posture he aped from old, grainy black-and-white films of Adolf Hitler, Hoffman muttered darkly for a while, then came to a halt at a large situations map spread on a plank table.

"Right here," he shouted, finger stabbing Cheyenne. "And only days after we ran out the Rebels there and established a major defensive position. Ben Raines must have his entire army with him. He would not dare attack so strong a position otherwise."

Colonel Webber cleared his throat, reluctant to bear further bad news. "We have also lost radio contact with the detachment in Laramie," he informed Hoffman.

Hoffman looked like a man with an attack of apoplexy. After his face had gone white, then red, and white again, he gasped out an incoherent jumble of words, some in Spanish, others in German. He kicked a table leg, then pounded a fist on the map. Then both fists. At last he regained command of speech.

"This has to be a diversion by Raines. He can't have wiped out the entire force at Laramie. Maybe he's jamming the radios. It has to be something minor. It must be. But, if we cannot reach them by radio, how can we order them to reinforce Cheyenne?"

"We cannot, obviously, Herr General Field Marshal," Webber felt emboldened to say. "There is more, Herr General Field Marshal."

"What? What else can there be?"

"The—ah . . ." Webber's face molded into an expression of distaste, "Alien Secretions are reported as having engaged Raines on his way to the Cheyenne area. They were completely annihilated."

"Blut und Donner!" Hoffman bellowed. "Blood and thunder," he repeated, liking the phrase. "Can anything else interfere with our orderly progress?"

"That I do not know, sir," Webber replied quietly.

"I want," Hoffman began with a wide circular gesture over the map, "I want every unit within a hundred miles of Cheyenne mobilized at once and sent there."

"If I may suggest, Herr General Field Marshal," Webber cut in. "It might be that Ben Raines does not have his entire army with him. We could be seriously weakening other positions to draw off so many men."

"Cheyenne is the key. We must hold onto that territory or the whole of my plan goes awry. I will have Cheyenne secured, gentlemen. It is up to you to see I have it. Dismissed."

"But, Herr—"

"No 'buts,' Webber," Hoffman snapped, a hand held up in caution. "By expending ammunition and lives, the Rebels will be weakened and forced on the defensive, fighting isolated guerrilla actions while I, the brilliant *Führer*—yes, I have decided it is time to claim my rightful title—while I conquer and subdue everything from Canada to the tip of Baja California. Cheyenne drains the Rebels of blood. Cheyenne is the pivotal point of a line that will extend our eastern border on Rebel territory north to south from Minot, North Dakota, to Sanderson, Texas.

"With our American Nazis as a sound base, I can build an unbeatable force to take on the rest of the United States in the spring. Go, now, and get busy with all of this. Your *Führer* has spoken.

Colonel West greeted Ben Raines with a broad smile, then he produced a worried frown. "I gather Tina has her neck stuck out quite a ways at Laramie."

"No more than usual," Ben dismissed.

He knew that West and Tina planned to marry once the fighting ended for all time. That day, the cynic in Ben told him, would likely be far in the future. West made a good prospect. He was handsome, healthy, a damn fine soldier, completely dedicated to the Rebel cause. What disturbed Ben about the relationship could be attributed to a factor that could be traced back to the days of Ancient Greece.

A commander had to consider the chance that the emotional involvement of lovers serving in combat units might cloud the military judgment of one or both. Not that West had ever exhibited such instability, nor Tina, for that matter. Just the opposite, in fact. Both had a fierce pride in their professionalism. West's next remark only reaffirmed that.

"I gather you're out here to get a look at our enemy. I've detailed a main battle tank and two BFVs to accompany you. Also a platoon of my best."

Ben cut him a gimlet eye. "You've been talking to Georgi and Lamar," he accused.

"It might be that we did discuss certain matters," West hedged. Then his personal concern entered the picture. "Dammit, General, if you won't cover your own ass, we have to cover it for you."

Ten minutes later, Ben and his team set out in a small convoy toward the black-shirt lines around the destroyed heart of Cheyenne.

Tina Raines looked up from the map with a cold light in her eyes. Unaware of Hoffman's order to direct all available forces into the battle of Cheyenne, she saw this evidence of increased Nazi action around Laramie as an attempt to dislodge her small detachment from the airport.

She was right in part. The Puffs were down and drinking, Tina added to her equation for holding the field. If they could get off again, before a major assault, everything would be all right. Although the Nazis had no idea of the airfield's importance, they knew about the Rebel occupation and would seek to neutralize it on the way to Cheyenne. She had to consider that, also. It turned out she had less time than expected.

Mortar rounds struck the grass median strips between runways and walked toward the control tower and administration building. Light artillery shells slashed into the terminal, completing the destruction carried out by Rebel troops during the campaign to exterminate the Night People.

Camo uniforms mingled with the loose, rumpled outfits of Brodermann's regular SS. They came in a determined wave that spread out across the runways and pressed in on the defending Rebels. Conscious of the short range of her Sidewinder, Tina grabbed up an M-14 and set the selector to single-fire.

153

That recoil smarted, Tina acknowledged as she put a round through the chest of a screaming fanatic halfway down the main runway. It didn't get any better, she discovered as she continued to fire from her vantage point in the control tower. Time to relocate, she decided when a mortar round impacted fifty feet from the slender concrete spire.

They had beaten back the first assault. Tina had moved the CP to the hangar where the Puffs sat fueled and ready, but unable to take off. Bodies littered the runways and shell holes pocked the surfaces. The Rebels worked to make repairs during a lull in the fighting. They had even managed to take a few prisoners for interrogation.

What Tina learned set her mouth in a hard line. It also verified what their intel people had developed from other sources. Fanatical Americans of the SS Hoffman Bodyguard brigade had joined forces with SS Brigade Leader Brodermann's troops. She reached Ben with this information while his recee detachment swept along the Nazi lines around Cheyenne.

"Really, Eagle, these homegrown Nazis are more Germanic than Hoffman's South American variety. They all have German names, even those who are of evident French, Irish, or Italian origin. They all chanted *Sieg Heil* while we tried to interrogate one of them, so I had the questioning done in another room. They sang old Nazi songs, too. Still are, for that matter."

"Remember my order for no quarter," Ben reminded her, tight-lipped.

"Yes, sir, General Daddy, sir," Tina answered stiffly. She had never liked killing unarmed men, with the uniform exception of the creepies. Never a Rebel had shed a tear over those slime.

"Knock it off, Tina," Ben growled, the closest he usually came to harsh discipline of his children.

"Yes, Eagle. I can see your point. We may have time to get the Puffs up if they get the corpses off the runway soon."

"Do so. I want a major assault to begin before more reinforcements reach these black-shirt bastards."

"Is it that bad, Eagle?"

"Worse. Hoffman is calling up people from everywhere and they are streaming into the triangle held by the black-shirts. We're taking more casualties all the time. So, hold what you've got, sweetheart, and get those birds in the air."

Fourteen

Tango Alpha One and his wingman screamed down the runway nose to tail and rotated smoothly into flying their craft. Small arms fire began immediately from the left side of the runway. A brief, shattering roar from a door gun silenced that. At 20 rounds a second slapping into the position of the hidden gunners, nothing living survived. The command pilot reached Ben Raines at Colonel West's CP.

"Welcome to the party," Ben responded dryly. "We have forward air controllers and guides in place." He gave the frequencies they would be operating. "You'll work inward from the friendly panel markers."

"Roger that, Eagle. Concentrate them and cream them," Chuck summarized.

"I will be mobile after your first pass on this side. Eagle out."

Chuck Yount wondered what the general meant by that. Mobile from where? To where? He shrugged it off and concentrated on flying his airplane. It took only minutes to approach Cheyenne. On the ground, Chuck could see small figures swarming toward defensive positions. Time to ruin their day.

"Foxtrot Gulf X-ray, this is Tango Alpha One. Over."

"Tango Alpha One, this is Foxtrot Gulf X-ray. Observe orange marker panels forward of all friendlies. I have you in visual and am passing you on to Foxtrot Charlie One."

"This is Foxtrot Charlie One. Tango Alpha One, I have a fire mission. On a heading of two-eight-niner, pick up panel markers. Deliver free fire to the north and east of those markers."

"Roger, Foxtrot Charlie."

"Your field of fire has a depth of 480 meters. You will observe tanks in the northern quadrant of your fire zone. Sustain maximum autocannon fire in this area."

"Roger. Enabling now."

With all systems armed, the lumbering C-47s became deadly dragons. They spit fire that scorched the Nazis below. In the initial salvo, the Puffs shuddered and appeared to come to a halt in the air. Individual gunners picked up a rhythm to their targets and the illusion dissolved.

From the belly of Tango Alpha One, the 75mm autocannon opened up on a company of main battle tanks, the superhardened shell casings easily driving through the light armor over the engine compartments. Tanks are designed to take on the enemy face-to-face. Their thickest armor is located on the face of the turret and driver's compartment. Their bellies and rear decks are vulnerable to all but small-arms fire.

So when the big gun hosed down the backsides of the MBTs, they began to erupt in nasty red blossoms, black-tinged harbingers of doom. Diesel tanks went first, followed by the superheated ammunition magazines inside the armored behemoths. The barrels of their main guns whipped through the air like skinny telephone poles in a tornado. Turrets lurched upward, revealing sheets of orange-red flame from inside the tank bodies.

Slowly a modicum of control developed in the pandemonium of the sudden, violent attack. Lines of tracers sought the slow-flying C-47 Puffs. Chuck heard the familiar gravel-on-a-tin-roof sound of rounds impacting the skin of his craft. Unconsciously he winced. Ground fire could be a bitch.

That which pierced the sides of the fuselage generally came in at high enough an angle to punch out the top with little harm done. Rounds that raked the belly were another story. During the battle for Los Angeles, Chuck had a door gunner who took a .50 caliber round through the foot. The flight deck had a light armor flak shield under the pilots, which would stop small-arms and nearly spent .50s, but one of the latter could produce the granddaddy of all crotch traumas. That's what bugged Chuck as he altered course under direction of the forward air controller.

"Fire mission! Fire mission! Tango Alpha One, I have a fire mission. Jesus, where'd they get all those tanks?" Taking a firm grip on his cavorting nerves, the FAC read off the coordinates of a whole column of armor advancing to the north of the demolished city.

Chuck leveled off onto the new heading and checked the expended-ammo indicator for the 75mm. "Foxtrot Charlie One, we're down to twenty rounds for the big gun. Over."

"Then cook them, Tango Alpha One. Descend to level one-five-zero and sew napalm along that column."

Chuck glanced back into what had been the cargo compartment. A quick count of the ovoid gray containers produced a grin. "Roger that, Foxtrot Charlie One."

At 150 feet, the ground fire became a sustained hailstorm on the skin of the Puffs. Risking their lives, the crew unloaded napalm canisters in a long, steady line. Rivers of flaming goo splashed along the column of MBTs, wrapping them in sticky, burning death. An abrupt, loud clank from the port engine nacelle jerked Chuck's attention that way.

Black smoke began to pour from the cowling.

Quickly Chuck hit the fire extinguisher and cut the throttle. His copilot feathered the prop. Regretfully, Chuck keyed his mike.

"Foxtrot Charlie One, we took a hit in the port engine. We're going to have to abort. Over."

"They'll run right over us," the FAC protested. "We've hit them with everything we have. You're all that's holding them back."

Chuck hated it, but he had no choice. "Let me check our base and find out the status on the other two birds. I'll contact you before we're out of range. Tango Alpha One, out."

From the jump seat, the flight engineer leaned forward and changed frequencies. Right away the good news leapt at them. "Tango Alpha One, where are you? We've been trying to reach you, over."

"You got me. What's your ETA Cheyenne?" Chuck asked rapidly.

"Ten minutes."

"We took a hit in one engine," Chuck told him. We've turned back. Go for it, ol' buddy." He gave the frequency used by the FAG and FAC and signed off. To the flight-deck crew, he confided, "It's going to be dicey landing. They may have hit the wheel, too."

"Nothing like landing on a flat tire," the flight engineer grumbled.

"We'll see."

Three minutes later they flew by the incoming Puffs. A wing-waggle greeting was exchanged and the aircraft bore on their separate courses. The C-47 flew like a lead brick. Chuck fought the control column and throttle to nurse more altitude. They were too high for the ground effect and too low for a normal glide slope. When they labored to 500 feet, he gave it to the copilot and contacted the tower.

"We're not in the tower anymore," Laramie told him. "The black-shirts mortared hell out of it."

"They came again?" Chuck asked.

"They're still here," came the reply.

"We'll make a pass and dust them off, then we've *got* to land."

A minute later he had the runway in sight. "Winds at two-six-eight, at fifteen, gusting to twenty, altimeter three-niner-niner-five."

"Roger, Laramie." To the right-hand seat, "Gear down. Flaps thirty percent."

Servomotors whined and the landing gear lowered. Chuck would have sold his soul for a look at the port wheel. Well, they'd know when he set the bird down. One of the ground crew must be manning the radio, Chuck decided when the radio crackled to life.

"Both down and locked, looking good."

True to his word, Chuck led the two aircraft down the runway from the west, both door guns blasting at the scrambling figures below. An APC bounced on its carriage with the impact of a hundred rounds. Parts began to fall off. Then they were past the apron and over the threshold. Chuck fought to bring about a smooth 180 far enough out to pull off a normal descent.

He sideslipped to line up the centerline as he crossed the threshold on the way in. Lower now, lower. The venerable Douglas airframe shuddered violently as they dropped through two hundred feet. Now a hundred. The runway streamed by below, littered with corpses. Chuck felt the landing with his fingertips. Lips tightly compressed, he judged the right second and flared out.

On a single engine, the overloaded C-47 dropped the last few feet to the runway like a stone. The plane lurched to the left and a shower of sparks sprayed out from the trailing edge of the wing. So much for appearances, Chuck thought. The tire was flat after all. Throttling back, then powering up, he fought to keep the wounded craft from groundlooping.

Metal shrieked in protest. Vibration gave Chuck a quadruple image of everything from the instrument panel forward. Gradually the cripple slowed. An intersection flashed past and Chuck made ready for the next. He never made it. With a brief, mighty moan, the port gear strut gave way and the wingtip touched concrete. In a shower of cement dust, the C-47 swung a quarter-turn and came violently to a stop.

"Switches," Chuck snapped. Blood trickled down from his forehead where it had made contact with the yoke. "Everyone out. Out now."

Vehicles raced toward them. At the sight of flames crackling up around the left wing, they stopped at a respectable distance. Chuck and his shaken crew did a fast 220 dash to shelter behind the nearest APC as the gas tank let go. They hugged the armored side while a firecracker rattle came from detonating ammunition. Another belly-shaking *whoomph* came from the starboard fuel bladder, then only the crackle of flames.

Chuck looked at the white faces of his crew. He wondered if he shared their pallor. He forced a grin. "Like they say, any landing you walk away from is a good one."

For all their awesome ferocity, not even the Puffs could hold back the surge of Hoffman's black-shirts. Shouting and singing Nazi songs, their American counterparts led the way. When the flying gun platforms ran out of ammunition and turned away for Laramie, the Rebels recoiled from the advances made against them.

General Striganov wore a mask of bitter regret as his troops retreated over ground hard-won only two days earlier. Colonel West and his mercenaries fought a holding action to the west of the Nazi lines. Ben's R Batt functioned as a flying squad to plug holes wherever they appeared. Only one place benefited by the determination of the NAL to hold onto their positions around Cheyenne.

Fighting remained heavy at the Laramie airport, yet the enemy inflicted few injuries and did little damage. The Nazis that remained to harass the ground crew refueling the three remaining C-47s had only ancient 60mm mortars, and few of those. When it got real hairy for Tina, Ben summoned Thermopolis.

"Therm, I want you to take the Headquarters Company and break out of here. Get the hell on to Laramie and reinforce Tina."

Captain Thermopolis looked concerned. "You mean the whole shootin' match?"

"Everyone. Leadfoot and Wanda, and Emil Hite, too. Take two Abrams with you. It's a fifty-mile run from here, so take along a tanker truck."

"Good as done, General. But who'll be watching you?"

Ben cut his eyes to the short figure by the doorway of the mobile CP. "I've got Jersey. What else do I need?"

"Flatterer," Jersey griped, aware she was blushing.

Thermopolis and the HQ company reached Laramie an hour and twenty minutes later. They rolled along the drive to the long-term parking lot in the middle of another assault by the screaming Nazis. Therm collared a harried-looking young corporal and asked where he could find Tina Raines.

He pointed to the parking ramps in what used to be the general aviation section. "She's out there. Cap'n Young got wasted and she took the company. There's hell to pay, sir. Good thing you got here."

Instead of the confusion of a hard-fought defense, Thermopolis found calm and order among the fighting Rebels. Tina was with two platoons making ready for a counterattack. She seemed cool and laid back to the ex-hippie.

"Daddy sent you," she accused when she recognized Thermopolis in his combat gear.

"We heard you had a lot on your hands. You don't look all that threatened."

"Even the best of all plans won't survive contact with the enemy. That goes double for these Nazi scum. They've been trying to take us since we got here last night."

Emil Hite came forward, tripped on the knee-level sag of his rifle sling, and nearly bowled Tina over. "I have been summoned by my dear friend and benefactor, Ben Raines, to come to the rescue of fair maiden," he bubbled. "To commemorate the event, I have created a new dance."

"Not now, Emil," Tina said, face squinched in reaction to this announcement.

"Oh, but it is most significant. A power dance, a sign that the Almighty favors the Rebels. It will strike fear into the hearts of those heathen Nazis. They will turn and run at sight of it."

"Oh, no doubt," Tina replied dryly. "Likely, anyone would."

"I am wounded. Please, O Radiant daughter of the Great Ben Raines, let my people perform the dance before you launch this counterattack. And," Emil added with a droll rolling of his eyes, "it might help to call down your mortar cover on their anti-Semitic heads while we do it."

Tina could not help laughing. "You old fraud. I suppose the theme of the dance is a mortar crew in action?"

Emil looked startled. "How did you know?"

"Because I know you, Emil. And what I didn't know, Daddy taught me."

"Oh, poo! But you will let us do the dance?"

"They have snipers," Tina stated, one eyebrow raised archly.

"We have body armor," Emil countered. "Come, children," he called to his troops, who looked like what they were, grizzled combat veterans, rather than the docile sheep of a guru's placid flock.

Led by Emil, the former Children of the Eternal Light through Blomm spread out on the runways, in the no-man's-land between opposing forces. Looking self-conscious, a young woman — assistant gunner on an M-60 — produced a tambourine and began to shake it and strike the head with strong fingertips. A bongo joined in. Two guitars made their appearances and produced the melody. Emil, standing in front of them, led his combat team in the dance.

It came out something like a combination between the Shimmy, with a little Watusi and some Frug thrown in. Emil varied that with ungainly leaps into the air, wrists bent and fingers steepled together, pointed downward. No doubt the mortar rounds, Tina snorted. Nevertheless, she ordered the mortars to open up.

The first sniper round took one burly dancer in the chest protector of his body armor. He sprawled on his butt, a surprised expression lighting his face. He came to his feet with an H&K assault rifle at the ready.

"That does it. Enough, Emil. Enough of this. I wanna kill Nazis," he growled.

"Oh, spoilsport," Emil pouted. "You'll get your chance."

Mortar rounds rained down in the Nazi assembly area where a new assault was being organized. One of the 81mm bombs must have hit an ammunition truck. It lit off with a tremendous roar while white smoke, flame, and debris flew into the air. At Tina's order, the three tanks with her light company, and the one brought up by Thermopolis, surged forward.

Main guns barked and sent out gorgeous smoke rings, transfixed with tongues of flame. The coaxial guns fired as the M-1 A Abrams MBTs snorted and ground upward to maximum speed. The Nazis had nothing like them. Their MBTs were more like old Shermans. Most of them mounted 90mm guns at maximum.

One by one they were blown apart by the husky Abramses. Panic infected the infantry. Unheeding of the scything effect of machine guns, they jumped from their positions and joined the fleeing survivors of the mortar attack. At sight of this, Tina waved an arm over her head, signaling forward.

"Let's go," she commanded.

The Rebels ran far enough to become winded in their heavy body armor. At last the infantry closed with the black-shirts. Face twisted in fear, one of the demoralized hatemongers turned on Tina with a savage roar.

She cut him down with the last round in her M-14. She bent and laid it on the ground. Then she swung the Sidewinder around from her back and drew back the bolt. At close range it did a better job, she reasoned. On both sides the fighting raged.

Tina took stock and started toward the hottest center of action. She chopped into two Nazis with three-round bursts that left them spinning away to eternity. Another ran at her with an AK-47. The small bayonet on its muzzle looked like a toy.

Unwilling to be played with by the likes of that, she raised the Sidewinder slightly and plunked three rounds in the American black-shirt's sternum. He took two more steps, dropped his weapon, and sprawled at Tina's feet. She heard a bolt fall on an empty chamber and turned that way.

"Damn," a young Rebel panted. "I lost count." He reloaded as Tina turned her attention to the general situation,

It appeared that Emil's eager acolyte had gotten his wish. The feisty little guru had been surrounded by desperate men with flat eyes and the drool of terror on their lips. What they didn't know was that it was they who were surrounded. Emil's little band fought like wildcats. A thick billow of smoke covered the action for a moment.

When it cleared, Tina saw Emil hopping from one foot to the other and prodding five prisoners with his rifle. A general silence began to fall on the battleground. Quickly, Tina evaluated the results.

"Get the BFVs up here," she commanded. "We're going after them."

Their chase ended with only a handful of poorly trained American Nazis. Tina's RT operator solved the mystery for her. "The SS received orders to scatter and rendezvous later. They're headed for Oregon to preserve their numbers."

Tina looked at the pitiful remains of "Supermen" who crouched fearfully on their knees, hands behind their heads. "All right. We get a breathing spell. The Puffs took a heavy beating in that hangar. Check for me on repairs." She started to walk off, to let the Rebel troops deal with the prisoners, then paused, a new idea blooming. "When he hears about this, I wonder what Daddy will decide to do?" she asked no one in particular.

Fifteen

Ben Raines's decision on what to do came easily and, to him, seemed obvious and predestined. He ordered an all-out attack in the wake of the devastation left behind by the flying gun platforms. The Puffs had shredded the columns of reinforcements. That left the already shell-riddled occupiers of the Cheyenne triangle to overrun.

"A piece of cake," Cooper had called it, earning a scowl from Jersey.

"Don't be such a glumph," she complained. "You've been around long enough to know what cornered rats will do." Her green eyes blazed. To Ben, "We are not, I gather, going to take this one sitting down?"

Ben favored her with one of his brilliant smiles. "Not at all. Coop, have the Hummer ready in fifteen minutes. We will, of course," he added in a grumble, "have our usual shadows along."

A platoon from HQ Company, augmented by three MBTs and a pair of Bradleys, spent much of their time spoiling Ben's fun for him. At least that's the way he saw it. The artillery opened up just then, ending effective conversation except that at the shouting level. With Jersey in tow, Ben stalked out of the CP and headed for his armored Hummer.

Dr. Lamar Chase met him halfway. "We're down twelve percent of our effectives, Ben," the medico complained. "What was that old saw they taught at the War College? That a loss of twenty percent was a total defeat, right?"

Ben gave Chase smiling benefit of his wisdom. "The troops they were talking about weren't Rebels, Lamar. Keep that in mind. Can you scrape together any sick-call victims and walking wounded to man posts in the rear?"

"I could," Lamar Chase began tartly, "if I was inclined to do so. Those men are entitled to as much care as the bed-ridden."

"Well, my old friend, the time has come, as the Walrus said, to talk of other things. Please incline yourself to rounding up those fit for limited duty. We're going to push those Nazi bastards out of the triangle and send them running to Hoffman in Oregon."

"Casualties are heavy," Lamar returned to his own pronouncement to reinforce his determination to prevent conscripting of the lesser injured. "But this is asking a lot of those men and women."

"And they'll do it, by god, because they're Rebels," Ben affirmed.

Georgi Striganov opened the assault on the north and eastern sides of the Nazi defenses. R Batt also pushed from the east, against the blunt short side of the triangle. Colonel West cut through the thin line to the south and swung around to attack from that direction. That opened a corridor for retreat to the west. Ben knew that Tina pursued the survivors of the airport battle in Laramie westward, with stragglers headed for Cheyenne. With a little luck and some creative radio operation, the demoralized blackshirt contingent might crash into their beleaguered comrades and each think the other the enemy.

With Tina gnawing on the rear of one unit, the impression could be created that the stragglers were in fact Rebels. Those fleeing Cheyenne might exterminate them with minimal expenditure of Rebel ammunition. Balancing this and a score of other demanding details in his head, Ben Raines started off to follow the first wave into the breech. R Batt struck stubborn resistance at once.

"Eagle, we have a light battalion in strength facing us," came the report from Stan McDade.

"Keep humping, Falcon. We're right behind you and Georgi is going to swing in behind us," Ben responded. "Let me know when you break through."

Jersey cut shrewd, calculating eyes to Ben. "You figure to go in with R Batt's lead elements, General?"

"Close to it, Jersey."

"Too damn close, if I know you," she grumbled.

"Now, Jersey, I'm following the restrictions imposed by subordinate commanders. I'll put up with all these babysitters and I won't lead the initial charge. I'm keeping to the letter of the law, so to speak."

"Yeah, but not the spirit," Jersey gave acid tongue. "I'm willin' to bet you expect to be not more than two blocks behind the lead squad."

"You heard the lady, Cooper. Make it so," Ben announced with a chuckle.

"Dang you, boss, you shoehorned me again," Jersey complained.

All around Rebels advanced, spread out as skirmishers. Squad control was maintained by hand and arm signals, while the radios got a good workout coordinating platoon actions and above. The mortars walked in a short fifty yards ahead of the advancing Rebel troops. A flicker of yellow flame from the basement window of a collapsed building caught the notice of a sergeant near Ben's Hummer.

He directed his squad's fire on the machine-gun nest until his assistant squad leader lobbed a blooper round from an M-203. The firing pin of the GLAD (Grenade Launcher Attachment Development) round ignited the primer, which in turn set off the propellant charge, which developed 35,000 fp of energy. The high-low propulsion system functioned normally and the burning gases expanded into the larger chamber, which reduced the energy to 3,000 foot-pounds per square inch. Good enough to dislodge the 40mm projectile, propelling it through the barrel with enough force to travel to the target at a velocity of 250 feet per second, with a right-hand spin of 37,000 rpm, sufficient to arm the fuse.

It struck the window casement with a loud crack, which got swallowed in the detonation of the grenade. When the smoke and dust cleared, the machine-gun barrel lay skewed downward and only dead men sat behind it. Ben Raines noticed and nodded approval.

"Good shot," he observed.

Ben's Humvee leapt forward, as Cooper made an effort to catch the advance squads of R Batt's assault. Fighting the wheel, Cooper careened around shell holes and avoided exposed steel I-beams that jutted into the roadway from collapsed buildings. All of these, Ben noted in passing, had considerable sign of rust. More Rebel handiwork in eliminating the Night People.

Charging Rebels recognized Ben's vehicle and gave friendly waves and "V" signs of their confidence. When the expressions on Rebel faces changed to surprise and worry, Ben tapped Cooper on one shoulder.

"Better stop here and wait for our hand-holders. We've about outrun our people," he instructed.

Jersey bit back a sharp retort, but could not resist a pointy needle. "About time you thought of that, boss. The next face we mighta seen could have been ol' Herr Hoffman's ugly puss."

"I'd be only too happy to get Field Marshal Hoffman in range," Ben riposted dryly.

Peter Volmer thrust the handset away from his face

with enough force to make the RT operator stagger when it impacted his chest. "I have ordered every available *Sturmgruppe* to the relief of the defenses at Cheyenne, yet our good field marshal demands more of me." He turned to his executive officer, Gerhardt Yodel, a scowl deepening his high brow. "We are taking losses far out of proportion to the Rebel strength. Three *Standarten* have been repulsed at Laramie. *We can't afford to lose three companies!*" he shouted in unconscious imitation of Hoffman's rages.

Yodel looked nonplussed. "What is it I should say? Our men are superbly motivated, well-trained, their courage is beyond question. Perhaps this final commitment will do it. And, there is that other matter."

"Yes, of course," Volmer calmed himself, the glitter in his eyes changed from anger to shrewdness. "Bring in *Standarteführer* Dracher. It's time we employed our Werewolves."

An orderly summoned the battalion commander of the special *Werwolfen* unit. An organization of highly trained, totally dedicated soldiers, they represented Peter Volmer's extra ace in the deck. They had undergone intensive instruction from the age of eight. Every one of them was fanatically dedicated to Peter Volmer and to Nazism. A sharp rap on the door announced the arrival of *Standarteführer* Sigfried Dracher.

"Come," Volmer commanded.

With a crash of hobnailed, glossily polished black boots, the battalion CO entered and marched smartly to a position precisely centered on Volmer's desk. Dracher's right arm shot forward and upward in a perfect Nazi salute.

"*Heil Hitler! Standarteführer* Dracher, Sigfried Mannheim, reporting as ordered," he piped in a voice still unaltered by the advent of puberty.

Peter Volmer returned the fifteen-year-old's salute. "At ease, Dracher. I am positive you shall be pleased by what I have to tell you. Your battalion is being activated at last. Every boy down to the age of eleven. Full field uniforms and equipment."

"We are going to Cheyenne?" Dracher asked expectantly.

"No-o-o-o," Volmer answered slowly. "Yours is a special mission. One of optimum importance to our victory. You carry a high enough clearance that I can speak frankly. General Ben Raines is not going to stop with Cheyenne. Oh, have no doubt," Volmer hastened to add at sight of the consternation on young Dracher's face, "Cheyenne is going to fall to the Rebels. After that, from my evaluation of Ben Raines, I am certain he will not be able to stand still for the duration of winter. You and the *Werwolfen* will remain on alert and mobile until it is determined where next Ben Raines will proceed.

"It will then be your honor and duty," Volmer revealed with relish, "to move swiftly and with great cunning in effecting the capture of Ben Raines. There can be no failure. I am counting on you and your magnificent young soldiers to do what many others have failed to accomplish."

Pride exploded on Dracher's boyish face. "I am already greatly honored, *Herr Hauptsturmbannführer*. We will not fail you. I have been dream—er, devising plans that we could employ to do that very thing. Thank you for this trust and for the chance to prove our faith."

"Remember," Volmer cautioned. "No failure will be tolerated. Death before dishonor. For the *Führer* and the Fatherland, *Sieg Heil!*"

Resistance intensified as the Rebels pushed the black-shirts back on themselves. The range had closed to the point that artillery and mortars had to remain silent. That brought rejuvenated hope to the defenders. Fighting became hand-to-hand through the tumbled remains of Cheyenne's suburbs. It slowed the Hummer containing Ben Raines and his team to a

172

crawl. When yet another spatter of rounds sang off the armor, Ben's patience evaporated.

"You have it in reverse, Coop? I can walk faster. Let's get out of this thing, kiddies, and have a little look around."

"Now, boss," Jersey cautioned from beside him.

"What's to worry? We have a platoon all around us, three M-1As, and those BFVs. All I'm saying is I can keep track of what is happening better if I can see where we're going, not where we've been."

In the usual manner, Ben Raines had his way. Jersey and Beth left the vehicle together, eyes alert, weapons at the ready. Ben followed, with Corrie at his side, while Cooper whipped the Humvee out of sight amid the rubble.

"Where are we?" Jersey asked first.

"That's the junction of old U.S. 85 and I-80 behind us," Ben indicated. "Which puts us in a suburban part of Cheyenne that must have contained a shopping mall. We're on the edge of what used to be a large parking lot."

"When in doubt, shop," Beth muttered.

"Born to shop," Corrie responded with a giggle.

"What's all this nonsense?" Ben demanded. "You are both too young to know anything about the compulsion to consume that advertisers directed at women before the Great War."

"But we had grandparents," they chorused.

"My grandmother told me all about it," Beth carried on. "How the merchants put up Christmas decorations the first of November, the cartoon shows—whatever those are—aimed at merchandising children and creating demands for products. How every conceivable occasion had been turned into a holiday, complete with a wide variety of greeting cards and appropriate gifts to be purchased. And about how women were encouraged to believe that the ideal stress reliever was a shopping trip to the mall. And that there was only one organization that

173

fought against it, called NOW. But I suppose it should be called THEN, now."

"Please, don't add to the confusion," Ben said, laughing. "Let's spread out and find whatever the advance squads left behind."

They found it almost at once. Three camo-clad American Nazis reared up among the folded masonry walls of the complex ahead and opened fire. In perfect order, Ben and team went to the ground and returned the favor. Jacketed slugs struck sparks off the stone and stucco rubble and howled off into the sky. Right then, six more black-shirts popped up to their left and poured rounds into their exposed position.

Slugs and chips of decomposed macadam flew past Ben Raines's face. The big Thompson in his hands bucked and snorted and two of the Sieg Heiling bad guys in front of them went down, drilled by .45 caliber lead. He gestured their direction for the team's benefit.

"We have to move. Forward looks the best idea."

Cooper's CAR-15 stuttered and another body fell, this time on their left. Three Nazis jumped up to race toward them. Beth downed one, Cooper another, the third did a Thompson tango as Ben ripped his guts open. As one, they came to their feet. Boots clomped on the crumbling paving as they streaked toward the sole, startled Nazi in their path.

He threw up his hands. His weapon clattered in the rubble. "Sorry," Jersey said, tight-lipped. "No prisoners." And shot him.

Right then one of the Bradley Fighting Vehicles caught up to Ben's Hummer. It sprayed the remaining Nazi trash on their flank and found itself in a disagreement with a pair of the light tanks Field Marshal Hoffman had assigned to Volmer's American cruds. One of the 75mm guns flashed and the BFV went bright white inside, rapidly going through blue to yellow, orange, and red.

"Aw, shit," Ben murmured, choked up. "They died protecting me." He sounded for once as though he regretted his hare-brained adventuring.

"Yeah, and we'd better be hauling ass, boss," Jersey put in. "Those tanks can cream us in an eyeblink."

Ben made a swift study of the hole out of which the American Nazis had appeared. It revealed itself to be the crumbled side of a subterranean vault. At one time a bank had done business here in the mall. He pointed to it with the muzzle of his Thompson.

"Down there. My bet is it's a bank vault. If they don't see us, they can't hurt us."

Secure from the view of the enemy gunners, Ben made a quick appraisal. "Pop a round from time to time from that blooper, Coop," Ben suggested. "Keep them around and interested, but at a distance. Because if that Bradley came around, the Abramses can't be far behind."

From outside came a frightful roaring as some three hundred screaming Nazi fanatics swarmed onto the parking lot.

Sixteen

Abruptly, as though cleanly sliced with a knife, the terrain changed. To the west of the line of demarcation, early fall retained its light touch on the land. On the other, winter had arrived with a vengeance. Tina Raines looked on with wonder as big, fat flakes of snow fell all around the column. She had ignored those Nazis who had fled in the direction of Cheyenne. Enough Rebels had gathered there to handle a company or so of demoralized troops. Her pursuit of those black-shirts who sought to rejoin their comrades in the west had been conducted at full speed along State Highway 130. She had them now.

According to the last transmission from the scouts, speed and nature had conspired to deliver the shattered storm troopers into Rebel hands. Snow had been falling for several hours here in the Medicine Bow Mountains. Tina gauged the accumulation on the level at about eleven inches, with drifts to five and six feet. Up ahead, the scouts reported, drifts had built to an incredible fifteen feet. Progress had slowed due to the wet, heavy blanket of white.

It had trapped the fugitive black-shirts in the narrow pass between Kennaday Peak to the north, at 10,810 feet and Medicine Bow Peak to the south at 12,013 feet. The highway to the west, already badly deteriorated by years of neglect, had been blocked so solidly that it would take days to clear it. With unscalable heights to both flanks, they could only turn back.

And behind them came Tina with two-thirds of her effective force. She maintained spotty contact with the Laramie airport. Although enemy troops had been observed streaming by in the direction of Cheyenne, none had engaged the lightened defenses around the terminal. Repairs were proceeding on the Puffs; at last report, nearing completion. They should be back in action in time to kick the living crap out of the reinforcements being sent by the head Nazi. A quick glance ahead showed Tina the long, curving approach to the pass.

"Let's halt here and get everyone in their white camocovers," she directed.

Like a lazy snake, the Rebel vehicles pulled to the verge and the troops dismounted. Their breath forming plumes of white vapor, they dug into equipment bags and came up with hooded blouses and baggy trousers of a neutral white color. Pullover covers for their helmets came next. Properly outfitted for the conditions in the Medicine Bow Mountains, the seasoned Rebels took advantage of the break in the long ride to relieve themselves and a few to light up smokes.

Other preparations went on also. From side compartments of the trucks, the drivers produced large canvas bags, heavy with tire chains, and hydraulic jacks. While the Rebels stamped feet and swung arms to relieve stiffness, the drivers set about affixing the driving aids to the rear wheels. Tina chafed at the delay. Then produced a rueful smile.

"They're not going anywhere," she spoke aloud with cold satisfaction.

"What's that, Colonel?" her RT operator asked.

"Nothing, Vargas. Just an observation on our enemy up ahead."

Silvia Vargas eyed her CO with admiration. "You are always so . . . calm. Every time, combat makes my *pantalóncitos* too small." She suppressed a giggle.

Tina Raines rarely shared girly confidences but felt compelled to do so this time. "Me, too. My panties sort of shrink up in the crotch."

Big-eyed at this revelation, Silvia blinked. "Really? It never shows . . . that you are scared, I mean."

"Silvie, we're all scared, every time. The trick is that we try like hell to keep anyone else from knowing it. You came up with that last replacement roster from Base Camp One. By then the fighting was all but over, and we enjoyed two months free of engagements. What you've seen in this campaign so far is mild, compared to what we're about to walk into. Even a little house mouse will turn on you when cornered.

"I want you to stick to me like a second skin," Tina changed the subject, drafting her plans as she spoke. "In the folds of these mountains, communications are going to be the key. We won't be able to see our people across the way. The terrain and this snow will cut visibility to about two hundred meters."

"That's bad," Silvia observed.

"No, that's good," Tina countered, and explained. "The enemy won't see us, either. If we do this right, it could be a cakewalk."

Relieved, Silvia smiled. "You make it sound easy."

"This highway is a bottleneck. We'll use two of the M-1As as a stopper, flank the Nazis, and blast hell out of them before they figure out where we are located. Now, I want to talk with the platoon leaders. Come along with me."

Tina and Silvia walked along the line of trucks, APCs, and armor. Tina summoned the subordinate troop leaders and they gathered at the rear of the convoy. Tina addressed Captain Thermopolis first.

"I'm placing you in command of the armor, Therm. Keep one platoon of headquarters with you to seal the way out. Leadfoot, those scoots of yours won't be any good in this weather. Take your people up on the slope of Medicine Bow Peak and flank the enemy. When the right time comes, I want you to come down on them with the full effect. You know what I mean. 'Run, the barbarians have broken through the walls of Rome,' that sort of thing."

Grinning, Leadfoot nodded. "I gotcha, Colonel Lady. We'll handle it, no sweat."

"Scrounge some whites. Those black leather jackets make you stick out like bears hunting a place to hibernate." To the other platoon leaders, "Lieutenants Strongbow and Harmon, take your people to the north side of the pass and flank the Nazis in the same way. Carry anything not heavy enough to make noise."

"I can horse a couple of eighty-one mike-mikes up there," Strongbow urged. He thought of the long-ago times when his Hunkpapa Sioux ancestors had fought the Blackfoot in these mountains. Now, he believed, he was fighting somewhere *significant*.

Tina thought a moment. "Two men on each baseplate. We don't want any noise. The diesel engines on the M-1As will keep their attention fixed down this direction. We want to keep it that way. Now, when everyone is in place, the Bradleys will scoot forward to a position just short of exposing themselves. The tanks will advance to where they can angle rounds over the rise and into the saddle of the pass. Fire will lift in exactly five minutes. We'll push forward from your positions, Harmon, and here at once. Fire from the Bradleys' fifties and chainguns will provide grazing cover.

"When they start to break and run, that's when the Goths attack Rome," Tina pointed out with a nod to Leadfoot.

Leadfoot's mustache waggled in amusement. "We'll go through them like—what was it that old general said?—crap through a goose."

"Don't be too efficient," Tina warned. "You might overrun and come under fire from Harmon's platoon."

"Okay. No problem. We'll keep shootin' an' shoutin' and herdin' them this way."

"You got that right, Leadfoot. The idea is to drive them on the armor and the troops held in reserve. We can finish them easily that way. Go back and brief your men."

General Field Marshal Hoffman, *Führer* of the Hemospheric Reich (self-proclaimed), and commander of the New Army of Liberation Expedition (North) sat up with a stricken expression. He had left strict instructions never to interrupt his late-afternoon nap. He fought to wipe the tendrils of sleep from his brain, which spun with the terrible news he had this minute received.

"What? This cannot be! I will not allow it to be," he shouted, froth forming at the corners of his twisted mouth. "We cannot, must not, lose Cheyenne."

"We haven't as yet, *mein Führer*," Col. Rupert Hertl, the G-1, hastened to reassure the leader. "The report is of a full-scale attack, with resistance crumbling. The bulk of reinforcements sent by Col — er — *Hauptsturmbannführer* Volmer should be arriving at any moment. They will be fresh and will repulse the Rebels easily," he added confidently.

"They had better," Hoffman responded petulantly. "Why hasn't General Brodermann's SS struck the Rebels and driven them from the field?"

"You ordered them to fall back and hold the high passes, *mein Führer*. And to make ready for the southern probe."

Recollection awakened in Hoffman. "Yes, so I did. You did well to awaken me, Hertl. Go along now, I'll join you in the communications center shortly."

"Have you any message for the commander at Cheyenne?"

Hoffman's smile had a bleak nature. "Oh, yes. Tell him to hold on, under pain of court-martial and the firing squad."

In a matter of seconds, Field Marshal Hoffman would have more bad news to digest.

"Open fire," Tina Raines said tightly into the mouthpiece of her radio handset.

High-velocity 120mm main guns on the M-1As barked with their characteristic ringing blast and sent smoke rings lazily into the snow-clogged air. Jetting gases from the muzzle brakes sent snowflakes to dancing in spirals. Millions of the lacy lamellae winked into steam in the tremendous muzzle bloom. Quickly as new charges could be rammed home, they bellowed again. The 4-inch mortars on the BFVs added their own counterpoint to the big guns. Charged with the tension of the moment, Tina waited out the five minutes of the bombardment.

In the impact area, terrified Nazis kicked, gagged, and screamed out their lives. Shells burst with shock waves powerful enough to dislodge the heavy layers of snow above the summit of the pass, where they had become bogged down in drifts. It cleared tree limbs in twinkling cascades. Bits of shrapnel buzzed, moaned, and whirred through the underbrush and the huddled soldiers with equal indifference. Detonations echoed off the mountain peaks until they became one blended cataclysm of doom sound.

"Cease fire," Tina announced when the second hand of her wristwatch next clicked up on the twelve. "Strongbow, open up with your mortars. Machine-gunners, pick your targets carefully. Bradleys, take your positions." Tina paused and took a deep breath. "That does it here. I'm going forward."

Her executive officer took this in with a disapproving frown. Then he shrugged and cocked a lopsided grin. He'd long ago decided that all the Raines's were battle-crazy.

Tina, with a three-man bodyguard, strode purposefully toward the crest of the rise that overlooked the area of the pass where the Nazi troops suffered terrible punishment. Silvia Vargas stuck to her CO closer than a shadow. By the time Tina reached a vantage point, the Bradleys had slewed into position. The big .50 calibers began their deep-throat rumble. Then the ringing clatter of the 30mm chainguns spooling up to operating speed reached her ears. Vibrant with the excitement of battle, Tina Raines looked down on the result of her planning.

Dark figures lay sprawled grotesquely in the show, which had been stained from light pink to dark red around them. Fully two hundred fighting men remained on their feet. Mortar rounds dropped out of the afternoon sky and cut down more of them. The machine guns scythed through their ranks with awesome finality. Here and there Tina saw isolated centers of disciplined activity.

From one of those, a man-shape emerged to kneel in the knee-deep snow and level a long tube over his shoulder. Flame spurted backward from his position and Tina instantly saw what to expect.

"Button up!" she shouted warning to the gunners in the BFVs as she dived for the protection of a snow-filled roadside ditch.

Two gunners made it in time. Although it did them little good as the rocket-propelled grenade slammed into their vehicle and its shaped charge sent a jet of burning gas through the light armor. Fragments of shrapnel killed the pair on the nearer Bradley an instant before the first exploded in a thunderous crash and ball of flame.

Chunks of metal moaned by overhead and Tina ducked low in the ditch. Then new fury claimed her. She rose, knees shaking and stalked toward the undamaged BFV.

"You bastards," she growled, eyes fixed on the rocket gunner who was being reloaded by a crewman.

Tina negotiated the three external steps in a smooth, limber economy of motion. Her nimble fingers unhooked the harness of the chaingun operator and let him slide down the hatch. Quickly she took his position and swung the multibarrel weapon toward the Nazi marksman.

Explosive 30mm shells churned ground across fifty feet as Tina tracked him, then they struck home in flesh. Literally blown asunder, the black-shirt cartwheeled through the air in several directions, his RPG a dented, useless tube of metal on the bloody snow. With telling effect, she hosed down the rest of the crew and exterminated that strong point. Still firing at a new point of resistance, Tina slapped a palm on the inside of the hatchway.

"Take me down there," she commanded.

"Wait," Silvia yelled from the side of the Bradley. "You said to stick with you and I'm not halfway up this thing."

"Hold it a mo' for my RT," Tina relented.

Silvia joined her, and they jolted over the crest and down the road toward the embattled Nazis. "What should I do?" Silvia Vargas asked, bug-eyed.

"Get that man out of there and take the Fifty," Tina told her. "You can shoot, can't you?"

Pride lighted the young Mexican-American's face. "Qualified expert on all our machine guns," she responded.

"Then let's go hose down some supermen," Tina quipped.

Harmon's Rebels had gotten into motion by that time. They streamed out of the tree line to the north, firing in short bursts as they ran downhill to the pass. Those black-shirts with enough wits about them threw grenades and took defensive positions behind their stranded vehicles.

Actually doing something served to rally them. They steadied down and began to inflict casualties. Then the big Rebel MBTs rumbled into view at the high point of the road east. Footsoldiers flowed around them and started down on the unnerved Nazis. A bull-roar came unexpectedly from the slopes to the south.

"Hot damn, boys!" Leadfoot shouted. "Let's go scrag Nazi ass!"

Hooting, yelping, and wailing, the Sons of Satan

poured down on the thoroughly demoralized black-shirts. Penned in by snowdrifts and armor, faced on three sides by advancing infantry, the American crud of Volmer's command deteriorated into panic.

One less-feverish noncom judged rightly that the smallest unit committed against them came from the south. He assumed command of escape-minded Nazis near his position and led them that way.

They closed within a few feet before they realized that the howling madmen were not merely swinging their arms around over their heads. Their gloved hands held length of motorcycle drive chain. Studded with razor blades, these improvised weapons brought quick, bloody ruin to the bold sergeant's plan.

Blood spurted and Nazis fell, writhing and shrieking on the ground. Here and there among them, rifles and pistols cracked a final farewell to the slashed and helpless black-shirts. When the last one had been rendered harmless, Leadfoot rallied his followers.

"Fun's over, boys," he informed them in a stentorian roar. "Now pick your targets and fire slow — ah — *ly*. Fire slowly," he repeated, conscious of the hard hours he had put in in secret with Thermopolis to work on his manner of speaking. Hell, it weren't no crime for someone to try to improve himself, right? Down below he saw the undamaged Bradley advancing into the teeth of the last resistance.

Tina and Silvia slashed swaths across the desperate and frightened black-shirt troops. The Bradley afforded them fair protection, except for grenades, Tina reminded herself. She lined up on five Nazis who took careful aim and fired with calm control. The 30mm chaingun rattled their death knell and fell silent.

Gradually the entire pass quieted. The acrid odor of powder smoke and coppery bite of blood scent filled the air. In less than five minutes, only the moaning and screams of the wounded could be heard. Tina's exec brought her a count.

"We lost twenty-five KIA, forty WIA. There's about

ninety-five Nazis unharmed, a hundred twenty-one total alive."

Silvia's voice came small and wonder-filled. "What
makes them hate us so? What could twist someone to
join such a sick, terrible thing?"

Suddenly, Tina realized that Silvia asked a question
she had never had fully answered. Curious, she dismounted from the Bradley and walked to where the
prisoners had been corralled behind some barbed wire
hastily strung between trees. She motioned to one with
officer's pips on his collar.

"I'm curious. You appear to be a reasonably intelligent person. You're clean and careful in your appearance. Why did you throw in your lot with these losers?"

"Why not?" he snapped. "What choice did any of us
have? Do you remember back before the Great War?
Remember how the government conspired in acts of
genocide against the white race?"

"What are you talking about?" Tina asked, truly ignorant of where this might lead.

"Quota hiring, for one thing. Had to be a nigger to
get a job. Got hired ahead of more-qualified white
men. Look at the welfare fraud. Black bitches gettin' fat
and sassy on money taken out of our pockets. Lived in
better places than most whites. There was quotas for
school admissions, too. My kid couldn't go to medical
school because some jigaboo who couldn't add two and
two and come up with four thought he wanted to be a
doctor. The last straw for me, lady, was when the
courts, even the Supreme Court, issued decisions that
implied one could not discriminate against whites.
That what would be considered discrimination against
other races was the just deserts of white men. And the
unrestricted flood of foreigners brought in, put up, and
supported on welfare, free medical treatment, taking
jobs, taking places to live, and spreading all sorts of
exotic diseases everywhere. And no one dare com-
plain."

Tina had heard it all before, in one version or another. What pained was that she, like her father, agreed on some issues. Where these whiners and complainers differed from the Rebel way was in the solutions they had chosen to apply. She told this specimen as much.

"Then why do you not leave these degenerate, race-mixing Rebels and join the only True American Way?" he demanded, the capital letters evident in the zeal with which he delivered his words. "We're going to win, don't you know that? *Sieg Heil!*"

Stifling a shudder as though she had touched something slimy, Tina turned a cold stare on the American Nazi and gestured to a Rebel trooper nearby. "Take him away and . . . do the usual."

"Away where?" the Nazi demanded.

"We're going to process you like we do all other enemy prisoners who refuse to be enlightened," Tina told him blandly.

"How's that?"

"By firing squad," Tina stated with a calm, composed face.

Seventeen

Silence had held over the immediate area for a good fifteen minutes. Ben Raines took the handset from his ear and peered thoughtfully at the patch of blue sky visible through the rubble-guarded entrance to the vault where they had taken shelter. The news he had received appeared to have energized him.

"Looks like we can get out of here soon. Estimates are we have pacified about two-thirds of the triangle. I have to tell you," he went on, grumping at the circumstances that had put them there, "I feel like an idiot, sitting it out in here while everyone else does the fighting."

"Look at it this way, General," Jersey appealed. "It gave you a chance to test your theory that the Rebel army would function equally well without you."

"Don't get cheeky with me, Jersey," Ben growled. "Dammit," he exploded a second later, "I'm getting to sound like an old fogey. All right, they clobbered my bodyguard platoon and had us pinned down here. Nothing we could do about that. Too many reinforcements coming in for the black-shirts. So why am I so pissed?" Ben gave a lopsided grin and came to his feet. "Let's pull up stakes and go find someplace where there's still some action."

Cooper made it to the top of the ramp of dirt and debris that led to the breech in the wall. His head had barely cleared the opening in the three foot thick slab of concrete and rebar when he dropped flat, mouth open in shock.

"Holy shit, there's about five hundred screaming Nazis out there."

"What? Let me see," Ben demanded.

He crept up the incline on hands and knees. Slowly he raised his head for a clear sight. Ben's eyes widened as he took in the swarming scene in the parking lot. More black-shirts had somehow gotten in behind the Rebel advance into the Cheyenne triangle. Now they boiled over from the streets and the interstate onto the cracked and frost-heaved blacktop of the parking lot. Quickly, Ben lowered his head.

Not fast enough, he discovered when a shout roused the milling Nazis outside the bank vault. "Over there, I just saw something move."

"A rag," some unseen black-shirt ventured. "Or a wild dog."

"No. It looked like a head, with a helmet on it."

"A dead guy?" a distinctly Boston accent asked.

"No, it moved, I tell you. I'm gonna go see."

"We'll cover you," his fellow Nazis offered.

Bootsteps crunched over long-ago-broken glass and the crisp weeds of summer, to grow louder as they approached the cavelike opening into the vault. Ben eased his Thompson into position, then thought better of it. He slid the Desert Eagle .50 caliber out of his holster and thumb-slipped the safety. A head, shoulders, and torso flashed through his field of view too quickly to make note of characteristics. Then disembodied camo-covered legs filled the space. Ben tensed.

Bent low, the young Nazi peered into the rent in the vault wall. His eyes went wide and he opened his mouth to yell. "By god, there's someone here, all ri—"

Ben's .50 Desert Eagle made an enormous roar and cut off the hail to the other black-shirts. The fat slug entered the Nazi's head through one cheekbone and splashed the inside of his helmet with the contents of his skull. The body had barely fallen to one side before the ground around erupted into geysers of dirt. A crackle of small-arms fire followed. Ben propelled himself backward to land hard on the floor of the strongroom. Two slugs impacted at the spot where his head had been a moment before.

"Bring a grenade," one Nazi demanded. "Hurry. Place may be full of them."

Trapped. The entire team had last, individually characterized, thoughts.

Betrayed, Jersey thought. Screwed by the fickle finger of fate. I'll never get to know if Ben Raines has any feelings for me besides trust and loyalty.

It isn't right to die like this, Beth fought against destiny. I wanted children, a home.

Fuckin' Nazi scum, Cooper blazed in his helpless anger. I hate having shit like that finish me off.

Well, hell, we should have moved out earlier, Ben blamed himself. Then the crackle of static on Corrie's radio distracted his thoughts. Eagerly he reached for it while his team kept up sporadic fire to discourage any close approach by the Nazis.

"This is Eagle," Ben said, dry-throated.

"Eagle, this is your Magic Dragon," came the laconic voice of Chuck, the C-47 jockey. "Officially that's Tango Alpha One, with two little chicks at my side. We be one minute out. Any idea what we should do?"

"That I do, Dragon." Quickly Ben gave a heading that would take the Puffs obliquely along the mall and parking lot.

"Make that two-zero seconds, Eagle."

Ben could already hear the drone of the big radial engines. The sweetest sound in the world, he rejoiced. Jersey ran her magazine dry and searched for a fresh load. Ben put the Thompson to work in loud, punishing bursts. Half a heartbeat later the world turned into bedlam.

Steel, copper, and lead rained down from the Puff. It cut a swath high, wide, and handsome through the press of enemy personnel. Its deadly armament hammered and yammered. Body parts levitated and fell back to smoking ground. American Nazis died in generous quantity, screaming in hate and pain to the very end. When the cacophony of Rebel shells ended, only the cries of the dying could be heard. Chuck's call was answered at once by Ben.

"We, ah, managed to suppress your problem, Eagle. We're gonna go over and he'p out your friends. Then we be gone from here back to Base Camp One, by way of Wichita to give these crates a drink. It took a long time to patch holes in them and then the icing started when we rolled them out of the hangar. Oh, say, ice storm and snow on its way here from Laramie. ETA about twenty minutes. Y'all take care, now, hear?"

Big white flakes descended in undulating curtains on the hushed expanse of the parking lot. Odd, Ben Raines thought, only the first week of October and it looked to be a heavy snowfall. He recalled the old, hackneyed barb about Wyoming. "I'd like to spend the summer there this year, but I'm busy that weekend."

Already a pristine blanket of white settled on the cooling corpses of the Nazi aggressors. Ben surveyed the astonishing number of dead lying in fan-shaped rows, the narrow part nearest the vault he and his team had so recently occupied. He didn't need close calls like that. Engine racing, a Bradley sprinted up and halted sharply, to rock briefly on its undercarriage. The vehicle commander levered his way up through a hatch.

"General Striganov's compliments, sir. The triangle is secured. Prisoner count is taking place now. Oh, and the general found this in the headquarters CP. It's addressed to you."

Ben took the flat, rectangular package from the sergeant and studied it. His name had been written in precise strokes on one surface. Whoever had put it there was an accomplished calligrapher. Then he saw that the "s" in Raines looked like an "f" with the back half of the crossbar broken off. German script, Ben recognized.

"Thank you, Sergeant," Ben returned to the matter at hand. He opened the parcel and frowned. It contained an old videotape. "Do you know whether General Striganov found the equipment to operate this thing?"

"Yes, sir, he did."

"Wait one, then. We'll get saddled up and follow you back to the enemy CP."

Twenty-seven minutes of dodging burning Nazi equipment, shell holes, and other obstacles brought Ben and team to the former black-shirt command post. Gen. Georgi Striganov greeted his commander affably and directed him inside. Jersey took her usual position, eyes sharply gauging every possible trouble spot. Georgi pointed to a relatively normal looking television set, although as a breed they had been effectively extinct for ten years. A slight oddness in the position of the controls, and a brand name as foreign to Ben as the language in which it was written, revealed its South American origin. Beside it sat a VCR.

"When I saw these, I figured from the weight that you had received a videotape, Ben. I left it up to you to find out what it contained."

"Then we'd better get to it," Ben said as he approached the equipment and inserted the tape in the slot.

Memory served Ben as he turned on the television and VCR. He set the recorder and TV to channel 3 and punched the play button. Nothing but black-and-white snow. He tried channel 4. Same result. On inspiration he tried 13. Blue sky and the rugged terrain of Wyoming came onto the screen.

"How did you figure that out?" Striganov asked. In the days before the Great War, when VCRs were plentiful, only members of the *nomenkultura* were permitted to own them in the old Soviet Union.

"You need a neutral channel for VCR feed," Ben explained, as Nazi troops flashed onto the monitor. Then he snorted with amusement. "I figured that since in the bad old days the Latinos would rather die than copy anything American, they would go to the opposite end of the channel selection."

Ben put the tape on hold and gestured to the manned communications station. "Oh, before we get into this, do you have a link to Base Camp One?"

"Of course."

"Good. Have your RT bump Cecil Jefferys for me." The call went through quickly. "Cec, this is Ben. The Puffs are on their way home. They did a fantastic job. Pulled my spuds out of the fire for sure. I want you to have a bottle of your special, rare, hundred-proof, twenty-year-old bourbon waiting for the command pilot and his crew when they reach there."

"It pains me to part with it," Jefferys joked. "But, considering the circumstances, I think I can make the sacrifice. Good news on Cheyenne. Georgi has already advised me."

"You do that, Cec. And how's the exercises going?"

A spate of profanity followed. At last Cecil Jefferys gathered his breath to snap, "You don't want to know. I twisted an ankle on the treadmill yesterday, and it took a threat to send the doctor off to Alaska to keep from being shoved into a bed again. I've already started the wheels turning for resupply. If you have secure airfields, you can expect the first within nine hours."

"Good. We need that," Ben responded. "You take care of yourself, Cec. Eagle, out." He turned back to the television and started the tape.

Cold outrage grew by the minute as those inside the CP watched. The firing squads and hangings for captured Rebels they expected. When it got to the garrottings, General Striganov exploded with fury.

"Borjemoi! Kotorohye solip'shim!"

White-lipped with rage, Ben spoke tightly. "They're sons of bitches all right, Georgi Alexandrovich. And it's about time we treated them like the rabid dogs they are."

Scenes of torture and degrading forms of execution followed. They so upset Beth and Corrie that they excused themselves from the command post. When the

192

Nazis started in on Rebel women and children, even Ben, hardened though he was, felt the hot bile rising in his throat. Hoffman's minister of information had in mind provoking Ben Raines into making some rash, ill-conceived blunder.

Far from that, what he accomplished was to awaken the fires of hell in Ben's eyes. Very carefully, conscious will at maximum to control his demeanor and words, Ben sifted alternatives and courses of action.

"Prisoners? How many do we have?" he asked in a choked voice.

"Close to six hundred eighty," Striganov answered. He had trimmed down some in the last few weeks, Ben noted idly. His broad Ukrainian face reflected all the anguish that racked Ben.

"Terminate them all. Every last one. No. Save enough to drive truckloads back to Hoffman."

"Ah, General, there were some women and children among the survivors. Families of the officers," Colonel West offered cautiously.

Ben's icy stare unnerved the mercenary colonel. "The kids nine and under go back to Base Camp One. All the others . . ." Ben started to pronounce their death sentence, then plucked out a possible advantage they might represent. "They can accompany the drivers back to Hoffman. What they have to tell the other wives and children could prove useful to us." He paused to suck in a deep chestful of air. "My initial order stands: no prisoners, no quarter, no mercy for all of Hoffman's god-damned army. No exceptions."

"That might be a bit rough on the Latinos among the rank and file," West probed again.

"Let it be!" Ben snapped. "They can either assassinate that son of a bitch and return to their own countries peacefully, or die with the rest. Because, gentlemen and ladies, I intend to make Field Marshal Jesus Diequez Mendoza Hoffman pay more dearly for this than even that sadistic kraut bastard can imagine."

Eighteen

Immediately, Ben Raines settled into a command conference. He scribbled notes on a Base Camp One version of a yellow legal pad while the various unit commanders assembled. In consideration of size, the meeting convened outside the Nazi CP. After receiving verbal reports on the condition of men and equipment, status of supplies, and preliminary results of prisoner interrogations, Ben consulted his lines of squiggles and began to outline the new plan of action.

"It appears we will be able to conduct the major portion of the game plan as devised. From here on, we hit on the flanks. Roll up the enemy lines in fast, hard strikes. To assist that, I'm calling up all gunships, Puffs, and two-thirds of our fixed-wing air-ground support and interceptor aircraft. Each of you is to designate and fully brief forward air guides and controllers to liaise with them. Questions so far?"

"What about food and medical supplies?" Dr. Lamar Chase asked.

"On the way. We hold everything east of here, and now the Cheyenne and Laramie airports. Expect the first cargo flights in—" Ben glanced at his watch. "Seven hours forty minutes, give or take fifteen minutes. Lowboys will be leaving to bring up additional tanks, to be employed in the southern half. These mountains don't make good armor country."

"What about the weather?" That from West.

"Our best guess is that the snow is of short duration. Higher altitudes may be another story. There is no snow, according to Ike McGowan, from Denver south. Real Indian summer weather through all the central and southern plains. Back to the high passes. We've secured Medicine Bow, but it is blocked westward by drifts. If you've no further questions, we can get on to troop dispositions." No one made a comment. Ben looked at his notes and began again.

"Take note of this one change. Headquarters Company is staying on the assault. Therm, I want you to take your company, Leadfoot's bikers, and Emil's followers and push on to Shoshoni on US 20/26. There, half, under Leadfoot and Wanda, are to turn south on State 135 to secure the Riverton area. Make a note and respond accordingly. There is a Shoshoni/Arapaho reservation near the town of Riverton. Any people still there may or may not be friendly to the Rebel cause. If you can recruit them, more than better." Ben paused and refreshed himself from a bottle of crystal-clear cola that bore a South American brand name.

"General, are you going to be with us?" Thermopolis took the opportunity to ask.

"No. My plans now are to head south toward the Denver area of operation and link up with Ike McGowan. I can coordinate from there with good commo and be able to move with R Batt as a quick-reaction force where needed."

Thermopolis frowned. "Then what are the rest of us to do?"

"Ah, here comes the best part," Ben said brightly. "Thermopolis, you will take the other half of your command and proceed from Shoshoni north, pushing the remnants of the SS ahead of you, to the town of Thermopolis. That's right," Ben added with a chuckle, "Thermopolis is going to Thermopolis."

"There ain't no justice," Thermopolis wailed.

Beth appeared at Ben's side. "Bad news, General. Colonel Gray's vehicle struck a land mine just outside the

Denver AO. Dan survived, but he is reported as severely concussed, and has six broken ribs and a dislocated hip. A Doctor Hutchinson at the MASH unit says that the colonel is out of it for the duration."

Ben's scowl could have melted titanium. "Dammit. Of all times." He sucked in air. "All right. Buddy to take command of Dan's battle group, and becomes XO to General Ike. They are to proceed as ordered. I will be in Denver within two days. Anything else, Beth?"

"No, sir."

"Thank goodness for that. We'll get on with this. Georgi, you will advance northward, rolling up the Nazis all the way to the Canadian border. Use I-25 as your main line of communication. I want the entire northern sector closed off and secured with units on every east-west road within two weeks."

To Colonel West, he instructed, "You are to continue west on I-80. It is obviously the best supply line open to Hoffman due to the weather. Spread out, and whenever contact is made with the enemy they are to be reduced. Don't worry about getting spread too thin. Within three days, Colonel Danjou's French Canadians will be in position to assist you."

This time, Corrie and Beth came to Ben's side. They wore worried frowns and held a commo flimsy. Ben noticed them and reached for the message form.

"What now? Oh," he cut off at notice of a familiar name. Silently he read on. A shake of his head accompanied a heavy sigh.

"More bad news, it seems. Is this the complete text?" he asked.

"Yes, sir. As much as came through. The transmission was from a long way off and badly broken up," Corrie explained.

"I'll read it," Ben told his commanders. " 'Hoffman's Nazis have hit us hard, many losses. Moving north.' It's from General Payon down in Mexico. I gather he means Rasbach when he says Hoffman, but it's all one in the same. We have to do something." He paused, thinking earnestly while muttered conversation ran though the subordinate commanders. At last Ben raised his head, jaw set firmly in a sign of decision.

"Corrie, have the team ready for immediate departure. Stan," he said to R Batt commander McDade, "I want R Batt ready to move out in half an hour. Level Three alert status." To the curious, concerned expressions of the rest, he enlightened them. "I'm going south to help out my old friend, General Raul Payon."

Book Two

While the man who called himself *Führer* of the Western Hemisphere and the Fourth Reich, Field Marshal Jesus Dieguez Mendoza Hoffman, played hide-and-seek with the Rebel army of Ben Raines, the older and wiser General Frederich Rasbach fled the United States for sanctuary in South America. General Rasbach found conditions markedly changed in the months they had been gone.

In Venezuela, Brazil, Argentina, Uruguay, Bolivia, Paraguay, and Chile, the people had risen up and overwhelmed the State Secret Police (*Servicio Secreto*) — which Hoffman had wanted to call the *Geheime Staats Polizei* (Gestapo); fortunately, as Rasbach saw it, the *Reich Bundestagen* of all Nazi countries didn't agree — and the civilian government. For a while anarchy reigned in the streets of Rio de Janeiro, Buenos Aires, Valparaíso, Montevideo, Asunción, and Sucre.

General Rasbach's return at the head of a division and a half of seasoned troops quickly ended that. Over the next two months, he set about restoring Nazi authority, although his heart was not in it. For all the posturing of his father and grandfather before him, Frederich Rasbach had always harbored a secret belief that Nazism, like all socialist regimes was essentially flawed. His grandfather had been high up in ODESSA (*Organisation der ehemaligen SS-Angehörigen*), as had his father. Their ar-

201

guments for racial purity and the superiority of the Aryan race failed to convince young Frederich.

But he was a loyal and dutiful son. He joined the youth organization, later the Secret Army Organization (SAO), which became the National Army of Liberation. Now, duty dictated that he must restore order, fill the ranks of the New Army of Liberation, and return to extricate Jesus Hoffman from the consequences of his folly. General Rasbach quickly noted an oddity in his dual role.

Restoring Nazi power and recruiting an army seemed to work at cross-purposes. No sooner had his storm troopers subjugated the people of one metropolis and recruited fighting men, to move on with the army, than the campesinos rose up again and ousted the Nazis in government. His black-shirt divisions received such a hot reception in several areas that General Rasbach was forced to write them off. At least temporarily, he told himself.

In the end, he had rallied scattered troops, to add to recruits, put together three divisions, with armor and artillery support. Popular sentiment still waxed so strongly against the Nazi regime that Rasbach took ship at once, to land in Nicaragua.

He had intended to transit the Panama Canal and come up the west coast of Mexico and the United States, securing territory for Field Marshal Hoffman as he went. He found the canal in the hands of anti-Nazi partisans. So on to a more-sympathetic climate. Which he found among the former Sandinistas of Nicaragua. He landed there while the Rebels with Ben Raines recovered and resupplied after their final onslaught against allies of Hoffman's NAL. His hosts greeted his army warmly, if a bit apprehensively. They, too, had maintained a cadre from the old days and schooled their children in Marxist revolutionary theory. After tactful negotiations, they easily accommodated the differences between Marxism-Leninism and National Socialism. Gen. Frederich Rasbach had found a new home.

One that he used as a staging area for a return to Mexico. His forces sailed from Puerto Cabezas, around Cabo Gracias a Dios, and on to Veracruz, Mexico. There he landed against slight resistance while Ben Raines chased Nazis westward across Kansas and Nebraska.

"I am not a Zachary Taylor," he announced, knee-deep in the surf during the initial assault landing. "We are going to keep this country for ourselves."

Spearheaded by armor, General Rasbach's divisions made a blitzkrieg slash across the narrow waist of Mexico. With secure bases on both coasts of the country, his army turned north. While the American Nazis fought desperately against the attacking Rebels at Cheyenne, General Rasbach spread his forces out on the Plain of Guerrero to face the army of General Raul Francisco Payon.

Monumentally courageous in their defense of the homeland, the soldiers of General Payon offered stiff resistance. In the first day of fighting, General Rasbach lost two regiments of relatively green troops. Staggered by the carnage, he drew back and formulated a new plan. Sending all of his armor and a third of the remaining troops eastward, General Rasbach swung them into position to make a flanking attack in depth against Payon.

Two days went by with only minor skirmishes and probing actions. Then Rasbach's two tank regiments and three of infantry worked their way westward. Traditionally, General Rasbach opened the engagement with artillery. The Mexicans fought as well as they could, trading round for round of heavy shells. When counterbattery radar located the Mexican emplacements, Rasbach ordered his massed armor to move on them and roll up the Mexican positions.

"Por Dios y patria!" the Mexican troops cheered, and threw themselves onto their attackers.

By nightfall of that day, Cheyenne had been surrounded. The Mexican defenses south and west of Mexico City crumbled. Through personal charisma and brilliant planning under stress, Gen. Raul Payon maintained a large degree of order over the withdrawal. For all of their haste, the retreating Mexican army left devastation in their wake. The enemy would get little benefit from what they took.

General Rasbach pursued relentlessly. Accepting a calculated risk, General Payon elected to halt the army's flight on the Plain of Chapultepec. General Rasbach's advanced units arrived three hours later. The Mexican artillery, already disturbingly low on ammunition, opened at once. When General Rasbach, a student of history, heard of this, he marveled at the similarity to that long-ago battle in the same place against the American invaders under Taylor. He made mention of it at his staff conference early the next morning.

"Well, gentlemen, if the Mexicans insist on playing out an historic battle from a century and a half ago, the least we can do is oblige them. If only we had some Marines."

"Pardon, my general?" his G-3 asked diffidently.

"Marines," Rashbach was reported as replying. "The American Expeditionary Force sent the Marines against the Mexican defenders of Chapultepec Castle in 1847. Beat them rather severely, or so the history books say. I rather expect that we shall do even better."

They did so, and quickly. By late afternoon Chapultepec had fallen and the victorious soldiers of General Rasbach blew through the decimated ranks of General Payon's Mexicans and headed out of Mexico City on a rapid drive for the border.

One

"And Caesar's spirit, ranging for revenge . . . come hot from hell, shall in these confines with a monarch's voice cry 'Havoc!' and let slip the dogs of war . . ."

Wm. Shakespeare,
Julius Caesar,
Act III, Scene 1

Back in the saddle, and running true to form, Ben Raines made plans on the fast drive to the Denver AO. Denver was weak, barely holding against the Rebel might Buddy Raines threw against it. It would fall in a day, Ben estimated. He would be there to see it.

But not to stay for long. Colorado Springs was back in Rebel hands; Pueblo no longer existed. That left all points south yet to consider. Beth handed Ben the latest intel sheets and he thumbed through them quickly, speed-reading the highlights.

Hoffman's regulars of the NAL, a good half of Brodermann's SS, and a pestilence of American Nazis had established nests in Santa Fe, Santa Rosa, and Alamogordo, New Mexico. From there, they cut a line to El Paso, Texas. They also controlled Raton Pass from Trinidad, Colorado, through the mountains to Raton, New Mexico. A damn lot of territory. And all of it, until recently, secure Rebel country.

"Hoffman's worse than a plague," Ben muttered to

himself.

"What's that, General?" Beth asked.

"Oh, ah, nothing, Trixie," Ben responded, using the nickname that had become an in joke between them.

Recently, Ben had blundered upon Beth alone in a copse of southern Missouri birch. She had been trying on long-forgotten civilian clothing. The cut and styling was blatantly feminine. When Beth saw Ben, she let out a startled yelp, then recovered quickly.

"Trixie McGuire at your service, sir," said Beth coyly, batting her eyes. "Would you buy a girl a drink, mister?"

The incident had been all but forgotten by both. Trixie had stuck. Now, Beth produced a mocking pout and indicated the yellow pad on which Ben scribbled. Ben sighed and nodded.

"Just deciding how many Nazis we are going to have to kick hell out of to reach Raul Payon. The answer is simple. Too damn many."

Beth cut eyes to the situations map on one wall of the mobile CP. "You got that right, General. If Hoffman hadn't picked up so much of this American crud, we could walk through them in three days."

Ben smiled gently at her confidence. Her belief in the Rebels notwithstanding, general and specific knowledge was what made the difference between private soldiers and generals. Given the best possible scenario, Ben knew, it would take more like two weeks with the forces he would have at his disposal.

"Maybe so," he offered tentatively. "If we had the whole Rebel army at our backs."

"Coffee, boss?" Jersey put into the conversation.

"Yes, gladly. When we shift to the Hummer, that's one luxury I'll miss. Coffee from a thermos, rather than hot and fresh," Ben lamented.

He sipped gratefully and immediately set to marking down the force he would organize in Denver. The R Batt of course, with its five companies, one of M-1A Abrams tanks, plus the two Apache gunships on trailers and six 4-inch mortars on BFVs. In Denver he would send Buddy's command, three full battalions, southeast, around the mountains on Colorado 71 to Rocky Ford and La Junta, then come at Trinidad from the northeast, on U.S. 350. The R Batt, and a third of Ike's command, would proceed south on I-25, toward Trinidad, while Ike would leave a small force to hold Denver and take the rest south on U.S. 287 into Oklahoma, then turn west to take Raton. With the pass secured, they would join forces and advance on the Mexican border.

It would do, Ben decided. Barely.

General Field Marshal Hoffman could barely contain his fury. Not only had they lost Cheyenne, but his incompetent intelligence people had lost contact with Ben Raines. Where had he gone? How many of the cursed Rebels went with him? Where would he show up next?

"This is an impossible situation. Get *Hauptsturmbannführer* Volmer here at once. Fly him here," General Field Marshal Hoffman demanded.

"Immediately, *mein Führer*," Col. Hertl gulped.

A nervous runner from the communications van appeared in the doorway. "A message, *mein Führer*," he blurted. "Denver is under attack."

"What!" Hoffman exploded. "Impossible. There aren't enough Rebels out there to overwhelm us at Cheyenne and immediately assault the Denver area of operation."

"The message, sir," the uncomfortable *Gefreiter*, or private, muttered as he extended the flimsy.

Colonel Hertl snatched it from him and handed it to Field Marshal Hoffman. His dark eyes scanned it quickly. "Light probing actions," he read aloud. "Sporadic sniping. Patrols ambushed." He turned a glittering gaze on the other staff officers. "It appears to me to be nothing more than guerrilla action by some of the survivors of the Rebel outpost. If it is no worse than this, we can ignore it for the time being."

Col. Joaquin Webber cleared his throat. "I beg your

pardon, *mein Führer*, but it was yourself who told us that we could never, never ignore anything involving Ben Raines."

Hoffman looked thoughtful for a moment. "Yes, of course. Our primary objective is to locate Ben Raines. Then eliminate him. That is why I want Volmer here. He has a plan, he says, that should work perfectly. While we pursue that, we can afford not to worry about Denver."

Ben Raines knew all about the Nazi defenses in the Denver area before he got there. So, his orders were brief and to the point. "Reduce them," he stated coldly. "No quarter. None are to escape if at all possible."

Buddy Raines and Ike McGowan spent a day covertly positioning their battalions. Then they struck with a ferocity not seen since the campaign against the Night People. Artillery shells made railroad ripples through the pale blue sky to crash into the mountain-rimmed valley that once housed the major population center of the entire state of Colorado.

One would think that with the destruction forced on the Rebels by the creepies, nothing would be left that could burn. Not so. Piles of rubble took flame, as did Nazi vehicles and three ammunition dumps. These latter soon erupted in thunderous explosions that rocked the basin. The vaunted Mile High City became a charnel house.

For the Nazis trapped there, it more resembled a crematorium. High-explosive rounds alternated with incendiary projectiles. Then, right on the heels of the walking barrage, yowling Rebel soldiers charged the remaining black-shirt positions.

"We're making headway, Ben," Ike McGowan reported delightedly. "Another hour and we'll have suppressed all resistance."

"Good. Keep at it," Ben responded from the Hummer. "We're following R Batt into the southern sector."

"Keep your head down," Ike advised. Ben's soft

chuckle answered him.

A blackshirt-manned MBT spun on one tread around a low mound and braked abruptly. The turret motor whined and the main gun swung to engage the target. The gyro-stabilizer kept the image in the sight steady although the carriage of the tank still rocked from the sudden maneuver and equally rapid braking. Carefully the gunner tightened the focus and lined the crosshairs exactly on the low, squat vehicle that darted across open terrain ahead of the tank. His thumb reached for the fire button that would blast the Humvee out of existence.

Only a fraction of a second of consciousness remained to the gunner after his brain recorded a loud, metallic clank against the side of the tank. Then a stream of molten metal and fiery gases blew into the turret from an inch-diameter hole that had been forced through the skin by the shaped charge of the ERIX antitank missile, fired by an alert Rebel.

Blobs spun around the circular walls of the cupola, and the ammunition stores ignited with a tremendous roar. The main gun slammed up and down an instant before the entire turret took off like an ungainly vulture. Inside the Hummer, Jersey lightly tapped Ben on one forearm.

"I think that kid out there just saved our bacon, General."

Attracted by the explosion, Ben eyed the demolished tank and nodded slowly. "If we were into the practice of giving out medals, he'd get one," the Rebel general remarked.

"Right now, I'd like to take him by the ears and hang a big ol' lip lock on him that would use all his pucker power," Jersey informed the team.

Cooper wanted to say something about preserving that on tape for posterity, but his unexplainable timidity around Jersey prevented it. Ben suffered from no such compunction.

"Why, Jersey, I thought you only kissed cows."

"There's a lot you don't know, bossman," Jersey quipped back. The high planes of her face, accented by a frame of dark hair, glowed with mischief and once more reminded Ben he suspected she had some Apache blood in her background.

"Cooper, take us somewhere from which we can see the action," Ben commanded.

"After that tank, General, I think we're close enough to the enemy. Maybe go higher? That knob ahead looks good."

"Do it," Ben accepted.

There had been houses there once. Expensive, exclusive suburban homes of the elite of Denver's upper-level executive class. A cracked roadway led to a cul de sac that had accommodated five houses, two on each side and one at the apex of the circle. A decorative fountain had one time sprayed water in the center of the paved drive-around. No doubt small children had splashed in its basin on hot summer days, Ben surmised. While their older brothers and sisters cavorted in the quartet of swimming pools that gave evidence of their former existence by crumbled tilework and depressions in the ground behind four of the demolished houses.

Ben directed Cooper to park in front of the largest pile of rubble. Jersey got out first. She gave the area a quick check and stepped aside, M-16 at the ready, and nodded an okay to Ben to emerge. Beth stepped out on the opposite side, her heart-shaped face turned to survey their backtrail. Corrie lugged her radio along as she exited. Taking the lead, Ben brought the team around one side of the big house at the end and they looked down into the basin. Shells still fluttered overhead to fall into the basin.

Plumes of smoke and debris rose in huge columns as the rounds detonated. Ben swung his extended arm in an arc. "They've been driven back on themselves. That should create a nice confusion," he observed. "We'll go down there, where those tanks are slugging it out. By the time we get there, Ike's lead element should be well into their assault."

"General," Jersey protested. "You ask me, I think we've got a good place right where we are. We can see everything that's happening."

"But not clearly, Jersey," Ben contradicted. "We might as well be a mile behind the lines as up here."

"General, there's a vehicle headed this way," Beth advised him, a slight edge in her voice.

"Ours or theirs?"

"Theirs, I think."

"Oh, great," Cooper complained. "And us with no way to go except through them."

"A remarkable idea, Cooper," Ben said lightly. "Yes, I think we'll do just that."

"Huh?" Cooper blurted. "We don't know what they might be carrying."

"The question is, do we want to stick around and find out?" Ben bantered, exhilarated by the prospect of a fight.

"There's more of them, on foot, coming up this side of the knob," Jersey warned. "Looks to be about fifteen of them."

"Back to the Hummer, folks," Ben cheerily suggested.

Returned to the light armored vehicle, Ben and his team had only time to take their weapons off safety before the careening truck slewed to a halt some fifty yards away. It spilled men onto the ground who opened fire before they could take aim.

Bullets cracked over Ben's head and he took a firm grip on the old thunder-banger in his hands. The .45 slugs from the Thompson stitched across the chests of three Nazis at a cost of only eleven rounds. Cooper, kneeling behind the motor compartment, loosed a 40mm grenade from his blooper. It detonated on the stake side of the truck. Thin shreds of shrapnel whizzed through the air and flesh with equal ease.

Men screamed and threw up their arms, to topple facefirst in the dirt. Ben dispatched the remaining pair with two 3-round bursts from his Thompson. One Nazi, only slightly wounded by Cooper's grenade, crawled forward relentlessly, his eyes fixed on the tall, rangy figure of Ben Raines. Ever so slowly he eased his rifle into position.

Never taking his gaze off Ben's crouched frame, he worked the butt into the pocket of his shoulder and blinked oily pain sweat from his eyes. The front sight blurred slightly and the black-shirt silently cursed it. Then the picture came into sharp focus. He took a deep breath and began to take up slack on the trigger.

Before the hammer could trip and drive the firing pin forward, Jersey pulped his head with a sustained burst from her M-16. His first dying spasm set off the rifle and sent a round close over the top of Ben's left shoulder.

"Thanks," Ben curtly offered to Jersey.

That left them with time to take up new positions and change for fresh magazines. Then the screaming Nazis crested the top of the knob and ran toward Ben and team across the scraggly, unkempt lawn of the big house.

"Welcome to the party, assholes," Jersey spat as she sent a short burst into the lead three black-shirts.

A small black spheroid flew from the hand of one to bounce on the lawn and roll a couple of feet closer to the Hummer. "Grenade!" Cooper shouted.

Everyone ducked behind the Humvee and the hand bomb exploded a second later. Fragments rattled off the light armor of the general-purpose vehicle and scarred the paint. Ben wet suddenly dry lips and cut his eyes to the Nazis. They had bounded to their feet and rushed dangerously close to the Hummer. He chopped at them with the Thompson until the fifty-round drum ran dry. In a smooth, agile move, Ben rested the hot barrel against the side of the Humvee and drew his .50 Desert Eagle.

His first round splattered a black-shirt thirty feet from them. His next two crippled another hatemonger. He could see the glint of desperation in the eyes of the next Nazi he shot.

Felled as though a switch had been turned off, the dead

black-shirt bounced twice when he hit the ground. Ben pumped his next round into a screaming face not ten feet from where he stood. His last round ended the uneven contest by blowing away the back of a Nazi's head who, had he had a bayonet on his rifle, could have skewered Ben with ease.

Ben looked around at the unmoving bodies. "Well, that's over," he panted.

"General, you still want to go down there?" Jersey asked dubiously.

"Of course. What are we waiting for?" Ben told her, enjoying himself.

Two

Peter Volmer climbed from the cramped rear seat of the two-place, Argentine-made Blanca. Painted silver, it bore the black cross emblem on the fuselage and swastika on the vertical stabilizer. He stepped onto the ramp of a small airfield gouged out by Nazi engineers near the spacious ranch house at Wallowa Lake in Oregon. He was greeted by General Field Marshal Hoffman.

"Heil Hitler!" Volmer saluted his leader.

"Heil," Hoffman responded idly, then instructed this most-powerful American Nazi. "Oh, by the way, it is *Heil Hoffman,* now. I have decided to take up the mantle of my true position as *Führer* of the Western Hemispheric National Socialist Alliance."

"Uh! Ah — congratulations, *mein Führer,"* Volmer stammered. "The world is ripe for a strong leader. You have summoned me for some matter of grave importance, *mein Führer?"*

"Yes, I have. We'll discuss it over cakes and coffee. Come to my headquarters."

Ten minutes later, an orderly served strudel and *kaffeekuchen* to an uncomfortable and impatient Peter Volmer in Jesus Hoffman's office. They stood to lose a rare and important opportunity, Volmer thought, by frittering away time on these amenities, as though it were 1938 in Berlin. From the way Hoffman rambled on, Volmer knew that the newly made *Führer* took himself seriously in this matter. Jesus! Cakes and coffee while

214

the Rebels consolidated their victories at Cheyenne and Denver. At last Hoffman got around to the business at hand.

"Tell me, er, *Brigadeführer,*" Hoffman slipped the promotion in slyly, "what exactly is this plan of yours to rid our *Reich* of Ben Raines?"

Volmer raised eyebrows. He had not missed the change in rank. Equal now to Brodermann, eh? Well, so be it. He had worked hard, made sacrifices for the Party. And his men had fought well, all things considered. Game-playing and politicking didn't suit Peter Volmer, but he decided it to be the best course under the circumstances.

"Did I hear you correctly, *mein Führer? Brigadeführer?* I — I am honored."

"Your men number enough to qualify as a brigade," Hoffman said expansively. "At least they did before . . . Denver. But no matter. I had decided to promote you, so I shall. Now, please enlarge on your plan."

"Thank you, *mein Führer.* It is my intention to employ my *Werwolfen,* in fact they are already shadowing the column of Rebels, led by Ben Raines, that is moving south out of Denver."

"Excellent. Go on."

"With all due respect, *mein Führer,*" Volmer shot his gaze around the room, at the staff officers, "I feel that this is so sensitive a plan that it must remain classified Highest Secret. That way we are assured of success."

Hoffman understood at once. He nodded and addressed the staff. "If you gentlemen will excuse the *Brigadeführer* and myself?" After the disgruntled staff had filed out of the room, Hoffman leaned forward in anticipation. "Now, tell me, Volmer. Tell me everything."

Quickly and concisely, Peter Volmer laid out his grand scheme for snaring Ben Raines in an inescapable trap.

Denver had gone well. The Nazi enclave in the Denver Basin had fallen with minimal losses for the Rebels. By the time Cooper had driven Ben Raines to the point of greatest action, it had become a rear area. Ben pushed on, only to find the complete destruction of the black-shirt units a done deal. After a few hours' rest and a hot meal, Ben organized his tactical commands and pushed on to the south.

Rolling up the Nazis in the southern half of Hoffman's vaunted "Eastern Wall" proved far easier than Ben anticipated. Before long, he and the R Batt breezed along I-25 south two days ahead of all the other units, except for Buddy's task force, assigned to Raton Pass and surrounding area.

"The last time through here," Ben noted irritably as the Hummer struck yet another huge pothole, "we did too damn good of a job wrecking the bridges and roadway."

"You can say that again, General," Cooper agreed over his shoulder.

"Keep your eyes on the road, Cooper," Jersey snapped. Cooper gulped and looked front. Jersey grinned, her face swathed in an aura of innocence.

"General," Beth began hesitantly, unsure of how to present her information. "Do you realize we are out ahead of the forward scouts by at least an hour and a half?"

Ben Raines pondered that. "Hummm. I suppose we are." Then he lightened up. "What do you propose we do about that?"

"Maybe we should slow down and let them catch up. If General McGowan learns of this, he'll be having a fit."

"If we go any slower, we'll be standing still," Ben complained. "We're doing what, Coop?"

"Twenty-five miles per, General," Cooper sang out.

"See there? We're south of Colorado Springs, south of Pueblo, and no sign of resistance. If we move along smartly enough, we can link up with Buddy outside Trinidad."

Fifteen minutes later, the obstructions in the highway began to take on a more orderly appearance. Half a mile further, they became part of a concrete maze that narrowed to a single lane for the movement of anything either direction. When Cooper came upon a phalanx of railroad rails, slanted and sharpened in such a manner as to prevent escape from the maze, Ben ordered a halt.

"This is interesting," he remarked dryly.

"Do you think the black-shirts built it, General?" Beth asked from the seat next to Ben.

"I doubt it. They weren't here long enough. But it is man-made, deliberate. I'd like to take a closer look." Ben reached for the door to the Humvee.

Immediately, heavily armed men and women rose among the blocks of concrete. They wore flowing white robes, the women with hair to their waists, the men with beards and hair almost as long.

"Step out of that car, strangers. Keep your hands in sight and no fast moves," said one of them in a sepulchral voice, heavy with menace.

Several of the women among the ambushers clapped their hands, then pressed them together in a prayerful gesture. "Praise the Lord!" they chanted.

Their men proved more prosaic in their actions. They came forward and quickly snatched rifles from the hands of Cooper, Beth, Corrie, and Jersey. When Jersey resisted by not releasing her grip, she received a sharp backhand slap to the face.

"You son of a bitch!" she barked in outrage.

"Easy, Jersey," Ben Raines cautioned. "I think we've found a group of religious wackos."

"So I gather," Jersey grumbled. Suddenly scarlet suffused her face. "Dammit, General, I've let you down again."

"Not really. These folks were in control from the time we entered their traps."

"No talking," a bulldog-faced man snapped.

One, obviously the leader, looked down at Ben Raines and his team from his astounding height of seven foot one inch. "Identify yourselves," he demanded.

It took some energetic prodding from rifle barrels to get any response. "My name's Cooper," Ben's driver stated sullenly.

"Beth Simms," the shapely young woman answered.

"Corrie Granger," Corrie identified herself.

"They call me Jersey," came resentfully.

"I am General Ben Raines of the Rebel army."

Several of the women covered their faces and shrieked in what sounded like genuine terror. A few made the sign to ward off the evil eye. A number muttered prayers. Surprise washed over the gaunt, drawn face of the giant.

"The Great Satan himself," he roared. "Our Aryan brothers have warned us of you."

"Y'mean this bunch is in with the Nazis?" Jersey asked Ben *sotto voce.*

Big, long ears picked up her whispers clearly. The tall, lean specter bent toward her and spoke again in that hollow, vibrant voice. "No, little lady. We are not a part of the Nazis. Although they share with us a belief in the purity of the white race, they refuse to recognize the authority of *Gawd*," he actually said it like that, drawing out the word from a mouth that formed a perfect "O". "They would also be our masters and not partners, so we dealt with them otherwise."

"How's that? I'm interested," Ben said conversationally.

"We ask the questions, Satan Raines," the huge man thundered. "Your life is forfeit if Gawd so decrees. We are taking you to our settlement, where you will be given a trial and your fate decided."

"If you are going to give us a trial, the least you can do is tell us who you are and who are these people?" Ben insisted.

"These Brothers and Sisters are the Assembly of the End of the World. I am their pastor, Brother Armageddon."

"You were right, boss," Jersey whispered. "A bunch of wackos."

"Silence!" Brother Armageddon bellowed.

"R Batt knows," Corrie told Ben in a whisper, accompanied by a wink.

"Who is R Batt?" Brother Armageddon demanded.

"Why, he's the Rebel god," Ben lied outrageously.

"Heathens," several of the Assembly hissed.

"Devil worshipers," others denounced all Rebels.

"Out of your mouth you have condemned yourselves," Brother Armageddon thundered in righteous indignation. Then he turned to his followers. "Number One, you and Three and Four, bind the hands of the women."

A young woman, who out of her stark robe and stringy hair would have been attractive, hesitated, shrank back into the ring of End of the Worlders. Brother Armageddon glowered at her.

"Wives, obey your husband," he roared.

Ben wondered if he ever spoke in a normal tone. He also noted the implication of polygamy. Armageddon made it clear that a woman's lot would not be ideal among these fanatics. Then, from the direction of the Hummer, he heard a faint click that interrupted the steady, low-level flow of static, followed by two more. Corrie's Mayday signal had been heard and acted on by R Batt. The three clicks indicated that whoever had come forward had them in sight.

That didn't guarantee that they could reach Ben and his team in time. Conscious of this, Ben Raines decided to stall for as long as he could. Fortunately, they had so far neglected to remove his big Desert Eagle .50 pistol from the holster. That could prove useful. Summoning his knowledge of more-orthodox religions, Ben prepared to argue with Brother Armageddon.

"Tell me about this god of yours," he urged Armageddon. "I would like to know more."

Unable to resist the desire to obtain yet another convert, Brother Armageddon willingly walked into Ben's trap. "Why, He is the god of the universe, Lord of all. It is He who brought on us the Great War, as punishment for our wicked ways."

"I can't argue with that," Ben offered with a rueful

chuckle.

Brother Armageddon looked surprised. "Why, no one can. Not even the Great Satan Ben Raines. He also visited us with the plague, to purge us of nonbelievers."

"It appears to me that an awful lot survived," Ben remarked.

"Why, that was His will, to which we all must bend," Armageddon explained in an almost-conversational tone. "Can't you see it? It was all explained in the Book of Revelation."

While receiving this lesson in theology, Ben had been watching from the corner of his eye while camo-clad Rebel scouts and snipers had been slithering through the underbrush. Now, three more clicks came from the radio Corrie had left turned on in the Hummer. Ben let himself relax into the familiar calm before action and decided to punch up the pressure somewhat.

"What about the Antichrist? He hasn't had his thousand-year reign and yet you say this is the end of the world."

Brother Armageddon looked confused a moment, then swelled his chest and roared at Ben, "It is you! You are the Antichrist, Ben Raines!"

"I don't think so," Ben answered as his hand closed over the grip of his Desert Eagle.

He whipped it clear as the two Assemblymen most directly in line to fire on Ben's team jolted backward and fell to the ground. "Run, girls," Ben commanded.

Although trussed like turkeys for the chopping block, Corrie, Beth, and Jersey took off to the meaty sound of bullets impacting in flesh. Cooper made a dive for the religious fanatic holding his beloved CAR-15 while Ben sent a round toward Brother Armageddon.

Ben's bullet cut through the cloth of Armageddon's robe and did no harm. An angry shout from another of the holy-joes forced him to change targets. Ben found himself looking at the muzzle of a Remington 700 in excellent condition as he triggered another shot. The big .50 slug smashed into the chest of the man with the

Remington. It drove him backward, feet windmilling, and he dropped the rifle. Ben put a safety shot in the End of the Worlder's gut as a fusillade broke out from the hillside to Ben's right.

With the team and Ben safely out of the line of fire, the Rebels opened up on the religious crazies. Armageddon began at once to bellow orders. His followers responded with alacrity.

"Retreat! Scatter and hide from the imps of Satan," Armageddon bellowed.

Giving no resistance, the flock ran off over the hilly ground, soon to be lost from sight. The Rebels ceased firing. Cooper came to his feet with his CAR-15 trained on the man who had formerly held it.

"I got one, General. Maybe he can tell us something about his crazy boss."

"I will tell you nothing," the man said stoutly. "God is my protection and my seal."

Ben Raines bent over him, his composure ruffled by this encounter. "A little of Dr. Chase's babble juice and you'll be telling us all the intimate details of your great-grandmother's love life," he growled. When a couple of Rebel scouts trotted up, Ben indicated the captive.

"Take him off and chemically debrief him."

Answers began to reach Ben quickly. Brother Armageddon, it turned out, had been born Archibald Culp. He had operated a cult before the Great War that sounded like a GM plant: the Assembly of the Body of Jesus. His latest scam had come out of the turmoil of the war and plague that followed. His present headquarters lay in a valley beyond North La Veta Pass in the San Isabel Mountains, part of the Rockies. They numbered about 250 effective fighting men, supplemented by 75 women with combat experience. They would, the captive insisted, bring havoc down on Ben Raines and all Rebel servants of Satan. Ben gave this and the immediacy of his mission to aid General Payon considerable thought. Frowning, he announced his decision an hour after encountering the End of the Worlders.

"We can't leave that large a nest of armed idiots behind us," he declared. "They could cut our lines of communication and supply, raise hell with the troops following us." He turned to Bull McDade. "Stan, get the R Batt ready to advance on La Veta Pass. We're going to take out Brother Armageddon and then move on."

Brother Armageddon might be a few bricks shy when it came to theology, but he proved adept at military matters. La Veta Pass had been mined, and more tank traps abounded. Ben Raines traveled directly behind the spearhead of the R Batt column. The flash from behind them lighted the interior of the Humvee.

"What was that?" Corrie asked, surprise clear in her voice.

"Antitank mine," Ben said tightly.

"Eagle, we took a hit," crackled the tank commander's voice from Corrie's radio.

"Unass that thing," Ben barked unnecessarily. Corrie was already relaying the same information.

Flames leapt up around one tread and shattered bogie wheel when the hatches flew open and the tank crew bailed out. One Rebel tanker cried out and went to his knees when a sniper's bullet pierced his thigh. The turret on another of the three M-1As swiveled to the hillside and the coaxial .30 MG stitched a shroud for the hidden gunman.

"Peace and nonviolence, my ass," growled Jersey.

"To quote our friend Emil from a few years ago, 'There's nothing like highly motivated self-interest to stimulate a reliance on arms,' " Ben quipped.

Jersey made a face. Outside, the tank reclaimer had crawled forward and started to pull the wounded Abrams out of the way. Ben nodded to it. "Corrie, have them clean out some of these dragon's teeth while they're at it. Use explosives if necessary."

"Getting right on it, General," she said cheerily. "Maybe we should have someone up here to probe for mines?"

"You're learning, girl," Ben complimented.

Two long, tedious hours went by while the part-time engineers with R Batt cleared the roadway of obstructions and hazards. At last the convoy got under way. Much of the snow had melted, and patches clung to the shaded southern slope. The ditches to either side of State 160 ran like fresh mountain streams. Ben urged greater speed. He was eager to make a finish of the religious fanatics and be on the way to Mexico.

The Rebel advance came out of the pass and down a long, winding grade into the valley with still five hours of daylight left. When they hit the valley floor, Ben ordered them to spread out, and raced forward with the point platoon. His heavy armor protectors rumbled along behind, second best in the speed department. In the distance he saw a cluster of buildings, all of recent origin and apparently crudely built.

From there came the first mortar rounds that began to shower down on the Rebel point.

Three

Colonel McDade posed a thorny question to Ben Raines while Ben and the point platoon scrambled to avoid the mortar rounds. "Same rules of engagement as with the Nazis?"

"Negative on that, Stan," Ben responded, shouting over the ear-slamming blast of mortar rounds. "Any of the younger women who want out, and all kids under twelve, to go to Base Camp One. If most of these people stop hearing the bullshit Armageddon is spouting, there's hope for them. At least I'm betting there is."

Ben considered changing his mind on that a few minutes later when he spotted three X-shaped scaffolds on a hillside behind the cult's meeting hall. Two wretched individuals had recently been crucified on a pair of these. Ben pointed it out to the occupants of the Hummer.

"Want to bet those aren't stragglers who accidently wandered into the valley recently?"

"No bet, boss," Jersey stated, tight-lipped. "What kind of crapheads would do a thing like that?"

"The sort we've just run—Look out!" Ben ended in a shout.

A huge old earthmoving machine had lumbered directly into the path of the Hummer. It bore down on them, its tall stack belching black diesel fumes. Cooper cut to the right, then swung straight to no avail. Twelve-foot-high tires rumbled by close enough to shake the Humvee. The articulated vehicle rammed past and reversed itself with surprising speed. Ben lowered a window and tried for a shot at the operator's cab.

His Thompson rapped out a three-round burst and the slugs sang off the thick plates of counterweight on the nose of the bright yellow monster. The worn engine clattered as the driver poured on full throttle. Cooper spun tires in loose soil as he fought the wheel of the Hummer. Roostertails of dirt fanned out from the rear of the armored vehicle. Ben tried again and managed to put two rounds through the radiator.

Ben reached to the combat harness snugged over his shoulders and slipped a grenade from its retainer. "When I say to, brake hard, Coop, and throw the wheel all the way to the right."

Cooper nodded, and Ben pulled the pin. Clasping the spoon tightly, he squeezed his broad shoulders and chest out the window and freed his throwing arm. The earthmover loomed over them, rapidly approaching for a broadside slam. Ben slipped the spoon and shouted in the same instant.

"Now, Coop. Hit it!"

Foot heavy on the brake, Cooper spun the wheel to the right as Ben's count got to two. With a savage roar, the story-and-a-half machine flashed past the Humvee. Ben lobbed the grenade on three.

"Gun it!" Ben shouted. "Get the hell out of here."

The grenade plopped through an open door on the side of the cab and went off immediately. Showers of safety glass bits mushroomed outward. Many had instantly been washed with a spray of blood. Driverless, the formidable monstrosity rumbled on until it struck the stone structure that served as the cult's meeting house.

Its nose rose upward while the dirt-hopper portion continued forward. Upended, the drive unit snapped the gooseneck and fell on top of the rear portion. Ben took his first secure breath in a long minute. It tasted sweeter than clear mountain air on a frosty morning.

"Great improviser, ain't he?" Jersey gasped out.

"Corrie, check with the point," Ben requested, ignoring Jersey.

"You're . . . going on?" she asked, still unsettled by their close call with the rampaging construction equipment. "Here," she answered a second later, chastened by her knowledge of Ben Raines.

"We've come under heavy fire at a low building, looks to be mostly dug into the hillside. Some sort of bunker. They've got machine guns," the point lieutenant reported to Ben.

"I don't need to tell you your job, Lieutenant Crowe, just see that you neutralize that place."

"Yes, sir, Eagle. I have men bringing up a wire-guided rocket now. My assistant squad leaders are using their bloopers."

Ben smiled tightly. "You're doing everything I would. Keep up the good work. Eagle out."

Terrible blasts and the ruffled air of cannon rounds in flight advised Ben that the tanks had located the mortar batteries. Once they got knocked out, it would be just a question of mop-up.

"Lady Gloria, this is Eagle," Ben radioed, to contact the tank nearest them, which he recognized.

"This is the Lady, Eagle. Sergeant Gomez commander, sir."

"Are you using beehive, Gomez?"

"Roger that, Eagle. Also gas."

"Jesus," Ben ejected forcefully.

"Oh, not *that* gas, sir. Just the nausea and pepper stuff."

Ben chuckled, and spoke to the team. "Stan's right on top of it." To the tank commander, "Good hunting, Lady. Eagle out."

Unbidden, Cooper set out in the direction indicated by the point leader's report of heavy action. The building looked odd, all right. Like part of a castle from the Middle Ages, cut off and transported to Colorado. Narrow firing ports allowed for interlocking fire to protect the approaches, and lateral ones provided for the traverse of machine guns. Not a bit of glass or a doorway could be seen.

"They go in and out by way of a shaft from above," Ben surmised to the team. "It's going to be a bitch to dig them out of there. Direct fire from the MBTs is the best bet."

"What about one of the four-inchers on a Bradley, General?"

"I knew you were going to be worth something someday, Cooper," Ben jested back. "Corrie, get one over here pronto."

It arrived in a shower of churned-up sod. Ben talked to the commander, who studied the situation a second and suggested that the Rebel personnel be cleared from the area.

"Then I'll put a HEAT round in there and crack some eggs," he added.

"Go for it," Ben urged.

It took ten minutes to disengage and pull back the Rebel troops. Then the Bradley lined up and pumped a 75mm high-explosive antitank round into the stone face. The delayed fuse allowed the hardened steel nosecone to punch through like a single-jack drill, a cloud of dust and rock chips in its wake. A soft crump followed, then the front of the blockhouse bulged outward and came apart like a watermelon shot with a 12-gauge punkin ball.

"Hit the magazine," the Bradley commander observed in an awed, quiet voice.

Immediately, resistance slackened. World's Enders tried to surrender, to be shot down by hard-faced Rebels. The rest, driven by desperation, hung on to the bloody end. Ben thanked the Bradley crew and then added, "Keep up the good work. I'm going after Brother Armageddon."

"Brother who?"

There hadn't been time to fully brief everyone in R Batt, Ben realized. He explained as the distance between the Hummer and Bradley widened. The search soon became futile. Either the cult leader had perished in the bunker or he had somehow managed to evade the steel-tipped dragnet of Rebel troops.

After half an hour, Ben had to admit to himself that somehow Brother Armageddon and an unknown number of followers had managed to escape from the valley. "No doubt," he told Colonel McDade and the other officers, "they took State 150 west in the early stage of the assault. I had him figured for a guy who'd be careful to cover his ass. Only I expected it to be some sort of hidey-hole. At least he's been reduced to a harmless irritant. Clean up the last of this mess and we'll move on south to Trinidad."

Peter Volmer sat at a desk in the office accorded him by the *Führer*, Jesus Hoffman. The walls were covered with maps, the desk with the latest intelligence summaries. Somewhere out there, Ben Raines prowled the countryside. Peter Volmer literally ached with the desire to capture and exterminate this insult to their superiority.

He made repeated circles and arrows on the acetate overlays of the maps. Only one of them truly represented the whereabouts of Ben Raines and his Rebels. Slowly, inspiration came to Volmer. Reports of Rebel attacks continued to come in from the northern end of their eastern wall. Yet, more came from the south. Denver had fallen. Fleeing members of his own American Nazi Party had reported Rebels in large numbers advancing southward along the line from Denver toward the Mexican border. Reports of the use of the Rebel call sign Eagle had all but ceased to exist in the north.

Volmer's troops had managed to obtain several Rebel radios intact, complete with scrambler units. Fortunately for the Rebels, the operators had managed to destroy the SOI and SSI (Signal Operating Information and Standard Signal Instructions), leaving it a hit-or-miss operation to intercept and descramble Rebel communications. They had managed to establish that the majority of "Eagle" calls came from the southern end of the defensive wall. And "Eagle" had to be Ben Raines. Satisfied with that interpretation, Volmer decided to act.

He left his office for that of his personal communications officer. Rather than draft a message and have it sent through normal channels, he trusted his own people more. He excused the operator on duty and sat at the radio console. On a white pad he drafted his message and opened a channel to the headquarters of his Werewolves.

"This is Werewolf One, *Brigadeführer*," Siegfried Dracher announced when he responded to the summons to his communications van.

"Excellent, *Standartenführer*. After considerable investigation and evaluation, I have come to a conclusion regarding your major assignment. From here on, the project is classified Most High Secret, and code-named Eagle. You are to take your command and proceed at all possible haste to the vicinity of Carlsbad, New Mexico. There you will deploy, set up your diversion and the principal ruse, and stand by to intercept the subject of Eagle. Is that clear?"

"*Jawohl, Herr Brigadeführer*," young Dracher replied, his voice breaking.

"You are to remain out of sight from even friendly forces until you are able to effect the intercept. You are to operate in absolute secrecy throughout and to carry out your mission in such a way that no one knows the identity of the troops involved. Do you have any questions?"

"*Nein, Herr Brigadeführer*."

"Excellent. You're a good boy, Sigie. Remember that boating trip two years ago on the lake?"

Volmer could not see Dracher blush furiously on the other end. Dracher vividly recalled that trip. To his eternal self-contempt he remembered every detail. "Yes, *Herr Brigadeführer*. It was the high point of my life," he forced himself to say.

"Well, then," Volmer offered in a rush. "What you are about to accomplish will become the new high point, I assure you. There is nothing you need? No last-minute questions? You are to maintain complete radio silence until the mission is completed."

"There is nothing. I understand, *Herr Brigadeführer*."

"Fine, *Standartenführer*. Volmer, clear."

Now, Ben Raines, he thought fiercely after setting down the stand microphone, your days are numbered.

Tiny slits of headlights materialized out of the darkness north of Trinidad, Colorado. Silhouettes of canvas-topped trucks, lowboys, and tanks took on substance in the wash of pink light that intensified in the east. Ben Raines and the R Batt rolled along I-25, five miles north of the city. A brief flash from a shielded high-intensity light slowed the column. Ben directed the Hummer to a spot at the base of a rounded hill. There he and Jersey climbed from the back of the vehicle.

Ben greeted his son warmly, with a big Latin-style *abrazo*. Buddy stepped back, his dark hair floating out from under a headband on the light dawn breeze. "Dad, you look worried."

Ben dismissed it with a wave of his hand. "We ran onto a band of religious nuts. Why that sort of thinking holds such fascination for people I don't understand. Anyway, we fought."

"Yeah," Buddy responded. "We monitored the radio traffic. Is it true that they crucified two people?"

"They'd done it to more than that before we got there," Ben answered tiredly. "The weird practices of these cults is so counterproductive to survival, it's a wonder they haven't all died out."

"Well, there was Sister Voleta."

Ben winced at Buddy's mention of his mother. That had all been history for several years. But the boy had a point. For all her craziness, Sister Voleta had held her organization together and even enlarged it since way before the Battle of New York. Her ultimate downfall had come, Ben believed, from the internal decay of her sick cult as much as from the deliberate campaign he had directed against the woman who had borne this strapping young man before him. He decided to cut to the chase.

"What are your dispositions around Trinidad?" Ben

asked his son.

"We're deployed to the east and here in the north. I was thinking that the R Batt might want to take the south side of the Nazi positions to prevent them from slipping down to the American SS holding the pass or on to Raton."

Ben's grin flashed in the first intense white glow of dawn. "You know, you're about ready to take command of this whole shebang."

"No, Dad. I could never do that."

"Oh, I don't know. Whatever, I had the same idea. We'll pass through your lines to the east and close off access to Raton Pass."

"Are you going to do it by day?" Buddy asked.

"No. We'll settle in under the trees and wait for tonight. I figure they must have observers out."

"Oh, they do. They know we're here, but haven't done anything about it so far."

Ben smiled grimly. "When we bite them in the ass, they'll do something. Now we've got to get these vehicles out of sight and I'm for some breakfast. Join me?"

"Sure, I can always eat," Buddy offered enthusiastically.

"So I've noticed," Ben said dryly.

Obersturmbannführer (Lt. Col.) Erik Klein commanded in Trinidad. He was a cautious man by nature, and relatively well-read in military subjects. Unfortunately for him and his troops, he suffered from a severe lack of respect for the Rebel army. He spent most of the day Gen. Ben Raines arrived outside his area leafing through reports of his intelligence staff and other observers. As the evidence of Rebel positions grew, he noticed one glaring error.

"Whoever is commanding this Rebel scum has made a terrible tactical mistake," he remarked to his executive officer. "They assume that, if attacked, we would move north toward the *Führer's* bastion in Oregon. He has closed off access to the east, naturally, to preserve Rebel territory, but placed the rest of his force to our north.

Should the situation require it, that allows us to withdraw to the south and join our *Kameraden* in Raton Pass."

"Ummm. I should think they would be aware of that," Major Richard Gross observed.

"It is said General Raines remains in close touch with Denver and Cheyenne, both in Rebel hands as of now. This might be some young, untried commander," Klein opined. "No matter. See to it that contingency plans are made for us to take advantage of that omission."

"I will at once," Gross replied.

Thirty minutes later, at 1640 hours, the Rebel shelling began.

It caught the American Nazis by surprise. Rounds from 155mm guns dropped in the rear areas of the SS defenses, blasting two field kitchens to steaming ruins. Tents and vehicles suffered mightily. One Six-by hurtled into the clear mountain sky, trailing a stream of fire from its ruptured gas tanks. Casualties began to mount.

Other rounds fell on the entrenched positions of the line companies. Rebel FOs had the advantage of the heights around the Nazi defenses. They called in pinpoint fire on machine-gun nests, armor, and armored personnel carriers. Whizzing shrapnel kept down the heads of SS troopers. Confusion in the rear echelon escalated into pandemonium. By the time darkness fell and Ben's R Batt got on the move, the Nazis were in no condition to take note of it. *Obersturmbannführer* Erik Klein summed up the situation in a mood of white-lipped, impotent fury.

"This Rebel commander may be lacking in tactical experience, but he is painfully aware of the value of artillery. Damn the man! And damn Ben Raines."

Four

Ben Raines turned away from the map on the wall of his mobile CP. "Buddy is putting on pressure to the north and east. The Nazis would have to push through the ruins of the city to head west. I think it's time to load up in the Hummer. We're going to have some visitors soon."

Concern colored Jersey's words. "Boss, you haven't had a full night's sleep since before we met those holy lunatics."

Ben stifled a yawn. "Don't remind me. We'll be in Santa Rosa before I get the chance, the way I see it."

Ten minutes later, inside the Hummer, pathfinder scouts reported light probing action by the black-shirts. Ben leaned forward and spoke to Cooper. "Take us up with those pathfinders. I want to see what we're facing."

A twelve-man patrol had been allowed to slip through the advance screen of R Batt. Ben observed them from the Humvee while they did a fairly professional job of reconnoitering the old interstate south toward Raton Pass. Ben keyed the mike when the last of them went past the deep shadows where the Hummer sat.

"Stop them three hundred meters short of our main lines," he commanded.

There would be more to follow, he knew. They came twenty minutes later. Three trucks, escorted by armored personnel carriers. Ben let them come up close, then gave the command to fire.

"Stop them here and then pull back to form a pocket," he concluded.

Streams of tracers slashed into the unprotected trucks. Screams came from the occupants, some of whom tumbled dead onto the roadway. The APCs reacted instantly, disgorging ready troops, who spread out and returned fire as well as the darkness allowed. One of the squat, slant-sided vehicles geared up and raced directly for Ben's Hummer.

"Bail out, people," Ben advised as he hit the door latch.

He hit the ground rolling and came up with his Thompson ready and yammering. Forty-five slugs spanged off the light armor of the rampaging APC. It continued to swell in size as its engine raced. Then Cooper fired a grenade round that dropped behind the armored front into the open-top troop compartment. It went off with a fearsome flash and bang.

Concussion disabled the driver, who fell across his controls. That caused the armored vehicle to veer to the right and run past the Hummer with engine screaming. It proceeded on to the verge of a ravine and launched out into space, before settling nose-first into the streambed below.

In the abrupt silence that followed the APC's end, Ben caught sight of half a dozen black-shirts rushing their direction. They might be intent on a rescue attempt, but Ben hadn't the luxury of giving them the benefit of a doubt. Vertical tongues of flame spurted from the compensator on the muzzle of Ben's tommygun. The lethal hot lead chewed into running men, who tumbled like rag dolls thrown by an angry child.

"This is getting too personal," Jersey suggested from her place beside him. "Let's get back in the Hummer."

"It's just getting exciting," Ben protested, a fierce grin spreading his lips. He saw movement to his left and turned the Thompson in that direction.

Bullets sprayed the darkness and a scream came from one unfortunate Nazi. Ben paused to change the drum magazines and put his old faithful back in action. In the

234

interim, more of the Nazi horde came pelting out of their compound outside Trinidad.

"There's too many of them, General," Beth declared. "We'd better draw back while we can."

Ben chucked a grenade at a clump of disorganized Nazis and followed it with a trio of five-round bursts. Not so numerous, nor so crazed as the creepies, the black-shirts kept coming in disciplined rushes. Reluctantly, Ben gave council to good advice and climbed into the Hummer. Cooper kicked the utility vehicle to life and they scooted out of there only seconds ahead of the Nazi armor.

Wire-guided missiles came into play as the rumble of heavy tanks filled the night. Ben and his team strained to watch what happened behind. Night became midday within a second of impact by the Rebel missiles. In the aftermath, the Rebels withdrew according to Ben's plan.

"Well, we certainly got their attention," Ben quipped as he reached for a plastic bottle of Colorado spring water.

"We've been trapped!" Major Gross shouted as he burst into *Obersturmbannführer* Klein's operations center.

"Easy, Richard, what is it now?" Klein asked tiredly.

"Somehow, the goddamned Rebels positioned troops to the south of us. Reports from the surviving officers of the retrograde force indicate a strength of at least a battalion. They have armor and a madman who single-handedly destroyed an armored personnel carrier and some eleven footsoldiers."

"One man?" Klein demanded, incredulous. Then he thought it through. "Ben Raines. By God, we've got Ben Raines caught between us and the troops in the pass. Get on the radio and alert Miller to send a reconnaissance in force this direction. We have a chance to destroy the Rebel high command." Smirking, Klein went to the map table. "Show me exactly where our men came under fire."

A messenger rushed inside the operations center, eyes wild, face ashen. "Rebels are inside our eastern lines,

Herr Obersturmbannführer. The northern sector is collapsing. Major Pritz fears a general route in the making."

"Damn them. Damn the Rebel *Schwein!* All right," Klein went on, recovering his temperament. "My orders are for every command to restore order and to realign for immediate movement to the south. We'll push into the Rebels there and perhaps overrun Ben Raines," he added, eyes glowing.

Tightly fitted into the protective platoon of Rebels, the Humvee occupied by Ben Raines sat on a promontory overlooking the fighting below. Corrie, eyes alight with satisfaction, presented the radio handset to Ben.

"Buddy on the line, General. All resistance in the Trinidad operational area is crumbling. He reports several columns of Nazi vehicles headed south."

Ben spoke into the mouthpiece. "This is Eagle, go, Rat."

"We're coasting through the Nazi fortifications, Eagle," Buddy's voice crackled back, robbed of emotion by the scrambler.

"Roger that, Rat. Only, don't you think it is a little too easy?"

Buddy paused to consider. "Not when they're running directly toward you, Eagle. And I do mean running."

"We'll be waiting," Ben assured his son. "What say you come in on them from behind?"

"My thoughts exactly," Buddy handed back. "You know, I'm sure glad *I'm* not fighting you. You can be as devious as hell's host at times."

"Why, thank you, Rat. I take that as a compliment. Report when you link up with your northern elements and head after the Nazi scum-suckers. Eagle out."

Ben sighed as he handed back the instrument. "Buddy's feeling his nuts. Even with that scrambler unit, I can tell he's having the time of his life."

"Only you hope he don't stick his neck too far out and get his head chopped off, huh, boss?" Jersey put Ben's disquiet into words he would never say.

Rather, he gave her a tight-lipped nod. "I want to get a look at this retreating column of Nazis. Coop, can you find enough side roads to take us up close?"

"Now, General," Beth objected. "You are supposed to stay right here with the platoon."

Ben made a face. "Ike McGowan's been chewing again," he speculated rightly. "People, Ike's three hundred miles away, and Chase is with him, so I think I can tend the store without their help."

Grinning, Cooper turned to eye the general. "I've already worked out a route that should do it for us."

"You two," Beth complained with a toss of her long locks. "Men are all alike. Always off on a lark. The only difference between small boys and grown men is the size of their toys."

"And how dangerous they are," Corrie added as an afterthought.

"The toys or the men?" Ben asked, picking up on their banter.

"Both," Beth and Corrie chorused.

Cooper hadn't need to take to the roads. Ten minutes later, the advance elements of the Nazi retreat to Raton Pass slammed into the Rebel lines.

Laughing, Cooper started the Hummer and eased along with the protective screen for Ben Raines. "Looks like they got here before you could go look for them, General."

"You got that right, Coop. Let's see if we can find any of their command elements. I've an idea these are mostly American Nazis. Without a head, they'll be easily scattered."

"Why so, General, if I may ask," Beth queried.

"Remember the mob in that drive-in back in Nebraska? They fought us rather well when Volmer was there. But they came to pieces when he skinnied out on them and took all the leaders except for one."

"You're right, boss," Jersey added her bit. "And Tina called them more Nazi than Hoffman's storm troopers.

237

They're strong on theory and singing songs, but not had the chance to become good fighters."

"Combat troops don't come from singing the "Horst Wessel Song" and spray-painting swastikas on synagogues — or whatever hate activities they thought up after the Great War," Ben agreed. "Corrie, bump R Batt commo and have them triangulate the center of most outgoing Nazi radio traffic."

Jersey gave Ben a wink. "You're going ahead with it, aren't you, boss?"

"Whatever gave you that idea?" Ben asked with a feigned look of innocence.

After twenty minutes, during which Ben consumed two hand-rolled cigarettes, Corrie gave him the word. "We have a choice of three places. If I can see that map, Cooper." She oriented herself quickly and identified the locations, pointing them out to Ben.

"Here, and here. And right here, directly in front of us."

Mischief flashed in Ben's eyes. "Any preferences?"

Cooper got them to the eastern, or right, flank of the Nazi movement toward Raton in quick order. To the surprise of the team and Ben Raines, they slipped from their lines through the vangard of the approaching black-shirts without being challenged. Ben recklessly made a quick decision.

"Let's find that comm van. I think we should pay them a call."

"Need we remind you that we're out here without the platoon?" Beth asked quietly.

"All the more reason we got away with this so far," Ben countered. "If we play this right, we can wipe out the entire command center for this column."

"Colonel Ike won't like you taking those kind of chances," Jersey mentioned.

"I suppose not. But remember what Napoléon said: *'L'audasse, l'audasse, toujours l'audasse.'* "

"What?" Jersey asked, nose wrinkled. "My French ain't so good."

"Napoléon advises us to be audacious, always audacious. We'll just walk in there like we belong and blow up their comm van."

Jersey threw her free hand in the air; the other held her M-16. "The man's lost his marbles."

"Hide and watch, Jersey," Ben suggested.

Give or take fifty yards, Cooper drove them to the exact spot indicated on the map. Without satellite oversight, Rebel tracking was a little lacking in accuracy. Good enough, though. What looked like a large refrigerated, dual-wheeled truck, painted forest-camo colors, bristled with antennas as it rolled along a state highway that paralleled I-25. Road conditions and shelling harassment from Buddy's Rebels had reduced their progress to a brisk walking pace.

At Ben's direction, Cooper swung the Humvee in beside the thick-walled truck. Ben and Jersey stepped from the halted Hummer and caught up with the rear of the Nazi vehicle. A lift gate served as a stoop outside a low door. Ben plucked a Rebel version of the M-26 fragger from his battle harness and pulled the pin after he had climbed to the platform.

Jersey, eyes as nervous as the rest of her, kept watch for Ben. He rapped on the door and it opened a moment later. The staccato rattle of radio voices came from the interior. Ben looked the surprised Nazi in the eyes and tossed the grenade beyond him.

"Adiós, asshole," the CG of all Rebel forces said before he jumped from the lift gate to the comparative safety of the road.

A wild scream of terror preceded the explosion of the grenade. In such confined quarters, with its thickened walls, the little strips of wire shrapnel did terrible damage. In a flicker, all communication with this column ceased to exist.

"On our way, children," Ben declared as he returned to the Hummer.

* * *

Ben had Cooper remain behind the lead elements of the Nazi retreat. Confusion and fear haunted the common troopers. Most naturally assumed that any vehicle that drove about purposefully within their ranks had a reason for being there. What they didn't know was what that reason happened to be.

"We'll work our way to the other flank and take out that comm center next," Ben advised his team.

"General, we're likely to get our ass in a crack," Cooper protested.

"You, too, Coop? I thought you were on my side."

"Coop is right, for once," Jersey added. "Our necks are stuck out far enough. *Yours* is stuck out way too damn far."

Ben helped himself to coffee from the large stainless thermos. He considered rolling another cigarette, but his tobacco supply had dwindled in the past week. "Jersey, we're simply doing some creative terrorizing. Get these people unhinged and we won't have near so many to fight in the pass."

Jersey grinned, more her old self again. "Now, that's something worth taking a chance or two, for sure."

"And I promise, no one will have his or her neck out far enough to feel the bite of an ax," Ben put a cap on the topic.

Captain Thermopolis had his hands full of Nazis that night, too. It had grown bitterly cold in the high country around Casper, Wyoming. The Headquarters Company, reinforced by the bikers of Leadfoot and Wanda, had stalled out against heavy resistance. It called, Thermopolis decided, for some creative thinking.

"Leadfoot, some of your bikers have old coal-scuttle German helmets, don't you?"

"Yeah. A few," the huge ex-outlaw biker replied.

"Anyone taken a few souvenirs from the modern Nazi slime?"

Leadfoot's brow wrinkled in concentration. "I could

scrounge maybe twenty armbands, some death's-head cap badges."

"These American vermin wear cammies almost like our own. How'd you like to report in for duty with the Nazis in Casper?"

"You're shittin' me?"

"No, only too serious. At least the ruse of you all dolled up in Nazi regalia might hold up to get you past their sentries and pointed in the right direction for the headquarters. The rest will be up to you."

A grin replaced Leadfoot's worry lines. "We'll kick the shit outta them."

"I certainly hope so," Thermopolis advised. "Oh, and be sure and come back."

Leadfoot gave Thermopolis the universal gesture of an extended middle finger. Then, with a wolfish expression, he set out to organize his bikers.

Twenty minutes later they rolled into the rubble-strewn streets at the outskirts of Casper. *"Heil Hitler!"* Leadfoot greeted the first Nazi he saw.

"Where have you been?" an American voice answered him. "It's *Heil Hoffman* now."

"No shit? What brought that on?"

"Our South American friend has declared himself *Führer* of the Americas. It should have been Peter Volmer's place to do that," he complained. "Where'd you come from?"

"Out west, by way of down south," Leadfoot gave confusingly. "We come to join up. Goddamn, how we hate Ben Raines."

"Who don't? You gotta check in at headquarters."

"Where's that?" The American black-shirt gave Leadfoot directions through the remains of Casper. Leadfoot *"Heiled"* him again and the bikers took off.

"Now what do we do?" Beerbelly asked over the rumble of Harley engines.

"We go to the headquarters like good little boys and blow them off the fucking map," Leadfoot informed his second-in-command.

"Just like that?"

"Yeah. Just like that," Leadfoot echoed. "We got satchel charges, which our good brothers can plant while we're inside bullshittin' with the brass, there's enough plastic explosive to plant in the can and other places, timer fuses, too. They'll have a real party there about three minutes after we pull out."

"That's cuttin' it kinda close," Beerbelly objected.

Leadfoot gave him a vulpine "V" grin. "Makes it more exciting. I've gotten sorta bored lately."

Leadfoot took three bikers into the headquarters building, a converted modular home that had somehow survived the years of depredations. There he strung a line of crap for the officer in command while his subordinates got busy planting plastic explosive in unobtrusive places.

At last, satisfied that Leadfoot and his companions were genuine, the commander assigned them to an area of the perimeter and dismissed them. Back on their hogs, they rode laughing wildly into the darkness. It was the last the Nazis of Casper would see of them.

With a ripple effect, the explosives blew the modular house into a cloud of splinters and totally eliminated the leadership of the black-shirt troops. A huge fireball rose in the night, and flames continued to burn while Thermopolis launched an attack that totally exterminated every last Nazi rat in the nest.

Five

Five Rebels died in the first assault on Raton, New Mexico. Ben Raines considered that an acceptable loss figure when three hundred goose-stepping Nazi slime died in the same three minutes. Resistance outside Trinidad had become a screaming rout after Ben and his team visited the second communications van of the black-shirt withdrawal from the area. Following quickly on the heels of the demoralized troops, they discovered the message had carried clearly to Major Miller, who commanded at the pass.

Ben's Rebels found the pass deserted. Only a few random rounds came from the last Nazi tanks to join in the race for Raton. Jubilant Rebels followed. The pace slowed when booby traps and land mines began to take a toll of vehicles and men. Ben Raines waited out the delay impatiently, knowing that it gave opportunity for the commander in Raton to strengthen his positions.

He had done that, Ben learned in that first bloody three minutes. Unwilling to spend Rebel lives unnecessarily, the advance stalled out while landing gear got unchained and crewmen fitted main rotor blades into position on the Apache gunships. In less than half an hour, the ungainly warbirds received a checkout and cleared for flight. The AH-64s lifted off all but silently in clouds of dust and leaves.

Ben Raines, back in the Hummer, watched their insectile shapes cruise past overhead and line up on the

243

targets below. Ben admired the courage of the crews who manned these aged craft. Each had logged more hours on its airframe than the manufacturer had ever dreamed possible, yet they faithfully served the Rebels' needs.

Their four wing hardpoints flashed fire as mixed bags of eight Hellfire missiles and thirty-six 2.5-inch rockets sped off to bring mind-numbing destruction to the black-shirts. From turrets slung under their bellies 30mm chainguns made a path of destruction that Rebel troops could follow into the heart of the Nazi resistance.

Shock and confusion became frantic disorder. Ben urged Cooper closer to the crumbling resistance. The Hummer leapt forward and slewed around a burning black-shirt tank. Everywhere death seemed to come with unexpected ferocity. The radio squawked and Corrie offered the handset to Ben.

"Eagle, this is Rat. We've come on a large pocket of stiff resistance."

"What are you looking at, Rat?" Ben came back.

"The bastards are dug into hillsides. A lot of them, and they have buried armor so we can't use the ERIX missiles. Plenty of infantry, too."

"Hang on, Rat. Corrie, bump R Batt, I want to talk to McDade." When Bull McDade came on the line, Ben explained what he wanted.

"I don't know, Ben," Lieutenant Colonel McDade responded. "Those rockets aren't as reliable as the old Sov BM-21s."

McDade referred to the 122mm 40-tube multiple launch unit mounted on a truck bed. Rebel R&D had made close duplicates from some General Striganov had with his army in Canada. Two batteries traveled with R Batt. Ike McGowan had more with his command. Trouble was, the Rebel version lacked much of the sophistication of the 1964 Soviet version of the old Stalin Organ of World War II.

"I remember Georgi had some with him when we first locked horns," McDade went on. "Some blew up as they left the tubes, as I recall."

"Yeah," Ben agreed. "Only our R&D people have bore-safed them. It was a matter of Soviet indifference to human life and lousy quality control. Besides, Buddy needs something strong and nasty to crack bunkers with indirect fire. It's worth the risk."

"A big ten-four to that," Lieutenant Colonel McDade approved. "We'll pull them up now."

"I knew you'd jump at the chance," Ben replied.

"I'm kind of curious to see them unload on something besides big buildings," Stan McDade joshed back.

Ben called Buddy next. "Rat, you've some special equipment on the way. Hold what you've got and wait for the roar."

When it came, the rockets in ripple-fire impressed everyone, even those who had experienced it before. In less than thirty seconds, the forty tubes of each battery unleashed their cargo. With a flight time of less than a minute for the maximum range of 16,395 yards, each salvo delivered .76 tons of HE on the Nazi bunkers in a tight pattern of repeated shocks.

Not even reinforced concrete, of which the black-shirts had very little, could withstand such a cataclysmic pounding. The bunkers collapsed in fountains of dust, dirt, and cement chips. Along with them, the defense around the old town of Raton fell. Major Miller threw up his hands in alarm and despair and led the pell-mell flight southward to Santa Rosa.

Ben Raines watched from a hillside as the rout grew in numbers of demoralized "supermen." He had allotted three days to reduce Raton, given the refugees from Trinidad and the intact command from the pass as reinforcements. Buddy happening on and destroying their main line of resistance so early had provided them with time to spare. Ben gladly allocated a full day to preventive maintenance and R&R.

An enterprising squad of Buddy's headquarters company located a large herd of wild cattle in a side canyon in Raton Pass and had selected a few to provide fresh meat. That left enough to ensure the survival of the herd and to allow for a large barbecue for all hands. After weeks of Dr. Lamar's patent glop, they quickly cleaned the piled-high tables and mopped up any stray juices with slices of fresh-baked bread. Some of the Rebels braved the cool highlands air to splash and cavort in the inviting waters of the north fork of the Cimarron River.

Stuffed full of spit-roasted beef and vastly superior Nazi rations, Ben Raines relaxed for the first time since Cheyenne. Jersey stood watch and even diverted would-be visitors, while Ben lay under a bullet-scarred tree.

"The boss is sleeping," she declared. "Give the guy a break, huh?"

Thermopolis and Headquarters Company did not receive such a break when their advance stalled out some five miles from Shoshoni, Wyoming. Thermopolis carefully considered his options and tactical choices, as he had been taught by Ben Raines. In the end, he summoned Leadfoot, Wanda, and Emil Hite.

"Those Nazi pricks have us stopped cold," he began his briefing. "Leadfoot, and you, Wanda, I want you to take your bikes and get around on the west side of their operation. Emil, you and your people will take the south. The rest of the company will handle the north and east. The idea is for you to make all the noise and confusion you can when we open up. We want those crud to think they are overrun and caught in a box."

"My girls will love this," Wanda remarked. "Just thinking about us gets those black-shirt pukes pissed off."

Leadfoot produced his wolfish grin. "Me'n the boys can come on like Atilla the Hun. We'll scare those fuckers so bad they'll be crappin' *tomorrow's* breakfast."

"Never fear, O wise Day Star of Hippiedom, we shall perform to your specifications," Emil chimed in.

"Okay, okay. The thing is, you need to get right in among them before you open up with the diversionary action," Thermopolis urged them. "Use suppressed weapons, knives, that sort of thing, to take out OPs and perimeter guards."

"When do we do this?" Leadfoot asked.

"Tonight. Well after dark, when the goose-steppers are sacked out. You'll be in dark clothing and grease paint. Oh, and another thing. I've had the company armorer work up some gimmicks to help identify friend from foe." Thermopolis produced a small, springy metal clicker, unaware he had reinvented one of the devices used by Allied troops on D day in World War II. "One click to question, two clicks to reply friendly." He demonstrated.

"Everyone will have one of these?" Wanda asked.

"By the time you are ready to pull out, yes," Thermopolis assured her.

"I can hardly wait," the leader of the Sisters of Lesbos responded.

Ghosting along with the mufflers reducing the exhaust of their Harleys to whispers, the Sons of Satan navigated by the gridlike layout of country roads. Dressed in black, their faces smeared with dark camo grease paint, only the chrome on the motorcycles picked out the light of the stars. Leadfoot had a good feeling about this raid. After they had demolished the headquarters in Casper, he and his men had wanted badly to get roaring drunk.

Although not teetotalers, the Rebels frowned on that. Particularly when armed and in a combat zone. Alcohol and gunpowder did not mix. Now he and his followers were out doing what they did best. Beerbelly, on point, braked his scoot and raised a hand to signal a halt. Leadfoot coasted up beside him.

"What gives?"

"Up ahead. That low mound." Leadfoot could vaguely make it out in the dim light. "I'd say there's two of them in there," Beerbelly went on. "Only damned if I don't think they're both stackin' z's."

"Why not? They're watching the back door. They don't expect any Rebels to the west of them, right? What say we slide up and pay a call?"

Experience gained even before they allied with the

247

Rebels let the ex-outlaw bikers advance on their unsuspecting prey with ease. Close at hand, Leadfoot noted that a hollow had been dug out and the dirt used to form a breastwork. Branches had been laid over all and covered in leaves. Two black-shirts slumbered inside, lulled by a long period of inaction and boredom. Leadfoot raised the muzzle of his suppressed Uzi, and the bolt clacked as he stitched one Nazi with a neat three-round burst.

Beside him, Beerbelly dispatched the other black-shirt with equal élan. "This must be State 789," Beerbelly observed of the road they traveled. "That bridge we went over would be the one across Boysen Reservoir."

"Good figgerin'," Leadfoot complimented. "We turn east now. You done good, Beerbelly. Keep a sharp eye."

Half a mile farther on, they came to a roadblock. A long, slender lodgepole pine had been trimmed and rigged as a drop bar across the road. Two bored sentries manned the barricade. Soft whaps from silenced weapons ended their lives before either could shout a warning or fire a shot. Leadfoot pointed to a small, ramshackle tear-drop trailer to one side of the road.

On tiptoe, three bikers angled over to the door. Braced for anything, the one in the center reached out and opened the sagging, holey screen. The door swung out at a touch. A sleep-muffled voice spoke inquiringly from inside. Swiftly, the trio swarmed in and made short work of the off-duty guards with razor-sharp knives.

"You do good work," Leadfoot praised his men as they emerged from the trailer. "I wonder how Wanda is making out?"

Wanda and the Sisters of Lesbos had skirted close to the northern edge of town, to avoid the problem of crossing the reservoir. With their backs to the water, they approached the shattered town from half a mile west. Two squat MBTs blocked the onetime residential street the Amazons scouted from behind rubble heaps. One of the girls touched Wanda's arm after they had surveyed

248

the actions of the inattentive crews who sat or stood outside their tanks.

"Watch this and be ready," the young Sister urged.

She stepped out into the open and sauntered through the darkness toward the listless Nazis. Finally one of them, a sergeant in command of one tank, noticed her. "Who goes there?" he demanded.

Without altering her pace, she walked right up to him. "Hi there, big boy. D'you like to fuck black girls?"

Outraged at this insult to his racial purity, the blackshirt sergeant flushed scarlet and spoke with a voice choked by hate. "You degenerate slu—"

His outrage got choked on a gush of blood as the Sister of Lesbos shoved an eleven-inch knife into his gut and wrenched it upward. More of the deadly women materialized out of the night and quickly slashed the life from other unwary Nazis. Two of Wanda's girls dropped down the hatches of the MBTs to slit the throats of the drivers. Greatly pleased with their success, Wanda rounded up her command. "Let's move on into town, girls."

From the corner of one eye, Emil Hite saw furtive movement to his right. Tensed, he positioned his assault rifle and squeezed on the clicker in his left hand.

Click!

Click—click!

"Oh," Emil Hite sighed in relief. "You're a friendly."

"Nein," came a guttural reply. "I watched you Rebels infiltrating, learned how you identified one another, killed one, and took his noise-maker."

It was not the high priest of the Great God Blomm, nor even Emil Hite, con man supreme, who responded. It was Emil Hite, Rebel soldier. He shot the Nazi through the heart. The 22-inch suppressor on his assault rifle swallowed the detonation of the cartridge and the smug black-shirt fell on his face in the waste-choked street of Shoshoni.

"That was close," Emil panted.

"You did all right," one of his closest followers remarked as he appeared out of the dark. "We'd better move on."

"Ah, Ezra, it is you. That one, he tricked me."

"Could have been any of us. What time do you have?"

Emil checked his watch. The faintly glowing hand pips and numbers indicated less than ten minutes to the assault by Thermopolis and the company. "We need to hurry. Is everyone spread out?"

"Yes. Let's go."

Emil took three steps and tripped over the loose sling of his assault rifle. His inept foot caused the weapon to be yanked from his grasp. It clattered on the ground. At once a figure loomed in front of them.

"Who are you and what are you doing here?" an American voice asked.

Emil clicked at him and got no reply. The Nazi swung the muzzle of his rifle to cover Emil, and Ezra did the only possible thing. He shot the black-shirt through the head. Reflexively the man triggered a round that sounded like a 155 going off in the stillness.

"Was ist das?" a muffled voice demanded.

"We're under attack!" came a frightened shout.

A shrill scream came from Emil's left. "They're in among us," another black-shirt shouted in alarm.

Suddenly an intense flood of white light came from a large halogen flood mounted on a former telephone pole. Emil and Ezra stood out in its glare. Despite his klutzy nature, Emil could act swiftly when needed. He snatched up his rifle and did what any good Rebel trooper would. He shot out the light.

New darkness changed to a red-orange glow as Headquarters Company mortars opened up.

Howling like demons, Leadfoot's Sons of Satan swarmed toward Emil. The little con artist clicked his clacker furiously. Laughing, Beerbelly swept up the minute ex-leader of Blomm's children in a huge bearhug.

"Get to killin' Nazis, li'l feller," he roared.

Keening like the shades of the Inferno, Wanda's Sisters

of Lesbos brought terror and death to more swastika worshipers. Muzzle flashes began to light up the foreground as the stunned Nazis recovered their senses and started to offer resistance.

Leadfoot lobbed a grenade through the window of a trailer and ended the lives of six muzzy-headed American Nazis. Thermopolis, with the second wave of his company, advanced steadily into town. Frightened, disoriented black-shirts tried to surrender, only to be gunned down by grim, vengeance-hungry Rebels.

"Remember the kids from Kansas," became an oft-repeated rally cry.

Within five minutes the first vehicles started a mad race for the causeway bridge over Boysen Reservoir. They met more of the Sons and Sisters, along with claymores and shoulder-fired rockets. An ammunition truck erupted in the heart of the demolished city and added a bright mushroom of roiling flame. At thirty-three minutes into the operation, Thermopolis declared the Nazi cantonment totally suppressed.

Ben Raines spoke briskly into the mouthpiece of the handset. "That's good news, Therm. I assume you have everyone patched up and ready to move out to Riverton and Thermopolis?"

"Oh, yes. Emil got a broken toe. He's limping around and making a big thing of playing the invalid. We took eleven KIAs and twenty-three WIA. Nobody missing, except some Nazis."

"They won't be mourned. Keep it up. I want pressure on them in the north for as long as you can hold out. Resupply will be at the Casper municipal airport as soon as flights can get out of Base Camp One. I'll have Georgi detail enough men to keep the roads patrolled and open. Eagle, out."

Ben returned the handset to Corrie's keeping and picked up his binoculars. An excellent pair of twenty-power optics with superior light-gathering properties, the field glasses picked out individual details of the vista below their position on a ridge on the right side of U.S. 54/66, five miles outside Santa Rosa.

Santa Rosa, being built on a series of hills and the valley floors between, Ben evaluated, would be much like laying siege to Rome. Intel indicated that the Nazis had one battalion of Hans Brodermann's regular SS and one of American SS defending the partially rebuilt town. Added to that were the remnants of the black-shirt garbage that had abandoned Raton, Tucumcari and other, smaller outposts. Taken as a whole, it provided a formidable obstacle.

Impatience chafed at Ben Raines. His commitment to aid Gen. Raul Payon weighed heavily as he considered the efforts made by the Nazis in Santa Rosa to make use of rubble, natural terrain, and man-made obstacles to consolidate their position. He was glad when Ike McGowan's three battalions rolled into the assembly area. With him came Dr. Lamar Chase.

"I hear you've been risking your life again, in spite of all the good advice you've been given," the rotund doctor complained in the pitch of a musical saw.

"Yep, Tubby. Every word is true. I've been eating your outrageous imitation food for nearly two weeks," Ben quipped back. "Today I dined on delicious fresh beef."

"Cooked rare enough to moo, no doubt," snapped the disapproving medico.

"How else?" Ben was enjoying this. He decided, though, that the time had come to get serious. "Have you received enough supplies to support a major campaign? We're facing a tough go here at Santa Rosa."

"We can handle it," Dr. Chase said, frowning. "Why do you suppose they picked this place for a major stand?"

"It's a crossroads of the Southwest," Ben told him. "From here you can access Flagstaff and points west, Santa Fe, Albuquerque, and everything south of there."

"Well, damn them for being smart enough to know that," Chase snapped, then launched into another pet worry. "I'm concerned about Cecil Jefferys. He keeps

252

chewing on me to release him early from his recovery program."

Ben started to answer when a young corporal appeared in the doorway of the communications van. "General, we have General Payon on a secure channel."

"I'll come at once," Ben responded. "I'd like you to tag along, Ike, Lamar."

Inside the van, the high-altitude advantages to radio communication became clear when the sharp, nearly static-free voice of General Raul Francisco Payon came through the speaker. "Well, my friend, I hear you are in a messy situation up north of us."

"Not so's you'd notice, Raul," Ben stated calmly. "The usual run of things when dealing with Hoffman and his black-shirts. How are you situated?"

A sigh, colorless over the scrambler, preceded Payon's reply. "We were betrayed at Chapultepec by the politicians. They welcomed these Nazi *cabrónes* like liberators. I sometimes suspect that all politicians are corrupt and seek only to exercise absolute power over everyone else. I also believe that at least half of our crop in Mexico are secret Nazis. But I wander. We were forced to withdraw to the central highland. There we fought a few indecisive battles and again we retreated northward. We are now on a line between Parral and Ciudad Camargo."

"Where does that put you in relation to Rasbach's dispositions?" Ben asked next.

General Payon chuckled. "We hold the high ground, once they get out of the mountains. I have discovered that the *bandidos* are at least loyal Mexicans. The outlaws who used to rob our trains are now fighting guerrilla actions against Rasbach, who is bogged down in the steep passes around Torreón."

"How are you and they supplied?"

"We have air cover and supply drops from Ciudad Chihuahua some sixty kilometers north of us."

"Can you give me a time frame?"

"A week. A few days. Hours, if Rausbach's men can clear the boulders and refuse from the passes. He has

253

some good engineers with his army. They are working in spite of the snipers and bandit raids."

"How long can your, ah, guerrillas hold out?"

"With better supply arrangements, indefinitely. Alas, Ben, our planes are few and small. If only we had the big cargo craft the Rebels use."

"I understand, *amigo*. But considering the distance involved and the refueling problem, it's out of the question. Hang in there, we'll be joining you within the week."

"I look forward to it, my friend, Ben. *Adiós.*"

From outside, the rumble of armor, moving fast and with a purpose, alerted the commanders of a new development. "Let's take a look," Ben suggested as he put up the mike.

Nazi tanks had rolled out of Santa Rosa and lined up for a classic desert tank battle. Rebel MBTs raced to oppose them. The first of the big guns let go with long lances of muzzle flame and pearly smoke rings. Crews with ERIX missiles hurried to get into position to support the Rebel armor. With all attention centered on the developing battle, it came as a surprise to hear the rattle of small arms and yells of alarm from the rear of the Rebel positions.

Ben Raines directed his attention that way and saw a wave of white-robed people rushing the Rebel rear. In the center, beard and hair waving in the air, came Brother Armageddon, urging on his demented followers.

Six

When Ben Raines received confirmation that Archibald Culp/Brother Armageddon was indeed leading this new assault on the Rebel assembly area, he immediately left the CP to get a first-hand view. Cooper delivered them in somewhat-tumbled condition in a now-vacant tank park. From where the Rebel general had been minutes before came the continued rumble of the armor battle.

Ben and his team spilled from the Hummer, and Ben put binocs to his eyes. A rapid count of the advancing skirmishers brought a muffled curse from his lips, then he asked in an uncertain tone, "Where in hell did he come up with this many troops?"

Jersey plucked a stem of grass and chewed on it. "With Hoffman on the loose, I'd say every crack-brain in the country has come out from under his rock."

"Brother Armageddon has made that obvious," Ben replied dryly. "Even so, it's been less than a week since we cleaned out their snake pit." Decisiveness replaced his surprise. "We haven't time to fool with these people. I want Ike's infantry to turn back this way and roll over the assholes. We can only hope the Nazis aren't in radio contact with that son of a bitch."

"That's no problem, General," Corrie offered sweetly. "As you know, there's jamming equipment in all of the comm vans that hasn't been used in a while. The blackshirts can be put off the air in no time."

"Do it," Ben commanded, then blinked in surprise as a

six-by-six roared up out of a draw directly in front of them.

It had a snowplow blade fixed on its front and a ring-mounted light machine gun on the extended cab. The driver aimed the jolting monster directly at the Hummer. Everyone scattered. With less than fifty yards to cover, it looked as if the truck would cream Ben's favorite transportation in seconds.

A light of zealous madness shone in the eyes of Archibald Culp as he and his six-man bodyguard established a forward observation post and urged the screaming mass of his fighters on past. So agitated had he become that his words spilled out in jumbled confusion.

". . . them, gonna we . . . get . . . must . . . moving keep."

"Say what?" blurted a former redneck, recently converted to the Assembly.

"He is speaking in tongues, Brother Cash," a longtime follower explained inaccurately, a hand on the forearm of Brother Cash.

"Sound like he be drunk to me," Brother Cash went on.

"Don't say that," the scandalized convert demanded. "Brother Armageddon hates the demon Rum. Hates all alcohol. He has never allowed a drop of pernicious waters to cross his lips."

That wasn't entirely true. Archibald Culp had been checked into an alcoholic rehab center by despairing parents when he was seventeen. He had been released as clean and sober nine months later. From then until the "Spirit" touched him at age thirty, he was in and out of every detox clinic in Southern California.

"There — there," Brother Armageddon shouted, a long, trembling finger pointing to the Rebel rear area. "They are gathering to fight us. The Angel of the Lord shall smite them. The Archangel Michael shall descend from Heaven and lay waste all the vanities of Satan."

"It'd do better to get them snowplow trucks up here with their machine guns," Brother Cash muttered. "Them fuckin' Rebels don't worry none about angels smitin' 'em. They just kick ass an' take names."

"You have fought them ere this, Brother?" the faithful disciple asked in awe. "We never did before they came to our valley."

"Oh, I done fought Ben Raines before," the redneck allowed. "Fought him in Loos'ana, fought him in Geo'gia, fought the bastid in Arkansas last summer."

"What's it like?" the fascinated End of Worlder asked.

"Ben Raines was plumb mean back home. Battled like a madman in Geo'gia. In Arkansas, there was this bull nigger across the river. He talked some bad shit against us white folk. Ben Raines an' his Rebels kilt damn near ever' one of them. Then he turned on us. That's when I knew he was sure enough crazy."

"Bring up the fiery swords of the Almighty," Brother Armageddon interrupted.

"He means the machine-gun trucks," the true believer interpreted.

"I know what he means. 'Bout damn time," the redneck grumbled as he keyed his radio.

His was the last message that got out before jamming began. It brought half a dozen huge, powerful trucks with snowplows for armor, and machine guns mounted over the cabs. The beds had been filled with heavily armed members of the Assembly and their new recruits.

"I've seen stuff like this before," the redneck advised. "But this time, with them Nazis on one side an' us on the other, I got the feeling Ben Raines is gonna get his."

Obersturmbannführer (Lt. Col.) Kurt Nagel had lived through the Rebel vendetta on Field Marshal Hoffman's army. He had thought he had seen the full gamut of Rebel ferocity. What unfolded now left him gasping.

"Liebe Gott!" he swore to his executive officer. "Who are those troops attacking the Rebels? They are not any of ours."

"No, *Herr Obersturmbannführer,*" Major Guttmann responded. "Before the Rebels began jamming us, we had radio contact. Their leader claims that they are Aryan brothers, who have come to help us against, ah, against the, ah, 'Great Satan Ben Raines.' That's really what he said. He said they are the Assembly of the End of the World and have a safe conduct pass from the *Führer.*"

"Well, well, nothing surprises me in this mad country anymore. Whoever they are, they are being slaughtered by the Rebels." He pointed to a BC scope. "Take a look. The Rebels take no prisoners. Men who try to surrender are shot down or bayoneted or clubbed to death. It's—it's *barbaric.*"

Guttmann stepped back from the battery commander's scope, his face ashen. "Perhaps it is a mistake to defend this area so aggressively. Do you think they would treat our men like that?"

"Very likely," Nagel stated coldly. "It is reported that Ben Raines has declared no quarter for any NAL soldier. As to your speculation on our defending this portion of the Eastern Wall with anything less than our utmost, it is a sentiment that *Brigadeführer* Brodermann would not approve, to say the least. No, Guttmann," he went on through a sigh. "We must defend the Santa Rosa complex to the last man, for *Führer* and fatherland."

Unable to react in time to raise the plow blade, the driver of the road maintenance truck died in a shower of safety glass fragments and .45 slugs as Ben Raines's Thompson chopped a ragged line across the windshield. His body slumped to the left and the vehicle turned that way. Jersey had hacked a crooked stitch up the torso of the machine-gunner, silencing the weapon.

At the last minute, she had to jump to her left to avoid the deadly edge of the blade, which slammed into the front fender of the Humvee. The loud scream of rending metal came clearly over the yammer of the engine and pop of small-arms fire. The Hummer slewed to the side on loose gravel and the driverless truck careened by.

Riflemen in the rear opened up as the truck rocked by, and two 5.56mm rounds struck Ben's body armor, stinging him with the force of impact. Then Cooper fired his M-203. In a *bloop-bang* zero time frame, the 40mm grenade exploded in the truck bed. Ben Raines hosed down the screaming survivors, and silence accompanied the wobbling vehicle to its encounter with a large boulder.

Stunned, Jersey looked hard at Ben, noted the holes in his body armor. "If you were a cat, boss, you'd be down to only a couple of lives. This whole campaign has been screwed up from the start."

"Complaining, Jersey?"

"Who, me? No, sir. I wouldn't dream of complaining, sir. Everything is just hunky-damn-dory, General Raines, sir." She drew a deep breath and bellowed, "Goddammit, that nut in the truck almost scared me enough to wet my pants."

"Me, too," Ben admitted quietly. Then, "Remember the pucker factor, Jersey."

Cooper prudently kept out of the exchange, intent on reloading the blooper under his CAR-15 and taking aim at another truck. An ERIX crew had discovered the mobile machine-gun nests and eliminated one in a huge fireball. More of the holy lunatics poured over the lip of the draw to their front and Ben put his Thompson to good use.

Three of Brother Armageddon's followers went off to their brand of heaven when Ben washed them in their own blood. Although firing in tight three- and four-round bursts, a respectable pile of shiny .45 brass accumulated to Ben's right rear. The faithful old Chicago typewriter ground out deadly copy for the enlightenment of screaming End of Worlders. Ben estimated he had some ten rounds left in the third drum when Ike's battalions of infantry slammed into the ragged companies of kooks.

They died screaming, howling, begging for mercy. The biting tang of wet copper filled the air, tinged with burnt powder. It gave Ben a moment to wonder what went on in the armor battle. He sought Corrie and her radio.

"Bump Ike and ask him how the slug-out is going with the tanks."

"Already done, General. Ike says he'd like his infantry back now, if possible. Our gunners are better than theirs. The Nazi armor is pulling back into town."

"Good. Tell Ike he can have two battalions as of now. We'll need the other to mop up on this collection of filth."

In common with the executive officer of Brodermann's regular SS troops in Santa Rosa, *Obersturmbannführer* Alex Young of the American SS began to have doubts about the wisdom of making so strong a defense in the hilly city area. He had witnessed with growing horror the obliteration of the fanatical group calling themselves the Assembly of something or other. What he saw and learned chilled Lieutenant Colonel Young's blood.

Nagel and the others of Brodermann's officers may have thought they had seen examples of Rebel ferocity. This gave them an entirely new lesson. In the hiatus following the uneven tank battle and slaughter of the religious lunatics, Young drafted his own report for the eyes only of Peter Volmer.

"The man Brodermann has in charge here," he wrote, "seems determined to get every last one of us killed. Not necessarily his own men, Peter, but ours. He has a withdrawal plan that places us as the rear guard, with orders to fight to the last man to keep the Rebels from following the main column too closely. Somehow, the Rebels have brought together the strength of an entire brigade. All of that power is leveled at Santa Rosa. Surely a word from you would change our new *Führer's* mind about last-ditch stands?"

Young sighed and looked up from the page. "I'd gladly kill for a bottle of cold beer," he said absently.

A youthful aide perked up. "Really, sir? Only, you won't have to kill anyone for it. Our—our South American friends seem to have plenty of it. I'll only be a minute."

"Sep, you are marvelous. You've proven to me that there still are miracles. Even if they are small ones. Yes, get me one, by all means. Get half a dozen if possible and you can share with me."

Sep had barely returned when the Rebel bombardment of Santa Rosa began. Artillery rained down in sheets of deadly steel.

Three burly Rebels brought Brother Armageddon to Ben Raines. The false prophet's hair and beard were smeared with bloody mud. His robe was in tatters and only the wild light in his eyes revealed any former part of the fanatic in him. He had lost a shoe somewhere and walked with a pronounced limp. He was bent forward with pain and exhaustion so that when Ben stood, they were nearly eye-to-eye.

"So, Mr. Culp, you've played out your string."

"It is not over, Satan Raines," Culp muttered in a ghost of his former voice from the crypt. "And I am Brother Armageddon. You will address me as such under pain of Gawd's punishment."

"I'm afraid God has abandoned you, Mr. Culp," said Ben with steel-edged words. "It is now up to the Rebels to mete out justice to you."

"I deny you the right to judge me," Armageddon snapped back, his old self rallying.

Ben laughed, loud and long and hearty. "You sorry little shit. Deny all you want. The fact remains, you are in our hands and we will decide your fate according to our laws."

Armageddon's head rose slowly. "You . . . have . . . laws?"

"Oh, yes. We also have chaplains with the Rebel troops, and a lot of sincere believers in one religion or another. Three of them are holding you right now; a Buddhist, a Catholic, and a Jew. You were so busy preaching ignorance and hate, glorifying plural marriage and, no doubt, incest, that you hadn't time to learn the least little thing about your self-proclaimed enemy."

Renewed anger choked Armageddon. "We do not tolerate incestuous relations," he bellowed nearly in full form. "Of course, a father must instruct his daughters in the . . .

261

dutiful arts . . . but that's not the same thing."

"Oh, certainly not," Ben dryly taunted. "Let's see if we have it all? "You've engaged in acts of war against the Rebels, committed polygamy, screwed your daughters, crucified innocent men, and I suppose women—"

"Heretics, unbelievers, defilers of our sacred temple, servants of the Antichrist!" Armageddon bellowed.

"Oh, fuck this!" Ben Raines roared back. "You three, take him out and hang him."

"What about my trial?" a suddenly sobered Archibald Culp asked.

"You've had it, you scumbag asshole. I am sick unto death with sanctimonious hypocrites like you. The world is a hard, cruel, unforgiving place, bad enough without your sort coming along with some disgusting absolutist, half-baked theology that panders to the lust and greed of a few, who become your cadre, and feed enough bullshit to the sheep to fertilize every garden in Rebel territory. Mister, if you sincerely want a look at the Antichrist before you die, I suggest you get a mirror."

Grinning, the three tough Rebels frog-marched a screaming, kicking Archibald Culp out to meet his deserved end. Jersey rolled her eyes and made a show of mopping her brow.

"Jeez, boss, you sure told that shithead off. I knew you supported religious freedom in Rebel territory, but I never knew you felt so strongly about it."

"We learn something every day, Jersey," Ben said lightly, feeling good about the disposition of Brother Armageddon.

Corrie called from her place by the Hummer. "I have a Lieutenant Colonel Young on the horn, General."

"Hummm. Rats and sinking ships, Jersey."

Jersey winked. "Right you are, boss."

His voice came tinnily over the radio, set for a Nazi frequency. "I am Lieutenant Colonel Alex Young, an American in service to *Führer* Hoffman, and co-commander of the NAL forces in Santa Rosa."

"*SS Obersturmbannführer Alex Jung,*" Ben coldly pronounced in German. "Commander of a battalion of American SS filth."

A gulp and long pause followed. "Your intelligence is excellent, General Raines. It was not believed that you knew American Nazi units were present here."

"We even know what color shorts you're wearing and what brand of toilet paper you use." Then Ben gave him his best Bogart impression. " 'Of all the saloons, in all of North Africa, he has to come into mine,' eh, *Obersturmbannführer?* Well, I've come, all right. What do you want to talk about?"

"Ah — er — terms, General Raines."

"There is but one term for those who fuck with the Rebels. Unconditional surrender, followed by execution of all war criminals."

"Those are rather, ah, harsh terms, General," Young gulped.

"Not to those who are getting the shit shelled out of them right this minute," Ben snapped. "Let me talk to the real commander of the Santa Rosa complex, *Obersturmbannführer* Kurt Nagel."

Shaken by the intimate knowledge of their inner workings the Rebels possessed, Alex Young paused several seconds before answering. *"Obersturmbannführer* Nagel is not available at the present, General Raines. He — he —"

"He's running like a scared rabbit at the head of a column headed for Santa Fe," Ben concluded for him.

"Just — so. I am in command here at present. Can we not discuss more, ah, civilized terms, General Raines?"

"No."

"But, surely, General —"

Once more, Ben's impatience flared. "Fuck this! Raines out." He turned to Corrie. "Bump Base Camp One. I want Cecil to prepare all tactical air units. Buddy, Ike," he addressed his son and Ike McGowan, who had just come up. "We're going to pull out all stops. I've just called in air. I'm on my way to help General Payon."

Seven

"Dammit all, this just doesn't figure," Thermopolis exclaimed as he turned away from the blank view ahead.

Thermopolis was finding Thermopolis more to handle than he had expected. It had become rough sledding. Literally, he thought ruefully, sleds might be the thing. A low, leaden cloud cover spilled large, wet flakes over the ground. Icy gusts of wind created snow flurries that spun and danced across the hilly terrain, cloaking trees and turning the world gray-white. The radio crackled and he acknowledged.

"This is Leadfoot. You said to report when we had the enemy in sight. Well, we do. A whole shitpot full. They come pourin' outta the cellars in that wrecked town like the Devil himself was after them."

"Be precise, Leadfoot," Thermopolis instructed. "How many?"

"Dozens. Ah . . . I'd say at least three hundred. An' they're crack troops, too. Reg'lar SS scum from down South."

"Any sign of American Nazis?" Thermopolis queried.

"Huh-uh. Not so far. We're pullin' back."

"Give us five, no, ten minutes, then do that."

"I don't think we've got ten minutes."

"Do your best, Leadfoot. Thermopolis out." He cut hard gray eyes at the lieutenant next to him. "We take 'em off the road. Set up an ambush and let Leadfoot lead the black-shirts right into it."

"Good as anything in these conditions," Lieutenant Walker agreed. "They sure won't be able to see us."

"Get everyone into winter camo," Thermopolis added as an afterthought.

Twenty-five minutes later, Leadfoot and his bikers blew through the ambush site with 350 black-shirts gnawing on their behinds. When Leadfoot made out the snow-muffled outline of an M-1A, he guided his flock past and laid down his hog. Steam hissed a cloud from his muffler. He made a quick check of his trusty Uzi and had the honor of firing the first round in the ambush at an overeager Nazi who came pelting after the Sons of Satan on a battered old rice-burner Honda.

Nine-millimeter slugs exploded the eager beaver's head in a cloud of chips and pink spray. The Honda continued to carry him past the sprawled Sons of Satan. Leadfoot looked for another target. Thermopolis appeared at his side.

"Nice going, but did you have to bring so many?" he asked the biker.

"Didn't want to leave anyone out."

"That's what I like about you, Leadfoot. Generous to a fault," Thermopolis quipped. "Now, what about the town?"

Fire erupted from the ambushers, to be answered by the Nazis. Leadfoot winced. "There ain't any. Torn down and scavenged off long ago. These dudes been living in cellars, basements, such-like. With this storm settlin' in, they didn't even know we were there until one of the boys got careless. They have a couple of small field pieces. We booby-trapped them. Also a couple of heavies with flamethrowers."

Thermopolis rolled his eyes. "Not what I want to get mixed up with. Total numbers? Any idea?"

"Ummm, no. Could be a battalion in there. Could be more or less. From what we seen, they're all SA regulars."

"That's not good. That Brodermann's SS and the others from Hoffman's crowd are tough," Thermopolis calculated out loud. Bullets cracked over their heads and

265

bodies began to pile up fifty yards in front of the tank.

"Time to be movin'," Leadfoot observed.

"Don't I know it," Thermopolis agreed. "Say, ol' Thermy, time to get your old ass moving."

Faced with the knowledge of sure death, the American Nazis in Santa Rosa dug in and fought with the tenacity of the regulars who had deserted them. Buddy and Ike found themselves holding the heights of the old "Motel Row" at the eastern end of town. Their troops spread out for half a mile to either side of U.S. 54/66 and settled down to dogged slugging matches with the enemy. That lasted through a day and a half.

Then the Apaches Ben had left with the main force joined with Puffs and light B-25 Mitchell bombers (rescued from the old Confederate Air Force) rained steely death on Santa Rosa. Fifty-caliber machine guns in the Mitchells kept down the heads of SAM gunners, which opened the pathway for the slow-flying C-47 Puffs. In a thirty-minute display of air power, the Rebels trashed more Nazi vehicles and armor than since the initial travesty invasion by *Führer* Hoffman's pick brigade. Bombs flattened those buildings constructed since the Creepie War and set rubble heaps to blaze.

Over the drone of departing engines, Ike McGowan made a grim announcement. "Now we go in and clean out the rest."

Buddy Raines had volunteered to lead the mopup with his reinforced regiment. He nodded to Ike's observation and informed the senior Rebel commander, "I'll be up front in my APC."

"Like father, like son," Ike sighed in a way that made the cliche new and original.

True to his father's style, Buddy went in behind the point squad of the point platoon. Through the commander's periscope, he kept sharp eyes on smoldering ruins and sprawled bodies. Their central thrust followed the highway through town. Down in the first valley, past the shattered remains of a truck stop, a rivet-gun clatter on the skin of the APC announced the presence of some live black-shirts.

Buddy spoke into the boom mike of the headset he wore. "Thunderer, this is Rat. We've got an MG emplacement about two hundred yards to our right. Come on up and squash it."

"Ten-four, Rat. Be right there."

Buddy continued on, indifferent to the .30 caliber rounds striking the APC. They made it noisy, but not dangerous. An M-1A Abrams rumbled into place behind the personnel carrier and swiveled its turret to the north. The coax machine gun opened up to suppress return fire, then the tank commander popped up through the hatch and put the big .50 MG into action.

It took only seconds, Buddy noted with satisfaction as he progressed into the lowlands of Santa Rosa. Near a small, ancient, adobe church, the APC jinked to the right to avoid the stubby, broken-off base of a fountain. Grenades crashed sharply outside and three of the point squad went down, two of them biting off screams of pain from shrapnel wounds. A split-second later, some thirty screaming black-shirts charged the survivors and the APC.

Lt. Col. Alex Young stared bleakly at the rapidly changing symbols on the situations map. Dedicated to the monolithic Staff Command system, he rarely got out in the field with his troops. The little blue, green, and red grease pencil marks carried no human aura. It should be easy to watch the red ones growing more numerous and not experience emotional shock. Yet he had a growing sensation of being a man repeatedly punched in the stomach.

"We outnumber them," he stated wonderingly. "How can they do this?"

"They fight like demons, *Herr Obersturmbannführer*," an aide told him. "You saw what the Rebels did to the troops of that religious fanatic."

"We will not sacrifice the lives of these brave men for nothing. Order an immediate withdrawal. We will head west, take the interstate as far as we can. I should have accepted their terms," Young added sadly. "None of my men have committed war crimes."

Obersturmbannführer Young's order came too late for the units locked in battle in the church square. Black-shirt troops swarmed over the point squad and killed the survivors. Shouting in anticipation, they rushed the APC. Buddy Raines answered them with the chatter of a .50 caliber. Heavy, half-inch slugs ripped flesh and burst heads.

"Back us out of here," Buddy shouted to the driver through his headset. "We need a better position."

"No can do, Colonel," came the answer. "The guys in back saw them put mines under the wheels."

"Put those troopers out the rear to clear the mines and scatter these assholes."

"Yep. Good idea, Colonel."

Buddy opened the breech cover and slapped a fresh belt of .50 ammo into place, then shut the lid and charged the gun. Once more its roar brought terror to the Nazis in the plaza. Buddy took three painful hits in his body armor, which momentarily blurred his vision. His hand relaxed on the toggle trigger of the .50.

Anticipating this effect, a wide-eyed Nazi leapt onto the fender of the APC. He shoved the muzzle of his assault rifle toward Buddy's face. Swiftly, Buddy snatched his 10-inch Ka-Bar and jammed the wicket point into the Nazi's forehead. To his surprise and Buddy's, the cold steel slid into the brain behind that shelf of bone and blinked out the lights. His trigger finger never even got the message to fire.

Buddy yanked his knife free and shoved the corpse off the fender. "I always had doubts that would work," he spoke wonderingly.

"What's that, sir?" the driver asked in Buddy's ear.

"Uh—I just stuck my knife in a Nazi's head."

"Bet that smarted some."

That broke the grip of mortality that had dazed Buddy Raines. He began to laugh and to clean out the last of the black-shirts not eliminated by the twelve men from the APC. He completed the task in time to reply, "No, not as long as you keep your fingers off the blade."

Brigadeführer Peter Volmer exploded in a fountain of curses. He realized he was getting to sound like Hoffman and cut them off in midspew. "This will make me look like an idiot," he snapped.

In a gesture of confused impatience, he ran a hand over his bald dome. Sensitive fingers picked up the presence of stubble. He would have to get the barber to shave him again. His cold blue eyes pulsed with an angry glow as he considered the message form in his other hand.

"Ben Raines has been positively identified *on the road to Alamogordo!* Not heading for Roswell and Carlsbad. *Alamogordo!* Why didn't you jerkoffs in Intelligence anticipate this?"

Nervous, his face pale and lips trembling, Volmer's G-2 responded spasmodically. "I—I—we—er—we naturally assumed that the objective of the Rebel campaign was t-to reduce o-our East Wall defenses a-a-and open the Pacific Northwest to attack in the spring."

You do not 'assume' anything, especially when dealing with Ben Raines," Volmer barked through thin, colorless lips. "There is an old canard that says, 'Military Intelligence is a contradiction in terms.' You people make it appear a truism. Find me Ben Raines and find out why he is going to Alamogordo."

"Zu Befehl, Herr Brigadeführer," the frightened man cracked out with a click of heels. *"Heil Hoffman."*

"Oh, for Christ's sake," Volmer blurted disgustedly. *"Heil!"* That outburst behind him, his keen brain began to settle down and consider options. After a while, he spoke to an aide. "Draft a message to *Standartenführer* Dracher. To Commandant, Werewolves. Target has changed positions unexpectedly. You are to move all Werewolf units to vicinity Alamogordo and Los Cruces ASAP. When in position you will await contact with target. All other orders stand as issued. Volmer, *Brigadeführer*, SS." He paused, gulped water directly from a carafe. "Do you have that? Read it back to me."

His aide complied and waited expectantly for more instructions. "Copies to?" he asked tentatively.

"To no one. My mistake is obvious enough by now, without rubbing the *Führer's* nose in it." Like his supreme leader, Volmer began to pace the floor as he verbally built a fantasy of eventual success. "Now, my fine Ben Raines. You have nowhere to go. There is only one connecting road through that desert. I know it. You have put yourself exactly where it most helps my plan. Within a week I will have you in my grasp."

Cooper gave a quick glance over his shoulder, relief over the news he bore clear in his voice. "That used to be La Luz we just drove through. At the bottom of this downgrade is Alamogordo."

"Thanks, Coop. Any word from the pathfinders, Corrie?"

"Not so far. Should I rattle their cage?"

"Might be wise, considering how close we're getting," Ben surmised.

"Oh, dear," he heard her say a minute later. "I'll give you Eagle."

"This is Eagle," Ben spoke.

"Eagle, Bronkowski here. We've hit a whole hornets' nest on the far side of Alamogordo. A black-shirt popped a scooter before we even knew they were there. We had to pull back, but they know we're coming."

"Not your fault," Ben consoled the unhappy scout. "Are you in contact at present?"

"Negatory, Eagle."

"Then hold what you've got and wait for us to come up. How many are there?"

"More than we can count. Probably a battalion in strength, maybe more."

"Don't take chances. ETA with the lead element in two-five minutes. Eagle out." To his team, he advised, "We'd better stop here and get into body armor. There's a crowd of unhappy campers waiting for us down there."

Ben's estimate of the situation proved violently true. As his Hummer and the advance company of R Batt churned through the damaged streets of Alamogordo's northern suburbs they came under mortar fire. Twice the Humvee rocked on its springs from close hits. Shrapnel did a hailstorm on the light armor. Ears ringing, Ben gave the devastation around them a once-over.

"Tell me, one of you, what kind of person would name a town Fat Poplar?"

"Huh? What do you mean, Boss?" Jersey queried.

"You speak fair Spanish, Jersey. *Alamo* is a poplar tree, right? And *gordo* means—"

"Fat. Gotcha, boss. You're right. It would take some wild sort of guy to come up with that for the name of a city."

"Chances are it was a bureaucrat," Ben opined.

"How do you figure that, General?" Beth asked.

"Well, you kids wouldn't remember. But back before the Great War, the only reason for the existence of Alamogordo was as a bedroom community for the workers at White Sands Proving Ground. That's just southwest of us. We'll be going through it in a couple of days."

"What did they do at White Sands?" Corrie asked.

"Tested rockets. Also nuclear devices," Ben answered. "It was established as part of the Manhattan Project way back in World War Two. Enrico Fermi worked there at one time. Also the American rocket pioneer, Goddard. At one point, more than twelve thousand people were employed at White Sands. Tract houses sprawled over all these mesas around town. The government project brought boom conditions to a sleepy little Mexican-

American village, built around an adobe plaza with, yes, a big, ancient poplar in the center of the square. That, of course, was one of the first things that got sacrificed to 'progress.' Well, enough of the travelog. We have to lay plans for kicking hell out of the Nazi garrison."

"You can still amaze me with your vast knowledge of these out-of-the-way places, General," Beth remarked.

"Nothing to it, my little chickadee. Just have faith in your basic travel guide and Triple-A road atlas," Ben responded, laughing. His remark abruptly sobered Ben. One hell of a lot had happened since the last days of the American Automobile Association. Too much of it lay on his hands.

"First off," he began, organizing his tactical situation. "We need to get the Apaches in the air to clear the mortar-battery forward observers off the heights to the northeast and southwest of what will be our IP. The troops can use the ruins of the city to mask their deployment. We're going to want to hit them on a broad front. Shock effect all the way." Ben paused, considering his next order of engagement. "Georgi would love this. All armor forward, including APCs. Just like the old Red Army in the Great Patriotic War."

"What was so patriotic about the Great War?" Cooper asked.

"World War Two to us, Coop," Ben explained. He examined the folded map on the clipboard strapped to one thigh. "Hummm. We can bring up R Batt's snipers with the big .50s and put them on the mesas cleared by the Apaches. Target officers and lead NCOs. Time for the gloves to come off, I think. All 105s and above to load CNDM shells for first five salvos. HE and flechette rounds to follow. Apaches to be refueled and armed and fly close air support for the infantry, which will follow the armor into the black-shirt MLR. That, I think, should do it tidily."

"Gosh, General, that even scares me," Beth assured him with a crooked smile.

"Let's hope it scares the head Hun defending Alamogordo," Ben offered.

"General, counterbattery radar says they have the mortar batteries bracketed," Corrie informed Ben.

"Good. Have them relay coordinates and order Perkins to open fire as soon as the guns are laid. We need to bust their butts before too many people are shoved into too small an area." To Jersey's quizzical expression, he added, "We could still lose this one, kid."

Eight

Faced with only the remains of a battalion inside the ruins of Thermopolis, Thermopolis gauged his task to be easy. The ambush had gone perfectly, with over 275 enemy KIA. It would give any prudent commander cause to seek surrender terms. Not so the hardcore Nazi in charge at the small Wyoming town. In addition to the flamethrowers, he had another as-yet-unknown weapon. Although not professing to be Nazis, a large number of Americans had volunteered to join in the fight against the Rebel forces.

Their leader had sworn foul oaths against Ben Raines and vowed to sacrifice every last one of his followers, and himself, to ensure the destruction of all Rebels within range of the town.

"I could understand such a pledge if it meant the downfall and death of General Raines," the South American Nazi had countered, curious as to motive.

"We once were many," the hollow-eyed specter before his desk replied. "We lived as we chose after the Great War. Then Ben Raines and his vile Rebels came hunting us. They killed without mercy; men, women, children. They used nerve gas and other abominable devices. Those of us who survived . . . have been forced to — change our ways, our appearance, live again in cursed da — But that is another matter, not of your concern. We are experienced fighting men and women and hate Ben Raines and his Rebels to the point of distraction. We will not fail you."

"Your assistance will be appreciated," the black-shirt colonel had responded indifferently.

Now, with two-thirds of his force destroyed by a mere company of Rebels, he sought to turn these rather odd allies to his advantage. Maj. Ernesto Kruger was not prepared for what he encountered in the underground home of the American leader. He came to them at mealtime. An unfortunate choice, as he soon discovered.

His stomach churned at the sight of what appeared disturbingly to be a roasted human thigh laid out on a large platter in the center of the table. Perhaps it was bear, he hastened to assure himself. There were a lot of them around now that man did not occupy their former living space. And the — meat had been skinned.

"Join us in our humble fare?" the American had asked, deep-set eyes aglitter with some secret jest.

"No, ah — thank you. I just left my dinner table," Kruger responded, stomach jittery.

"Oh, well." The American leader passed slices of the meat to those around the table. It smelled sweet, like pork, Kruger thought. "You came about your defeat by the Rebels," he fired at Kruger.

"That's — yes, I did. They hit us rather hard in an ambush, the snowstorm, you see. I wanted to be certain that your people would still fight to keep the Rebels out."

"Without question. We'll fight. But I am sure you know that you will lose."

"Why is that?"

"By our count, the Rebels have less than a company in strength, yet they wiped out twice their number in one fifteen-minute battle. And that in conditions of limited visibility. No, don't take that wrong. Your troops are fine. Excellent, in fact. They performed outstandingly against the small, partisan armies of the countries you dominated in South America, and against native peoples, primitives with spears and blowguns. They did well against a determined enemy in Venezuela, Colombia, and the Central American Alliance. Even the venture in Mexico went well."

"So, then, why is it inevitable that we shall lose?" Kruger demanded.

"Without exception, those nations were weakened by the presence of my — our — ah, co-religionists, if you will. My point is, all of this did not prepare you to face the Rebels."

"That is patently ridiculous," Kruger spat in outrage at this insult to Nazi superiority.

Suddenly the weird American's face swelled and the cords stood out in his neck. *"We almost ruled the entire world, you silly Nazi clown! We know what the Rebels can do."*

Kruger recoiled as though he had been slapped. Who were these strange people? A chill began at the base of his spine and grew to engulf his soul. At last he mastered enough control to frame a retort. "Then why are you willing to fight?"

"Because we hate Ben Raines. Anything that hurts him gives us pleasure. And, we are willing to die for it. Tell me where and when you want us and we will be there. Now, our food is getting cold and dining has very special meaning to us."

Smarting at his dismissal, Ernesto Kruger departed from his allies with an impression of having escaped something dark and sinister. *"Santa Maria, y todos los santos,"* he breathed prayerfully, meaning it for the first time since childhood.

Somehow the Nazis got some rods shoved up their asses, Thermopolis thought at the sight of screaming, raging men charging the Rebel forward lines. Through the magnification of his field glasses, he discovered that women fought in the company of the maniacal defenders of the Thermopolis Quadrangle, as he had dubbed it.

Women? Maddened to the point of attacking with bare hands, at that. Where had he come across that before? He asked his executive officer.

"The creepies, man," Bags — short for Bagh Savita — Rivers answered.

"Thanks a bunch, Bags, man. What we need is an instant replay of those bastards," Thermopolis complained. "Have our people got those flamethrowers spotted?"

"Yep. Came in a minute ago. I sent snipers to deal with them. Should be hearin' any time now," Bags advised him.

Big custom .50 sniper rifles had a distinctive blast to them that set the bull-barrel, long-range blasters apart from any other firearm. Thermopolis heard one kick in a second later. Another followed in a heartbeat. He produced a broad grin.

"Scratch two firebugs."

"What do we do about these dudes who are clawin' and bitin' at our people?" Bags asked.

A shiver ran up Thermopolis's spine. "They really doin' that?"

"True thing."

"Bags, we could be in some deep shit, man," Thermopolis underestimated. "Back up every patrol with a light machine gun. Take no chances. Frag every hidey-hole that's uncovered. And, no prisoners. None, no matter what. See that they are shot, and from a distance, not knifed."

Bags Rivers developed a sickly expression. "Don't lay that on me, man. It sounds like we're fightin' the creepies again."

Thermopolis spoke with a slight catch in his throat. "I dunno. It could be."

Electrified by the similarity in behavior of the defenders of Thermopolis to the Night People, the Rebels renewed their determination. Careful, calm deliberation by Thermopolis-the-man led to a sudden and final upset of the Nazi dream for the town. Within three hours, squad mopups on a block-by-block basis got under way. Thermopolis could count himself another victory.

Apache gunships blew the FOs off the peaks around Alamogordo like so many winter leaves. While they sanitized the area, Rebel units spread out across the middle of the wreckage of the town and prepared to advance against the black-shirts.

Spearheaded by the armor, BFVs, and APCs, the Rebel assault struck terror into the hearts of the American Nazi defenders. Advancing behind the heavies, the infantry crunched over the ruins on the flat mesas that once were home to thousands of workers at White Sands. What structures had not been cannibalized for firewood were blown into clouds of splinters by the 4-inch mortars, firing flat-trajectory like tank guns, and the recoilless rifles of the mobile infantry.

"Eagle, we have a hot spot over here on the south side of town," came a call to Ben's headquarters.

"You're that far already?" Ben asked in surprise.

"Roger that. They melted in front of us until we got here. There's some kind of big compound, cyclone fence with razor wire on top. Wooden barracks, a mess hall. Also somethin' that looks like big prefab ovens."

"I'll be right there," Ben snapped.

With directions provided by the R Batt company commander, Cooper got Ben there in fifteen minutes. That came after much dodging of enemy mortar and machine-gun fire. What Ben Raines saw culled up images of grainy film shown at the Nuremberg War Crimes Trials.

"Another of Hoffman's 'improvements for America,' no doubt," Ben observed acidly. He took the mike from Corrie. "Yankee Two-four, Eagle here. Can you punch through to that place?"

"Roger that, Eagle. We've got the wire down on two sides. I'm taking some casualties, but we're ready to jump off now."

"Let me find you first. Eagle, out."

Cooper raced the Hummer around one side of the apparent concentration camp. He tried hard to not flinch at the wall of flickers from small-arms fire. With his usual élan, Cooper slewed the Humvee into place beside a man who exuded command authority. Jersey, then Ben, emerged from the utility vehicle.

"Yankee Two-four?" Ben queried.

A warrior bred, the company commander nodded acknowledgment of his general instead of bracing and saluting. Ben liked that. "General. We captured a CP earlier. According to the marks on the map, this is a labor camp. Looks like old pictures of Dachau to me."

"My thinking exactly. When we go in, watch out for collateral damage."

The company commander's eyes narrowed. "You think there are civilians in there?"

"There could be. Whether or not, we have to take this place. What say we go give Hoffman an enema?"

Ben and his Thompson, accompanied by Jersey and the team, went in alongside the company commander. Two hate-mouthing Nazis appeared in a second-floor window of one barrack and Ben ended their day, and their lives, with a spray from the heavy old subgun. Screams of agony, rage, and terror grew to a chorus of misery as more Rebels poured into the camp. Jersey shot a black-shirt who held a stick grenade poised to throw.

It dropped to the ground at his feet and went off. End of story for him and three others. A trio of walleyed Nazis tried to surrender. Snarling Rebels cut them down. Then, with a short spurt of fire from the far end of the building at the center, all resistance ended.

Ben wiped his face with the back of one hand and reached for his canteen. After a long gulp, he gestured to the sturdy structure where fighting had ceased. "Let's go see what we've walked into."

What Ben found raised his eyebrows and his anger by a few degrees. Pathfinders from the assaulting company herded a dozen small, uncertain, hesitant figures before them. In the smoke-darkened light of late afternoon, Ben discovered them to be small boys, he judged to be from ten to thirteen. All had smudged, tear-stained faces, grubby hands, and rags for clothing. But they were clear-eyed, with cherubic features and neatly crew-cut hair.

"What have we here?" Ben asked the corporal in charge.

"Internees, according to this boy here, General."

"Y-yer General Ben Raines?" a towheaded lad of twelve or so chirped doubtfully. When Ben nodded affirmatively, he threw himself forward and hugged Ben around the waist with thin, dirty arms. "We're safe! We're really safe at last," he wailed.

"I'll—be—goddamned," was all Ben could manage.

Ben Raines turned away from the field stove and handed a mug of hot chocolate to the towheaded young-ster who had been so demonstrative. The boys had been cleaned up; the Rebels had found a total of twenty-four of them. Within the limits of a predominantly adult organi-zation, clothing had been provided to cover their seminakedness. Fighting still raged in one corner of Ala-mogordo, but the time had come to discover what these children might know.

From some of the others, Ben and his interrogators had heard horror stories of enslavement, torture, parents killed by the Nazis before their children's eyes. He had also obtained hints that there was another camp, somewhere up in the Sacramento Mountains to the south of town. Most had indicated that this lad knew the most about what had happened.

Ben had so far learned that this boy was named Jimmy Riggs. He was twelve and, apparently by tacit agreement, spokesman for the rest. He wore his patched and washed shorts, a Rebel camo T-shirt that hung to his bare knees, the armholes sagging well down thin arms, and worn sneakers. Jimmy accepted the cocoa eagerly and took a deep sip. It left a pale brown mustache on his puckered upper lip.

"Now, Jimmy, I have some questions I have to ask you," Ben explained in a far-more-kindly voice than used for his regular interrogations. "Some of them may be painful to answer, but everything you can tell me will help. You can be sure of that. First off, how long did the Nazis hold you captive?"

"I—uh—I don't know, Gen'ral Raines," Jimmy piped.

"It was a long time. At least a month."

That tallied with what the others had said. "What about your parents? We didn't find any adult prisoners in this compound."

"Th-they—they—" Tears welled in Jimmy's eyes and he choked off his voice.

"I think I can guess the rest, Jimmy. The Nazis hurt them?"

"Y-yes. Some kids' folks never came with them. My m-mom a-an' dad—they—they went away. I—we boys think the nasties killed our folks."

"I'm sorry, son, but I believe you're right. Do you have any idea why we found only boys? There were no girls here."

"Th-the girls . . . they—uh . . ." Jimmy lowered straw-colored lashes over cobalt eyes and dropped his voice to a whisper. "They took them somewhere else. There's another camp, where they have a lot of boys, and girls, too. To—to use for their dir—dirty fun."

For all his compassion for the child, for any children, Ben's anger exploded. "Goddamn them! Do you know where they took the girls?"

"I—I'm afraid to say. What if they found out I told you?"

Ben reached over and ruffled Jimmy's brush of crew-cut hair. "Nothing will happen to you, Jimmy. We're kicking shit out of them." Ben bit his lip. *You don't say "shit" to a twelve-year-old,* he admonished himself.

Jimmy giggled. "Good. I hope you get that Major Brauer an' kick him in the balls. He—he tried to—ah—pester me."

Ben's eyes narrowed. "Is Brauer a short, fat guy with a little mustache?"

"Y-yes."

"No problem, Jimmy. I blew his brains all over the wall of his office with this." Ben lightly touched the butt of his .50 Desert Eagle.

Jimmy sighed heavily. "Okay. Then—then I guess it's safe to tell you what I know. I—I heard some of the guards talkin'." His face twisted in childish disgust. "They were

Americans, can you believe it? Spoke English good as me or you. There's this place in the mountains to the south, the Sacramento Mountains, right? These guards were talkin' about how the big-shot officers went there for R&R, whatever that means."

"Rest and Recreation," Ben provided.

"Huh! Recreation, all right. They had the girls up there, an' some boys who wouldn't make a fuss over it, to fool around with."

He'd heard enough, Ben Raines decided. His blood boiled whenever he learned of kids being misused in any manner. When someone picked them for sex toys, he lost all composure when it came to dealing with the perverts. And right now he figured to deal with those responsible for this atrocity.

"Do you know where this place is?" Ben asked tightly.

"No — not exactly. But I could show you how to get most of the way there."

"Would you do it, Jimmy?" Ben asked eagerly.

"Sure. I'd go with you if you want."

A frown creased Ben's brow. "I'm not so hot for that idea. The place is bound to be guarded."

"This was guarded an' you managed to get me an' the others out," Jimmy reminded him.

Ben fought a smile. "All right, we'll do it. Jersey," he raised his voice. "Where's the rest of the team?"

"Cooper's with the love of his life." She meant the Hummer. "Corrie's chowin' down. Beth is helping clean up some of the other kids."

"Leave her, then, and Smoot. Get the rest together, get a light semiauto rifle for Jimmy here, and we're going to hit the road."

"No sport jobs around, General, but I can get him an M-16."

"Do it."

"Where we headed, boss?" Jersey asked.

"We are out to bust the Nazi big wigs' brothel."

Nine

At Ben's repeated urging, Cooper put the pedal down on the Hummer. Little Jimmy Riggs sat up front and pointed out various landmarks with which he was familiar.

"Look! See—see that rusty pile of metal?" he chirped somewhere in the middle of the White Sands Proving Ground complex. "They say that was one of the first rockets tested here. It was up on a stand, once, to show off. Why did they test rockets?" he asked innocently.

"So men could go to the moon," Ben simplified.

"Who'd want to go to the moon?" Jimmy returned.

"Did someone feed this kid some uppers with his canned hash?" Ben asked jokingly. Then he relented and spoke in his teacher's voice. "Back before the Great War, before even your dad was born, men had dreams of exploring space, going to Mars, to the other planets. We did, too. Only it was machines for the most part. Men did stand on the surface of the moon. They planted an American flag there. It's still up there, as far as I know. Small, powerful robots, called space probes, were shot into space and visited Venus, Mars, the outer planets. One even went off out of our solar system. Then the dream died," Ben concluded with sadness evident, "along with almost everything else good in our world."

"The Great War, huh?" Jimmy asked.

"That's part of it. But it began long before that. Politicians convinced themselves that their offices were a 'career.' They thought they had been elected for life and acted with all the arrogance of that self-delusion. They openly looted the public wealth to brazenly buy votes from every loudmouthed minority and special interest. They pandered to the criminals, the worthless, and the incompetent. They encouraged a cult of victimism, in which no one was required to be responsible for their actions, and particularly for their crimes or failures. It was always someone else's fault. Not surprisingly, at the same time, the politicians and judges coddled criminals and persecuted their victims.

"Society glorified drugs and sex and violence, encouraged by the deviants in the media, entertainment, and government. We became a morally and economically bankrupt nation," Ben summed up sadly. "And that didn't happen only in our country, Jimmy. Look at what went on in South America. The politicians began by accommodating the Nazi fugitives from Germany after the Second World War, and see what that got them. Oh, hell, here I go preaching again. And probably pitching my spiel above your head."

"Oh, no, sir. I understand everything you said, Gen'ral Raines," Jimmy answered quietly.

Was that a note of bitter cynicism in the boy's voice? Ben asked himself. Considering what he had been through, he had come by it honestly. A silent minute later, Jimmy pointed ahead.

"We're going to start up into the mountains. Maybe— maybe you can have Mr. Cooper slow down so I can look real hard at the country?"

"Sure, Jimmy. Back it off some, Coop, if you please," Ben instructed.

Above 3,000 feet in San Agustin Pass, snow began to fall. Strong drafts through the cleft in the red-brown mountains caused it to swirl in thick, tornado-shaped billows. Jimmy's face became pinched and closed as he studied the country.

284

"It was somewhere around here that the trucks with the girls turned off, Gen'ral Raines," he said quietly.

A few minutes later he became agitated and pointed excitedly at a narrow side road. "Is that it, Jimmy?" Ben asked.

"Yes — yes, I think so," he squeaked.

"Take a look, Coop," Ben commanded.

Cooper slewed the Hummer into the opening, tires creaking on four inches of new fall. They eased along, with not even fences to show a sign of human habitation. After the third mile, with a high, overhanging wall of rock ahead, everyone agreed this was not the road. With greater than usual care, Cooper navigated back to the snow-swept concrete surface of U.S. 70/82. They continued upward.

Near the summit, at 3,900 feet, Jimmy again showed signs of alert energy. He pointed the Hummer onto a decrepit, rutted dirt side road. Again they didn't see a sign of life for the first mile. Then, around a bend, a high chain-link fence snapped into sharp focus during a spate in the whirling flakes.

"That's it!" Jimmy squeaked. "I bet it is."

Ben Raines patted the boy on one shoulder. "Go on, Coop. We'll take a better look."

Indeed they found a compound, enclosed by sagging fence and rusted razor wire. Tall access gates closed off the road. On one, a sign identified it as a part of the old security system for White Sands. It read MONILE PATROL 1 AND DET. 3, AIR SURVEILLANCE (RADAR) CO. B. (USA).

"We might have something here, Coop. There are no guards in that shack."

"Or they're hiding from us," Jersey suggested.

"The guards I heard talking said there weren't many men on duty up here," Jimmy offered.

"Then, let's go wake up whoever is here," Ben declared.

Dismounted from the Hummer, the team approached the gate. Cooper checked out the sentry box and signaled it empty. They entered through a personnel portal. Ben had insisted that Jimmy remain behind in the Humvee.

He had an M-16 to keep him company, and with the motor running it was warm.

Jersey came upon the first guard. She silenced him with a butt-stroke to the throat. He went down gagging and suffocating. Cooper knifed a fat guard in what might have been the guardroom. After a quick circuit of the compound, they gathered at a large barrack building. Dim lights glowed from dirty windows, indicating the presence of a generator.

"We'll take the end doors, front and rear. In two minutes, we all go in together," Ben instructed.

"One of those doors is goin' to have to go beggin', boss. I stay with you," Jersey insisted.

Ben snorted his irritation, but agreed. When the second hand indicated the end of two minutes, Ben kicked in the door and Jersey went in first. High, shrill shouts of surprise reached Ben's ears a fraction of a second before he followed Jersey.

They found kids, all right. Each one a fanatical member of Peter Volmer's Werewolves. Firing began at once, with the advantage to the crazed Nazi kids. Like their leader, Ben Raines, the Rebels had an instinctively protective attitude toward children. That made even the deadly Jersey a bit slow with her trigger finger.

For all that, her slugs reached two kiddie black-shirts before the weapons they aimed at Ben Raines could discharge. They went down with severe wounds, rather than killing shots. Intense pain in ones so small rendered them helpless. Shouting *"Sieg Heil!"* the little monsters swarmed around and over Ben's team. Ben went belatedly for his .50 Desert Eagle a moment before a stout lad of fourteen drove the butt of his FAL M-2 rifle into the back of Ben's head. Blackness swamped the Rebel leader as other blows felled his team.

A murmur, like the surf on a gentle strand, reached the mind of Ben Raines. Slowly the blackness turned to gray. Slivers of pain lanced through his head as he tried slowly to raise his eyelids. After a long rest, he made another effort. The murmur turned to human speech.

At least, Ben thought it to be human. It did sound like high, sharp twitters of birds. Suddenly a voice heavy with authority cut through the chirping and brought silence.

"Achtung!"

Ben forced his lids up to a strange sight. He estimated some forty little tads standing at rigid attention all around him. Their faces were clean-scrubbed and glowed with health. All had crew cuts, their hair ranging from cotton white to soft brown. They all wore short black trousers and brown elbow-length shirts. Each had a swastika armband. The authoritative voice spoke again.

"Comrades, our beloved leader, *Brigadeführer* Peter Volmer."

"Heil Hoffman!" the little Nazis barked.

Peter Volmer here? Where was "here"? And how long had he been out? Ben puzzled over these questions muzzily while he fought to maintain focus with eyes that burned and throbbed.

"My dear Werewolves, I am immensely proud of you. When I learned of the presence of Ben Raines near Alamogordo, I immediately made arrangements to come here. First I must compliment your commander. *Standartenführer* Dracher, you planned and executed your mission splendidly. I will personally recommend you to our *Führer* for the First Class Order of the Iron Cross."

"Thank you, *Brigadeführer*," young Dracher blushingly blurted. "What are we to do with these Rebel swine?"

"I think we shall leave them alive. Let them try to live with the fact they are responsible for the mighty Ben Raines being captured by the mere children of the Master Race." He laughed heartily for Peter Volmer, a sort of strangled "Haa-ha, haaa-hee—haa!"

Again, Dracher called for silence as the boy Nazis picked up on the laughter. Volmer nodded his approval and Ben Raines glowered at him from the floor. Then Volmer reached behind him and made a come-here gesture.

"The real hero of this engagement — the star actor of our little drama, shall we say — is young *Abteilungführer* Heinz Gruber."

Volmer brought forward a pale-faced boy in the uniform of the Werewolves. With outrage and sick disgust, Ben Raines recognized their ever-so-cooperative guide, Jimmy Riggs. The two pips of an SS squad leader sparkled on the shoulder tabs of his brown shirt. On one side of the collar were the SS runes, on the other an old U.S. Army officer's infantry branch insignia. Volmer ran lengthy, pallid, spatulate fingers down the long lobe at the back of the boy's head and along his neck in a possessive, intimate touch that made Ben's stomach lurch.

"You did well, Heinz," Volmer praised. "But what else could I expect from my most efficient *Standartenführer?*"

Heinz/Jimmy's face glowed with ecstasy. A promotion! And not a little one, to Company Commander at that. "Th-thank you, *Brigadeführer.* I — I don't deserve the promotion, I only did my job."

"And excellently, too. We have the great Ben Raines in our grasp now. The ultimate destruction of all Rebel forces is at hand. And it is entirely due to your superb acting ability." He turned to more-mundane matters. "Clean out this place quickly, leave not a trace. Dump these Rebel scum in their vehicle. Ben Raines is to be bound securely and made ready to be moved. He is coming with me. So, Heinzi, are you," he concluded, again stroking the boy's head.

Ben Raines could contain his revulsion and humiliation no longer, sucking in air he roared with all his powerful voice, "You sick, pervert son of a bitch!"

Jimmy's small Nazi foot, in an ankle-high boot, kicked Ben back into unconsciousness.

When the headquarters comm unit reported that nothing had been heard from Ben's team in an hour and a half, Buddy had a stab of apprehension. Since he found himself occupied in the finishing-off of Carrizozo, he could do little about it, except worry.

AH-64 Apaches made their final runs three hours after communications had lost contact with the Hummer. With their "black hole" exhausts, they made hardly a sound as the insectile forms peeked over a ridge and positioned themselves to unload their terrible ordnance. Nazis died like ants on a griddle as missiles, rockets, and thousands of rounds of 30mm swathed through them. Even those dug into supposedly secure holes retained flash impressions of the nosecones of Hellfire missiles an instant before white-hot oblivion embraced them.

By the time the fledgling village of Carrizozo—rebuilt by Rebels the previous year—had been fully suppressed, Buddy's gnawing preoccupation with Ben's whereabouts had reached the head-scratching and lip-chewing stage. Relief flooded him when his comm unit beeped and he heard the welcome words.

"Rat, we've just heard from Eagle's team."

"Good," Buddy replied briskly. "Where is Eagle and what's he up to?"

"Uh, Rat, like I said, we've heard from the *team*. General Ike thinks you should come over here."

A cold hand grasped Buddy's spine. "What do you mean? Come out with it. Is Dad okay?"

"We, ah, don't know." The uncomfortable RT operator had the mike taken from her hands. "Buddy, this is Ike. You'd better come over here. We've gotta talk."

Conquering potholes, blown bridges, and rockslides, Buddy made the ninety miles to Ike in Roswell in two hours. He entered his senior commander's CP with a face drawn and gray. Ike, he quickly noticed, looked the same.

"Here's what we've got," Ike said curtly after greeting the young Raines. He pushed the play button of a tape recorder.

Jersey's voice came through the background static. "This is Eagle team. I gotta talk to General Ike, uh, to Shark." Crackling airwaves followed while the RT patched the channel to Ike, who was assaulting Roswell at the time. It gave Buddy time to wonder why it was Jersey and not

Corrie. He soon learned when the connection was made.

"Uh — Shark, this is Eagle Team. They, ah, they've got Be — Eagle." Ike's bluster followed. "I know. It was my fault. I take all blame. The Hummer is out of order. Cooper is trying to reattach the distributor cap and plug wires. It happened about four hours ago. We're still up in San Agustin Pass. The Nazis, *kid* Nazis, jumped us, god-damn them."

Buddy stared blankly while she spoke. Her disclosure that Ben Raines had been captured by the most vile enemy, except possibly the Night People, the Rebels had known stunned him. Now he croaked out his question when Ike turned off the recorder and keyed the mike.

"How's the rest of the team?"

"Is that Rat? Well, Beth's all right. Sore and damn mad. Corrie got a hell of a lump on her head. Sick to her stomach right now, so I'm doin' the talkin'."

"What about you?"

"I don't matter," Jersey, filled with misery, fired back. "I dropped the ball. I let the boss get taken by those rotten little bastards. I'm losin' it, Rat, Ike. I'll never forgive myself. I — I don't even know if B-Ben's still alive!" A sound like a ragged sob ended her transmission.

Ike's slow, patient voice got her back on the air. After several deep breaths, Jersey related the entire story from the beginning. Expressions of alarm passed among those in the comm van. Ike questioned Jersey in his easy drawl to make certain everything came out.

"You say those kids the R Batt found in Alamogordo were part of this Werewolf outfit?"

"Roger, Shark. I felt hincky about that all along, those kids being there, all convenient for us to rescue. Way I see these Nazis, they'd kill any witnesses. Oh, shit! There's most of them still there. Somethin' ought to be done about it."

It being Buddy's AO, he took the mike. "Some of them still are," he replied to Jersey's worry. "Others we packed up an hour ago and sent them off on a supply plane to Base Camp One. We'll take care of it right away. When will you

290

be back to Alamogordo?"

"Whenever Cooper gets this thing running again. I don't want to come back. I want to go find the boss," Jersey said with anguish.

"We all do. I'll be there in two hours. Then we'll take care of those baby black-shirts. Meet me there and we'll organize a search for — for Eagle. Rat out."

Ten

Buddy Raines came back to Alamogordo boiling with rage. He'd never trust a kid again. Wide-eyed little deceiving sons of bitches. And they had his father. Who knew what tortures the Nazi bastards would use on Ben Raines? Radio messages had alerted the military police among the Rebels.

Part-timers, they were volunteers for policing rear areas, directing convoy traffic, and all the details attended to in a military community. The captain who served as provost marshal to Buddy's command met him outside the administrative building of the fake Nazi concentration camp.

"What are your orders, Colonel?" he asked briskly.

"We're going to round up those Nazi brats damn fast," Buddy snapped.

"Sir, some of the guys who are missing their own families have sorta taken them in. After all, once they were cleaned up, they were kinda cute little tykes."

"I'm calling this Operation Diaper Vipers," Buddy stated coldly. "Those kids are trained killers. Consider it like having a cobra in your hooch, Captain O'Malley." At the top cop's puzzled expression, Buddy explained. "It comes from that old war in Vietnam. Dad told me about cobras and hooches. Snakes are cold-blooded. They like warm places. A hooch was a dugout shelter, usually with a thatch roof, for one or two men. Sleeping men put out a lot of warmth."

"I follow the rest, sir," O'Malley responded with a wince. "We handle the kids with care."

"Right. You'll be in charge, but I'm coming along to pick up every one of them."

"Five of the boys are still right over there in the barrack, sir."

"Good. We'll start with them. Pick five of your MPs and bring them along." Buddy loosened the .45 in his belt holster.

Five small boys sat in a tight circle on the floor of the main dormitory room of the barrack. They had been engaged in an earnest, whispered conversation when the door burst open to reveal Buddy Raines, face darkly clouded with his anger.

They were good, Buddy had to admit. All five looked up with guileless, friendly expressions. "Spread out, get on your bellies, arms over your heads, legs apart," Buddy snapped.

"Wh-what? Is this a game?" one lad chirped.

"This is like the nasties did to us," another whined.

Buddy stepped further into the room and MPs followed him. At their presence, with the bands on helmets and brassards on arms, the Werewolves' eyes widened. Buddy growled at them, with full intent behind the menace.

"Do it, or I'll kick you clear the fuck across the room."

An MP knelt at the side of each supine boy. Expertly they bent the small arms down to the small of childish backs and secured the wrists with plastic riot cuffs. Then they began searching. A small pile of boning, filleting, and utility knives began to grow. Buddy studied it and felt a chill.

"I imagine the cooks will be interested to learn where their missing cutlery was found," he observed dryly. "Take them somewhere and lock them up. Have interrogators stand by to chemically debrief them. Let's go get the others."

Operation Diaper Vipers went quicker and easier than Buddy had anticipated. Before an hour had passed, all but one of the boys had been rounded up. The embarrassed, red-faced Rebel who had "adopted" the boy who called himself Tommy Cook told them that the youngster had wanted to go look at the tanks. Buddy and the military police headed for the tank park.

They did not find Tommy there. Growing more concerned, Buddy suggested the search spread out. Captain O'Malley directed his men to every sensitive point. He remained with Buddy Raines. Their wait didn't prove a long one.

"MP One, this is MP Six," the radio in Pat O'Malley's hand crackled. He cut his eyes to Buddy Raines, who nodded a "this is your show" go-ahead.

"Go, Six."

"We found him. Only we got a problem."

"Ten-twenty, Six?" O'Malley asked.

"We—we're over at the ammo trucks, Captain." The strain in his voice had Buddy Raines seeing the sweat standing out on a young Rebel's forehead.

"Shit," O'Malley spat, then keyed the mike. "What's the situation?"

"The kid—the kid's standin' at the back of an ammo truck, in the center of a line of them. He's got a grenade. And he's pulled the pin."

"Keep him calm, Six. Talk to him. We're on our way," O'Malley instructed tightly. Then, to Buddy, "Colonel? You—ah, don't need to be in on this one."

"Yes, I do, Captain O'Malley," Buddy said flatly.

They found a pale-faced, frightened boy with a live grenade in his hand. He gripped it so tightly that his severely bitten nails made black crescents against whitened fingers. His bare knees shook so violently that the legs of his shorts fluttered. Buddy Raines took it all in and spoke softly to Pat O'Malley.

"Let me." He stepped forward and Tommy jerked his hand upward toward the tailgate of the loaded ammo truck. "Tommy, Tommy, it's all right, son. Just hold on and let me get that pin and put it back in the grenade. Then we can all relax. Listen to me, Tommy."

"My name ain't Tommy. I'm Dieter. Dieter Yaegel, a soldier of the Fourth Reich!" His thin voice grew loud and shrill. "I demand that you let me go and free all my comrades. Do it or I'll blow up everything."

"You don't want to die, Tommy — er — Dieter. Neither do we. Just let me safe that grenade." Buddy took a step closer to the terrified boy.

"No! Don't take another step. I'll do it. I swear."

"Dieter, my name is Buddy Raines. General Ben is my father."

Shock and confusion registered on the boy's face. He couldn't be over eleven, Buddy estimated. Buddy took advantage of the kid's confusion to take another step closer. A wild light came suddenly to Dieter/Tommy's eyes. Reading the boy's intent, Buddy made a desperate dive forward and hooked the boy's legs in a one-armed tackle.

He and Dieter sprawled in the dirt, the boy kicking and screaming. Buddy's free hand pried at Dieter's death grip on the grenade. He managed to wrench it loose and the arming striker smacked into the primer with a metallic click. Instantly Buddy let go of Dieter and came to one knee. He made a hard, straight pitch with the armed hand bomb toward the low basement window of a smoked-out house across from the ammo vehicles.

"Grenaaaade!" Buddy bellowed.

The light-green spheroid bounced off the bottom of the sill and dropped from sight. Two seconds later it went off. Every Rebel in the vicinity had hit the ground, and they all jerked in reaction to the detonation. Dieter sobbed wretchedly and pounded the ground with small fists. Buddy Raines came to his feet first. He reached down and yanked Dieter off the ground.

With cold, deliberate calmness, he carried the boy by the scruff of his shirt collar to a huge equipment tire that had been changed out. There, Buddy sat down, a lopsided grin on his face as he put the kiddie Nazi over his knees.

Dieter found his voice. "What're you gonna do to me?

295

What're you gonna do?"

"You're going to get what you, by god, should have gotten a damned long time ago," Buddy informed him as he yanked down the youngster's short trousers and underwear.

Then, amid Dieter/Tommy's shrieks, wails, and pitiful sobs, Buddy Raines administered a thorough and deliberately painful spanking. After the sixth application of Buddy's big, hard palm to the boy's buttocks, Dieter stopped wriggling and kicking. His tears continued to wet Buddy's camo trouser leg and his sobs became whimpers on the tenth smack. Buddy quit at an even dozen.

"That was one hell of a spanking," Capt. Pat O'Malley commented in an awed tone.

"Not a quarter of what he deserves," Buddy said thickly.

Restored to his feet, Dieter pulled up his shorts. His face held a strange expression. With effort he gulped back his hysterical sobs. His lips and throat worked and Buddy sensed he wanted to say something other than the defiance he had been uttering. He gave the boy an encouraging nod.

"W-we're part of the W-We-Werewolves," the boy blurted. Then, tearfully, humiliated and feeling betrayed by the Master Race, Dieter told everything he knew about the Werewolves and Peter Volmer. Buddy and O'Malley listened with growing horror and disgust.

"Mary an' all the saints," O'Malley gasped when the lad had concluded. "What kind of monsters would do that to kids? Pervert their childhood into something so twisted and violent."

"The world is full of them," Buddy answered tightly. "Dad said that at least this country used to be. All it takes is a sick mind and the right kind of hate. I'd like to get my hands on that son of a bitch Volmer. Which reminds me. Lock this one up and I've got to get on the horn to Base Camp One."

Cecil Jefferys took the call from Buddy that interrupted his supper. "What's that?" he asked in astonishment after Buddy had given his warning about the small boys soon to arrive at BCO.

"Exactly what I said. You've got a basket of deadly little monsters arriving on a cargo plane any time now," Buddy reiterated. "The Nazis call them Werewolves. They are well-trained, vicious, and deadly. Right now the ones headed your way don't know we've found out about them, so they'll no doubt play the role they used to suck Dad into their trap. Sweet-faced little boys."

"Don't worry, Buddy. They'll be taken care of the minute they step off the plane. Now what's this about Ben in a trap?"

"Oh!" Buddy responded in his surprise. "I thought you'd been informed about that." He went on to describe all they knew of Ben's capture."

"By damn, I'll mobilize my division and be on the way at once," Jefferys growled, outraged at this turn of events.

"No, General Jefferys," Buddy responded. "I can't give you orders, but Dr. Chase can. Right now I don't think Dad would want you exposing Base Camp to any possible advantage the Nazis could take from this. Let's wait and see what happens. We're mounting an expedition to go after Dad as soon as we can get clear from here. General McGowan is taking command in the field and will coordinate everything. I—I feel rotten about Dad being taken like this, but his team feels worse."

"You mean they survived?" Cecil asked, astounded.

"Yes. The Nazis left them unharmed. I gather this Volmer likes to play head games. But, we're on it, so just keep the home fires burning."

Cecil Jefferys decidedly did not like that, but he agreed in principle. After all, he was now C-in-C of the entire Rebel command. He had to coordinate from somewhere.

By use of repeated, vicious blows to the head, and later drugs, Ben Raines was kept unconscious during his transportation to where Peter Volmer had decided to confine the Rebel leader. The place chosen had been the result of careful consideration. He could have moved Ben Raines to *Führer* Hoffman's headquarters at Wallowa Lake.

That would have put all the eggs in Hoffman's basket. Peter Volmer had his own ideas as to whom it should be who became *Führer* of the American Reich. Now on an equal footing with Hans Brodermann, and ranked only by the *Führer* himself, Peter had ambitions to enlarge his power base. Everyone loved a winner. The man who captured Ben Raines and succeeded in forcing the surrender of all Rebel forces would be the man of the hour, as Volmer saw it. With General Rasbach's army behind him, and all of the American Nazis, he would be in a good bargaining position to present himself as the new *Führer.*

People would remember and admire the one who had defeated the Rebel pirates. They would back him, he knew it. For that reason, American and Mexican Nazis had secretly placed a battalion in the environs of Villa Ahumada, Chihuahua, Mexico. They controlled the entire area—in particular, a large, luxurious hacienda some ten miles out of town. It was there that Volmer and his Werewolves took the comatose form of Ben Raines.

Ben gradually regained awareness over the next two days. Still groggy, and seriously concussed, Ben could at first make little of his surroundings. He was nauseated, dizzy, his head throbbed and his vision blurred. On the third day at the hacienda, he began to retain food given him. His strength returned rapidly now.

By what he surmised to be midafternoon he had come to the conclusion he was being held in a partly subterranean room, a sort of dungeon. The door was thick, wooden, and barred from outside. He had a crude, narrow cot, a bucket to serve as a toilet, and a three-by-three-foot table on which he took his meals. Muffled voices from outside his cell grew louder as someone approached. The door opened and Peter Volmer entered, accompanied by a man Ben figured to be a doctor, from the small black bag he carried.

Without a word, both men approached Ben. The doctor peeled back Ben's eyelids and flashed a penlight into each pupil. He tapped and probed and at last nodded his satisfaction.

"Ah, it seems you are with us again, and at least conscious and rational enough to suit the purpose."

"What might that be?" Ben demanded.

"We're going up to the radio room and have a little conversation with your precious Rebels."

"Talk all you damn well please. We have a policy. The Rebels do not recognize hostages. Hostages are considered KIAs, and there will be no negotiations for their release."

Volmer chuckled condescendingly. "Come now, General Raines. I think an exception will be made in your case. Get up!" he snapped in a command voice. "You're to be the star of the show."

Considerable effort had gone into development of this Nazi stronghold, Ben reflected as they waited for a response from the Rebels in the elaborate radio communications center in a towerlike second-floor room of the hacienda. The windows in its rounded outer walls looked out over a sharp drop-off from the top of the mesa, on which the Spanish colonial ranch house had been built, to the desert floor below.

Ben had decided he was imprisoned in a Mexican hacienda when he had observed the large interior garden, with fountains, statues, and tall, ancient palm trees, the distinctive wrought-iron grilles on windows and doors, and generous use of arches. Stout, hand-hewn timbers formed the lintels of doorways and frames of arches. Yes, definitely Mexican in origin. Ironically, it raised Ben's spirits; it put him that much closer to General Raul Payon.

"I repeat, this is the Headquarters of the American Nazi Expeditionary Force in North America. We demand to speak to General Ike McGowan. Over."

Again, no reply came. Volmer gestured to a sergeant standing beside a table. The noncom picked up a captured Rebel long-range field radio and set it on the counter in front of the RT operator.

"Try that," Volmer commanded.

After careful study, the RT operator attached antenna leads to the proper terminals and turned on the set. He let it warm up, then repeated his message. A crackle of static came from the speaker, then a voice, made tinny and distant by the scrambler.

"We copy you, Nazi scum. General Ike isn't available at the moment."

Volmer made an impatient gesture. "Give me that." He took the mike in hand and pushed the talk button. "This is *Brigadeführer* Peter Volmer. I demand to speak to General McGowan of the criminal Rebel forces at once, or to someone else in authority. We are holding General Ben Raines as a prisoner of war."

"Then why didn't you say so, asshole? I'll get someone right away."

Ben cut his eyes to Volmer's livid face. "Didn't I tell you, Volmer? It's Rebel policy to write off hostages. And they don't like Nazis."

"Shut up!" Volmer barked. "You will speak only when told to."

Although it hurt his head to do so, Ben laughed at Volmer.

"This is Lt. Col. Buddy Raines, Volmer. What is it you want?"

Ben laughed again at the surprised gape Volmer's mouth formed. "Your — son? Does he outrank your General McGowan?"

"As a matter of fact, he is subordinate to Ike. But he is in charge of one of the task forces headed this way to kick your Nazi ass."

Volmer missed the indication that Ben knew he was in Mexico. "He will do, then." To Buddy, he spoke into the mike. "We are holding your father as a prisoner of war.

We are willing to discuss repatriation. There are, of course, certain demands, conditions if you will, affixed to returning him."

A heavy sigh from Buddy. "We do not deal with terrorists or hostage takers. If General Raines is indeed your prisoner, we insist he be afforded all the rights and protections of prisoners of war."

Volmer lost it for a moment. "You are in no position to demand anything! You will listen to our demands and do as I say. There will be an immediate cessation of hostilities by Rebel units against forces of the National Army of Liberation and the American Nazi armed forces. Within twenty-four hours, you will present a detailed plan for the laying down of Rebel arms and the peaceful dispersal of your troops. Further, you will present a plan for the surrender of all Rebel war criminals for trial before the High Reich Tribunal. Within forty-eight hours you will present a detailed plan for the delivery of all Rebel-held territory to the New American Reich. At the successful completion of these terms, General Raines will be repatriated. Are those terms clear?"

After a long, tense thirty seconds, Buddy answered. "I stated at the start that we do not deal with terrorists. I have as yet to receive proof that you indeed hold my father and that he is alive."

Volmer uttered a muffled curse. "Arrogant whelp. I expected as much," he directed at Ben. "Here, talk to that obnoxious son of yours, order him to meet my demands."

"I'll talk to him, but I'll not order him to surrender. Even if I did, he'd refuse," Ben responded.

"Just—talk," Volmer snarled.

"Buddy, this is your Dad."

"Yeah, Pop. I think the scrambler is flattening your voice a lot, but it's you, right?"

"Sure, son. I'm alive. And I'm pissed off."

"So are we. Are you all right, Pop?"

"I'm fine, son. So far they haven't pulled any fingernails."

"Then hang in there, Pop. Don't worry. What does

301

Jersey always dream about as the perfect dessert?"

Ben produced a big smile. "She longs for a big, gooey, hot fudge sundae."

"That's a big ten-four, Pop." He went off the air for a moment, then, "Let me have that Volmer mother again."

"This is *Brigadeführer* Volmer," Peter said icily. "Show some respect for your superiors, you repugnant woods colt."

"You're the *bastard,* Volmer. Pop legally adopted me a long time ago," Buddy said flippantly.

Ben fought to suppress a big, warm smile. Buddy never called him "Pop." It was the boy's way of telling him something was brewing. Ben's spirits bloomed.

Volmer battled his rising fury and forced his voice to remain stern and demanding. "Your old-home week was touching. Now, you know your father is alive. We will deliver General Raines as specified immediately you comply with our terms."

"Sorry, can't do. You know the rules, Pop. There's nothing we can do. So I guess this is goodbye."

"Wait," Volmer shouted into the mike. "General Raines — your father — mentioned torture a moment ago. He is telling the truth . . . so far. But that can change. I'm giving you this ultimatum. You have one hour in which to reconsider, or your father will be minus one finger. We'll send it to you. Now get busy and reach agreement to comply with my terms. Volmer out."

Eleven

An hour later, one in which Peter Volmer alternately threatened and harangued Ben Raines, the RT again contacted Buddy Raines. Volmer had summoned Heinz/Jimmy, who stood close to the mike in Volmer's hand, while the Nazi chief caressed his neck and shoulders. Ben felt his natural revulsion at flagrant perverts rising sour and hot in his throat.

"Well, Colonel Raines. Are you ready to capitulate on our terms?"

"What were those terms again?" Buddy asked, sounding like a man trying to stall for time.

"You know them perfectly well. All hostilities against NAL and American Nazi troops to cease at once. Twenty-four hours to devise a plan to have all Rebel units currently engaged against us or in reserve to lay down their arms and return peacefully to their homes. Immediate surrender of all war criminals, whom we shall designate. Forty-eight hours to devise a plan to turn over all Rebel-held territory to the American Reich."

"Yeah. I thought that was what you had said." Usually mild-mannered, Buddy's voice grew hard as he spoke again. "I'm sorry, Pop. I'll miss you. But, it's no deal. As far as those Nazi scum are concerned, they can go fuck themselves."

Immediately, four burly American black-shirts grabbed Ben Raines. With considerable effort, despite his recent condition, they wrestled him to a table. There one splayed his left hand flat on the surface. Another raised an SS dagger and swiftly brought it down. Its keen edge flashed blue-white in a shaft of sunlight a moment before it severed the tip of Ben's pinkie finger. The blade made a loud, solid thud in the wood.

Volmer had keyed the mike while this went on and now Jimmy provided a convincing scream of agony. "Here comes the finger I promised you, Buddy Raines," he declared, voice dripping with venom.

Ben bit back his own pain as the Nazi thugs stanched the flow of blood and bandaged his left little finger. He had lost the tip, but he had never screamed. He trusted that Buddy would know that had been faked.

"Get him out of here," Volmer ordered his henchmen. To a staff officer, "See that the fingertip is delivered to Rebel lines." Then into the open mike, "We will wait twenty-four hours after you receive our token of affection for a more reasonable reply. Volmer out."

When he heard the news later that day, *Führer* Hoffman was elated that Ben Raines had been captured. But he wanted Raines dead, not in custody. What sort of game was Peter Volmer playing? He contemplated the possibilities while he sipped a congratulatory brandy. Then he had Volmer contacted by radio.

"You have Ben Raines. Execute him," he snapped harshly.

"Patience, *mein Führer*," Volmer soothed. "Consider the opportunities this gives us. By having Ben Raines alive, I have already caused his son to act irresponsibly. He has flatly refused the terms given. He has sworn and acted like a petulant child. We can use that to force the entire Rebel command to surrender in exchange for the life of a single man. One we can then try for war crimes and execute anyway."

Hoffman thought on it and began to chortle. "By Wotan and Thor, I like your style, Volmer. You really have him? You have Ben Raines locked up securely where the Rebels can never find him?"

"Absolutely, *mein Führer*. He is going nowhere. I have already contacted the Rebels and demanded their surrender." Volmer omitted the rest of his terms. "By this time tomorrow they will receive a little token of my — our commitment to this course. Twenty-four hours later, I will renew the demands."

"What is this token you speak of?"

"The tip of one little finger belonging to Ben Raines."

"A man after my own heart! I've a mind to promote you to field marshal, Volmer."

"I would be honored and flattered, *mein Führer.*"

"Single-handedly you have accomplished more than all my fine generals have come close to doing. Yes — yes, by god, I will. From this moment, *Brigadenführer* Volmer, you are a *Feldmarschall* in the New Army of Liberation, with all the privileges and authority of that rank."

"I'm — astounded." And Volmer was indeed. He had not expected this. It made his chances of becoming *Führer* even better. "I'm also grateful. We will work diligently to insure the immediate defeat of the Rebels, *mein Führer.*

"Excellent, Field Marshal Volmer. Oh, one thing. I want you to be prepared to turn over General Ben Raines to General Rasbach, immediately he arrives from Torreon."

"But, I . . ." Volmer forced himself to silence. He was not at all happy about this, but he had no choice . . . at the present. *"Zu Befehl, mein Führer."*

Contrary to the long-held belief of Ben Raines that the Rebel cause would survive his loss without a ripple, reaction spread with the same speed as the word of his capture. The troops were stunned. A number reacted by summarily executing a number of prisoners who had been taken without firing a shot. The command structure reeled like a drunken man.

Cecil Jefferys contacted every field commander individually and in conference calls. Efficiency began to plummet so rapidly that it had a visual effect. Nothing significant got done. Dr. Lamar Chase came to Buddy and Ike with ominous news.

"Out of your two commands, over three hundred on sick call this morning. Not a blamed thing wrong with any of them. They just wanted to talk to someone about the general being captured. That's a quote. Some of them actually plotted to get to where those kids are being held and string them up. Now, that's more in line with Ben's way of thinking reactions should go," the portly doctor added, "but hardly suited to the circumstances.

"The bottom line, gentlemen, is that we can't afford to have better than two companies turning out for sick call every day until something is done to get Ben out of there, or we acknowledge Cecil Jefferys as the new Commander in Chief."

Buddy frowned darkly at the medico's words. Lamar Chase blinked and cut his eyes from Buddy Raines to an equally stormy-visaged Ike McGowan. "What did I say? Did I say something wrong?"

"No," Buddy replied cautiously. "Not wrong. Only something that shouldn't be mentioned."

"Meaning what?" Hands on pear-shaped waist, Dr. Chase looked as though he would pout. Then comprehension struck him and he brightened readily. "Oh. That's it. You've got something laid on, right? About Ben, I mean."

"Yes, Doctor," Ike McGowan, as senior, elected to say. "Only it is not to leave this command post, understood?"

"Sure. But there's no such thing as a disloyal Rebel. Except for communications security, we've never had such classifications of things as being secret or top secret."

"That's right, Dr. Chase," Ike agreed. "Of course you've heard about the darling little kids we took in? Well, there's nothing to say that there aren't more of their kind, and adults, at that, among the civilians that have been filtering in since we stomped the black-shirts."

Lamar Chase looked thunderstruck. "You're right, certainly. I'll keep it to myself. I'm glad, though. Glad

306

Ben ain't gonna get to find out if we can get along without him."

Buddy relented and revealed more to the good doctor. "The Nazis who have him aren't at all shy about using the radio. We're working on a way to pinpoint Dad's exact location. When we have that, we do something about it, and damn fast."

Jesus Diguez Mendoza Hoffman had not gotten to so high a pinnacle by being ignorant of men and their motivations. It took him less than a day to figure out what Peter Volmer might be up to. Coupled with reports of lowered morale among the Rebels, he made a decision to act in a manner that should ensure the unquestioning loyalty of the troops and the adulation of the people at home. He had not been made aware that General Rasbach had all but been thrown out of South America and that the Nazi governments were in utter disarray.

"The time has come," he declared at a general staff conference, "to go on the offensive. Our forces are to start immediate counterattacks at Billings, Montana, and Thermopolis and Riverton, Wyoming. The objective is to push the demoralized Rebels back beyond Miles City and Cheyenne. There are to be no faltering, no defeats, no retreats. Any officer failing to carry out his assigned mission will be shot."

"It's like the old days on the Eastern Front, in the Third Reich," Col. Jouquin Webber confided to Manfred Spitz, the G-3, after the conference broke up. "My grandfather used to tell me about it."

"Yes. We've all heard . . . stories. Hitler got a bomb in his bunker for it, didn't he?"

"Are you suggesting—?" Webber blurted back, white-faced.

"No—no. This is a new *Führer,* a new *Reich,* and an entirely different sort of enemy." Pea-soup-thick mockery could be read in his eyes.

Hoffman's new offensive began within fourteen hours.

In a lightning strike, Thermopolis and HQ Company got pushed out of Riverton, and then Thermopolis. They regrouped at Shoshoni and reported they were holding what they had left. Colonel West had his battalions scattered from Billings in front of a blitzkrieg that pitted a hundred main battle tanks against his dozen. To conserve precious resources—ground could always be retaken—he was forced to retreat. The ignominious run from the enemy ended on the Custer Battlefield.

Gen. Georgi Alexandrovich Striganov found out what it must have been for the Germans facing Marshal Zukov outside Stalingrad. Reeling from a continual artillery pounding, his valiant troops wound up with their backs to the rock walls of the Bighorn Mountains, outside Sheridan, Wyoming.

Gen. Cecil Jefferys, still deeply grieved over the capture of Ben Raines, read the reports of crumbling Rebel resistance all through the northern portion of the Nazi's vaunted Eastern Wall. That bothered him even more. For all practical, military purposes, he knew he had to consider Ben as expendable and dead. He was spoiling to get into the fight. But he also had to admit he had a great reluctance to assume overall command of Rebel forces.

"Dammit, Annie," he blared to his aide. "What's gotten into these people? They're actin' like Ben Raines is all there is to the Rebel program for a new start. Can't commanders command and troops follow orders and fight?"

"Don't ask me, General. If you want my opinion, I'd say it's you who should be commanding about now. These people need a real leader. With General Raines—out of the picture, it has to be you."

"I want to fight those Nazi bastards. Want it in the worst way. You know that."

"I do. But you are still thinkin' of taking your troops into combat as a subordinate commander. You're *in charge now.* Ben—the general would want it that way. He put you here for that purpose. Don't you think he's countin' on your right now?"

General Jefferys gave her the oddest expression. Then his mahogany face split in a broad grin. "By God, girl, I think you're right."

Dr. Lamar Chase stood in the aisle of the recovery ward of the field hospital outside Las Cruces, New Mexico. In his agitation, he used his clipboard like a conductor's baton. "You are going to get out of those trousers and get back in bed. Dan, you suffered a fractured skull, severe concussion. Hell, man, you admit yourself to still having moments of blackout."

Col. Dan Gray glowered at the doctor and reached for his shirt. "Doctor, we all have to do what we can to infuse our Rebels with new spirit. I can't, I won't, accept the fact that Ben Raines is already a casualty of this war with the Nazis. Dammit, Lamar, we're losing on every goddamned front but this one. If there's any way of getting Ben back, do you want him to come home to that?"

Dr. Chase pondered that a moment. "Jesus, you're right. But, I'm not authorizing you for full duty."

"I don't expect to return to full duty. I want to coordinate with Ike and with Buddy, participate in the planning. Do something to restore morale. If these kids see a man who is technically still on medical rehab reporting for duty every day, it'll spark them to new efforts. At least I'm hoping it will."

Ben Raines stared at the wall opposite the bunk on which he sat. His left hand throbbed. At least he didn't have red lines shooting up his arm. The amputation had not gotten infected. He felt drained, weaker and more helpless than ever in his life. His mind snapped out of neutral when he heard the scrape of the bar outside the door to his cell and the rattle of a key in the lock.

Heinz Gruber/Jimmy Riggs stood in the doorway

when Ben looked up. The man and the boy studied each other for a long, silent minute. Then Heinz/Jimmy stepped into the cubicle. He had yet to speak when Ben broke the silence.

"How can you do it?"

"What? Keep you prisoner? It's easy." Heinz/Jimmy giggled.

"I mean, how can you wear that uniform, knowing what it represents?"

"I *love* what it stands for, General Raines," the boy glowingly replied.

"Perhaps you're not old enough to understand. Your father was yet to be born when Hitler spread his poison over Europe."

Heinz/Jimmy's face flushed. "Adolf Hitler was a god! I didn't come here to discuss my beliefs."

Ben persisted. "What about your, ah, relationship with Peter Volmer?"

Heinz/Jimmy hesitated, shrugged, would not meet Ben's eyes. "Nothin' wrong, I guess. Pet — Field Marshal Volmer got a promotion from the *Führer* himself. He is a powerful man, a field marshal," he repeated. "He can — have whatever he wants." The youngster's lower lips trembled. "M-my folks sent me to him, to raise as he wanted me to be. Th — they said it was a great honor." He squared his shoulders, recovered his childish arrogance. "I c-came here to give you the latest news. Your Rebels have lost the will to fight. They are being driven out of every place they captured recently. All — all except the regiment your son commands. They are fighting like crazy men. But even they are not making advances. The Rebels are helpless without you, General Raines. They will soon collapse."

Ben stared at the boy, not wanting to believe. His face must have reflected his thoughts, because Heinz/Jimmy blurted suddenly, "It's all true. It's not propaganda. I — thought you would want to know."

"You haven't done me any favors, Jimmy," Ben said sadly.

310

"I am Heinz Gruber, *Standartenführer* of the New American Reich!"

"Banner Leader, eh?" Ben translated the rank. "No, you are Jimmy Riggs, a troubled little boy. I don't hate you, Jimmy. It's your parents I'd like to kill for turning you over to that sick monster, Volmer. And I'm willing to bet your name really is Jimmy Riggs."

"I am Heinz Gruber!" Jimmy shouted again, over his shoulder, on the verge of tears, as he rushed through the door and slammed it shut behind him.

"God help you, boy," Ben said to himself, and he meant it.

Long hours crawled by after Heinz/Jimmy left Ben alone. Haunted by the news of Rebel defeats, Ben found himself forced to reevaluate his importance to the Rebel cause. He had been so certain that the Rebel leadership would settle in, after a short period of adjustment, and carry on should anything happen to him. He wasn't after all immortal. The day would come when he was too old to carry on the affairs of the Rebel state. Or he would be dead.

Granted, his cold logic told him, that would ideally not happen during the middle of a difficult campaign. War should end some time. Hopefully before he became unable to administer the Rebel army and its territories. Ben recalled his speculation on the hillside in Kansas. It looked now as though he would not live to again see those amber waves of grain.

No, he had failed the Rebel cause. He had not properly prepared his co-commander and his subordinates for the ultimate time when he was gone. As it stands, he compelled himself to accept, they are not able to go on in a business-as-usual manner.

Ben didn't like the conclusions he reached. But after hours of reflection, he had to accept, at least intellectually, their validity. It gave him cause to do something else he had been neglecting to do. He had to plan an escape.

Twelve

Three guards came to Ben Raines's cell with Peter Volmer. Volmer seemed subdued, his bald dome shiny with sweat when he removed his black SS hat. His manner was somber, too, not so ebullient as before.

"You're coming with us," he announced to Ben.

"I have a choice?" Ben prodded.

"Don't fence with me, Ben Raines."

"Where are we going?"

"You are going to make another radio broadcast. A very important one. It has become evident that resistance continues, albeit lacking the spirit with which you fired Rebel hearts, General. So, it is time for all of North America to hear of your captivity."

Volmer and his SS guards took Ben from the hacienda. In an Argentine model of the *Kugelwagen,* they drove across the flat mesa top to the distant town of Villa Ahumada. There, a tall steel-girder antenna mast advertised the presence of a commercial broadcast radio station. At Ben's appraising look, Volmer elaborated on the station.

"This is not any mere jerkwater Mexican broadcast studio. Oh, no. Here we have a one-hundred-thousand-watt clear-channel station. I have made arrangements for other transmitters on your Rebel tactical nets to be available also. You will speak into a battery of microphones. Quite impressive, wouldn't you say?"

"What if I refuse to speak?" Ben taunted.

"You'll speak, or you'll scream for mercy."

312

Inside the building, they went through a thick double-door baffle into a small studio. An array of microphones faced the slant glass window of the control room. Volmer began speaking to the men at the console.

"You may begin the music now." An aide handed him several sheets of paper.

Two SS thugs positioned Ben beside Volmer behind the microphones. Ben wondered how anyone could look so smug, yet have deep worry furrows on his brow. Volmer scanned the typed lines on the page and looked up for his cue. A red light flashed on and beside it a sign that read ON AIR. An SS man in white shirt and black tie raised his arm, elbow crooked, then snapped his forearm down, index finger pointing at Volmer.

"This is Field Marshal Peter Volmer of the New Army of Liberation. Today you will be witness to a momentous occasion. The notorious war criminal, General Ben Raines, has been brought here to announce his capitulation and the end of the so-called Rebel government. I give you, now, General Ben Raines."

Ben remained silent. Volmer shot him an angry look. Ben gave Volmer a crooked smile. After an embarrassingly long period of dead air, Volmer snarled angrily at Ben.

"Get on with it, General Raines. You will order your troops to lay down their arms. You will order all Rebel civil authority to surrender their territory to representatives of the New American Reich. Do so at once!"

"You can go to hell," Ben said levelly. Then, speaking rapidly, Ben had his own message for the Rebels. "I call on all Rebels to rally around your commanders and fight to your utmost, *using all means at your disposal.*"

"Get him out of here!" Volmer shouted, completely off balance.

"Fight as though I were there beside each and every one of you," Ben continued as the SS guards dragged him away.

Out in the corridor, after Volmer had attempted to regain some of the effect he had hoped to create, Ben faced the shaken new field marshal. Volmer was white-faced with rage.

"You'll not do that to me again," the American Nazi chief declared. "I'm going to break you, Ben Raines. I'm going to turn your mind to pudding." To his aide, he barked, "Get on the radio to the hacienda. Tell them to prepare the sensory-deprivation chamber."

Fuck this! Cecil Jefferys decided. He had heard the broadcast and Ben's message. Heart surgery or no, if Ben wanted the Rebel army to go balls to the wall, he *had* to be in the field.

"Dr. Chase has given strict instructions," Cecil's doctor protested. "You are not to resume full duty status for at least another month. General Jefferys, I simply cannot let you return to full duty, let alone lead a force into a combat situation at present."

"Sorry, Doc, this time you have nothing to say about it," Cecil told him, dark face alight with his eagerness to get into harness. "Ben Raines is a prisoner of that Nazi scum, they'll probably kill him for that broadcast. That makes me Commander in Chief of the Rebel army. I intend to take that army all the way to fucking South America if I have to in order to snuff out every last one of those bastards."

"But your medication," the medico bleated.

"Send all your little pills along with me. I'm taking the home division to what used to be Amarillo, Texas, to set up a unified field command." With that, Jefferys stomped out of the hospital and walked to his office. He had a spring in his step that had been lacking since before the operation.

At his staff conference half an hour later, he began outlining how he saw the upcoming campaign. "We can't use nuclear; the tactical units of Hoffman and Volmer are too small and widespread to make that practical. Ben said use all means, so we can use gas shells and aerosol application. I want those loaded onto cargo planes immediately.

314

All artillery that is transportable by air is to go also. Ammunition, fuel, and food are to go forward also. We'll leapfrog men and matériel all the way until contact is made with the enemy. Troop movements will begin at 1300 hours today. I want the whole division mobilized immediately after noon chow."

"General, what about those rednecks down in Bayou Gatoon? They've been getting bolder of late," Colonel Morris remarked.

"We're leaving enough personnel behind to deal with those inept scumbags. Hell, a couple of squads from the Middle School UMT class could handle them."

"Ah, General, only boys and girls twelve and over are qualified on the M-16."

"Ain't we got enough of them?" Jefferys teased, laughing, his spirits high once more. The staff joined him, then sobered to listen to the rest of Cecil's planning to date.

Buddy Raines looked toward El Paso, Texas, from a high, conical hill on the edge of what used to be the Fort Bliss Military Reservation. He noticed only minimal activity on the part of the Nazi troops who occupied the ruins of the suburbs. That suited him fine.

"We'll go through them like a dose of Ex-Lax," he remarked to his battalion commanders.

"What's that, Ex-Lax?" Lieutenant Colonel Morris asked.

"A laxative from the old days," Buddy explained. "Dad told me about it. Came in the form of small chocolate squares. He said it really turned you loose. Anyway, it appears they are not expecting us. Or at least not this early. Deploy your men on a broad front, armor up front, and we go in at sixteen hundred. By the way, General Jefferys is on his way to Amarillo with a division. He's assuming overall command."

"We're doing all right, aren't we?" Morris asked.

"We are, but in some places this thing with Dad is playing hob with efficiency. In fact, we're getting the shit

315

knocked out of us up north. We've got a purpose, to get Dad out, now that we know where he is."

A grin opened a line of white in Lieutenant Colonel Morris's ebony face. "That was real obliging of Volmer to use that powerful radio station to show off on."

"Yes," Buddy agreed. "We'd still be trying if they had stuck to low-wattage transmitters. We have a perfect triangulation from the audio direction finders in the Apaches. Speaking of them, I want them up and hitting the area along the river when the assault begins."

The American Nazi co-commander in El Paso was sitting opposite his NAL counterpart in a modular home that had been converted to an officers' club. On the low table between them was a bottle of excellent Hueradura tequila from Mexico. As one they licked salt from the web of one hand, drained off the shooters, and bit lime. The South American bent to pour another round.

"I tell you, Fritz, the Rebels are all but defeated. They cannot survive without Ben Raines."

Colonel Fritz Rivera nodded and then peered at his American ally through his monocle. "Walter, you take too much for granted," he stated. "Ben Raines is not the whole Rebel army. We have fought them before. Once the rank and file, and their commanders, are over the shock of Raines's capture, they will come back at us with a vengeance."

Colonel Walter Hauber lifted his tequila. "Then we publicly execute Ben Raines."

"That, I'm afraid, would prove terribly unwise," Rivera responded a moment before his brows rose in astonishment and the eyeglass dropped from his face.

Outside the window of the O-club, directly in front of the Nazi brass, the blunt snout of an AH-64 Apache lowered into position. It hovered a moment while Colonel Rivera gaped in disbelief. Then it blew off a Hellfire missile that crashed through the window and exploded in the laps of the El Paso area commanders.

* * *

Death slashed at the Nazis around the former city of El Paso. It came in the form of 30mm explosive rounds, whirring flechettes from 105 and 155 artillery, and from the barrels of rifles in the hands of screaming Rebels, who charged into the unsuspecting black-shirts before many of them could grab their weapons. Rockets and grenades crashed and added to the carnage. Buddy Raines stayed close on the backs of the lead elements of the assault.

Riding a BFV, he watched closely as laser target designators flashed green and red across the battlefield, "painting" enemy armor for the smart projectiles fired by the 4-inch mortars in the Bradleys. His dad would call it a scene out of *Star Wars,* whatever that was, and refer to LTD spotters as Hans Solo. Even without those images of the past, Buddy still enjoyed himself.

"Take us in a little closer," he told the driver.

"Yes, Colonel, but—"

"I've got a feeling these crud are fighting without orders. I want to find out. Let's go get me a prisoner," Buddy replied.

Three Nazi slime ran at the BFV a quarter of a mile deeper into the rubble of El Paso. They had their hands over their heads. Eyes filled with fright glittered out of powder- and dirt-grimed faces. Buddy ordered the vehicle halted. He climbed out the door at the rear of the Bradley. He had his .40 caliber P7M10 in his hand, the muzzle steady on the chest of the nearest black-shirt.

"On your bellies," Buddy roared, then repeated it in Spanish.

Instant compliance. Buddy waited while two Rebels from the Bradley searched and secured the prisoners. Then he stepped forward and raised one Nazi to his feet. "Okay, put them in the Bradley, one at a time."

Inside, he asked the camo-clad prisoner, "Do you speak English?"

"Yeah. I'm an American. You've got no right treating us like this."

317

"You want to snivel, I'll kick your ass back outside where our troops have orders to take no prisoners," Buddy coldly told him.

"That's inhuman," the man wailed.

"Bullshit! Are you a member of the Super Race or a whining hanky-stomper?"

"I'm a guy who's scared shitless, that's what."

"Then try answering some questions and you'll live longer."

"What do you want to know?" the bound man asked, head hung.

"Start with your name. Then tell me who's running the show here?"

"I'm Victor Lawson. No—no one is running anything any more. W-we're drivers, see? We were with our staff cars outside the officers' club when one of your helicopters blew hell out of it. It was right at cocktail time. There ain't anybody left above the level of company commander."

Buddy produced a broad grin. "Well, Vic, that's nice to know. Thing is, can I believe you? Yes, I think I can. Where is this club?"

"Back the way we came from. It's still burnin'. It was one of those big, two-piece trailers they hauled down here."

"If you'll guide us, we'll go have a look." To the Rebel guarding Lawson, Buddy said, "Take him outside and keep him away from the others."

With a little difficulty, he got much the same story from the second black-shirt. Although Buddy's Spanish was good, the prisoner spoke a South American dialect that made understanding difficult. The third proved to be a defiant fanatic.

"I'll tell you nothing, you Rebel bastard," he snarled.

Buddy Raines eyed him icily, nodded, and spoke through a smile. "Okay. No problem. Open the door, Sam," he told the Rebel trooper. With the prisoner out on the ground again, Buddy put the muzzle of his H&K P7M10 an inch above the recalcitrant Nazi's nose and blew away the left side of his head.

"Now, let's go to the O-club," he said lightly.

* * *

Resistance in the El Paso area unraveled even faster than Buddy Raines had expected. His BFV had barely reached the smoldering remains of the former officers' club when reports from different companies came crackling in. He began to develop a picture of a battle rapidly concluding.

A large corridor had been blasted right through the middle of the defending line. Caught by complete surprise, the Nazis frequently chose to swim the Rio Grande rather than try to face the Rebels. They were not aware that the young man leading these yelling killing machines had every intention of going on into Mexico. Some blackshirts stood by their guns and fired until destroyed. Buddy climbed from the Bradley Fighting Vehicle to examine the remains of the modular house that had taken a hit from an Apache.

Instantly he jerked violently and went to the ground, unmoving. A second later the BFV crew heard the crack of the sniper rifle. One of Buddy's staff, Major Harmon, arrived a moment later. Everyone still hugged the ground, assuming the sniper to still be there, and Buddy to be dead.

Harmon ignored the possibility of a sniper and rushed to Buddy's supine form. He knelt and examined the young dark-haired man. Anger, doubled by what he found, burned in him.

"He's alive, no thanks to you," he complained to the BFV crew. "His helmet took most of the damage. Knocked him colder than last week's pea soup. He'll be all right, but have one hell of a headache. That's the trouble with you people livin' in those turtle shells," he complained of the crouching men. "You develop awfully thin skin."

He gestured to two infantrymen who had come with him in a Humvee. "Go find that sniper." To the immobilized crew, "Someone hand me a canteen. We have to bring Colonel Raines around."

By the time Buddy Raines regained consciousness, he

had been handed the largest single victory of his career with the Rebels. When the defenders had heard over their radios that the entire command structure had been wiped out, and heard it from one of their own — the American Nazi Buddy had questioned volunteered to broadcast it — they had given up in droves. Most had chosen to flee to the eastward, or south into Mexico.

"I don't remember tying one on," Buddy grunted as his throbbing head steadied enough for him to sit up.

"Sniper," Major Harmon advised him. "I have people out hunting him."

"How long have I been out?" Buddy asked.

"About fifteen minutes. That ballistic helmet took most of the shock, but you got a good rap on the skull."

In the distance, muffled firing could be heard as the diehards did just that. Harmon told Buddy that the Rebels now controlled all of the Nazi AO. Buddy made to rise when a short crackle of shots sounded from about a quarter-mile away. Harmon nodded in satisfaction.

"I think that takes care of our sniper."

"Good. I want to get on the horn to all batt commanders. We're crossing over into Mexico."

Juárez, being on the border, had suffered as much as El Paso from the ravages of the Great War, the plague, and the reclamation by the Rebels. Surprisingly, one bridge remained intact. Not the fancy, gracefully curved, prestressed concrete ribbon that once carried four lanes in both directions; rather, the old, stone two-lane bridge built in the late 1800s. When Buddy Raines arrived, behind the first wave that drove the Nazis out into the desert, he climbed from the BFV and stood looking over the devastation of a once large, prosperous city. His head still throbbed as his gaze went beyond the piles of Juárez debris to the south, toward a town called Villa Ahumada.

"Hang in there, Dad," he said softly. "We're coming for you."

Thirteen

Ben Raines floated in limbo. He experienced no light, no sound, no sense of movement or gravity. IV tubes in his arms fed and hydrated him and kept him in a mild drugged state. After the first few hours, he even lost consciousness of the tidal flow of his own blood and pulse of his heart. Slowly, a light began to form in his mind. Ben stirred, although not conscious of the movement.

With a powerful effort of will, he concentrated his consciousness and struggled to keep control of his mind. The light grew. *Symbolic,* he thought. *That's not a real light. But I can make it come and go.*

That realization encouraged him. After a timeless time, he began to focus his attention on days gone by. He visualized the itinerary of his lecture tour, shortly before the Great War. He had spoken at such prestigious institutions as Notre Dame, Stanford, Columbia, and Georgetown University. Often his speaking engagements had been interrupted by the brainwashed, loud-mouthed, politically correct offspring of the hanky-stompers.

Gradually his mind formed the pinkly scrubbed, baby-faced features of one long-haired, politically correct punk who had mindlessly chanted, "Get the Contras out! Get the Contras out!"

Too bad that the little idiot had his brain so drug-soaked that he didn't realize that with the election of Violeta Barrios de Chamorro the previous year, the Contra cause had collapsed in Nicaragua. The little mullet had become so enraged that he charged down the aisle and spouted his stupidity directly into Ben's face.

Ben had kept a blank expression, but covered the microphone with a big hand and spoke with soft, deadly force. "Shut the fuck up and sit down, you ill-mannered brat."

Stunned, the youthful agitator went silent. No one had ever spoken to him like that. This big, hard-faced man in front of him must not love him. By the time he stumbled away from the podium, he was on the verge of tears. Ben had finished the rest of his talk, "World Conditions and Their Impact on the American Novel," without further interruption.

Deprived of all sensation, the world drifted by for Ben Raines while he reviewed those terrible days of the robotic war called the Great War. Ben had done his share, more than most. Out of the ashes of that holocaust, Ben had pulled together like-minded people and established the Tri-States.

That had been fortunate for many. *Un*fortunately, time revealed that the politicians had survived the bombings and thwarted invasion. The left-leaning whiners and snivelers and would-be tyrants could not tolerate the idea of a state within the state, so they went to war against Ben Raines, called him a rebel and worse.

Rebel had become a label of pride under the leadership of Ben Raines. Impressions of those days brought on a touch of sadness, too. He recalled his first wife and the children they had adopted. How little time the demands of statecraft and war allowed for him to spend with his family. So precious few hours. And he had paid for that, Ben noted. At least Tina had survived.

Thoughts of Tina brought Ben inevitably to Buddy. For years he had not even known that Buddy existed. When they at last met, he had seen how time had weighed on the boy. A man grown, even then, Buddy had known nothing but fighting against overwhelming odds since. Which eventually brought Ben to speculate on what Buddy had in mind for rescue. Ben relaxed into picking that apart, and his delta waves altered dramatically.

Peter Volmer slammed his fist onto the counter under the observation window. "He's resisting it. Somehow he has found a way to stave off the process of breaking down his mind."

"We have been at it for less than three days, Field Marshal Volmer," a technician protested. "The subject has a strong ego, a powerful mind. It is going to take time."

"We don't have time. I'm compelled to face *Führer* Hoffman's impatience and counter his demands for the execution of Ben Raines. I have to tell him something. Are you sure there has been no progress?"

"Nothing measurable. If anything, I'd say the subject is enjoying a long, comfortable rest. One long overdue."

"He's not here for a rest cure," Volmer snapped at the technician. "Do something. Break him, dammit!"

By the end of the day in which Ben Raines established his defenses against sensory deprivation, the supply of gas shells for the 155s, 105s, and 4-inch mortars sent by Cecil Jefferys had arrived in all operational areas. Along with them came acrosol canisters for the aircraft. The deadly nerve poison was quickly distributed to the waiting batteries. Particularly glad to receive this ultimate means of subduing the enemy were Colonel West and General Striganov.

General Georgi Striganov had joined Colonel West at the Custer Battlefield and deployed his troops on the heights around the fateful "valley of Montana." West arrived at the hastily called staff meeting softly singing an old ballad.

" 'Do you hear their tomtoms ringing, Sergeant Flynn? Do you hear the Sioux out singing, Sergeant

Flynn? Do you hear the tomtoms ringing? It's a war dance they are singing, but they've yet to learn the words to Gerryowen. Gerryowen, Gerryowen, Gerryowen, in that valley of Montana all alone. There are better days to be for the Seventh Cavalry, when we charge again for dear old Gerryowen.' "

"What's that, Colonel?" General Striganov asked.

"It's an old song about George Armstrong Custer and the Seventh. It happened right here, June 25, 1876. Custer and 286 troopers charged seven thousand Sioux and Cheyenne warriors. The Indians ate Custer's lunch."

"So it amuses you to see us in Custer's boots?" Striganov asked.

"No. It amuses me to see us in the Sioux's moccasins," West answered levelly. "The gas canisters arrived half an hour ago. Hoffman's Nazis are making up to attack us. It strikes me that now is a good time to teach them something about Rebel arms and tactics."

Georgi Striganov smiled for the first time in days. "I do think you are right. We'll deploy at once."

"We hold the high ground. The terrain compels the black-shirts to come at us from below. The natural valley of the river will contain the gas long enough to be fully effective," West listed the rest of his plan. "I think we're going to give the Nazis a Little Big Horn of their own, with *Brigadeführer* Brodermann as Custer."

SS *Brigadeführer* Hans Brodermann was a troubled man. His approach to the Rebels holding out on crescent ridges from the northwest to southeast of his line of march had been confined to the course of the river they now followed. Constant, heavy probing actions by Rebel patrols dictated the course. He was not aware it was the Little Big Horn, and it would have meant nothing to him if he did know. The secret Nazi war colleges in Argentina and Paraguay spent a lot of time on the blitzkrieg invasions of Poland, Czechoslovakia, and the Ukraine, but made no mention of the United States military campaigns against the Indians in the nineteenth century. So he advanced in ignorance.

That lack of knowledge would prove quite costly in the next hour. The radio in his *Panzerkampfwagen* crackled constantly with reports of the point element and observations from along the route of march. The lead element had reached a big bend in the river, with a large fan-shaped floodplain.

"Aspen and birch trees are growing in abundance on the east side of the river and it appears there is some sort of cemetery on the shelves of a ridge due east and to the north of our position," the point company commander described. "There are Rebel troops up there. *Verdammter Mist!* They are firing artillery at us."

Even at his position in the center of the column, Hans Brodermann heard the soft crump of big guns firing shortly after the announcement. He slid forward on his seat in anticipation. Now the Rebels were going to stand and fight.

"Continue to the north," he ordered. "We will occupy the flood plain and engage the enemy."

"Sir, sir, General Brodermann, there's something terribly wrong. Those shells are bursting with only small explosions. I don't—I—" He ended with a terrified scream. "It's—gas—nerve gas," he choked out a second later, before his autonomic nervous system began to shut down and he died horribly.

Rebel artillery began walking in on the column. Fascinated, Brodermann watched them fall out of the sky and detonate by proximity fuses some fifteen feet above ground. His imagination supplied clouds of lethal gas spewing from the casings. Then the frightening realization hit him. *They had no protection against nerve gas!*

"Turn around," he shouted to those within hearing, and through the mike. "Turn back and get away from here at once." Was he imagining it, or had his vision started to blur? "Pull back," he kept urging.

Adrenaline, that's all it is, he tried to convince himself when his heart rate increased precipitously. His lips and nose felt numb. All of a sudden he lost control of his bladder and voided it in his trousers. Gripped by genuine terror now, SS *Brigadeführer* Hans Brodermann wondered belatedly what explanation he would make to God for all the wrong he had done.

Hard rounds began to fall then. Flechette and HE that slashed into vehicles and their occupants with equal ease. Heavy machine guns opened up, cut swaths through the numbed Nazis, and chewed up light vehicles. The main guns of tanks fired at point-blank range, destroying Brodermann's MBTs almost casually. Spasms began ten seconds later, and Hans Brodermann died in that valley of Montana all alone.

"Brodermann's entire command has been wiped out," Gen. Georgi Striganov reported to Cecil Jefferys, now established in Amarillo, an hour later. "Less than seventy-five escaped. They are thoroughly demoralized and are making no show of stopping to reorganize anywhere this side of Oregon. That gas worked wonderfully well. The major portion of one division is — is *bezizkhodnost*. How you say? They no longer can exist."

"Doveryai, no proveryai, old friend," Cecil responded.

"Trust, but verify," Striganov translated. "You know our old Russian proverb, eh? We already have pathfinders out keeping touch with them. They are no threat, believe me."

"That's good to hear. All tactical units currently engaged with the enemy are using the gas. It's a good thing that stuff breaks down in a matter of an hour or so. I'd hate to think of it blowing around the country for longer. Continue your advance, Georgi. Push it as far as the weather conditions in the passes will allow. We want Hoffman hurting so bad he hasn't time to worry about Ben."

A silence settled between the two old warriors. Georgi cleared his throat, to respond, "Yes. How are matters relating to that?"

"Ongoing, my friend. Those Nazi pricks have enough of our radios now to be able to descramble, so I can't say more."

"I understand. Good luck. Striganov off."

That brought Cecil Jefferys a small smile. Those Russians never could get American radio procedure down right. But the former Soviet general's question prompted him to another detail. He'd have to check with Buddy Raines about what was being done to rescue Ben.

Droplets of foamy spittle flew from the lips of Jesus Hoffman, self-appointed *Führer* of North America. His rage towered over any previously witnessed by his staff. The cause of his rancor was the news of the defeat and death of SS *Brigadeführer* Hans Brodermann and nearly all of his command.

"They planned it this way," he shrieked. "They picked the spot for its propaganda value and deliberately suckered Brodermann into place for the slaughter. I won't have it! I won't allow this horrid crime to go unpunished. Listen to me, hear exactly what I demand. We are going to begin a scorched-earth policy all along the Eastern Wall. When and if forced to withdraw from our fortifications, troops will destroy everything useful to the enemy. No food, no shelter, no bridges are to remain for the Rebels. All Rebels and their sympathizers in our custody are to be summarily executed. All nonmilitary supplies and buildings to be destroyed. They will see how terrible war can be. Far too late, but they will see."

"Jawohl, mein Führer," the staff chorused.

"We will begin at once. Now, get me Field Marshal Volmer on the radio," he snapped to an aide. When contact had been made, Hoffman gripped the microphone stand until his knuckles whitened. "Field Marshal, you are now second in command to me. Brodermann is dead, his division devastated and scattered. Everything depends upon you, now." Quickly he reviewed his demands for the new policy, then added, "It is up to you to see we do not fail. I'm counting on you, Volmer. Now, I must have immediate results with Ben Raines. He is to renounce the Rebel cause and disband the Rebel army at once."

"B-but we have not as yet implanted our 'new reality' in General Raines," Peter Volmer protested.

"Never mind that now. Just get him unplugged and on the radio to order general surrender. This is vital, Volmer. The Rebels are using nerve gas."

Shattered by this revelation, Peter Volmer could only stammer agreement and end the conversation.

They came for him minutes later. The same doctor who had first examined Ben Raines supervised his removal from the sensory-deprivation machinery. He was taken to a bedroom on the second floor of the hacienda. There Peter Volmer paced impatiently during the six hours that were required to elevate Ben to a satisfactory level of consciousness.

While he did, black news poured into the hacienda radio room from the northern sector of the vaunted East Wall. Colonel West, General Striganov, and Thermopolis had gone on the advance. They steadily rolled up platoon-sized Nazi units so fast that their capitulations tumbled over one another. Volmer cursed the Rebels and Ben Raines steadily.

When at last Ben Raines roused enough to sit upright with some help, Volmer came to his side and spoke earnestly. "This is your last chance. All Rebel resistance is crumbling. You are to go to the studio and order a general surrender. It is all you can do to save the lives of your precious Rebels. We'll get you dressed now and you'll come with me."

Half an hour later, three guards dragged Ben into the studio. Not everything that was real seemed real to Ben, and a lot of ghosts remained from his long effort to keep his identity. He did learn that Jesus Hoffman was in a three-way radio net, linked to the Rebels, as well as this radio station in Villa Ahumada.

When the engineer cued him, Peter Volmer spoke with falsely hearty confidence. "Attention, all Rebel commanders and all Rebel soldiers. You are about to hear from your supreme commander, General Ben Raines. You are ordered to obey what he says, without exception. General Raines."

Ben needed help to approach the mike. He wet his lips and summoned total concentration of his powerful ego and superlative mind to make this moment count in the most effective manner. "Jesus Hoffman, are you listening?" he asked.

"Yes, General Raines. Please go ahead."

"I'm glad you're hearing this. I want to tell you personally to go to hell. And, I suspect that hell is on its way to visit you as we speak. Whether I live or die, the Rebel cause will go on. I want to ask all Rebels to never lay down arms until the last Nazi bastard is dead or run out of our country. Never give up. *Allons revange!*"

When Ben called for revenge in the hated language of France, *Führer* Jesus Diguez Mendoza Hoffman lost it. He screamed incomprehensibly for several seconds, then addressed Volmer. "Field Marshal Volmer, you are to immediately prepare to place Ben Raines in front of a firing squad. He is to die at dawn."

Fourteen

A new spirit infected the Rebels. They redoubled their efforts against the Nazis at all points of contention, and then went hunting them. Defeats came to Hoffman's black-shirts so rapidly that he had to concede the northern sector to the Rebels. He began to pack up his headquarters to make a swift end run to join Field Marshal Volmer and General Rasbach in Mexico.

"I am not retreating," Hoffman snapped to his alarmed staff. "I am regrouping. We will come back out of Mexico and smash that arrogant Rebel scum. Mark my words on that. It's Ben Raines that caused this. Him and his glory speech. Why wasn't he cut off the air? Damn the man, damn him. But that will end. With Ben Raines dead, this new spurt of aggressiveness will burn out quickly. Then we will drive a wedge of armor up from the Texas border to the heart of Rebel country and finish them once and for all." Buoyed by this idea, he walked with some of his former strut to a low table where a plate of sweet cakes waited. Selecting one, he munched it thoughtfully. "Is that not a brilliant idea?"

"Yes, *mein Führer*," his dubious staff responded.

"Which reminds me. Set up a secure radio net. I want to talk to Field Marshal Volmer about tomorrow's execution."

Still smarting from the way they had been gulled by

the Nazi kids, Ben's team now had to face this threat of immediate execution. They fulminated with anger and a lust for revenge. No one blamed them and no one tried to talk them out of it.

"I want me a great big piece of this American Nazi bastard, Volmer," Cooper announced as the team sat about drinking coffee. No one had thought to reassign them.

"No more than I, friend dragon," Jersey returned. "Only how do we go about it? I know there's talk about going in after the general. But no one has done a thing."

"That's changing as of now," Buddy Raines informed them as he entered the orderly-room section of the mobile CP.

"You mean it?" Jersey asked, excited.

"I sure do. What do you say to a retrieval op against Volmer and the black-shirts holding Dad?"

"Wonderful. Show us the way," Jersey enthused.

"It'll be a small DA op," Buddy outlined for them. "Say twenty-one people. We'll go in at night."

"Now you're talkin', Colonel Raines," Jersey encouraged. "How are we going to avoid being seen all the way to this Villa Ahumada place?" she asked skeptically.

"Simple. We fly in. We'll pull a HALO jump and be deployed on the ground before the Nazis know we're there."

Jersey paled slightly. "C'mon, Colonel, Buddy," she pleaded. "You mean we're gonna jump in, at night, into unknown territory, with a high-altitude exit and low-altitude open?"

"Just so. The Nazis don't have any of the right kind of radar to detect us, so it'll be a breeze," Buddy passed off the danger.

"Awh, get real. You know how I hate airborne ops," Jersey wailed, already regretting the butterflies that would fill her stomach.

At his Amarillo headquarters, Cecil Jefferys stared at

the sheet of paper on his desk. A part of him approved entirely, even wanted to go along. A recovery drop mission just might carry it off. But he strongly disapproved of Buddy Raines leading the strike force. Even though the mission had been approved by Ike and Dan, he didn't like it at all. They could not afford to lose two Rainses in one campaign.

"I want a delay on this DA mission of Colonel Raines's," he announced to a surprised Ike on the radio.

"What about Ben's execution at dawn tomorrow?" Ike hammered.

"We know where they are holding him. We can put air on it and break up the party." Cecil withheld his main trump card.

"I don't know about that," Ike countered. "They just might carry it off inside where we can't reach them with air."

"Then we won't lay on an air strike. As it happens, I have received the deciphered text of a communication between Hoffman and Volmer that has a lot of bearing on this." Cecil reached for a flimsy in his "action" basket and read its content to Ike.

Three officers came with Field Marshal Peter Volmer to get Ben Raines half an hour before sunrise the next morning. They brought with them his laundered Rebel camo uniform. The baggy trousers and jacket of cotton twill and ripstop nylon fit him like a two-thousand-dollar Savile Row suit, if Savile Row still existed.

"Do you expect a final meal?" Volmer asked, gloating.

"Why bother? Do you expect to get some sort of propaganda mileage out of it?" Ben countered hotly.

"It's . . . customary. Oh, well. We might as well get on with this. The execution will take place outside the north wall of the hacienda. It will occur as soon after sunrise as there is light enough for the cameras."

"Ah, the fine Nazi zeal for documenting everything. I would have thought you had learned your lesson the last time," Ben taunted his captor.

Volmer bit back a retort and snapped over his shoulder to Ben. "Come on, then."

A five-man security squad waited outside the cell. They formed around Ben, who was marched through the inner courtyard and out a door on the north side of the large estate. A slow drum roll struck up as the escort paraded Ben in front of the assembled Werewolves and Nazi elite troops.

They halted him in front of an old, crumbling adobe wall about eight feet high. There the sergeant in charge tied Ben's hands behind his back. Exercising ritual care, the guards next bound him to a freshly planted stake. Volmer approached and sneeringly held up a black bag.

"To cover your head," he offered.

"I won't need that. You can stuff it where the sun never shines."

"A last smoke?" Volmer said, dragging out the procedure.

"No thanks," Ben said tightly.

"All right. Everyone clear away here," Volmer ordered.

Once out of range, Volmer drew his service weapon from the belt holster and held it at his side. He would deliver the *coup de grace*. With a final inspection of the scene, he gave an approving nod to the firing squad commander, a young lieutenant.

"*Exekutionskommando . . . Achtung!*" The squad snapped to attention. "*Bereiten Sie!*" The squad came to port arms. "*Beladen Sie!*" With crack precision they charged their weapons. "*Aufzielen Sie!*" Rifle butts came to shoulders, and muzzles steadied on the chest of Ben Raines. "*Schiessen Sie los!*"

Thirteen hammers struck thirteen bolts and drove thirteen firing pins forward on empty chambers. To his immediate shame, relief flooded through Ben Raines. He gulped a cool draft of early morning desert air and let it stream out through his nose. It was then that he heard the shrill, derisive laughter of the child-storm troopers and saw the grinning faces of their adult comrades. To one side, a battery of microphones stood before a slender podium. Volmer walked briskly to them, cameras panning to follow his progress.

"Rebel cowards. What you have witnessed was a dress rehearsal for the execution of Ben Raines. This has been done, and filmed, so that every one of you hopelessly misled Rebels will know for sure what is in store for Ben Raines. His execution awaits only the victorious arrival of *Führer* Hoffman."

Well, the arrogant bastard has given himself a new title, Ben observed.

Twenty people had gathered in the tightly closeted tent. Sixteen came from the elite pathfinders of Dan Gray's command. The other four were the members of Ben Raines's headquarters team. Only low-intensity red light illuminated the interior of the tent, to preserve the occupants' night vision. The double-flap arrangement of the light baffle swung wide and admitted a tall rock-jawed young man with a grim expression.

"All right, listen up, people," Buddy Raines began. "I'll keep this short and sweet. This is your op order. We all know the situation: Elements of the American Nazi SS *Leibstandarte Hoffman* are holding General Ben Raines captive in or around the town of Villa Ahumada, Chihuahua, Mexico. Sub One: enemy forces consist of an estimated light battalion, with the remainder of Peter Volmer's Werewolf company, estimated strength fifty combat trained boys aged ten to fifteen. Sub Two: friendly forces are what you see. We will be augmented by a rapid-deployment team from R Batt." Buddy paused to study the intent faces before him. He smiled briefly and nodded.

"The mission is to go in and get General Raines out. Ah — and to kill as many Nazis as we can. Execution, Sub One: we will form into three 7-man teams. I command Team Alpha; Hank Evans has Bravo; Jersey, you have Charlie. We will be inserted by HALO at 2315 hours tonight. Two: uniform and equipment standard night ops. Challenge for ID will be 'Tri-States,' answered by 'Freedom.' Every team member will carry a short-range, hand-held radio. During approach to the final objective, we'll use our standard click code to indicate movement. Three: issue weapons with eight spare magazines, supplemented by four frag grenades and two gas for all, with the following exception. A suppressed submachine gun will be carried by every third trooper. Pathfinder team leader will carry a homing beacon to be turned on when General Raines is located. Four: each team member will carry iron rations and water for two days. Resupply will be from the RDT." Buddy paused again, stepped to a small field desk beside a blackboard that had a list of names posted and a large aerial map of the area around Villa Ahumada. He drank from a metal cup of water and picked up a pointer.

"I am in overall command. On the ground, my team will be directed by Lieutenant Bob Simpson. Lieutenant Evans has his team. Jersey, hers."

"Hey, Colonel Raines, I ain't no officer. How come I'm leadin' a team?" Jersey asked, brow lined with concern.

"Because you are good. The best. Besides, it's your team that has to go in and take General Raines away from them. Now, team sergeants will direct fire against the objective. All right, let's go over the time schedule. I know you got it in the warning order, but there's no time for a rehearsal of this. We depart here at 2130 hours, climb to thirty thousand, and proceed south to the DZ outside Villa Ahumada. The jump is on for 2315. Police up the DZ and reach the Rally Point by 2325. We proceed overland to the initial objective. Checkpoints have been set" — his pointer tapped the map — "every twenty minutes along the route of march. We should be in Villa Ahumada at 0320 hours. We neutralize any enemy there. I've allowed thirty minutes for that. Try to keep one for interrogation. Intel indicates the best estimate for the general's location is this large hacienda ten miles outside the village. If this is verified, that becomes our primary objective. We will proceed there, to arrive at 0505 hours. Deployment time five minutes. Then we hit the place half an hour before sunrise, which is at 0617 tomorrow. Jersey's team takes out guards around General Raines and di-dis out of there. Cover fire for the initial exfiltration will come from your team, Hank. We take a vehicle if possible and head due north with all possible speed to link up with the RDT from R Batt.

"Okay," Buddy went on after a glance at his watch. "Since time is short, we'll go right into the jump briefing. There will be two passes over the DZ. Only two. First out is Nelson, our pathfinder. He will have a red and green strobe with him to mark the DZ. Red, of course, is for a wave-off. On the second pass, the sticks will unass the bird in reverse order. I'll be first out the door; Jersey, you'll be last."

"Why me? Why *me?* You know I hate to jump."

Buddy gave her a smile. "Don't worry, this is going to be jumpmastered by Sergeant Quinlan. He'll see you get out on time. Chute up at 2100, then equipment check. GP bags for all loose gear. Make sure you secure your oxygen bottles, we'll be breathing it for the first twenty thousand feet. Once on the ground, rigger-roll and police your area, then report to the RP. We'll bury the chutes there and move out. Questions?"

Several came, as to equipment details, fire control, and the usual on altimeter setting for the ADGs. Buddy was startled to learn he had forgotten that important item. The automatic-deployment gear was a HALO jumper's lifeline. Without it, he had to guess on when to deploy his parachute, and at night that could be suicide. At the last, Cooper put up his hand.

"Yes, Cooper?"

"I was wonderin'. What's the name of this town we're headed for? In English, I mean."

"It means Smoked Village," Jersey informed him. "An' we're gonna smoke it, all right, along with every Nazi scumbag around," she added with a bit of her former fiery spirit.

* * *

With a light, though deft, touch, the pilot put in a little left rudder and rotated the wheel so that the Argentine Blanca slipped left a little to line up with the center of the runway. A single landing light bored a hole in the night over Villa Ahumada. How he longed for the technology of his homeland. There they had ILS glide slopes and all the proper equipment for effortless landings in nearly any conditions. Here he had to rely on visual contact and marginal presence of inner marker beacons. To his surprise, the instrument panel IMB light flickered on and a beeping pulse came from the speaker over his ear. Half mile to the end of the runway.

Seated behind him, *Führer* Jesus Diguez Mendoza Hoffman gnawed on his lower lip and laced white-knuckled fingers around his drawn-up knees. He hated flying. It seemed such an unnatural act. He would go immediately to the hacienda and confront his field marshal. Volmer had better have the right answers. The pilot cut back the throttle and the little plane sank to one hundred feet. Hoffman swallowed hard and closed his eyes.

Tires squeaked at contact with the runway, and the little high-wing aircraft sped along the tarmac toward where a "Follow Me" truck lighted the way to the proper taxiway and the ramp beyond. *Führer* Hoffman began to relax. He even opened his eyes.

A mistake, he quickly discovered. In the near-complete darkness, he had no idea where they were going or why. He felt even more disoriented than in the air. Without warning, the pilot braked and cut the engine. The prop spun to a sudden stop.

Outside, a *Kugelwagen* waited to transport the *Führer* to the hacienda. Salutes were given all around and Hoffman walked stiffly to the open door. "Ah, Captain Elbe, am I right?" he greeted the officer standing stiffly to attention at the side of the vehicle.

"Yes, *mein Führer*. I'm honored that you remembered."

"When you visited Führer Headquarters with Field

337

Marshal Volmer I was impressed by your dedication to the Party and this campaign against the Rebels," *Führer* Hoffman flattered the young captain. "Now, take me to see General Ben Raines."

Jersey sat in the soft red light and chewed her nails. The rumble of jet engines pushed the Gulfstream upward toward an assigned altitude of thirty thousand feet. She felt an itch in her armpits and wanted furiously to scratch. Although she had gone just before chuting up, her bladder demanded attention.

"God, I hate this," she said to Beth, beside her.

"Truth to tell, so do I. I'll never understand why General Raines insisted we all take airborne training."

"Because sometimes he likes to jump in with Colonel West's mercs," Jersey patiently told her, although certain they had had this conversation a dozen times before.

"I wish he would stay on the ground, in the rear, where it's safe."

"There's a lot of people with a lot more rank than you who wish the same," Jersey advised. "I think I'm gonna try to get some Z's." *That's it,* she told herself, *sleep through it.*

All too soon, the light above the doorway to the flight deck flashed from red to yellow, then green. The door opened and Nelson, the pathfinder, went out. The Gulfstream spooled up to cruise speed and continued to the south. Three minutes later it started back. Sergeant Quinlan, secured on a tether, hung partway out the door and peered at the ground through light-gathering binoculars. At last he found what he sought and swung back inside. He spoke into the boom mike and the light flashed yellow.

"Get readyyyy! . . . Stand up! . . . Check your equipment!" This would not be a static-line jump, Jersey frightfully recalled for the twelfth time. "Sound off for equipment check." The count rippled down the sticks from rear to front. "Adjust oxygen masks and check your buddy."

Jersey tested the flow valve of Beth's O-bottle and tapped her on the right shoulder. Hers would be checked by Quinlan when she reached the door. Her gut muscles tensed as the burly jumpmaster sergeant opened his mouth to shout at them again.

"Stand in the door!" The sticks shuffled forward from front and rear of the Gulfstream. Suddenly the throttles cut back and the engines spooled down to a whisper. "Go! Go — go — go — go . . ."

And then it was Jersey's turn. She got a quick tap on the shoulder and then on the butt. "Go."

The solid platform of the floor of the jet disappeared and Jersey closed herself to a compact ball to drop the first twenty thousand feet. Then she would spread-eagle and stabilize for the long ride down another nine thousand four hundred. At six hundred feet AGL, her chute would automatically deploy. At least they said it would.

All of this raced through her mind in the brief second before she yelled into her face-covering oxygen mask, "What am I doing heeeeerre!"

Fifteen

By straining on tiptoe, Ben Raines could marginally see out of the tiny slit that passed for a window in his cell. His view was of the inner courtyard. He saw a solitary, small figure sitting alone on a stone bench. Moonlight from a thin crescent high above gave a faerie glow to straw-white hair. For all his years in combat, Ben retained excellent hearing. He thought he detected soft sobs coming from the silhouetted boy. The shoulders rose and settled in time with the thin sound.

After a moment, Ben realized who this had to be. "Jimmy," he whispered forcefully. "Jimmy Riggs. Come over here."

Electrified, the boy sat rigidly upright. "Who? Who is that?"

"It's General Ben, Jimmy. Come over here."

"N-no. I c-can't ever see you again," Heinz/Jimmy stammered, uncomfortable at this confrontation.

"Why not? You were at the phony execution yesterday."

"That's different. I can't see you because you are a—a bad influence."

Surprise elevated one of Ben's eyebrows. What had brought that on? "What do you mean by that?"

Reluctantly, Heinz/Jimmy rose and padded barefoot over to the wall that contained Ben's cell. He wore summer pajamas, with short sleeves and legs. Hesitantly he knelt down and peered into Ben's eyes. "I—I got to thinking about what you said. So I told Pet—Field Marshal Volmer that I didn't want *that* any more. That you had said it was per—perverse. He got mad and slapped me and told me I was not to visit your cell anymore. Then he—we—anyway. An'—an' he demoted me." Tears ran down Jimmy's cheeks. "The other kids don't like me any more. I'm—all alone. Is it true everything about the Nazis is bad?"

"I believe it to be, Jimmy."

"Wh-why did my folks want me to be one?" came his plaintive query.

"I can't answer that. I do know that it is not too late for you. You can change. We have schools in Rebel-held country. They teach the truth and you are free to say what you believe. You can grow up normal and happy."

"But they're gonna kill you when the *Führer* gets here."

"When is that, Jimmy?"

"Sometime tonight, I think. Field Marshal Hoffman ordered the firing squad for tomorrow morning at sunrise."

"Would you, could you, help me get away?" Ben pressed rather too quickly.

"Oh, General Ben, I would if—but it's not possible. The guards and all, and I don't have the key to your cell anymore."

"Think of something, Jimmy. Think hard. We have until tomorrow morning."

A sudden flurry of action made Jimmy jump like a frightened animal. Lights began to come on throughout the hacienda and harsh voices shouted orders. "It's the *Führer*. I've gotta go. But I'll be back, General Ben. I promise."

Without any more warning than the sudden appearance of the darker outline of hills against the blackness of night, the ground leapt up and slapped the soles of Jersey's boots.

"Shit!" she grumbled to herself as she let go at the

knees, swiveled hips, and dropped into a regulation PLF. So much for standing landings at night.

Quickly Jersey came to her feet from the parachute-landing fall, ran around the suspension lines, and collapsed her chute. A twist and slap on the quick-release box and she was free of her harness. Thank God she had remembered to guesstimate when to release her GP bag and let it depend below her. With that on one leg, she would have been a case for splints and a cast.

Quietly she rigger-rolled her parachute and carried it in a bundle against her chest while she walked down the tie-off line for the missing general purpose carrier. She found it twenty feet away. A check of the compass on her right wrist and she oriented herself toward the proper edge of the drop zone and headed for the rally point.

"What kept you?" Buddy's voice teased from the stygian shadows.

"I stopped off for high tea with the Queen of England," Jersey quipped back.

"Okay. Get that chute in the hole with the others and let's move out."

Separated by a quarter-mile, the three teams advanced in parallel lines, zigging and zagging periodically to comply with the indicated locations of their checkpoints and to thwart observation. They covered four times the distance to Villa Ahumada that way. At least, Jersey thought grumpily, they didn't have to do it on tiptoe to fool anti-infiltration sensors.

They reached the village on time for all the caution. "Hank, make a quick recee of the vil and see if there's any friendlies in there," Buddy Raines whispered into the mike of his hand-held radio.

Hank Evans grinned, a flash of white in the waning moonlight. "That's why we took these gas canisters, eh?"

"Roger that. What we don't need is a firefight to advertise our presence. You might verify the prevailing wind direction also," Buddy suggested.

Evans and his team melted into the darkness. Buddy waited for a long count, then bumped Jersey. "Be ready to move to the upwind side of this burg."

"Roger, Rat. We're gonna do the Big Sleep number on them, right?"

"You got that right. Rat out."

Twenty tense minutes passed for the Rebels while Evans's team did a quick check of the village for any friendly locals. When the sweep had been completed, he keyed his mike and spoke tersely. "It's clean. Southwest."

"Roger. From here on, no voice communications. Rat out."

All three teams had come to within a hundred yards of Villa Ahumada. They took a full half hour to move into position in the southwest quadrant of the village. When each Rebel trooper had reached a suitable spot, the team leaders reported by breaking the carrier wave of their transmitters with a single click of the talk button. Three seconds later, two more clicks.

Buddy Raines reached for his gas mask and fitted it into place, making sure to check the tightness of the edge around his forehead and chin. Then he took a small syrette from the pocket of his utilities and snapped off the protective cover of the needle.

He plunged it into his exposed forearm and squeezed out the contents. Only then did he free one of the two gas grenades on his harness, untape the safety handle, and pull the pin. In his mind he saw the other troopers doing the same. He drew a long, steady, deep breath and exhaled sharply. This shit was so damn scary.

With a soft, explosive pop, the grenade of nerve gas detonated and began to spew its invisible contents out onto the steady breeze blowing into Villa Ahumada. *Thirty minutes,* Buddy Raines thought, his gut tightening. It would be safe for them to go into town then. Technically they were free to do so now, what with the antidote injected and their masks. But he always considered it wise to let the lethal fumes dissipate before playing loose and personal with an exposed area.

At the indicated time, Buddy keyed his mike once, waited five seconds, and hit three more. The teams advanced into a deathly silent Villa Ahumada. At the edge of town, Buddy found the duty watch on a road barrier sprawled in death. Their features were contorted horribly and they had completely voided themselves. He waved an arm to advance.

Grim-faced Rebel troopers swept through the town. Everywhere the story had the same ending. Dead Nazis lay all around. A rough body count indicated at least two companies. The last place they visited was the radio station.

Lights glowed and to all appearances it was business as usual. Jersey and her team entered first. Immediately they discovered that the air-conditioning system was all too efficient. A groggy Nazi sat at the reception desk. His hand darted toward the rifle leaned against the dividing partition.

"Get him," Jersey shouted, voice muffled by her mask.

Cooper shot the black-shirt with his CAR-15. The suppressor on the end provided an eerie effect. Slapped back by a silent three-round burst, the Nazi tilted over his swivel chair and tumbled onto the thick carpet.

"Check the other offices, Beth," Jersey instructed. "Cooper, Corrie, the studios. I'm goin' to the control room."

No one in the inner core of the building had been affected in the least by the murderous fumes. Caught by surprise when black-cloaked Rebels burst into the empty studios, the engineers reacted slowly. Ordinarily they were not armed, and this fateful night proved no exception. When the baffle door flew open, they dived for the floor.

One of them died when he hurled a thick glass ashtray at Jersey. Her M-16 sounded loud even through the plethora of soundproofing. "Get up, you cruds," she snarled. "Hands over your heads."

That ended the battle for Villa Ahumada. Buddy put a German speaker and a Spanish speaker in the control room to handle any traffic, and the prisoners were herded into the larger studio. Buddy faced them with a cheerful expression and rubbed his hands together.

"The war is over for you 'supermen.' So, which one of you is going to tell me where Volmer is keeping General Raines?" When the tough Nazis remained absolutely silent, Buddy swiftly drew his P7M10 and put a .40 caliber S&W Magnum round in the forehead of the nearest black-shirt engineer.

"We'll try that again. Where is General Raines?"

Worried glances passed between the remaining two. Each took a deep breath and slowly shook his head. Buddy Raines walked slowly by them, then back. Without warning he turned suddenly and knee-capped the smaller Nazi. Screaming, the man fell to the floor.

"We're going to find out, you know. Where is he?"

Only moans answered Buddy. He walked up to the standing black-shirt and put the hot muzzle of the autopistol squarely in the center of the trembling man's forehead. *"Auf Wiedersehen,"* Buddy said quietly an instant before he triggered the round that blew out half of the black-shirt's brains.

"I'll tell you," the remaining Nazi blurted. "The general is being kept at the big hacienda west of town. It's twelve kilometers out there."

"That's the truth, right? You're sure?"

"Yes — yes. Only they are going to shoot him in the morning. Please get me to a medic," the man sobbed.

"You don't need medical help," Buddy told him casually as he shot the last American Nazi through the heart.

"That's cold, Colonel," Cooper stated in shock. "That's damn cold."

"Unless you've forgotten, they are all under a death sentence. Their actions put them there, even if my father hadn't ordered it. And we can't leave them behind alive. Let's get out of here."

Dawn had yet to become a pale pink band on the sawtoothed horizon when Buddy and the teams reached the hacienda. The area had been thoroughly scouted, and surprisingly no OPs had been located. Every Nazi in

345

the area had gathered in the hacienda. Buddy Raines considered his first moves in brooding silence.

"We'll set up two 2-man mortar positions. One here and one half a click away to the east. They'll provide cover for the exfiltration."

They had relieved the Nazis in Villa Ahumada of two old 60mm mortars and ample ammunition. Buddy lapsed deep into thought again. The aerial photos did not provide any info on the layout of rooms inside. His dad could be anywhere. And he had to move damn fast. Perhaps only minutes remained for his father to live.

"Hank, your team will provide the cover fire. Jersey, you and Dad's team go in first; we'll be right behind you. Now let's make tracks while there's still some darkness down there."

Buddy Raines jolted along a shallow ravine that ran in the general direction of the hacienda. Jersey and Ben's team pounded along ahead of them. They reached the walls of the hacienda without detection, though the pre-dawn glow grew steadily. Soundless, on tiptoe, the Rebels entered through a small gate they located in the north wall.

Immediately a drowsy sentry at a small table ten feet away snapped alert and reached for his rifle. "What are you doing out there?" he demanded, confused as to the identity of the troops who so suddenly appeared.

Buddy extended his left arm in a waving gesture that distracted the guard's gaze and stepped closer. His right hand whipped the Ka-Bar from its sheath and drove it between two of the Nazi's ribs and into his heart. He caught the body and eased it back onto the chair. With a quick jerk of the bloody knife, he sent the Rebels to spread out through the courtyard.

Jersey found another sentry at a small recessed doorway on the far side of the courtyard. She took him out with a garrote. The dead black-shirt had a set of keys on his belt. Jersey quickly surmised what that might be. She gave a low whistle to the others and started going through them for the right one.

By the time Buddy and the rest of Ben's team arrived, Jersey had the low door unlocked. She went through it bent double, M-16 leading the way. Cooper followed with his suppressed CAR-15. Instantly he shot over Jersey's head and splattered a black-shirt against a stone wall. The man died outside the cell assigned to Ben Raines.

In a rush, Jersey went to it and turned the key in the lock, threw aside the bar. The door creaked when she drew it open. The cell was empty.

"Well, General Raines, it is through the goodness of the *Führer's* heart that you had this comfortable room to spend your last night on earth," Peter Volmer spoke oilily, his personal distaste evident in his tone.

"Tell him I am grateful beyond belief."

"Come, General, no sarcasm. Your uniform has been cleaned and pressed and awaits you. The *Führer* says that you have proven a worthy adversary. He feels you are entitled to a good rest, a shave and bath, and a good breakfast before your, ah, date with the firing squad."

"He is too kind," Ben grated out, mentally counting his last minutes.

"Well, enough of this," Peter Volmer said lightly. "I'll leave you to your ablutions and a hearty meal. We'll meet again . . . for the last time . . . before the *parèdón* — the firing wall, as I've learned from my Latin American friends."

Volmer left the second-floor room where Ben Raines had been confined and walked along the as-yet-silent corridor. Dawn had not streaked the east and he had his own early breakfast to attend to. What a day! This day would be the ultimate test of Rebel resolve. He had no doubt that they would weaken in the end and give up. The fighting would at last be over and then, soon after that, a tragic accident to Jesus Hoffman would make him, Peter Volmer, *Führer* of the American Reich.

What a future to contemplate! It put a lightness in his step. Too bad about little Heinzi. But there were other beautiful ones from which to choose. First get rid of Ben Raines, then he would reward himself.

"He's gone," Jersey gulped, filled with the awful vision that they had arrived too late.

"It's not daylight yet," Buddy Raines encouraged. "We will have to get ahold of someone and find out where Dad is."

"If there's time, any time at all, I say do it," Cooper added his support.

"All right, spread out again and bag someone who has some knowledge," Buddy ordered.

"How about the cooks?" Jersey suggested. Her teammates looked at her as though she had farted in church. "No, hey, listen up. People get fed, right? No matter what is going on, right? And who knows who gets what and where better than the cooks?"

"The cooks it is," Buddy decided.

Two more Nazi guards died on the search for the kitchen. The Rebels found it at last and burst inside to thoroughly frighten four rotund Mexican women. Their shock set them to gabbling rapid-fire in Spanish. At last, Jersey quieted them enough to ask the important question.

"*El General no esta en la célda,*" one chubby woman replied soberly to Jersey's question.

"We know he's not in his cell," Jersey answered patiently. "Where is he?"

"*Arriba,*" the moon-faced cook replied. All three women pointed to the ceiling.

"*El segundo piso?*" Jersey asked. They all nodded enthusiastically. "All right, gang, we go upstairs," she told the team.

Buddy, Jersey, and the team found the upstairs deserted. Limpid light glowed from skylights above. Jersey caught her breath when she saw it. They all took different doors, weapons ready, and began to search. Jersey and Buddy came to the arched portal at the end of the hallway first. The door had not latched tightly. Buddy threw it

348

open and Jersey rushed inside, bent low, M-16 ahead of her.

Empty. A corner room, it had windows that opened on the north and west sides. The glass had been raised out of the way, which gave access to the ornately carved and colorfully painted wooden grillwork that blocked the openings. From the one on the north side, recessed in an arch, with a small balcony outside, accessible by French doors to one side, voices rose from the ground below.

"General Benjamin Raines, Commander in Chief of the Rebel forces, you have been tried by the High Reich Tribunal and found guilty of insurrection against the Reich," came the high, thin voice of *Führer* Hoffman. "You have been duly and properly sentenced to death by firing squad. It is our duty to carry out that sentence. Have you any last words?"

There followed a familiar and beloved voice that made Jersey's heart flutter. "Cut the bullshit and let's get to the chase."

"Very well," *Führer* Hoffman replied tightly. "Hood?"

"You might need it yourself. I hear you get squeamish at the sight of blood." Ben taunted.

"Enough," Hoffman grated.

Quickly he and Field Marshal Peter Volmer marched to their assigned positions. The firing commands began.

"Firing squad . . . Attention! . . . Present! . . . Load! . . . Take aim! . . ."

Right then, Jersey knew that time, which had been their enemy in this campaign since Hoffman's invasion the previous spring, had run out. She squeezed closed her eyes and bit her lip to keep silent the sobs, and whispered a farewell prayer for Ben Raines, the man she secretly loved more than anyone else in the world.

William W. Johnstone
The *Mountain Man* Series

The Wingman Series
By Mack Maloney